MW00770849

CHOSEN
THE NEW ORDER

CHOSEN
THE NEW ORDER

For Lisa —
Adventure Awaits!

Nov 14, 2021

NICK McPHERSON

CONTENTS

ACT 1: THE HUNT

ACT 2: ARRIVAL

ACT 3: THE NEW ORDER

DEDICATION

To Katie for your unwavering support through all the mental blocks and late night writing sessions; this book would not exist without you. And to your pursuit of higher education for providing me the time (and boredom) necessary to create the world and characters herein. And last but not least, to Bray and Jamo for your ceaseless, albeit inadvertent, efforts to derail all chances of completing this book with loving, chaos-filled joy. I wouldn't have wanted it any other way.

Much love,
—*Nick*

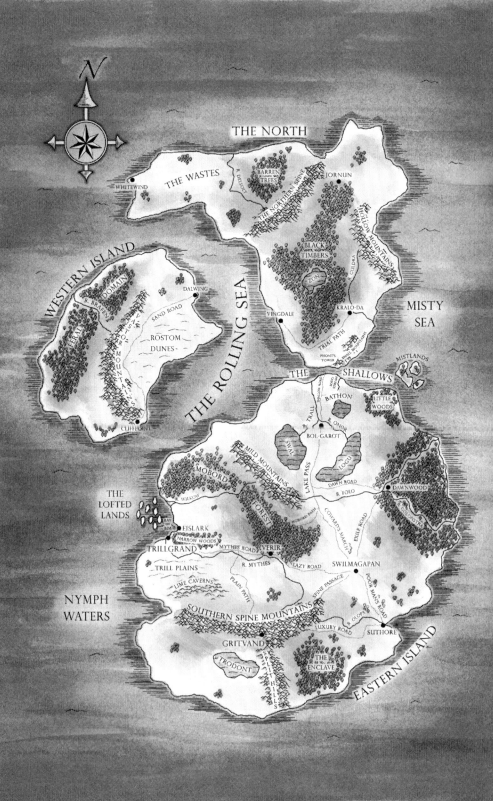

CHOSEN
THE NEW ORDER

ACT 1
THE HUNT

BANISHED

The old chiseled rock shone brightly in the afternoon sun as his shackles clanged down the open causeway. The heavy chains that bound his hands tightly to his hips rattled along the stone and made the effort difficult as they caught periodically on the less than smooth pieces, but being out in the open air mitigated the discomfort. The armed guards stationed on the walkway watched him warily, and the two in front and behind him as his escorts already had their swords drawn and at the ready. But Walding paid them no mind; he had no intention of pulling off an elaborate and daring escape. The new king would have his trial, fair and just, and the judgment would be handed down. And whatever the outcome, Walding would accept it. The world had seen enough violence at his hands without him adding any more to it.

He looked out between the guards on his left to see the sea, glittering reflections of sunlight catching the thousands of waves that washed towards the shoreline, as if they were coming to see the verdict themselves. The waves slammed hard into the rocks below and crashed upwards, misting above the edge of the defensive wall that they walked upon. The wall wrapped tightly to the shoreline and ocean below, built in among the rock centuries ago under the tenure of Lord Trillgrand himself when the city was hardly more than a large village. Exiting out the back of the castle, the wall's split could be seen ahead where half continued along the shoreline and around the rest of the city while the other half curved to the right to encompass the inner castle grounds. His escorts would be taking him right and down the slight slope to the Grandstand, where commoners and prestigious citizens could see him all the same. Walding felt drops of the salt water against his skin from the crashing waves, cooling and evaporating in an instant from the breeze and warm sun. It put a painful smile on his face.

He glanced back at the somehow pristine white stone of the castle, its grand arches bouncing around the structure like decorative sashes on a wedding gown, dotted at each arch's apex with the light blue banners of the capital city. "Endland's Diamond" was only a slight exaggeration; the castle was gorgeous, and the colors matched the gemstone's reflective nature, sun shining off the white stone and blue banners to give it the illusion of a soft glow. Grand ol' Trillgrand was a sight indeed. Another cascade of waves hit hard on the shoreline and erupted upwards, breaching the walkway's rail, a small shower sprinkling them as they walked. Walding thought in the back of his mind that perhaps Endland was shedding a tear for him. A quick jerk of his chains pulled his attention back to the path's split that they had nearly reached.

The inner castle wall they took sloped down before reaching the Grandstand, a small elevated platform set atop the main gate to the castle. A great many more guards awaited him there, armed with two short swords on their hips, all of them with the wheat-crowned Blue Heart emblazoned on their chest armor. At the center of the stage stood the new king, Lobran Sarn, in his white and blue cloak with a golden crown of wheat wrapped tightly to his brow and around his well-kept black hair. Next to him stood the head of the High Council of Wizards, Councilor Supreme Petravinos Morgodello, young for leading such a group. Only thin highlights of grey stroked his temples and his short beard of his otherwise light brown hair. Most of it was concealed beneath his large dark blue hat. Besides his hat, he too was adorned in the white and blue of Trillgrand, though his garment was more of a robe, loose and flowing compared to the king's fit and trim look.

A few other members of the council stood by as well, cloaked in the colors of their own cities, many leaning on their staffs for additional balance. They were accompanied by their lords, equally soaked in their city's crests and colors, all of whom whispered among each other. They were seated along the outer edge of the platform in a semicircle with a small gap in the arc for the escorts to pass through. Their eyes never left Walding once they saw him approach.

The escorting guards stopped Walding before the short set of stairs and clanged their armored fists against their breasts as a hard sea breeze blew through the procession, bringing with it the salty smell of the sea water. Walding breathed deeply as it rustled his now ragged blonde hair around his head, displacing long strands in front of his ice blue eyes. A flip of his head moved the hair back into place, but the motion caused the guards closest on the causeway and the platform to quickly draw their short swords and the escorts to pull heavily on his chains. King Sarn waved his hand gently towards them, causing the guards to relax, before he turned his back to the prisoner and walked to the far edge of the platform to address an unseen crowd.

"People of Endland! For I know I do not only speak with the city of Trillgrand today but with men and women from many of the great villages, towns, and cities of the Eastern Land, and perhaps from all of Endland." His voice boomed loudly around him, cutting through the sea breeze. "Here stands the last of the men responsible for the catastrophe at Jornun. And here stands the last of the men responsible for Endland's current safety. This man is on trial for the murder of thousands, as his counterparts have stood before him. But let us not forget his role in the banishment of the Grim King Kuor-Varz as we deliberate the fate of the Prophet of Philanti, the Lord of Storms, and Grandmaster of the Chosen Order, Walding Zarlorn." A great many boos echoed from beyond the platform that the king stood upon; angry and hostile the voices rose, drowning out the waves of the nearby beach. "Today we shall judge him, today we shall judge the last of the Chosen. Phont guide us in our examination and in our verdict."

The guards escorting Walding pulled him forward up the steps and toward King Sarn. The king had returned to his position in the half circle, sitting in a large stone chair that was roughly centered on the platform. The rest of the Lords and Councilors sat in wooden chairs that were far from permanent items on the platform; this was a special occurrence for this many people to be present at a hearing. The escorts pulled Walding through the semicircle to the far edge of the platform and pulled down heavily on the chains, forcing him to kneel before a sea of people. Their volume rivaled that of the ocean, 15 feet below the raised platform in a massive courtyard, packed together to watch one last judgment, one last sentence be carried out. They cried out as Walding knelt, and those nearest attempted to throw rocks and rotten food at him. Some found their mark, striking Walding in the face and torso, but they were quickly dissuaded by a platoon of armed Blue Heart guards standing at the ground level of the elevated platform, a small barrier of 50 or so men defending the gate. Walding looked over the people with sadness and understanding before casting his eyes downward to the rough stone he knelt upon.

Petravinos stepped forward from the now-seated council members, shuffling a few feet past where the king sat. He stood between the king and the accused, looking over the crowd who still jeered at the kneeling man. Somewhat nervously, he cleared his throat as he scratched the back of his hand with his beard before speaking.

"Walding Zarlorn, you stand accused, like your Chosen brothers and sisters before you, of the mass murder of the armies of the Free People of Endland at the Battle of Jornun. The great threat, Kuor-Varz, and his Grim were defeated definitively at this battle, but not by sword and spear, blood and sweat, but by dark magic. Though victory was achieved, your tactics pulled the life from thousands. Those that survived returned from the battle scarred, not with wounds and worn feet, but with time. Young men returned old, older than their fathers and grandfathers, clinging to a life that they had barely lived. Memories of loved ones were lost; feelings of joy and happiness were impossible to achieve. Those that returned did so as sulking husks of the men they once were, unable to live and love as they had prior to Jornun. And numbered among those were many descendants of the lords and ladies of Endland, including our great and now deceased king, Yorn Trillgrand. These are facts and truths expressed by the families of those whose family members have returned, seen firsthand by our new king, Lobran Sarn, seen firsthand by the lords of the Eastern Lands, and seen firsthand by the members of the High Council, myself included. Further, these facts have been confirmed and corroborated by many of the Chosen that have been judged before you. Walding Zarlorn, what have you in defense of these accusations?"

The sea of people quieted, the calm before the storm, a glass ocean waiting for a stone to be cast and the waves run through them. Walding looked out over the crowd and breathed in the salty air slowly, shaking slightly from the emotion he clearly felt at the recollection of the battle.

"Endlanders," Walding began, "the Chosen were faced with an impossible decision: to allow Kuor-Varz to continue his march of destruction, and doom Endland to an eternity of death and despair, or to end Kuor-Varz, whatever the cost. We now know that cost was high, far worse than anything we Chosen Grandmasters had thought possible. It was horrific and will forever haunt me so long as I breathe. But we did what we thought was right, and as a result, brought peace to Endland. I do not deny any of the actions levied against me as inaccurate or false. Judge as you see fit."

The crowd remained silent as the members of the High Council whispered agitatedly with their lords atop the altar. They deliberated for a minute as the sea of people rose in anger beneath them, murmuring to the kneeling accused. One voice rose louder than the rest of the crowd, setting them off.

"Murderer!"

The insult propelled others to cry out louder and louder until the sea of people swelled, angry fists rising like waves, their insults hurled like storm winds cutting at stone. Petravinos and the other council members walked to the edge of the stage and tried to calm them as the Blue Hearts atop the Grandstand swapped their swords for bows and the knights below fought back the

crowd with their massive blue and white shields. The people continued to push forward, attempting to climb for a chance to spit
their words directly to the accused's face or get close enough to
deliver a blow that might end him. Walding lowered his eyes to
the floor after his proclamation and did not lift them through
the turmoil, even as some large stones struck him, causing small
scrapes and gashes on his head and through his paper-thin tunic.

"Silence!" Petravinos roared.

At once the world was quiet, the voices of the mob vanished
like smoke in the wind. The ocean too went quiet, no waves could
be heard nor birds singing, and even as a powerful breeze blew
off the sea and whipped their skin, there was nothing but the
cooling sensation. Petravinos now stood next to the kneeling
Walding, a light wood colored staff in hand, with an intricate
raven etched in the top of the otherwise plain-looking stick. Pe-
travino's other arm was outstretched over the people who had
gathered. The crowd's attention, in their stunned silence, was
drawn to Petravinos who lowered his hand and stepped to the
edge of the platform.

"It is the decision of the High Council, with unanimous
agreement from the lords and councilors, as well as the king of
the Eastern Island, that Walding Zarlorn, from this day till the
end of his days, be banished from Endland. He is never to step
foot on its soil again, under penalty of death, and will on this
day leave us for all time. This is the verdict we lay for this man,
and by Phont's wisdom, let it be just and true."

Some of the crowd attempted to call out in protest, surely seeking harsher punishment, but their voices were stilled
as Petravinos and the other High Council members walked
forward in a half circle around Walding and began whispering quietly, some open handed and some of the more elderly
with staff in hand. Walding looked slowly, only now seeing the
scrubbed but charred stone he was kneeling upon, with remnants of those who had chosen to not go quietly. He eyed the
wizard councilors that stood around him, but none seemed
overly concerned with his subtle movements due to the burden of their incantations. He could stay put and be banished

or attempt escape and be smote. Either way, Endland would be rid of their murderous savior.

A small light appeared a few feet above Walding's head. It grew in size, flat like a plate as it widened, wobbling a few degrees arbitrarily as the incantations continued. Very soon it was wide enough for four men to stand inside, and the light that it emitted grew cold and grey, like a fog light through the mist. It wobbled increasingly as it grew, an unevenly loaded pottery wheel spinning rapidly, and the members of the council were fully entranced with their work. Sweat beads formed on their brows with the strain as their voices echoed in the otherwise silent world. Petravinos lowered his arms and, wiping his forehead with a cloaked sleeve, stepped forward next to Walding. Walding looked to him and over his shoulder to the lords seated on the edges of the platform soaking in the show, guards armed with bows all pointed to where he knelt.

"Walding Zarlorn, you are hereby banished from Endland. May the gods pity you when you at last greet them, for you will need their mercy for the crimes you have been found guilty of here today." He looked down and sighed a whisper. "At least it is not the Medius, old friend. I wish this was not our path but it will bring stability to the land. Please understand. Fortune unto thee, my friend."

"Until we meet again, Vinos," Walding whispered nearly imperceptibly and somewhat to his surprise in the silence as Petravinos stepped back into the half circle and continued with the others.

The whispering of the High Council was now bordering on shouting as the disc swirled and shook above his head. None noticed the position of Walding's hands, his pinky fingers and thumbs extended in his chains, too enthralled with the light show above him. Walding closed his eyes and the council lowered their hands, the flat light lowering with it, passing over Walding's body and landing solidly on the stone he stood on. It popped with a loud and long hiss, the grey light dissipated, and where Walding had knelt was now only air. The crowd's voice returned with the distant sounds of the shoreline as the High

Council broke their formation and returned to their Lords as Petravinos stepped forward to address the people once more.

"Go forth with Phont's blessings good people, knowing that His will has been realized. The Chosen are gone and Endland is safe. Fortune unto thee." A weak reply came from the crowd, not nearly matching their size, and they began to file out of the courtyard. Those closest to the front of the platform, those clearly most angry, remained fixated on where Walding had been, waiting for some trick to be exposed and Walding to show his face again for one last stone's throw. The armed Blue Heart guards stood vigilant with their shields before the Grandstand, but no one was keen on attempting to overtake them. Petravinos watched the crowd slowly disperse before turning to where Walding had disappeared. He lingered for a moment of mourning and then walked towards the rest of the council who had surrounded King Lobran Sarn on his throne.

"It is done, my King. The last of the Chosen is gone."

"Splendid, Petravinos. For a moment I thought we may have to spill some blood to slack the people's thirst." He spoke calmly and with little emotion as he swirled the last bit of wine in his cup.

"The people's pain is written plainly. It's been a difficult day for all of us, a difficult year. So much death, these ongoing trials, and the passing of King Trillgrand weighs heavy upon them," Petravinos said as he turned back to look upon the still disbanding crowd.

"Your words are true, Councilor Supreme. Such a tragedy to have lost him, and not at the hands of the Grim, but by his precious Chosen! But do not forget half my blood is his! The people will recognize the Sarn name once this glorious new age of Endland begins!"

"Yes, my King," Petravinos responded. "I suppose we are primed for a joyous time of prosperity now with Kuor-Varz gone."

"Yes, precisely, now is the time for celebration! The Grim are gone, the Chosen banished, and the world is at peace for the first time in nearly a hundred years! A new age is upon us! The time of the Chosen is over, now is the age of peace!" King Sarn exclaimed.

He raised his glass as the lords and ladies cheered loudly at the joyous proclamation. Petravinos bowed shortly and backed away from the group. They spoke loudly of their new king and followed him down the steps of the Grandstand back towards the castle as a set of Blue Heart guards moved in to flank them for escort. The High Council members followed suit, strolling down the walkway that overlooked the sea as a small patch of clouds cast a brief reprieve from the warm sun. Petravinos's feet did not immediately move, looking to the lone cloud that blotted the sun and sighed. He turned back to the banishment site where his friend had just been and knelt before it, placing his hand on the warm sun-soaked stone. He straightened after a moment,

"Let us hope, my King, that you are right."

WAVE TO A STRANGER

ooking out the window, Bryce's only view of the outside world, he could see that the leaves had nearly all turned to their autumn colors. That is, at least, on the trees that decorated the parking lot medians; those in the woods beyond were on their way but not in the entirety the ones in the lot were. Small short trees, the same ones that line the streets of nice neighborhoods, all pulsing vibrant yellow-orange like miniature suns. They nearly matched the actual sun as it sank behind the distant cloudy horizon, burning sharply through the evening air. A great many of the leaves had taken the plunge from their branches and now lay on the mulch bed and lawn below, dancing mournfully in the grass and wood chips if the wind caught them right, as if they may now be regretting leaping from their perch.

It was a picture that he had seen transform before his very eyes over the past year. Season to season, fall to winter to spring to summer and to fall again now. Through all his visits he had never had to spend more than a day or two at the hospital, but it was depressing nonetheless, especially considering they had not made much progress on a diagnosis. He hadn't gotten worse, which he supposed was a nice way to spin his predicament, but he hadn't gotten any better either. And it always seemed to happen at the worst time, like it was cognizant of when it would take hold.

He sighed and shifted his eyes back from the window to his room, looking at the lone basket of flowers sitting at the table at the end of his bed. His foster mom always went out to get a bouquet as soon as he had to come in, "Flower Power" as she always said. *"Nothing like some nature to bring in the positive vibes, right?"* She had always been positive through the whole weird ordeal, almost to the point of obsession and definitely to the point of annoyance. But he liked the flowers; between the view of the trees and the smell of the flowers, it was almost like being outside, which was a nice escape from the drab and dreary hospital rooms. He looked around for probably the millionth time at yet another tiny little room. The machines were there as usual, used for monitoring his heart and respiration rate when needed and probably a bunch of other stuff he didn't even know about. Most sat idle save the heartbeat monitor, its steady beeping counting away, a constant reminder of the time he was spending sitting around doing nothing. The plain grey walls solidified the staleness of the room, the same boring palette as all the other rooms he had been in. What bothered him most was how often he had frequented the place; the muted scenery had started to reach a level of normalcy. It was like going on vacation unexpectedly and then when you got there, you found out you're staying in a little crappy motel room, and you couldn't go outside because it was raining.

He closed his eyes as tears began to well in them from the frustration and took a deep breath to calm himself. He wiped them away with the back of his navy-blue sweater and looked out again to the mini-tree-suns in the cooling fall wind, wishing he could be crunching the fallen leaves under his feet as he played tag or catch or anything with his friends. Fall was his favorite time of year without a doubt, warm enough to still be outside but cool enough to not have to worry about the sun burning him to a lobster's complexion, as often happened in the summer. And Halloween landed right in the middle of it, which would be coming up tomorrow already.

He hoped that he would be able to go trick-or-treating this year, depending on how long his stint at the hospital lasted. Last year he had just had his first dizzy spell when he got home from school, derailing trick-or-treating and thoroughly pissing him off simultaneously. The only consolation he had was that his two buddies had been right here with him. They were getting a little old for Halloween now at 13, but up until last year they had gone out every year together as long as they could remember. But while most kids were picking their costumes and preparing to run around all night, collecting more goodies than one child should ever need, they all had been stuck here in this hospital, suffering dizzy spells, barfing their brains out, and seizing or sweating profusely among other strange and unpredictable symptoms. Mainly he just remembered being sporadically dizzy beyond imagination, as did his friends. Laying, sitting, moving, it didn't matter, the room spun all the same without apparent cause and without warning. He also remembered that the nurses had come around with candy, but the experience felt strange. The whole process had been reversed, him staying put while the candy-givers walked around distributing. It was just weird. And if he had to be here again this year for the holiday, he might just leave his light off and pretend no one was home.

"Hey Bryce!" came ripping through his daydream. He quickly wiped his eyes and averted them from the door, only casting a side-eyed glance. He knew the voice but it had startled him nonetheless.

"Hey Marge," he replied, hoping she had not seen the tears. Unfortunately for him, Marge didn't miss much; she was quite astute, even among moms. Had she been his biological mother, Bryce would have thought he got his observational tendencies from her. That is where the similarities stopped though; she was short and somewhat plump and Bryce was already taller than she, despite his being rather average in height. Marge had green puffy eyes, like she may have been crying or been suffering a mild allergic reaction, and well-kept, naturally dirty blond hair. Bryce's eyes were blue and keen, looking wise beyond his years, beneath a somewhat shaggy brunette top. But none of the physical differences detracted from her motherly instincts.

"Bryce, what's wrong dear, did you miss me that much?" Her tone shifted ever so slightly, though she played it off pretty well, still trying to maintain her initial level of exaggerated cheeriness. Bryce heard the slight deflection in her voice and saw the small wrinkle where her nose met her forehead, despite her best efforts; she had instantly become worried.

He had always had a keen eye for stuff like that. In school he often pointed out typos that he found in his text books or homework sheets to his teachers or he would predict what each of his friends would have packed in their lunches on any given day, and he was usually correct. He would play games with himself, trying to read people's expressions or pick up on patterns. It was a weird form of people watching for him and a great deal of fun. For instance, with the lunches, his buddy Zack almost always had chocolate pudding snack packs Monday through Thursday and then a more formal desert on Friday. And Johnny alternated between PB&J and ham and cheese sandwiches at a minimum every other day. He knew Zack had "family dinner night" on Thursdays, so leftover deserts on Fridays was only natural. Plus, pudding snacks usually came in packs of four. And Johnny was more of a personality observation. He had ADHD or bipolar disorder or something, undiagnosed by professionals, but Bryce would bet his whole life savings there was something there. Johnny had to be doing something new every so often or he'd create his own entertainment at the expense of everyone around him. If he had to have the same thing to eat two days in a row, he'd get so bored with it he'd end up playing with his food and making a sandwich man named "Hank." And that wasn't hypothetical; Johnny walked around with a ham and cheese sandwich on his shoulder for an entire day and talked to it like it was an actual sentient being. His food had to change for the sake of everyone around him. *"Variety is the spice of life B-man, or so they say."*

Rarely did they call each other their actual names, it was always abbreviated somehow. That or they went by their teacher assigned nicknames from grade school. Mr. Marles came up with one for everyone that went through his class. *The Rock* for Henry Powarski, who could do 27 pull-ups in a row and had a six-pack since the prime age of 7. Big Zack Kapule was *Papa Bear* for being a large human and for being acutely parental for his young age. Johnny Pragg was *the Joker*, and not for having a crazy maniacal laugh or for continually failing to outwit a man dressed as a bat, but for being genuinely funny.

Zack, Johnny, and Bryce even extended the tradition to the other kids at the hospital that they frequented so much. There was *Sniffs* or *Gags*, depending on which of the three you asked, for Martha Quinn who had terrible allergies or overactive nasal passages or something along those lines. It could have been a symptom of whatever she was in the hospital for, but honestly describing it as terrible wasn't descriptive enough. You don't get a name like Gags without literally making people gag from the disgusting nature of your leaky faucet nose. *Zep* was Kirk Lowel's nickname; he always always had an iPod going with some classic rock music. Bryce recognized some of the songs when Zep would let them listen, but Kirk could rattle off every line and band member and album, year it was released, on and on and on. Assigning the names helped the three pass the time while they were stuck in the hospital awaiting another "the tests are inconclusive" diagnosis.

"Bryce?" He suddenly realized he had still not answered his mother, whose concern was slowly growing given her son's slow response.

"Nothing, Marge. I was just thinking that's all," he murmured. To his surprise, there was no follow-up question. There are typically a range of anywhere from 2 to 47 questions that follow a mother's initial question, especially when the answer to that first question is "nothing." Instead, she walked over to the edge of his bed and pulled him close, brushed his brown hair out of his eyes, and kissed the top of his forehead before continuing prepping their dinner. He smiled softly. Bryce couldn't remember either of his parents, and only fragments of a time when he lived at an orphanage, but it had really just been Marge and Walt as long as he could remember.

"Your dad will be here in a few minutes and then we will have some dinner, OK? It's Sunday-Funday so I decided to bring your favorite! Burgers and beans!"

Bryce forced a smile and did his best to look excited. He did love burgers and beans, always had, but something about these "episodes," as the doctors called them, really put a damper on his appetite. It was all he could do to choke down some Jell-O or crackers from the nurses. The smile seemed to fool his mom, who smiled back and began to unload the Tupperware containing the beans. She had always brought food to the hospital on the first evening, ever since the initial episode last Halloween. It wasn't that the food at the hospital was bad per se, she just liked bringing in homemade food. Bryce thought it was because she wanted to help, and that by providing food to him she was somehow able to directly affect his health. He didn't know this for sure, but it made sense to him.

Bryce moved his gaze back to the window and the trees, bright and beautiful in the setting sun. A man was out in the yard now raking the droppings of the three trees into a heap. He propped a collection bag against the closest tree and gave a quick stretch before he started scooping handfuls of his pile into the bag. Bryce smiled jealously; he would take doing yard work over being stuck in his hospital bed in a heartbeat.

The man paused from his work for a second and looked up in Bryce's general direction while leaning lightly on his rake as he flashed a smile and waved. Bryce hesitated; there was nothing more embarrassing than waving back to someone who was never waving to you in the first place. Bryce ignored the wave and continued to look out at the leaves and the sun. It would be dark soon, though it wasn't quite daylight savings time so the sun still had some life around, but it was fading fast. His thoughts were broken as his eyes were drawn again to the man, who had increased the smile stretched across his face and started waving more erratically, his arm fully extended above his head and swinging like a pendulum. Bryce finally returned the wave by raising his hand but a few inches and opening his palm, to which the man finally ceased and merrily went back to his raking.

He was certainly in a cheerful mood for yard work. Maybe the man had the same appreciation for the fall season as he did. He watched him rake for a minute or two, imagining the smell of the leaves and the cool grass. He continued to pull off small piles, placing them gently into his bag, before he took another break and looked back towards Bryce's window again.

The hair on the back of Bryce's neck stood up and he shivered. Something about the man's gaze was unsettling this time around, and the man's smile, which appeared genuine at first glance, now seemed misplaced and forced. He was *too* cheery. Bryce watched as the man pointed towards him and held up three fingers. Pumping his hand as he went, he counted down with his fingers. 3, 2, 1.

"Hey kiddo!"

If his mother had startled him, his father had nearly stopped his heart. Bryce jumped and whipped his head around to see his father in the doorway, smiling and with a six-pack of soda in hand. The goose bumps that were on his neck had suddenly jumped across his whole body, arms and legs buzzing with the odd perception.

"A little jumpy today, huh, kid? You alright?" his father asked, walking towards him and putting the pop on the table next to the flowers. He took off his baseball cap, the same beat-up one he'd worn for as long as Bryce could remember, and ran a lanky hand through his grey and thinning dark hair as he looked to Marge for some clue as to why he had nearly given his kid a heart attack.

"He's OK, Walt, just doing some thinking, right, honey?" Bryce hated being called that, but he was too tired to argue.

"Yea, just thinking," he confirmed. His foster father's face twisted in an inquisitive wrinkle, his grey mustache twitching as his face did, but before he could continue, his mother touched his arm and recognizing the gesture, his face switched back to faux cheerful, restoring the long and worn crow's feet to his eyes.

"So is it suppertime or what?" his dad asked his mother with a jesting smile.

Bryce did not hear the response from his mother; he had just remembered the groundskeeper. He whipped around to spot the man through his window but he was gone. No rake, no leaf bag, most leaves still sitting on the ground, a job half-finished. The sun was still out, enough for another hour or so of work before it would be too dark to see. Bryce shivered again as the last of the goose bumps started to fade. It was quite the coincidence that the man had counted to his father's arrival. Perhaps the man could see through the window. Bryce closed his eyes again and thought about it. Conceivably, the man could see him in his bed through the window because he was fairly close to it and the curtains were drawn wide open. But seeing his dad walk in through the door was another thing. They were on the second floor and his room door was opposite the window a good 30 feet. The angles just didn't add up. But he *had* to have seen him; the man had pointed right at Bryce and counted down to the instant his dad had spoken. Bryce shook his head as he opened his eyes before chalking it up to an eerie coincidence.

"Ready for some food?" His mother's voice again brought him back to reality. Bryce peeked over to see a burger and a pile of beans on a paper plate for him. He smiled weakly and looked to his parents.

"Yea, let's eat!" he said with all the enthusiasm he could muster. The periods of fatigue were incredibly annoying, and he had to try to sell it as best he could or risk an excessive amount of motherly worry. She again seemed to buy it, and his mom began to prepare their own plates as his dad cracked open a soda and passed it to him. Bryce grabbed the bottle happily and took a swig, feeling the bubbly sugar jolt along his taste buds and, for a short while, he forgot about whatever was ailing him and enjoyed the makeshift dinner. With a smile he took a bite of the home-cooked meal and put the dizziness out of his mind.

A MAN OF
MANY LOCATIONS

The following morning Bryce was helped into a wheelchair by the nurses and zipped over to one of the therapy rooms for a group session. He could walk just fine now, as it usually was after the first day of being at the hospital. But in replacement of the dizziness, he felt as though his nerve endings were randomly being jolted in various locations. Even with his ability to walk restored, the nurses insisted on the wheelchair, and he had grown tired of arguing with them over it, so into the chair he went. Bryce didn't mind it too much anymore; it was kind of nice being whisked around. He would pretend the nurses were part of his security detail, like he was a crime boss, and that he was far too important to be troubled with the task of walking.

He didn't mind the sessions either. He had only been to a few, rarely did his being in the hospital coincide with the meeting day, but it was nice to be around other people of his same age and same health, or rather, lack thereof. Somehow knowing that there were other people going through the same thing, most often much worse things, made him feel a little better. As he was wheeled into the room next to Johnny Pragg, he extended his fist towards his friend in standard fist-bump fashion. He

was looking as comfortable as ever, always dressed in the latest
lounge wear: ragged sweatpants and a loose T-shirt with his ex-
treme-fluff slippers. He took more flack for those things than
was fair, but he wouldn't be caught dead in a potentially relax-
ing situation without them.

"Eagle, my man, how's it going?" Johnny reciprocated the
gesture as the weakest fist bump in the history of the world ensued, like two butterfly wings brushing against each other.

Bryce smiled and flexed his fist-bump hand, assessing his
lack of strength. "Doing alright Mr. J, how about you?"

"No more dizziness, but feeling weak as hell and I've got
those electrical buzzes all over my body. So, the usual for day
two of our stints here, eh?" Johnny uttered in his always sarcastic tone, a small grin rising under his thick-rimmed glasses.
His hair was short, almost a military buzz cut, and it made his
glasses all the more prominent on his round face. Bryce laughed
honestly.

"You should probably talk to the doctor or something, Johnny, get yourself checked out." They both laughed as Nurse Jan
walked into the room.

"Well, I see some of us are off to a great day!" the nurse exclaimed, taking her seat in one of the chairs around the circle.
If Bryce's mom was a positive person, Nurse Jan was queen of
the Royal House of Positivity. She was relatively new. This was
only the second time he had met her, the first being just a short
month or so ago in mid-September. It was almost frightening
sometimes how upbeat she was, which is saying something considering he had lived with his oh-so-positive mother for nearly
13 years now. Bryce thought it might be a nervous coping mech-
anism, her way of dealing with the overt sadness throughout
the hospital. That or she was insane. Johnny, who was always
looking for reason to talk, took advantage of Jan's exclamation.

"You know it, Jan! I mean just today, just wait till you hear
this. So, the day starts, ya know? And I wake up! What a day
right? What. A. Day." Bryce laughed out loud at his friend's ri-
diculousness as big Zack was wheeled in, the third member of
their trio, eating a Jell-O as his nurse pushed him into the circle
next to Nurse Jan. His tight crew neck sweater was struggling

to hold his body, and as always, he was dressed in a pair of cargo shorts and tennis shoes. Whether it was his large build that kept him warm or because he simply liked acting tough, he was always wearing shorts, even during the Cleveland winters. He had actually been sent home to change into pants by the school one day out of fear for his safety. On that day, Johnny made sure to comment about how bizarre he looked with actual pants on, like a part of the big guy was missing without his thick lower legs exposed. Zack slurped the last bit of Jell-O from his spoon and whispered something to the nurse as he handed off the empty container. The nurse, Micky, another newer face, smiled while reaching into his pocket and dropped another container into Zack's slightly pudgy hand. Zack gave Micky a finger-gun and a wink and then ripped the foil top off feverishly.

Zack was the only one of the three who still had most of his appetite through their episodes, symptoms and all. But he wasn't just a pudge ball, he was quite the athlete, more so than Bryce and certainly Johnny. He was just a big guy, probably a little less than twice the weight of Bryce or Johnny, who were both rather thin, but he was about three inches shorter than both his friends. He looked like the son of Bigfoot, the missing link, with his frizzy thick mop going every which way and nearly reaching his broadening shoulders. When he hit his growth spurt, and he certainly was bound to given his father's stature, he was going to be a monster. In the meantime, he was just a plump kid enjoying eating anything that was in front of him. He polished off the Jell-O he had just been handed as Nurse Jan began the session.

"You guys are just too much sometimes! And I am L-O-V-E-ing all this laughter, so let's carry it over to our session, OK? For today I want each person to start with something bad that happened to them this week and then talk about how that might improve. Then talk about something good that happened and how it might get even better! Let's go clockwise, so Zack you're up first!"

Bryce zoned out almost immediately. It wasn't that he was uninterested in what Zack had to say, but he often found it difficult to hold attention on his second day of an episode. Twice during dinner last night his mother and father had to snap him back to reality, and that wasn't including his loss of focus while observing the leaf-raking man. He found it easy to daydream when the episodes struck, almost driven to do so. And this time was no exception, thinking of the leaves outside, wishing he could be one, dancing and floating carefree with the wind. Whatever was going on with him and his buddies was horribly annoying. At first the doctors had insisted the three friends had taken some sort of drug together, huffed some glue or something outrageous. Being in a foster home only increased the condescending opinions about him, that somehow he was a bad influence on his friends who had more traditional families. "It is no coincidence that the three of them share the same symptoms," the doctors had continually said. Every time they came in it was the same accusations and every time the drug screening and testing had of course proved that they were all perfectly clean.

He zoned back in momentarily to glance around the group. Zack had finished speaking and was requesting another Jell-O from Micky, who again happily obliged. Martha Quinn had begun her round of sharing. She was a pretty girl, despite her knack for sneezing on *everything*. Her nose was like the eighth wonder of the world, the Snotagra Falls. Somehow Johnny was able to see past the stream of snot that so often flew from her face. *"Beauty's in the eye of the beholder, or so they say."* Bryce smiled and started to zone out again, back to flying as a leaf on the wind, but before he completely lost touch with reality, Martha said something that piqued his interest.

" . . . standing there, waving like a madman. I can't say I've seen him before but—"

"The groundskeeper?" Bryce blurted out, leaning forward in his chair so far that it almost tipped. He lurched back quickly so as to not spill onto the floor as Martha and most of the group looked over in surprise.

"No," Martha replied, looking a little confused, "he was delivering something, he looked like a FedEx or UPS guy or something." Bryce slumped back into his chair disappointed as his heart beat heavily in his chest. He thought for sure this might be the groundskeeper. "But the way he smiled and waved . . .

it was kind of . . . . I'm not really sure how to explain it." She continued. Bryce noticed that Johnny was leaning forward with the same enthusiastic attention, but before either could speak, Nurse Jan interjected.

"Martha, I'm confused. Is this the good thing that happened during your week? It seems like he was a kind person who brightened your day!" Martha sniffled loudly, holding back a surefire snot storm before continuing.

"Well, I guess it was a good thing. I think it just struck me as a little strange since I didn't know him. Most people don't really do that sort of thing with strangers, you know? But the really strange part—" She stopped abruptly to unleash a hurricane sneeze into the tissue she always had in her hand. Full category F5. If there had been a microbe city on that tissue, it had just been obliterated by Sniffs. Jan smiled at the girl to allow her to continue, but the smile did not match her body language. She seemed off to Bryce, who was unable to turn off his observational insight. She masked it well, but Jan seemed concerned. She was leaning forward slightly in her chair, as Bryce and Johnny were, and was twirling a strand of her dark hair by her ear nervously. She was always engaged in their sessions but something was up. Bryce watched Jan with intrigue as Martha continued.

"Well that was a little strange too. It seemed genuine but something about it was . . . I don't know. Creepy, I guess." Bryce swallowed hard as he continued to watch Jan's body language. Her face was fraught with a momentary shadow of concentration, her hazel eyes squinting ever so slightly before returning to her cheery facade. But Bryce saw it for the split second. Jan was concerned with something. Further, Bryce thought Martha's description sounded similar to the same guy that he had seen outside the other night raking leaves, although he couldn't really see his smile well enough to be able to classify it as "creepy" or not. It certainly matched the feeling though.

"Was that the strange part? Or was there more?" Jan interjected, flipping open a notebook and scribbling something quickly. Martha paused, looking up as if the answer was secretly written on the underside of her eyebrows. "I remember it was around the end of the day. My parents had just arrived for dinner when he walked past my door but then sort of paused and turned back and looked in my room and gave a smile and a wave and walked away." She looked back over the group realizing that it really didn't sound very strange at all and blushed fully. "I don't know what was so odd about it." She pulled her knees up to her chest in obvious discomfort and sniffled loudly again as she rested her chin on her knees and looked off to the side.

"It's OK, dear, it is a bit strange for delivery personnel to be in past the front desk, but no matter!" Nurse Jan paused and looked over to Bryce now. Jan should have been glad to have another jovial force like her around, waving and spreading good cheer in the name of positivity, even if it was from a slightly creepy stranger. But she wasn't.

"And Bryce, what's this about a groundskeeper?" Bryce looked at Nurse Jan and around the group. Others were shifting uncomfortably, looking from him to Martha. Johnny was still on the edge of his seat and big Zack had even stopped eating his Jell-O to listen.

"Well, I saw him yesterday. He was out front raking some leaves under the parking lot trees, and he waved towards me. I didn't think it was for me at first, but he just kept waving until I finally raised my hand. It just gave me this weird feeling, and then my dad . . . "

He trailed off as Nurse Jan motioned for Nurse Micky to come over to her. He dropped another Jell-O in Zack's hands and leaned over as she whispered in his ear, too quiet for Bryce and Johnny to hear from across the circle. They whispered shortly back and forth before Micky nodded and headed towards the session room doors without another word, clapping Nurse Bart on the shoulder and nodding as he passed. Bryce saw Bart's eyes widen before he gave Micky a 1-2 fake punch to the abdomen, but there was an air of discomfort around the room now as Micky shut the door behind him. Bryce looked at Johnny with a curious expression, which Johnny returned, as Bryce was suddenly struck with goose bumps down his neck and arms. He hunched his shoulders in discomfort and pulled his sweater closer around him.

"Thank you for sharing Martha, thank you Bryce. Now unfortunately we will have to cut this session short for today. Nurses, please return the children to their rooms. Kids, we will reschedule our session for tomorrow morning, OK? See you all at lunch!" Nurse Jan was already standing and walking towards the door as she spoke but managed a big cheesy smile as she left the room. The other nurses nodded in agreement and moved to their respective children's wheelchairs to whisk them back to their rooms. Johnny leaned over on Bryce's armrest as their nurses grasped the chair handles and whispered quickly to him.

"So this guy you saw, did anything stand out about him?" Bryce shook his head.

"No, not really, he looked average height, average weight, brown hair, nothing special really, it was just . . . weird." Bryce waited for the joke that so often left Johnny's mouth, but none came. He was looking at Bryce intently and very non-Joker like. Bryce thought a little more, trying to quench Johnny's appetite for description. Not tall or short, not fat or thin, short brown hair combed over to one side. Just an average-looking guy.

"I guess his hair was pushed to one side if that helps. I don't know really; he was just normal looking. Why?" Johnny smiled, pushed his glasses back up his nose, and extended his arm for another fist bump. As they made contact, Johnny whispered: "I think I saw him too."

Bryce's eyes widened in surprise as Johnny gave a wink, but before he could ask his friend anything else, the nurses had pushed Johnny out of the circle and back towards his room.

"Wait!" Bryce whirled around to see which of the nurses was escorting him back to his wing. "Bart! Can we go the long way and wheel next to Johnny? I've got to—"

"Sorry Bryce, normally I'd be happy to oblige, but Nurse Jan needs me in the lounge for a quick meeting. We've got to get you guys back ASAP." Bart shrugged as he said this, as if the gesture validated that what he said was truly out of his hands. Bart was a big guy, someone who looked like he had played linebacker through college, maybe even professionally, although Bryce had never asked him to confirm it. Thick forearms and a neck that was as about as existent as hard evidence of a flat earth, he was quite the imposing figure. Most people who met him were initially intimidated by his stature but soon enough it became apparent his personality did not match his "evil henchman" look. He was as kind as his muscles were big and was as strait-laced as they came, as was just reaffirmed to Bryce by his lack of enthusiasm in being a few minutes late to a meeting that was announced moments ago.

"Oh come on, it would only take a minute or two. Or why don't I just walk myself." He began to stand, pushing himself up from the chair's arms but was quickly pulled backwards by one of those massive hands laid firmly on his shoulder. "Sorry man, we've got to get you kids back to your room. No exceptions."

"But—" Bryce started before being cut off.

"No 'buts' bud, Jan's orders. She doesn't call an impromptu meeting unless something important has come up. Plus, I'm sort of the new guy, I got to make a good impression, you know? I can't not show when I'm the only one invited." Bryce's intrigue piqued at Bart's last statement as he slumped back in his chair, arms folded in a show of futile protest. He couldn't be sure what the topic of the meeting would be, but logically it was the mystery man. He could ask Johnny about what he saw soon enough, but Jan was clearly concerned with his and Martha's stranger sightings. He thought on it as Bart wheeled him into the elevator and hit the button for the second floor. Bart started whistling something terribly, often slipping into a high squeak or a soft nonmusical blowing sound as they waited. It was enough to knock Bryce off his train of thought as the elevator doors closed and the lurch of the machine tugged them upwards.

"Any idea what your meeting is about, Bart?" Bryce knew that he hadn't spoken to Jan; he just wanted Bart's opinion. Maybe he had noticed her investigative nature towards the mystery man like he had.

"I'm honestly not sure bud, Jan didn't really say anything except to Mick. Probably about some minor detail I'm not doing right. She can be a little nitpicky." He rubbed the back of his neck with one of his mammoth hands, tweaking his neck as he did so. "Our last meeting was 'an opportunity for feeling expression among co-workers.' It was horrible." Bryce laughed out loud as the lurch of the elevator reversed and doors opened. Bart gripped the wheelchair and pushed laughing lightly. "I wish that was a joke but it wasn't. It was an open-floor half hour for us to share how we felt about anything on the job force."

"Did you share anything, Bart? Any life-altering feelings you had to get off your chest?" Bart leaned forward over the back of the chair as they reached Bryce's room as Bart's laughter subsided.

"Honestly," Bart whispered in an austere tone and paused to build effect, "it could compete for 'worst half hour of my life.' And I've been stuck outside in a ditch during a blizzard." They both laughed at this as Bart parked the wheelchair at the edge of the bed. Bryce stood slowly, ready to combat any lightheadedness. After none came, he crawled into his bed, kicking off his moccasins as he did so.

"Have fun at your meeting, Bart. Hopefully, it won't be another 'feeling session.'" Bryce smiled widely at his jab, pulling a sheet over his legs as Bart smiled back and turned to exit the room.

"If I'm not here tomorrow, it's because I refused to share and was executed for lack of enthusiasm. Tell my story, Bryce," he shouted over his shoulder, causing Bryce to laugh again.

The boy glanced over at the wall clock and sighed as the sound of the wheelchair and Bart's footsteps echoed away, noting they had only spent maybe 15 minutes or so in their normally hourlong session. At least being in the sessions gave him something to do for some of the morning. He now had 40-something minutes of bonus time, time that would most likely be spent sitting in his bed twiddling his thumbs and looking out the window, as he usually did with his free time. TV was awful during the day; there was never anything on except news and crappy soap operas.

He quickly checked outside to see if the man was back to raking but without reward. The trees were by themselves today with no mystery man to be seen, just the leaves and the early morning fall sunshine. It seemed odd that this man was causing such a commotion. He supposed if it was really the same guy seen twice in less than a day it was cause for some concern. And if Johnny had seen him too, that would be three different sightings. A knock from his doorway pulled his attention. It was Johnny, that smug grin of his stretched on his face, and Zack with a granola bar of some sort half eaten in his hand.

"What would you say to a little adventuring, B-man?" Johnny asked as he pushed his glasses up his nose and leaned confidently against the door in his best "cool guy" pose. Johnny had always been one to stretch the rules a bit. Not to the point of serious trouble or danger, but enough to get some severe scolding from a whole slew of adults throughout their lives. Parents, teachers, neighbors, strangers—they had run through the gamut of potential discipliners. Not that the scolding was ever strictly Johnny's fault, but he always seemed to initiate while Bryce and Zack were always willing to tag along and contribute to the mischief. Once, the three of them had gotten sent down to the principal's office after playing tag in class while sitting at their desks. Sliding your desk back and forth to tag and dodge was evidently disruptive to the class. The game lasted about 30 seconds before the ruckus warranted their dismissal from the classroom. And as it were, Bryce found himself feeding into Johnny's shenanigans again today.

"What did you have in mind?" he replied, swinging his feet back over the bed and feeling for his moccasins with his toes.

"We're a little curious about what Jan and Bart are talking about," Zack said before he shoved the last half of the granola bar into his mouth and mumbled further, "We fink teh dree of ust hould habe been inbited." Johnny nodded, smiling and lifting one hand up towards Zack's mouth to shield himself from the granola crumb shower that was flying towards him.

"Yea, what he said."

Bryce stood and walked across the room to his friends. "I think we should excuse their lack of manners just this once and attend the meeting anyways, right?" Johnny and Zack both smiled and with a quick turn out the door they speed-walked down the hall towards the nurse's wing.

REQUEST TO THE COUNCIL

icky's ears perked up immediately at Martha's story, and even more so with Bryce's enthusiasm. This was eerily similar to the previous Hunt's reports, and he looked to Bart who met him with the same curious expression. They both knew what the other was thinking; time was now working against them to identify the Chosen. They had thought they were looking for an adult, not a child, but the odd out-of-place sensation was as common a sign as the Grim portrayed when they arrived, despite those bastard's best efforts to infiltrate unnoticed. It meant that the chances of someone here being Chosen just increased from questionable to certainty. And furthermore, if the Grim were just now making themselves known, it meant Mick and his companions were currently unknown to them. The element of surprise was still in play. He saw Jan motion him to her side and he took the few short steps towards her, fetching another Jell-O from his pocket to occupy big Zack. He bent close to her while plopping a Jell-O cup in Zack's eager hands as she leaned back in her chair.

"This sounds like a sighting, Mikel, two children having an unnerving feeling in the same day. I never would have guessed the Chosen would be a child but I'll speak with Bart, plan out how we can identify them. You must notify the High Council of our request for direct assault."

"Jan, are you sure about this, attacking the Grim openly? And why must I go? A letter could convey the message just as well as I could, and then I would be here to assist in the extraction."

"I understand what I am asking, but a letter cannot argue," Jan said. "We need a voice to make the case for us." Micky pressed his lips slightly in dissatisfaction.

"For the record, I am against leaving, but this is your Hunt. I will go now, just don't start without me, alright?"

Jan nodded while Micky pulled back from their whispering distance with a wink and a smile and headed towards the doorway. He firmly placed his hand on Bart's shoulder as he passed, "Got to go, hold the fort till I'm back."

Bart nodded in return before he began to fake box him with a few body shots. Micky dodged, joking as much as he could in such a serious situation before he exited the room, pulling the doors closed with a soft mechanical click. As soon as they had shut, he made his way down the hallway towards the lounge, walking as quickly as he could without drawing too much un due attention.

His heart was racing, and not from the brisk pace at which he now traveled. He knew this day would come eventually but not this soon. And now that it was here, he felt ill prepared. He had heard being on a Hunt was agonizingly anxiety-ridden, but it had not struck him at all until this moment. It was exhilarating and terrifying at once, but it all gave him a great deal of confidence now that Chosen had been confirmed; the Councilor Supreme was correct in sending a party to this world.

He opened the door to the nurses' lounge, ignoring the others who occupied the room, grabbed his old shoulder pack from his locker, and opened the leather drawstring. He rummaged through the bag, and feeling around he eventually found the amulet. Looking over his shoulder to confirm the other nurses were not too close, he pulled it out. It was a thin, golden-twined necklace with a small half-dollar shaped disk on the end, a deep purple and gleaming stone, and smaller rough disk-shaped stones entwined along the rest of the necklace. It was not exactly a fine piece of jewelry. The stone was unevenly cut and dispersed haphazardly throughout the chain, and the metal looked like it needed a thorough cleaning. He placed it back in his bag, slammed his locker, and exited the room, ignoring the judging looks the other nurses gave him for making such racket.

He made quick time through the halls and past the main desk before bursting out the front doors and into the parking lot. His brisk pace did not slow as he walked through the parking lot, blazing past the cars towards a nearby walking path that circled the hospital grounds. It was frequented by the doctors and nurses during lunch breaks and by the children, if it was allowed, but in the midmorning it was quite barren of activity, save a few birds that chirped in the trees at the path entryway. Wrapping through a corner of the nearby Metroparks, it was probably only a mile loop but something about getting outside the hospital and away from the structure was soothing, even if it was only for a short while. Micky, however, was numb to the calming nature of the trees today, keeping his impatient pace and racing further into the wooded portion of the trail.

He continued along the path until he was well among the trees, unable to see the hospital or parking lot he had just crossed. A quick check ahead and behind him assured he was alone and he quickly skipped off the paved trail further into the small forest. He walked in the wilds now, just brush and fallen leaves among the half-barren trees. The ground sloped downward quickly towards a creek, and after a minute, he was well out of view of the path above him.

There was a thick pine tree ahead, ideal cover, and he made his way towards it as an extra concealing precaution. Straining his ears, he listened for anyone that he might have missed, but hearing nothing but wind and leaves, he stepped behind the tree and reached into his pack again for the amulet, placing it around his neck. Gripping the purple disk of the amulet with both hands, which hung at the low end of his sternum, he breathed deeply and squeezed. With some force, the largest of the purple stones cracked between his hands, and he breathed calmly, keeping cadence of the inhales and exhales to maintain a steady rate.

The sound of the wind faded around him till all he could hear was his heartbeat. Another few seconds and that too faded to a light ringing in his ears, and when even that faded, he felt a sudden rush of wind and light and sound explode. His feet lifted from the ground beneath him as he squeezed his eyes shut even tighter and concentrated hard on his breathing. He had always hated shifting, and none had been worse than his cross-Realm travel to start his Hunt here. He anticipated his return to be just as unpleasant. His felt his limbs stretched outward as he consciously tried to pull them in close to his chest amid the roaring sound growing around him. It was impossible for him to tell how far along he was until it suddenly stopped as quickly as it had begun, and feeling solid ground under his feet again, he opened his eyes.

He was standing in a bare and open room, sun pouring in through tall stained glass, which covered the majority of the wall space. Where he stood was a lovely landscape of grass and small shrubs and flowers, a kind of greenhouse garden within the large room. Before him sat a woman at a beautiful ivory desk, quite contrasted to the dark stone floor it rested on. Aside from the desk, the room was bare save a few unlit torches along the walls and a door behind the woman. She was draped in a white and silver robe with her hair stacked and braided impossibly high upon her head with a thin blue ribbon weaved through her deep red hair. She was pretty, but not in an extravagant way; it was a simple and natural beauty that she exuded, and her lack of attention to her personal look only amplified it. She pushed her thick, crude-cut glasses up her nose and squinted as Micky walked towards the desk, swooning slightly from the shifting and still doing his best to maintain his calm breathing pattern.

"You are most certainly not Lady Janeph," she said coyly as she eyed the gruff-looking man in the very out-of-place hospital scrubs.

"I know this is unexpected, my Lady. I am Captain Mikel of Eislark. I am working with Lady Janeph on Trillgrand's Hunt, and I seek audience with the High Council on her behalf. It is of utmost importance and time is our enemy. Are they available? Is Councilor Supreme Morgodello here?"

The woman nodded, dropping her questioning eyes the instant he stated his name.

"Apologies, Captain Mikel! I had no idea you were part of her Hunt!" She gave a short remorseful bow. "The Councilor Supreme is away on business at the moment, but he has means for communication, as do the other members of the Council. But I am not sure your status will allow such a meeting. Lady Janeph may not even be granted audience. Well, I mean you are quite well-known, I know of you, but . . . ." She stopped and looked down embarrassed, pushing her glasses up her nose. "Forgive me, I don't mean to sound rude, I only mean to say it is up to the Council to decide to whom they speak."

"No trouble, milady. A sweet woman like you shouldn't worry about such things. What shall I call you?"

"Potrella, Captain," she quickly stammered as he smiled at her warmly.

"Potrella, lovely. I understand what I am asking is not of proper etiquette. But I must speak to them, on Janeph's request. I have news of our ongoing Hunt, and I suspect the Councilor Supreme will be interested in the recent developments." Potrella smiled, accepting his kindness, and gave a quick bow before standing from the ivory desk.

"We will request audience through the Council Circle," Potrella said. "Is Lady Janeph alright? For you to be back here without the Lady must mean something is amiss." She shook her head quickly in dissatisfaction with herself and again looked down in modest shame. "Forgive me, it is not my concern. Please, this way."

She motioned to the large oak doors behind her, bowing slightly again. Micky mirrored her in acceptance with a calming smile and pushed the doors open with both hands. Two Blue Heart guards met him on either side of the doors as he and Potrella walked into the hallway beyond. The guards clanged their dark blue chest armor with a similarly armored fist before resuming their unwavering stance. The newly acquainted pair walked silently past them through the marvelously clean sandy white stone work. There were many windows, most were open and allowed a small breeze to billow through the thin sheer light blue curtains. Aside from the guards, the hall was very much empty.

"So, how does this work, Potrella? Do they shift back to us to speak? Or is this more of a magic potion sort of thing? Janeph was scarce on details."

"No, sir, nothing like that. It is as simple as wearing some jewelry." Mikel scrunched his face.

"Jewelry? I know I am decent looking, but I'm no princess. And I don't know you well enough to know if this is a joke or not, which normally I would embrace wholeheartedly, but this meeting really is quite important." She laughed softly and brushed a loose curl of her deep red hair behind her ear.

"As amusing as that would be, there will be no pretending to be a princess today for you, Captain Mikel. It is a simple piece of jewelry, nothing that could disguise your scruff and scars into a woman's figure. And I do not think the Council would enjoy seeing a dress-wearing Lark delivering any news, good or bad."

Mikel smiled at the playful jab as they turned down a new hallway and another set of guards on patrol slammed their fists to their armored chests as they passed. Neither of them acknowledged the guards. Mikel was lost in his thoughts now, a faraway look taking over as Potrella observed his ominous body language.

"Is this ill news you bring to the Council, Captain?" He nodded grimly, still half in thought. "Have we lost another Hunt?" she continued, fidgeting with her hands as they walked in a nervous twitch. Micky shrugged half-heartedly.

"To be honest, from the reports I've read of previous expeditions, we may be in the best position yet for a proper extraction. There are signs that the Grim are near, and we now expect an abduction will take place in the near future, assuming they hold the pattern from previous reports. We need reinforcements or we will surely miss our mark or be overrun. Even with Janeph, Bartellom, and I, we are only three. A Hunt of 10 was lost but one moon ago, Gritvand's latest Hunt. I am sure you have heard. The only survivor informed that their Grim warriors came looking for blood, plentiful and powerful they are. Undoubtedly the work of the Dark One, if you believe he's still out there."

He looked over towards the young woman's enthralled face, anxiety plainly written in her eyes. He puffed his chest and smiled charismatically. "But Gritvand's Hunt did not boast I or my comrades in their ranks. Janeph is skilled beyond her years, she is a true Blue Heart. And Bartellom is as brute a warrior as there ever was; the battlefield is one of the few scenes that he can truly let himself fall back to his people's ways. And I have never been bested in sword combat, not since I was but a child. So, I suppose even if it just us three, we would manage. A few more men to bolster our forces, an ambush, a little luck, and we will finally bring a Chosen home safely. Nothing to worry about, milady." Potrella smiled as the concern melted away before she looked away quickly, blushing.

"You Larks and your swords. Are you so skilled among such a renowned group?" He winked as they reached a large metal door and maintained his alluring smile.

"I most certainly am."

She blushed further before quickly turning and pushing hard on the metal doors, a loud squeal emanating from the old hinges. The door looked to be older than any part of the pristine Trillgrand city that Micky had seen. It was made of worn wood and heavy metal, iron from his best guess, held together with giant iron spikes that jutted out crudely from the frame. It was quite unlike the rest of the white stone castle and hallway that they had just walked; the door was an eyesore to otherwise beautiful and flowing architecture. Beyond the doors there was a single circular room comprised of large logs and wooden beams with a raised and pointed roof. There were no windows; in place of the natural light hung torches every few feet along the exterior of the circle, and in the center was a large candle chandelier dangling from the thick wooden beams that supported the roof above him. Drippings from the candles smothered the iron chandelier like wax frosting on a metal framed cake, and small pools of hardened wax cluttered the floor beneath it.

Spaced along the perimeter of the room were short wooden racks, on each of which hung a tapestry of various colors and symbols. He recognized his red and white ship for his coastal city of Eislark before looking to the others. A golden tree for the city of Dawnwood, an orange hammer for Gritvand, the green and yellow river of Swilmagapan, Bol-Garot's hook and line, the crowned wheat of Trillgrand. Some racks stood bare; an additional torch mounted where the tapestries would have hung. Micky admired the detail in the Trillgrand tapestry again briefly before asking, "So, is there a mirror to get this jewelry set? I intend to look my best for the Council."

She took a step towards the center of the room and gestured towards the lone chair and table. "No mirror, Captain Mikel. You need only take your seat, wear the crown, and announce yourself. Any of the available Council will then assemble shortly or perhaps not at all. I really do not know." She motioned for him to take his seat and moved back towards the doors. "I must return to the shifting room. Fortune unto thee, Captain. I hope your meeting goes well."

"Until next time, Potrella." She bowed, quickly closing the doors behind her, leaving Micky alone in the strange room before he could rip off a flirtatious reply.

He glanced around skeptically, waiting for the group of wizards to pop out in some grand fashion as was their way. But when none came forward, he made his way to the lone seat and table at the center of the room beneath the chandelier and grasping the worn wooden handles at the edge of the chair's armrest, sat gingerly onto the tattered red leather. It creaked loudly as he rested his weight onto it and he tensed, shifting his weight to his feet, expecting the chair to give completely beneath him. It held, and he relaxed incrementally onto the chair until it bore his full weight. Slowly, so as not to load one side of the chair more than the other, he pulled a thin crown resting on the table next to him from its blue pillow. It had two intertwining silver twists with small engravings along the length of it. It was fairly plain and worn, the silver smudged and spotted in many areas, and was not at all what he would consider fine craftsmanship. He spun it in his hands as he examined it, trying to make sense of where the front should be. The symbols were gibberish to him and picking one randomly to be the front and center of the crown, he rested it gently onto his brow. The instant it rested atop his skin he felt a great weight go through his head and limbs, as if his bones had become filled with lead. He fought to keep his chin from resting on his chest. Clearing his throat and gathering his strength, he spoke in a loud but somewhat strained voice, "Mikel of Eislark, Captain of the Gull."

He shifted slightly in the chair as another loud creak echoed in the room. He was met with only silence. Micky looked around, flexing and lifting his limbs to judge the odd phenomenon. They were easily twice what they normally weighed, and it felt like he was moving them through molasses as he stretched and strained his fingers.

"Fortune unto thee, Captain Mikel, I am Petravinos Morgodello of Trillgrand, Councilor Supreme. You have our attention. Please state your business." Micky sat up as straight as he could with his increased weight, embarrassed by his experimentation. He was unsure if the Council could see him or only hear him, and nothing around the room indicated either way.

"Fortune unto thee, Petravinos!" he said loudly to the empty air, yelling to the unseen voice. "What an honor to be speaking with you!"

"Yes, indeed, Mikel, but let us speak at a normal tone, shall we?" Petravinos and a few other voices chuckled lightly at the barb, and Mikel shifted embarrassed in the old chair, its creaking echoing loudly around him.

"Forgive me, Councilor Supreme," Mikel replied in a normal speaking voice. "I wish we had met under better circumstances for our first audience, but I must bring news from the latest Trillgrand Hunt. First let me say that your suspicion was correct, this Realm does seem to point towards Chosen occupancy and we are very close to the individual."

"But not close enough, I suspect," replied Petravinos mournfully and asking Mikel to further elaborate, "Is that why you've come, to let us know that this Hunt too has failed?"

"Quite the contrary, Councilor Supreme." The empty air held its breath, Mikel felt the room tense in anticipation, as if the space around him was a living representation of the voices he spoke with. "We believe the Grim have made contact but they have not made an attempt on their abduction. They seem unsure of whom to target and are currently unaware of our presence. I imagine they have never needed to check for Endland Hunters as they always end up beating us to the target. Regardless, it is only a matter of time before they identify the Chosen and make an attempt at them."

There was a light grumbling across the room, echoing around him and through him, complete and heavy. Micky almost tried to remove the crown before questions were asked of him.

"And has your Hunting Party identified The Chosen?" A gruff deep voice barked through the air. "Why not simply send word via scroll and bring the extraction party in? The Chosen must be obtained at once! This may be the last effort to do so!"

"Yes, yes," came another voice as silky as the first voice was rough. "This personal meeting is a bit strange. With the Chosen identified, we've no time for trivial meetings. What—"

"Quiet yourselves," came Petravinos's old but powerful voice. "Allow Mikel opportunity to speak before shoving further inquiries down his gullet!" Micky cleared his throat uncomfortably as small beads of sweat began to grease his palms.

"I apologize for I know not to whom I speak, but I can answer your questions." He was cut off by the gruff voice before he could start his next sentence.

"You speak with Lodak Dalgor of Gritvand."

"And Nirilith Sholsun of Dawnwood," came the smooth voice.

"A pleasure, fortune unto thee!" Micky replied giddily, a child among famous wizarding heroes.

"Enough of the pleasantries!" Petravinos cried, breaking his chain of thought. "There will be a time for proper introductions and blathering, but it is not now. There is a great deal at stake! The Trillgrand Hunt is the Realm's last! If the Grim have been sighted, then we have precious little time to act to secure the Chosen. Lodak speaks true, Captain. If the Chosen have been identified, then a simple scroll would have been enough notification, your return here was unwise."

Micky replied frantically, stammering to regain some control. "Of course, Petravinos! But unfortunately, we do not know specifically whom the Chosen is yet. It has been narrowed to a group of children that are under our care, a few hundred that come and go."

"A few hundred *children*? Are we certain the Chosen is a child?" Petravinos asked beseechingly as Mikel again shifted in his chair beneath the tough question.

"The odd misplaced feeling has been felt through at least two different children, possibly more based on their reactions," Mikel began and breathed deeply in preparation of his hopefully convincing argument. "We've not been in such a situation as this, racing against the Grim to identify the target. Previous Hunts have always been at least one step behind them, often charging in as they complete their collection, or crossing swords with a well-prepared enemy. But for the first time, we are in close proximity to Chosen and the Grim don't know it. We have the element of surprise but are uncertain how to identify the specific target."

He paused and breathed deeply again, "We would prefer an ambush coalition be prepared and attack the Grim head on as they move for extraction. We allow them to narrow the field before we spring upon them—defeat the beasts and pull the Chosen back to Endland. Their identification methods are tried and true while ours are, well, rather nonexistent."

Grumbles rose throughout the air, much as Micky expected, though he could not identify any words as the entire council seemed to be speaking at once. His body quivered with the audible energy that ran through him and the air round him, but he pressed on, speaking louder to overcome the arguments that were flooding the space and to hopefully drown out the others.

"We are yet to extract any Chosen from any Realm because we are always late! The few we have sent prematurely to identification have been incorrect and are lost upon their arrival to Endland. Now we are on time but do not know how to identify them! A change of tactics is needed! We use the Grim to identify and we strike them to seize the target!" The arguing was so loud now that he was quite sure that nothing he was saying was being heard. "We must fight!" He cried out, "Will you send—"

"Silence!" Petravinos bellowed.

The command was met immediately by all, the rest of Micky's sentence suddenly getting caught in his throat. He nearly choked but managed to swallow hard and felt the words move down his esophagus. He tried to clear his throat to continue but no sound came out. He felt his lips and tongue move into what should have been words but the room remained still. He smiled in spite of himself; he had been cast against by the great sage Petravinos Morgodello! What power to cast across the land! The Councilor Supreme's voice came clear and wanting from the others, breaking the exhaustive quiet.

"Captain Mikel, this plan is a fool's plan. The Grim do not point a finger at the Chosen before selecting them. They take them silently and without warning." He paused, mumbling to himself under his breath. "I am sorry Mikel, but the Council cannot aid your Hunt. You are on your own."

Micky's eyes saddened, and he ran his hand along his temple beneath the crown in frustration. "Petravinos," Micky stumbled in his sentence, surprised at his ability to speak again, "I cannot say I agree, but I understand. What about setting up a shifting net? We could track the Grim as they enter and rescue the Chosen before they are taken from us!"

He was met with continued silence and sighed in defeat as Petravinos held his tongue.

"We will work to identify the target with the extraction team. I can escort them back to the Realm as soon as they are assembled."

"Perhaps that was not clear, Captain. You are on your own in terms of *any* assistance."

Mikel reeled in his chair as it creaked loudly from the sudden shift in weight. "Councilor Supreme, please I beg of you, I did not intend to insult the council. We were only seeking another method and thought an ambush might yield new results. Please, do not withhold aid as punishment!"

"Mikel, I apologize. But let me be clear that it is not from a lack of want that we must withhold aid," Petravinos said. There was a pause and even though the spell had worn off, no one uttered a sound. "We have all but depleted our supply of loose shifting stone." Petravinos finished as Micky felt his stomach drop. "We've eaten into Endland's shifting net, creating gaps in coverage. If the Grim find these holes, they can bypass our protection systems, flooding Endland with—"

"Petravinos!" A council member chided in harsh criticism of the information being shared. A short silence followed before a voice was cleared, assumedly Petravinos's voice, as he reorganized his thoughts.

"Mikel, we do not even have enough to send you back on your Hunt. We cannot risk larger gaps in the net. There are just pebbles available for use between all the cities of the Eastern Island, enough to send some scrolls perhaps, even that would not be guaranteed."

"Wait!" Mikel interjected leaning forward in the old chair. "Can't we spare the stone to send me at least? What is a little more stone if it secures Chosen for Endland? We're asking a two-person Hunting Party to do what none have accomplished, even with small battalions at their disposal! I must be there! You must let me—"

"I am sorry, Mikel, there is no way. If you knew the extent to which we have already depleted our nets, you would understand. Janeph and Bartellom are on their own. They are our only chance for Chosen to return now. May Phont guide them."

Micky slouched in the old chair, defeated and dumbfounded, as it creaked loudly in protest. There were only a few Hunting parties left, Janeph's being one of them. She must know what dire straits they were in, that their Hunt was perhaps the last opportunity to retrieve Chosen.

"Petravinos, we must at least use what is left of the stone to notify Janeph; she must know the severity of the situation. She must know that she and Bartellom are alone, that they must plan for a two-person extraction."

"We will do what we can, Mikel," replied Petravinos in a somber tone that did not instill any confidence in Mikel. "Are there any objections to sending the last of our free stone to Janeph and Bartellom in hope that it reaches them?" There were audible sighs from others but no formal refusal. "Come now, if there are words to be had, then let us have them," Petravinos continued after a few more moments of noncommittal moaning from the group.

"I do not see a better use of the stone at this point," the gruff voice of Lodak came clear through the air. "Gritvand's party has returned this morning empty-handed again. We've no means to send out another Hunt. Trillgrand's Hunt is the last." Audible discomfort echoed from all parties, including Mikel. "We must do all we can for them. Send the stone." This was followed with some murmurs, carrying over the distress from hearing of Gritvand's failure, but it soon transitioned to sounding overall positive.

"And what if it fails?" a high-pitched voice questioned aloud, unclear to whom the inquiry was addressed. Mikel started to sigh, before holding his breath remembering the sound would most likely travel to the High Council.

"If it fails, Lopi," came Petravinos's strong voice, "then the worst we have done is lost a small amount of stone into the Void. If it succeeds, we increase our chances of bringing Chosen to Endland for the first time in a century. A difficult decision, I know, but I think even you can figure this one out?"

A few short snickers echoed around the empty space before another voice shushed them like children in the classroom. An uncomfortable throat clearing from Lopi followed.

"I only meant, Councilor Supreme, if this fails, what comes next? What will Endland do with no Chosen and the Grim slowly finding holes in our defenses and our lack of means to Hunt for others?"

"Yes, yes Lopi, we all know what you meant, but this discussion is on the use of the few pebbles we have left, not the decisions to be made if the Trillgrand Hunt fails. It is our last chance for extraction, and as Lodak said, we must do what we can."

"Yes, but shouldn't the—"

"Enough, are there any justifications for holding this stone from the Trillgrand Hunt?" Lopi started to speak up again but was cut off as Petravinos rolled over his interruption. "No? Good. This meeting of the council has ended. Thank you, Captain Mikel of Eislark, for your report. The remnants of the stone will be sent to aid in whatever manner it can to Janeph's Hunting Party, along with a scroll detailing the gravity of their extraction. I will see to it personally that the letter is sent. Fortune unto thee and fortune unto Lady Janeph and Bartellom."

The other council members echoed their good wishes before the room fell silent. Mikel sat in the chair feeling heavier than he had when the crown first rested atop his head. The room felt larger than when he had entered, and he, quite small sitting in the center of the quiet. The air cleared, emptying as the presence of the council members dissipated and it returned to its regular lightness. When he was sure there were no more voices, he reached to his brow and removed the crown slowly, placing it gently back on its blue pillow. Covering his face in his hands, he prayed with all his might to every god he knew, and every god he had heard in passing, for Janeph's and Bartellom's safety.

5

UNDISCLOSED
INFORMATION

ithin a few minutes the three had reached the edge of the atrium at the center of the building. The hospital was kind of in a sideways cross formation, the long hall employee wing sprawling west, where the nurse's lounge was, and the three shorter wings extending north, east, and south with the atrium resting at the center of the cross inter-section. The boys stopped short of the second-floor railing and peered out below them at the front desk, glancing around for anyone that might question why they were not resting in their rooms.

The atrium had a beautiful circular glass-domed ceiling, which allowed the natural light from above to flow down to the ground floor. The bright blue railings of the balconies wrapped around the circular lobby at each level and overlooked the main check-in desk and lounge, which was loaded with couches and chairs with televisions set up around the edges of the space to entertain those who were waiting. At the edge of where the northern wing started stood the glass-cased elevator and in front of it, a large statue of the hospital founder or a prestigious donor; Bryce never actually bothered to check what the plaque at the statue base said. There were a few people sitting around watching some show on one of the TVs and a number of employees working at the front desk, some catching glimpses of the show that was on. Even with the built-in TV distraction, the boys decided it best not to walk directly in the path of the front desk employees and raise suspicion.

Each wing had a separate staircase that opened into the atrium so the boys elected to stay on the second floor and quietly circle from their current location in the northern wing to the nurse's western wing, then drop down the stairs to the first floor and hop down the hall to their lounge. Johnny was being an obnoxious spy as they entered the atrium, hugging the wall and shuffling half an inch at a time before cartwheeling past an unoccupied janitor's closet and holding up his fist for his friends to stop, looking side to side in dramatic fashion as literally no one walked by. Zack had to muffle his laugh as Johnny staggered on his feet and nearly fell over, the blood draining from his face suddenly.

"Damn dizzy spells," he said before either Zack or Bryce could ask, both knowing the feeling. "I don't get it, it's so random." They had all spoken about the odd symptoms in private to their doctors. A cartwheel shouldn't cause a kid to lose his balance, especially after repeatedly coming back with clean bills of health from every test that was thrown at them. By tomorrow or the next day they would all be cleared and sent back home, as they had for the past year. And then in another month or so, they would all wind up back in again.

They descended the stairs quickly, stopping at the midlevel landing and peeking down to the ground floor, analyzing for signs of any nurses that may be out and about. Bart walked past the stairwell opening towards the break room as they shuffled backwards and out of view. A few seconds of silence later, they continued down to the first floor and checked down the hall that Bart had walked. They caught sight of his back as he opened and closed the door behind him before they quickly zipped after him.

As they approached the doorway, they could already hear muffled voices speaking to each other. The group slowed to a shuffle, hunching and tiptoeing towards the closed door and listening intently. A few feet from the doorway, the boys lined single file against the hallway wall and pressed their ears to the cool grey paint to listen as best they could. Bryce was half listening, half being a lookout. They were horribly exposed in the middle of the hall and their hunching posture with ears to the wall screamed mischief.

Any adult would question their intentions if they walked by. Bryce poked Johnny's ribs, "Hey guys, what happens if someone see us? What do we say?"

"Shut up man I'm trying to listen!" Johnny hissed back and swatted Bryce's hand away, closing his eyes and concentrating on the sounds coming from the room. Bryce poked his friend again but without reaction, shrugged, and followed suit by pressing his ear to the wall.

"... on alert at all times. If any children see him or think they might have seen him, it is to be reported immediately. The kids must know this is to be followed strictly. They are to find a nurse and talk right away."

"And what about the other nurses, milady? We don't hold much power here. How can we express to the other nurses how serious this is without driving them to ask the basic question: why not call the guards?"

"We simply say security has already been made aware. Tell them I notified them, hopefully that will put an end to that line of questioning."

"What about the guards, Janeph?"

"The 'police,' not the guards."

"Right, the police. They may ask what's going on if another nurse alerts them."

"Yes, they may, but if we just stress it's been taken care of, that's really all we can do until Mikel gets back."

"I would bet we're going to get a lot of 'What in Phont's name are you talking about' questions. And speaking of our third member, when's Mikel returning from the Council meeting?"

"I forget the time change here, but I would bet he spends a day there and is back in another hour or so."

"Leave it to him to have a night of drinking before extraction, huh?"

They laughed together as Bryce pulled his ear from the wall. It was a strange conversation, but the bottom line was that Jan and Bart thought this guy was bad news, plain and simple, and everyone would certainly be on the lookout for him. His train of thought was broken quickly as Zack and Johnny straightened from their haunches rapidly, almost knocking Bryce's teeth together as his chin hit Johnny's back.

"Let's go!" Zack whispered, already tiptoe jogging back to the stairs. The group followed suit, running as silently as they could for a few steps and then quickly sprinting to the stairs. Bryce rounded the stairwell corner after Zack as he heard the door open down the hall. Johnny was right on his heels as they raced to the second floor, Zack never stopping as he continued to run up the next flight to the third floor.

"See you at lunch!" he whisper-yelled back down the stairs as he zipped out of sight. He sure could move for a big guy. Bryce left the stairs at the second floor and turned to salute Johnny, who gestured back and followed Zack back up the stairs, both staggering slightly from the physical exertion.

Bryce slowed his pace as Johnny left his sight. His head pounded and his breath came heavy just as it had for Johnny after his unnecessary, albeit funny, acrobatic display near the Janitor's closet. He walked the rest of the way to his room, averting his eyes to any nurses that questioningly looked his way and thinking on what Jan and Bart were so worked up about. Upon arriving to his room, he kicked off his moccasins and laid down for a much-needed nap before lunch.

———

6

THE CREEPY ONE

◇

After they got their lunches, Zack and Johnny moved towards Bryce in the cafeteria. His plate was still full and he was looking at the opposite wall blankly, mindlessly twirling his spoon on his food. His demeanor quickly changed the second his two friends approached.

"Mr. J, Papa Bear, how was the rest of your morning? Splendid I presume?" Bryce asked in his best British accent. It was terrible but he did it anyways.

"Oh, you know, tea and crumpets and staying in my room not eavesdropping on secret meetings, that sort of thing. It was quite the morn, eh Mr. Bear?" said Johnny as he sat next to him. Zack nodded in approval as he slid back his chair and sat eagerly at the end of the table.

"Yes, yes, all good things, chum. I even got me-self another Jell-O!"

Johnny grinned and shifted the accent back to Americanized English. "But the real question is, who is the groundskeeper slash delivery guy slash random visitor?"

"Who indeed," said Bryce, turning slightly to face his friends. "Nurse Jan sounded pretty worried during their meeting. And Bart sounded just as worried when he talked to our wing before I came down for lunch. I mean he is a big guy but he seemed nervous about this regular-looking dude. And he wouldn't give any details except 'Just call us if you see him.' Did Micky give your wing any details?" The two sat next to Bryce shaking their heads "no."

"He didn't talk to us, Jan did," Zack replied. "She said Micky had to go do or get something and would be back later. Must have been what they were talking about in their meeting?"

"Whatever," Johnny said as he ate and spoke at the same time. "Sounds like he was going to some bar since he was getting drinks, right? Forget Micky though, what do we know about this weirdo walking around? We know for sure Martha, you, and I have seen him so let's start there, but you haven't yet Papa Bear?"

"No, I haven't seen anyone odd that I can think of. That isn't exactly a lot to go on though, him just being 'odd.' What was he doing when you saw him Johnny?"

Johnny was digging into his mashed potatoes eagerly but paused between bites to swallow and respond with a clear mouth, opening his chocolate milk carton as he did so. His appetite was clearly coming back, as usual on the second day of an episode.

"Nothing really, he was walking through the hall like he was on his way to visit someone. I saw him walk by and then he doubled back a minute later to give me a wave. I hadn't seen him before but a friend in need is a friend in deed, or so they say, so I gave him a solid salute. He smiled like a psycho, which gave me the willies, and off he ran."

"But he wasn't dressed like a groundskeeper? Or a delivery guy?" Bryce asked. Zack raised a finger to pause the conversation while he attempted to swallow the fistful of food he had shoveled into his mouth. Johnny pushed his glasses up his nose in mischievous glee.

"Boy, he looks like Thud Butt from *Hook*, don't he? Right after they make the imaginary food into real food and get in that big food fight? You know?" Both Zack and Bryce looked at their friend with expressionless faces. On top of being so naturally funny, somehow in his short 13 or so years on planet Earth,

Johnny had seemingly managed to see every film ever created since the dawn of man and subsequently had memorized every important quote, scene, and cast member. Bryce would bet that he could out-quote the writers on their own movies if he needed too. It was a frequent event for him to name-drop someone or spit out a quote in a bizarre accent and only receive dazed and confused looks from his friends. Zack was continuing to chew still, so Bryce posed the question they both were thinking.

"Who or what is a 'Thud Butt'?"

"Oh, come on! You guys have never seen *Hook*? The next chapter in Peter Pan? With Dustin Hoffman? And Robin Williams?" Bryce and Zack looked at each other and shrugged together.

"I think I've heard of Robin Williams," Bryce guessed.

"Wow. Just, wow." Johnny paused and then closed his eyes, dropped his voice into a deeper tone, and rubbed his temples with his fingers.

"I'm surrounded by idiots."

"Ok 'Scar,' don't make me get Simba to kick your ass again," Zack said, finally able to speak after clearing his mouth of the miniature feast he had stuffed in it.

"Good, good!" yelled Johnny, "*The Lion King* is strong with this one! But I think we all can agree; Scar had the crown won, man. If he hadn't acted like such a hard-ass and told Simba he murdered his pops, he'd still be king. But no, he just had to play the cool guy card and start gloating, blabbing about his master plan when he was a wrist flick from victory. What an idiot," Johnny retorted in a more serious voice than was warranted for such a trivial conversation. Bryce and Zack laughed out loud before returning to the original topic.

"Scar had it won, but Simba was the rightful king. He would have found a way. But more importantly, now that Zack has cleared his face hole, what was it you were going to say?" Bryce asked, still smirking. Zack's face sobered and he leaned in closer to his friends, grabbing the roll off his plate.

"I was thinking about this guy after we got back to our rooms. So, here's my theory." The others rolled their eyes as Zack paused to take a bite from his roll. "What day waf it yefterday?"

"Uh, October?" said Johnny in his best drunk voice. Bryce ribbed him with an elbow in annoyance.

"Come on man, focus for like 30 seconds. It was Sunday, so what?"

Zack chewed and swallowed the bite he took and moved to shove the rest in his mouth before Bryce stopped him with a quick wrist grab. Zack scowled but allowed the restraint as he spoke.

"Do groundkeepers or delivery companies usually work on Sunday?" He said very matter-of-factly before he shoved the rest of the roll in his mouth, working right through Bryce's grip. Johnny and Bryce pondered as Bryce let Zack's hand go.

"I don't think so? The ground crew is a Monday through Friday operation probably," said Johnny, thinking it through as he spoke.

"And the mail is never delivered on Sundays. Could have been an Amazon thing? Don't they do Sundays?" Bryce questioned. Zack nodded and shrugged.

"I don't know, but I thought it was a UPS guy anyways?" Zack asked, as he snuck Johnny's roll from his plate.

"I don't think Sniffs knew what she saw," Johnny said, recollecting the morning meeting.

"So, assuming the guy was UPS or whatever and also a groundskeeper, he was posing as people who don't have any business being here on a Sunday? I guess that's weird, sort of?" Bryce said trying to convince himself it was as odd as Zack thought it was.

"I think so," Zack said with a clear mouth again.

"It's not that weird. Working that overtime, making that money, man. That's not abnormal," Johnny retorted as he plopped his applesauce with the back of his spoon.

"I guess that can be explained, but what is definitely weird are his clothes," said Bryce.

"What are you, a fashionista now?" Johnny jested as Zack giggled into his milk carton.

"No, I'm just a keen-eyed superhuman. Think about it. Why did this dude change at all? From a groundskeeper by me, to a UPS guy by you, to an actual visitor by Martha? If he wanted to get in, wouldn't it be easier and less suspicious to just dress normal from the get-go and be a visitor?" The others pondered this, eating as they thought. Zack chewed loudly and somehow gulped even louder before responding.

"Maybe he was like, scouting the area, you know? Like he was trying to figure where the best way to get in and around was so he disguised himself?" said Zack, looking for approval from his friends.

"I suppose that's possible," started Bryce. "When exactly did you see the mystery man, Johnny? Morning or afternoon or what?" Johnny scrunched his nose thinking as Zack took a spoonful of veggies.

"I think we can do better than 'mystery man' guys. How about Sir Creepsalot? Yea, yea, that's good. Ok, so Sir Creepsalot popped up right around dinnertime, maybe 5:30-ish?"

"Shut up, Johnny, I'm being serious," Bryce interrupted, a deep scowl on his brow as he took a sip of his milk. Johnny looked at Bryce with open confusion.

"I'm serious as a heart attack, man. Let's be honest. Sir Creepsalot is a way better name. And just because your nickname sucked and you lost another bout to the great Joker in the wonderful art of childish banter," Johnny looked to Zack for approval, which he refused with a crossing of arms and his own scowl, "doesn't mean you have to get all salty. You win some you lose some, or so they say, and today my wordsmithing outdid yours B-man."

"Not about the name, man! I could give a rat's ass about the name. When did you *actually* see the guy?"

"I think you meant to say 'When did I see Sir Creepsalot," corrected Johnny, his playful grin shining through as he spoke. Bryce would normally welcome such silly repartee from his friend, but Johnny was starting to really get under his skin. And what's worse was that Johnny's smile screamed *"I'm under your skin, and I know it!"* Bryce wiped his face with his hands in an act of frustration and sighed loudly so as to drive the point.

"Johnny, when did you see," another sigh, "Sir Creepsalot?"

"Ah yes, the creepy one. As I was saying, Nurse Jan had just dropped off my plate, which she said was 'cooked with all the love in the world' or one of her typically over-positive Nurse Jan lines, when I saw the guy, Sir Creep himself, wandering the hall. He just walked on by as Jan handed off the food, kind of glanced in towards me with a smile. But then another minute later after Nurse Jan had walked out, and I was digging into my lovely dish, he popped up again, looking in the doorway and gave a wave. And being the kind fellow that I am, I returned politely with a sergeant's salute."

"So he was already inside the building and you're sure it was dinnertime?" Bryce asked. Johnny looked to Zack incredulously, now apparently having Bryce under his skin.

"Zack, how could I make this any more clear?" Zack shrugged his shoulders looking down at his plate, realized it was empty, and grabbed the roll off Bryce's plate. Johnny marveled at Zack's appetite for a second before turning back to his other friend. "Yes, Bryce, I'm sure that I ate my dinner at dinnertime. The sun starts to set. In comes Jan. I eat. It's not complicated." Bryce stared at Johnny, unable to tell if he was being fooled with or not. It was impossible for this guy to be outside waving and then suddenly inside, new clothes, waving to Johnny. It had to be two people. Or twins or brothers or two totally random strangers. "Hello? Earth to Bryce!" Johnny said, knocking his knuckles on Bryce's brow. Bryce snapped out of his thoughts and retreated, batting away his friend's hand as he continued.

"Johnny, I saw the guy yesterday too, at sunset, outside, raking leaves. It had to be within minutes of when you saw him."

Johnny measured Bryce's face and body language as he replied. "What do you mean you saw him yesterday at sunset? What did he do, run from the yard up to my room so he could wave at me? Did he deliver that package on the way to my room too? Maybe he had time to mop the floor as a janitor too, and send a fax as—"

"Shut up, Johnny, I'm serious!" Bryce's lips were pressed in outright aggravation, forehead furrowed as his fist pounded the table next to his plate, which managed to stop Zack's non-stop eating and Johnny's buffoonery. Johnny glanced at Zack in surprise and turned back to read his irritated friend's reddened face. For a few moments there was stillness before Johnny suddenly burst into laughter. Zack looked at both of them, unsure of what to do as Johnny roared.

"Oh wow, you had me going for a second there man! That fist pound so convincing, so angry! 'Shut up Johnny, I'm serious.' Wow, that was good!" Zack started laughing along cautiously with Johnny now, joining in on what they both perceived to be quite the joke. But Bryce had not moved his gaze from Johnny, straight-faced and without the faintest hint of a smile. The two laughed a little while longer before Zack managed to look long enough to see his friend's somber expression and nudged Johnny.

"Hey man, I think he *is* serious."

Johnny looked up at Bryce and only laughed harder, borderline seizing in a throe of hysteria. "And this poker face! Bryce man, you're a riot! You can laugh now man. Go ahead and join in, you've earned it! That was a great deadpan, I've taught you well, haven't I, my little apprentice?" Bryce swiped his face with his hands in open detestation, took a calming breath and replied.

"Johnny, 100-percent serious, I saw him last night at sunset raking leaves outside in the parking lot. My parents were in my room and had brought me burgers and beans like they usually do when we first have to be admitted. Right when they got there, I happened to glance out the window and the guy waved up at me. I'm not joking." Johnny, finally realizing that his friend might actually not be messing around, sat up straight and wiped the tears from his eyes.

"That's impossible, man. I saw him outside in the hallway last night. I doubt he would have changed from raking clothes to everyday-visitor clothes that quickly just to come in and give me a 'what's up' wave. It was probably a different guy altogether. And sorry Zack, I think your theory of scouting was off. If he was inside already, why would he need to scout a way in?"

Zack shrugged at the dismissal of his theory. "What exactly did this guy look like in the first place?"

Johnny wiped the last of his giggle tears off his cheeks. "Yea, you're like the only one who hasn't seen Sir Creepy, huh? I think half the kids in the circle have seen him judging by their faces! The problem is he is just 'Joe Shmoe' enough that he probably describes about half the population of middle-aged white men."

"Just 'Joe Shmoe' enough?" Zack asked taking another massive bite of food off of Bryce's plate.

"Yea you know, average height, average weight, brown hair, normal, plain, bland, yadda, yadda, yadda, etcetera, etcetera. The only thing that makes me think he might be the same guy, and I emphasize *might* be," Johnny said as he looked to Bryce to calm his excited agreeableness, "is his odd waving habit and ridiculous smile. But let's be honest, waving and smiling to strangers isn't exactly odd behavior. Have you ever waved at a complete stranger? It's hilarious! They wave back to be nice but they have no idea who the hell you are!" Bryce and Zack both laughed in agreement.

"Yea, yea, everyone waves, everyone smiles, I get it," Bryce said still chuckling. "But did you see the looks Martha and I got when we were talking about him this morning? And then Nurse Jan canceling one of her 'sharing sessions' to have a private meeting with Bart where they talk about how to handle this guy being around? I'm sure you felt it too; something was strange about him."

"I think you mean, Sir Creepsalot," Johnny smiled back. Zack suddenly started coughing, spitting up food onto his chin and plate. It dribbled slowly from his lips and plopped loudly onto the cafeteria table as he tried to wipe his face and catch his breath.

"Chew your food; you're an animal!" yelled Johnny, smacking his friend hard on the back a couple times. He looked to Bryce with a smile, hoping he had recognized his quote but he was not looking. He was instead grabbing napkins from the table to clean up the mess Zack had just made.

"You alright there, big guy?" asked Bryce handing him the napkins, which he accepted and then covered his face in semi-embarrassment to hide the food across his chin.

"No *Matilda* recognition? Brother choking on a carrot? Danny DeVito? Nothing?" chimed Johnny. "Off the wall for sure, but it's legit." Johnny stopped as he caught the look on his friend's pale face. Zack's eyes were locked to the left, wide with shock as he obliviously patted the food spittle he had spewed.

"Does that guy over there in the doorway look familiar?"

Bryce and Johnny looked over and the blood ran from their faces. There was the man, standing in the doorway with that big stupid smile of his, waving away. They all looked down and away at once, all now pretending something terribly interesting was on the table or floor that was worth their undivided attention. Johnny took off his glasses and inspected them for dust that was not there, trying to look inconspicuous.

"Bryce—"

"Yes," Bryce said before he could even finish. "That's the guy that was raking leaves last night." Johnny exhaled onto both glasses and began wiping them gently with his shirt.

"Wow. Ok, so he was in my doorway yesterday. But he was also raking leaves. How can that be? And are you as creeped out as I am?"

"Yes," came the reply again, this time in unison from both Bryce and Zack.

"I'm going to call over Nurse Jan," said Zack, looking up and away from Sir Creepsalot's doorway. Nurse Jan, seemingly sensing their discomfort, was already walking towards the group. Zack gave her a half smile, grabbing his milk container as she approached.

"Is Creeps still in the doorway? Jan's on her way over here now." The other two were still looking down at the interesting nothingness on the floor.

"I'm not sure. That guy is kind of, sort of, definitely weirding me out though, and I'd rather not check," said Johnny, pretending to pick dirt out of his fingernails now as he visibly shuddered. "There is something about that smile that just doesn't fit."

"Hey guys, how's your lunch today? It seems like you're a little down about something, all hunched over here," said Nurse Jan, stopping a few feet from the table and crossing her arms in guarded concern. "You're not still upset about having our group session cut short today are you?" The boys sat silent for a moment, Bryce glancing up towards Nurse Jan and then looking back down.

"Nurse Jan, do you remember that guy Martha and I were talking about this morning? The one that we saw waving to us yesterday? And the one that Bart told us to tell you if we saw him?" She nodded approvingly, face undergoing a metamorphosis from cheery to dreary. "I think he is over in the doorway." Nurse Jan did not look up towards the door but continued to look at Bryce.

"How sure are you, Bryce?"

"Pretty damn sure, Jan," Johnny butted in. "Pardon the language but it is him, right B-man?" Jan scowled but it was hard to say if it was at Johnny's language or at his recognition of the man. She sat down next to the boys with her back to the door as Bryce nodded to reinforce Johnny's statement.

"John, you've seen this man, too?" Jan asked somewhat alarmed. He shook his head grimly.

"Something is up, ain't it, Jan? I mean, this isn't just some guy, is he?" She breathed in deeply and exhaled very slowly.

"OK, I need you boys to stay put right here, OK?" she replied, ignoring Johnny's inquisition. "Just stay put and talk among yourselves. And whatever you do, *do not* look towards the doorway. Just act natural and I'll be back in a jiffy." Her normal cheer and general good-vibes feel were gone, replaced by clear anxiety and a kiss of fear. She stood and walked to the far side of the cafeteria, doing her best to hide her haste as she power walked between the tables.

"You don't really think that guy is dangerous, do you?" Zack asked his friends, still looking down. Johnny shrugged.

"Who knows, Papa Bear, but Jan seems convinced he is," Johnny exhaled deeply as Nurse Jan had just moments ago. "But it's probably not even the same guy. We're all probably hallucinating or something and can't notice they're totally different people," Johnny suggested, trying to convince himself as much as the others.

"I doubt it J," Bryce interjected, "Nurse Jan wouldn't be acting so strange if he was just a normal guy. And she straight up ignored Johnny's question about something being up, so I'd say something is definitely up."

"Maybe he is looking for something or someone?" Zack proposed. "Like something at the hospital or a kid or something?"

"What the hell would someone want with a bunch kids in a hospital? And why not just go to the front desk like a normal person?" The three sat there for another minute contemplating the question, heeding Jan's advice, and avoiding looking towards the door. Bryce rubbed the top of his head nervously and sighed loudly.

"Look guys, what if—" Bryce stopped abruptly and shivered, a ripple of goose bumps stretching from the base of his skull down through his extremities as a headache erupted in his temples and caused his eyes to shut hard.

"Yes, yes, come now. Let's hear what the young man has to say? If you three friends put your heads together, I bet you can figure what exactly is going on here. I am assuming, of course, that you three are friends?" The voice was smooth like velvet and with a hint of deceit, like you would expect from a used-car salesman or a grimy lawyer.

The three turned and looked up to their left to see the man prompting all of the day's commotion and anxiety, Sir Creepsalot, standing before them. Blue jeans, sneakers, and a silver-white shimmering polo, with the "Joe-Shmoe" features Johnny had so aptly applied. Plain brown hair swept to the left over a plain face with a long nose which pointed somewhat above a pair of thin long lips. His slender sharp nose separated clean shaven and rosy cheeks.

The three boys said nothing, watching in incredulity that he was standing before them.

"I'm sorry, where are my manners? My name is James." He stuck out his hand for a shake, which was met by continued stares. He seemed friendly enough but the sheer bewilderment of seeing him face to face was blocking their motor functions.

James did not miss a beat and continued as if he had received the handshakes he was so clearly gesturing for. "And you three are?"

———

7

ALONE

Jan turned on her heels away from the boys, walking as quickly as possible without appearing in a hurry; she could not let him know she was here. She doubted the Grim would have a report on her, but Bartellom was large enough to draw even unsuspecting eyes. She crossed the room, trying to smile at the other children as she passed, and pushed open the doors to the hallway. As soon as the doors closed, she full on sprinted to the lounge, dodging staff and patients alike before crashing through the doors to the surprise of a few nurses occupying the room.

"Sorry, everyone!" she blurted loudly to the strange looks. "But has anyone seen Bart or Micky?"

"Sorry, Jan, I haven't seen either of them since this morning. But you did get some mail in. Were you expecting a letter from Camelot today?" one of the nurses replied as she gestured over to their mailboxes, snickering with the other nurses at her table. "Don't mean to be nosey, but I couldn't help but notice it. That's got to be a prank or something, right? Does the post office actually deliver wax-sealed rolls of paper?"

There was more laughter, still somewhat concealed, but Jan did not hear it. She quickly walked to the table without another word or glance to the others. She felt her heartbeat accelerate as her thumb brushed over the two blue ribbons across either end of the rolled paper and the crowned wheat insignia imprinted into the yellow wax seal. Taking it in her hand, she felt it was much heavier than a simple piece of rolled parchment. With a quick turn on her heels, scroll held delicately in her hands, she retreated toward the exit.

"If you see either of them, would you tell them I need to speak with them right away? I'll be over by the cafeteria. Thanks!" she yelled as she flung the doors back open to the hallway, not waiting for a response. The ribbon was already half off as the doors closed, and she quickly transitioned to freeing the paper from the wax's sticky grip. It gave and she found that pressed into the underside of the seal was a simple string maybe two feet long but intertwined in it were a series of small stones, shimmering purple. Most were as small as her fingertips, the largest maybe double in size of that, and at the end of the string was a golden coin of exceptional craftsmanship with a crowned grain engraved on one side and the distinct symbol of Petravinos Morgodello on the other.

"Hey Jan, aren't you at lunch now?" came a call down the hall from big Bart. A page went out over the intercom system for Bart and Micky which sapped the smile from the large man's face.

"What's going on, what's happened?" He stopped short of her, seeing the shimmering gold coin and purple stones. "Are those shifting stones?" he asked in a hushed tone.

"A gift from Trillgrand. And a note from Mikel."

Bart grabbed the letter immediately, to Jan's annoyance, and read for a few seconds before handing it back to her calmly. "He won't be returning," Bart said stoically as he crossed his arms and sighed deeply. "Why send us such small stones in his stead? What good are these to us? We already have ours plus a third set for the Chosen. This is hardly enough for a single shifting, especially considering it was partly used to send it here in the first place," Bart concluded, pointing to a number of the stones that were clear crystal, looking as if the purple color had been sucked out of them. Jan was half listening and half reading the scroll as Bart complained.

"The ambush has been rejected as well," Jan replied as she handed the note back to Bart and examined the stones more closely. He grabbed it and continued reading as he spoke.

"We thought that may be the case. But now they won't send Mikel back as punishment?"

"Perhaps you should read the rest, Bartellom?" Jan whispered mockingly. Bart obliged with a lip-pressed smile, and after a short minute, he crushed the small paper, his forearms rippling in frustration.

"So Gritvand's Hunt has failed, we're the last chance for returning Chosen to Endland, and there isn't any shifting stone left to send us any backup, even Mikel," he summarized through gritted teeth. "It would have been nice to know we were low on shifting stone *before* we sent Mikel back!" Jan rested an arm on his massive shoulder and held up the string of stone.

"We can try to set up a net at least. It will be small but perhaps it will be enough," said Jan thoughtfully. "It's a long shot but it's all we can do. And we still have the element of surprise. Any Grim who arrives won't be expecting a net, so we will have the advantage initially."

Bart took the string skeptically. "Jan, stones of this size will do nothing! Even with as small a zone to protect as this building. But somehow Petravinos expects this stringed gravel will help us stop the Grim?" Bart's muscles bulged in anger and he seemed to grow in stature momentarily.

"Peace, Bartellom, you must not lose your temper here. This will not halt the Grim, but it will at least let us know of their arrival and give us a chance." She sighed anxiously, fiddling with the string of stones. "And I fear we will not need to wait long. One of the children is surely Chosen; a Grim has just revealed his presence outside the cafeteria."

"What! When? Where?" Bart's aggravation was now evaporated completely, replaced by a storming rage as he attempted to brush past her. Jan ripped his arm with considerable force, which was surprisingly enough to slow him, and Bart turned back to her with his jaw pressed.

"Shroud your anger! The Grim do not know we are here and we must keep that way!" She ripped a large portion of the string and handed it to Bart as he opened his hand begrudgingly. "Your task is the net for now. Place them at the central point of the hospital. I will return to the children and try to give them some peace, and then hold the rest of the stones until we are ready for extraction. Last room of the northern wing is still empty, a bit of a dead end, but it will have to do. Hopefully we won't have to defend it for long."

Bart snorted in a frustrated exhale but nodded. "I will prep the net," he said gruffly and stomped off in the other direction with the string in hand, tossing the mangled note into a trash can as he went. Jan tossed the wax seal into the same can as she speed-walked towards the front desk to fetch security. They would only be able to offer a false sense of comfort, but for now, it was all she could do for the boys.

8

LIFE AND DEATH

N one of them said a word, their stares continuing up at him, none quite sure what to do now that the strange man had confronted them. James's eyes were the darkest brown, nearly black, pulling their gazes in like light to a black hole. They weren't sure they could look away if they wanted to.

"Well, boys, I do assume you have names, do you not?" James spoke with soothing charisma in a calm but strong tone. Shifting slightly, Johnny straightened in his seat.

"There are those who call me . . . Tim?"

Bryce smacked his palm to his forehead reactively, recognizing the reference immediately as Johnny did his best to hide his growing smirk. The man smiled as well, pulling back his extended hand which had still not received a shake.

"Ah, Tim, I had sworn you were Johnny Pragg." The boy's jaws dropped to the floor, and James let out a short light chuckle as he continued to display his giant smile. James now looked to the other two, reading them with his keen dark brown eyes. "And if I were to guess for you two, big man here is Zack Kapule." Zack scrunched his face slightly at the comment. James's face softened apologetically, realizing he may have offended the hefty child. "I apologize, Zack, that was rude of me to assume. But if I am correct, that would make you Bryce Blooms." He glanced over the group again before continuing and bore his wide grin at their utterly bewildered faces. "You must be wondering who I am and how I know this about you, yes?" James was met with more silent stares as they dealt with their current quandary. "Well, my dear boys, I can tell you all that and more, but I have little time to explain it all here. Let me start with the bottom line: I have come with a warning."

"Here's a warning for you!" Zack exclaimed. "Security is probably already on their way. Plus, everyone else here has seen you now, so we'll know who to look for if you show your creepy face again!" Zack spit with uncommon fire for the gentle giant. His manners almost never faltered, especially to an adult and even more so to a stranger. Even with his anger, the high pitch and quiver in his voice allowed his fear to shine through. Bryce noticed it immediately, mostly because he felt the same fear himself. James gave a small apologetic bow.

"Oh my, dear children. My apologies if I frightened any of you, there is no need for such wrath and certainly no need for any guards. You see, I'll be gone before anyone knows we've spoken." He gestured out towards the rest of the cafeteria with an open hand as he said this, bidding the boys to have a look around.

Bryce surprisingly noticed that the people at the table next to them had not seemed to notice the Creep was talking to them. He scanned the rest of the room and found that no one seemed to notice him. In fact, no one was noticing *anything*. After a moment he realized with terror that they were the only ones moving. It looked as if time had stopped. The boys watched in perplexity as the other children were in mid-bite, mid-sentence, mid-laugh, locked in time. Bryce looked closer and found that with concentration, he could see the nearly imperceptible movements of those around him, similar to the focus needed to see a slow cloud's passage through the sky. Martha moved as if she was about to unleash one of her viscous allergy sneezes, her eyes ever so slowly closing, her face contorting wrinkle by wrinkle. One of the cafeteria workers was pouring a large ladle of soup into a bowl for Zep, liquid suspended in the air like a chilled waterfall, floating gently downwards. Bryce looked towards the clock on the wall and found that the seconds hand was not moving but every five seconds or so. They were somehow the only ones functioning at a normal speed.

"What did you do to them?" Zack demanded, looking back towards James.

"Oh, not to worry, not to worry, no harm has come to them, they are just in a sort of time-out, that's all. They will be back in their normal states in another minute or so, not a clue as to what we've experienced. I've ways of manipulating such things, you see."

"What the hell does that mean? Who are you?" Bryce yelled now, his own fear beginning to manifest itself in his broken manners. He could feel his brain fighting itself to come to a determination on whether James was as dangerous as Jan had said or was as kind as he appeared.

"I am glad you asked, Bryce Blooms." James smiled and spread his arms wide, raising them to the sky, his silver shirt glittered in the artificial building lighting. "I am here to guide you and other children on the next steps of your spiritual journey," James replied sounding as noble as he could, but the boy's looks were pure skepticism. He ignored their cynical faces as his smile faded and he continued, "Heed my warning. Within the next day, children, you may pass. It is difficult to say exactly whom, I haven't quite pinpointed it yet, but certainly one of you will leave this Realm by this time tomorrow, probably sooner even. And if and when that happens to you, I will be here to be your shepherd into the afterlife, to guard you and keep you, to reassure you in your time of need and to help you into the great beyond." The boys remained still and silent as they tried to comprehend what they were just told.

"We're going to 'pass'?" Bryce finally questioned.

"Yes, it is what you assume, Bryce. You're going to die, well one of you at least." He paused here as if allowing time for the solemnity of his comments to sink in.

"Are you the grim reaper?" interrupted Zack, barely a whisper. James smiled his creep look at them and the three of them shuddered collectively.

"Not exactly. And I'd love to explain but unfortunately," he said, looking to a flashy silver watch, "I must go, taking this form is draining and slowing time in an entire building takes its toll. Perhaps we will meet again if you are the one I am here for. And, if you could do me a favor, don't tell anyone of our meeting. Not that they would believe you anyways!" James gave a strange bow, placing his left hand on his heart, his right hand facing the ground hand down with his palm open to the floor, as his right leg slid out and he flexed at the waist. It was quite honestly the most bizarre bow any of them had ever seen.

"Wait a minute! You can't just pop up, drop that bomb on us, and then disappear!" Johnny yelled angrily as James glanced up from his strange bow, perplexed. Johnny continued, "'Hey guys, I'm that stranger you saw the other day, all at the same time. Oh, and PS I'm a weird-ass death shepherd or something. PPS, you might be dead by tomorrow. Bye-bye!'"

Johnny was standing, face red with disbelief and lack of oxygen. "Now you'll stay here and tell us just what the hell is going on! How exactly do you know our names? Or that one of us is going to die? Is it this sickness that I have, that we have?" James smirked one last smile and melted into a smoky fog without another word as the world around them sped up. The sounds of the cafeteria slowly returned, like the volume had been turned back up on a television, and the slow-motion state dissipated. Johnny looked to Bryce and Zack, then out and around the cafeteria as the room returned to a normal pace, accelerating until the world was as it was before their brief meeting with James.

"How," Johnny started but then sat, unable to finish. The boys were motionless, processing what James had just told them, numb with confusion. Bryce scanned the room, looking for James or some trace of the smoke he had disappeared into, but found none. The tables around them spoke their conversations, the nurses and adults continued their chaperoning. No one had noticed, just as James had said. The three sat for a few minutes, none speaking, until Bryce finally broke out of the trance.

"Do you guys know anything about a 'spiritual shepherd' like he was saying? About anyone guiding the dead on their next steps or whatever?" They stirred slightly from their states of confusion. Johnny spoke up first after blinking away his muddled thoughts.

"No, not really. I always thought you went straight to the pearly gates, you know?" replied Johnny. "But I can try to ask the next dead guy I run into, he could probably shed some light on it."

"He has to be *something*, Bryce," came Zack, ignoring Johnny's sarcasm. "How else would he know our names? And didn't he put out a sort of, I don't know, calming presence?" Bryce nodded but did not say anything. Zack had felt the struggle too, the need to decide if this man was what he seemed to be: a normal looking, smiling, kind man/shepherd, or the dangerous individual Nurse Jan was so convinced he was. "And how else could he slow time!" Zack continued. "I mean, he freakin' slowed everyone around us to a snail's pace! And no one even knows it happened!"

"I don't know how that happened, or what exactly *that* was. This whole thing is so weird, maybe that's why Jan is so worried? Or maybe he is just a nice guy who happens to wave at strangers and also can slow time? That's a thing, right? Or maybe we're all having a shared delusion, like since we're all sick?" Johnny questioned aloud. Bryce rubbed his head again in anxiety and Zack wasn't even eating he was so worked up.

"His story seems bogus as hell though. And before . . . whatever the hell just happened, something felt off when we only knew him as Sir Creepsalot, didn't it? I know it did when I saw him. Johnny, you said the same thing."

"Uh yea, he was creepy as all get out. And now that we know he can slow time, I'm even more creeped out." Johnny trailed off and the boys were once again surrounded by their own silence.

"What are we supposed to do, Bryce? Do we tell Jan? Why would he ask us to keep our meeting a secret from her? If that really just happened, and he was telling us the truth, and one of us is really . . . ," Zack trailed off.

"One will be dead tomorrow," finished Bryce. With their mystery illness and going through the gamut of screenings over the last year, he would be lying if the notion of death had never crossed his mind, any of their minds really. They had all been trying to figure what exactly was wrong with them but they had not met a doctor who had said anything except "everything checks out." And now maybe one of them was going to bite the bullet.

"Why would an afterlife, whatever he is, come tell us we're going to die? That doesn't seem normal, does it? I mean, now we're going to be freaking out about dying for the next day. And it might not even be one of us at all," Bryce said aloud to his friends. Zack and Johnny thought on it, Johnny playing with his glasses and Zack finding his appetite and taking a spoonful of mashed potatoes off of Bryce's plate.

"I think we need to ask the other kids if anything crazy like this happened to them, you know? Have they met or talked with Sir Cree— er rather, James, or seen anything crazy like time slowing down, that sort of thing? I would feel a little better if I knew we weren't the only ones to interact with this guy, aside from a wave and a smile. And it's hard to say what exactly is going on, but for now," Bryce paused still deciding as he spoke, "let's keep Jan out of it. Just in case his warning is legit." Johnny nodded in agreement.

"We would sound like we had really been knocked off our rockers if we started blabbing about how we had all seen a dude stop time. They would throw every test under the sun at us, evaluations for days. I ain't doing that again, no sir," said Johnny.

Zack, looking less convinced about excluding Jan, shrugged reluctantly. "I guess I'm OK with that. But if he pops up again, I think we've got to tell her."

"I'm good with that. Let's talk to some of the other kids in the meantime, as many people as we can, and we will talk it over later tonight. And try to keep it on the down low," Bryce said as he motioned over to Nurse Jan who had returned with a security guard, both of whom were looking rather worried. The others nodded and awkwardly turned away from her as they walked quickly towards the table.

"Boys, I don't see the man anymore. Did he leave the doorway? Did you see which way he went?" Jan asked as she approached. The security guard behind her looked to the doorway and then across the cafeteria, surveying the area before heading to the door as he spoke into his walkie-talkie and exited into the hallway. Bryce looked to his friends before speaking up.

"We didn't look to the door like you said Jan. We didn't want to alert him." Jan frowned in disappointment at the lack of information but nodded in acceptance. The guard re-entered the cafeteria and was talking into his walkie-talkie over by the doorway, as Jan, still looking at the boys, spoke sternly and quietly.

"Please boys, this is very important. I need to know if this man has approached you in any way. I do not mean to frighten you, but it is critical to your safety and the safety of those around you that you tell me the truth."

Her gaze stopped on Bryce, who swallowed hard. He quickly tried to cover it by clearing his throat awkwardly but felt like Jan already knew that the man had approached them. Her vision was demanding and intent on him, and he felt his ears warm as he sat beneath it.

"We were waiting for you to come back; my guess is he split once he saw you come over. But we didn't look over at him so I can't be sure." Jan's stare remained on Bryce for another moment, processing his statement and body language before shifting her probing gaze to the others. She did not seem convinced.

"Very well. If any of you should happen to see this man again, please page a nurse immediately and avoid direct contact with him. Understood?"

The boys all nodded unknowingly in unison. Jan pressed her lips in acknowledgment and rose to walk toward the door James had been looking through. The security guard was waiting for her as he propped the door open.

"It's all going to be OK, boys. You have my word." And with that she left the boys to finish their food. Bryce sighed heavily once she was out of earshot.

"OK, well I'm pretty sure she knows we're lying," Bryce said. "That look was 100-percent skepticism." Johnny laughed lightly.

"Yea, we could have told her we were miraculously healed and we would have gotten the same look. Maybe we should hold off on questioning everyone till tomorrow at least? Let Jan and the other nurses' suspicion cool down a little bit?"

"If what James just said is true though, we will only have the morning to see if others have met him too," said Bryce, clearly not thrilled with the idea.

"True, but if Jan gets any more suspicious, she will probably work the truth out of us. And for whatever reason, that dude asked us to keep her in the dark," Johnny replied logically, a rare moment of directness from the Joker. "When a dude that can stop time asks you to do something, I think it's probably best to do it."

"OK, OK," Bryce replied. "Let's text anyone we've got numbers for, forget about face-to-face questions for today, and start talking to everyone tomorrow. First thing in the morning though, we've got to figure this out. Keep everyone posted, *capisce*?" The boys triple fist-bumped as they stood and threw out the remainder of their food. None of them were very hungry after having seen what they saw, even big Zack. They returned to their rooms for the evening, texting the few kid's numbers they had as well as each other about the conversation James had with them before sleep eventually took them all.

9

THE DREAM

◇

That night Bryce dreamed, and he knew it from the start of the dream, which he found odd and somewhat pleasant. Normally he didn't know the difference between the real world and his dream world until he actually awoke. Only after waking would he realize that what was happening in the dream world was strange and out of the ordinary. But this one was different; somehow, he knew as soon as it began that he was in his own mind, almost consciously traversing it.

He was in the hospital, or at least a version of the hospital, but what floor or wing he was on or in he could not say for certain. But the cool grey walls and the black and white checkered linoleum beneath his moccasins were unmistakable. He looked for a bulletin boards or pieces of furniture that would give him a clue to his location, but the walls and halls were uncharacteristically bare. And where a nurse or patient typically roamed the hallways, here it was empty, void of all life and activity and material. It gave him an odd sensation down his spine, and he found the hair on the back of his neck standing on end. Regardless of what his eyes were telling him, he felt as if someone was nearby, spying. He spun quickly to see if someone had snuck up on him but found only more desolate hallway. Bryce tried to ignore the watching feeling and chalked it up to the strange dream state he was in, a side effect of his being aware.

He shifted his gaze from the hallway up to the fluorescent lights above him, which quickly zoomed away, rising impossibly high before they snapped back and phased seamlessly into a tall glass ceiling. The strange transition threw off his equilibrium and he fell unathletically to his butt, flailing his arms like a toddler learning to walk. He took a second to rebalance and then with hands planted to the floor and leaning forward in an awkward squat, he regained his composure and looked around at the new ceiling. The hallway had widened into a room similar to the atrium in the hospital, large glass windows above showing the nighttime sky. A large bird sat atop the glass, pecking lightly for entry, fluttering its wings every so often in frustration. The moon above the bird was shining brightly, making it impossible to discern any features of the animal, but enough to partially illuminate the floor where he stood as shadows fought for their place in the room. The stars were doing their part as well to light the atrium space, twinkling above in the cloudless night. It was pretty but eerie, in the same way cemeteries can be hauntingly beautiful.

He glanced around the atrium and noticed there were only two paths as opposed to the four in reality, a left hall and a right hall from where he sat, neither of which seemed overly inviting compared to the other. He stood and turned to the left hallway, then back to the right, both plain, grey, and desolate. He shrugged and turned left, deciding that whatever way he walked, the dream would continue regardless. If his subconscience wasn't so definitive in its decision that he was dreaming and if the hospital was slightly more populated, he would have sworn he could have been awake still with how intuitive his thought process was.

Walking down the hallway he noticed that the walls had begun to show some similarities to the real-world hospital. The blank grey walls now showed room number directories and he could see doors up ahead. Bryce glanced at a few of the numbers as he came upon them, looking for some clue to where he was exactly. He passed room *101*, then illogically passed room *204* and then room *5@x* immediately after, all three right in a row. He shook his head in confusion as the feeling of the unfound eyes rested on him again, making him quicken his pace past the oddly marked doors. *3160* was the next room, followed by rooms *Llamamama*, *88 Vanilla*, and *POOL 5*. It was all nonsense until he came upon his room number, *207*. As he approached the room, the floor below him swayed like it might collapse, and Bryce jumped to the side of the hall instinctually out of fear and braced himself against the wall as he looked down.

The tiles had begun to give off the illusion of vibration, as if a motor had been switched on under the floor. His body did not feel any movement, however, contradicting what his eyes told him he was seeing. Half of his brain froze in confusion while the other half cooed in his head not to worry. Bryce hesitated, wrestling with his thoughts before reaching down to touch the clearly vibrating floor. It shifted around his fingers like shallow water, forming mildly between his fingers like a thin layer of potting clay and shaking ever so slightly between his digits. He pulled back his hand hurriedly and looked to it with concern. It was intact without any "floor" sticking to it. Bryce took a deep breath and lifted his right foot off the ground to inspect the bottom. The soft leather of his moccasins appeared as dry as his hand did. He placed it gently back onto the vibrating floor and swished his feet around, creating small ripples in the shallow puddle of bizarre tile. He stood for a few more moments, watching the floor buzz like it were made of a million tiny beads. Again, he wrestled with his thoughts before believing the latter half of his brain's plea not to worry.

He took a few more steps towards his door, cautiously reaching for footing as if the shallow puddle of the floor might suddenly drop to a deep pool, submerging him beneath the tiled floor surface. But the tiles never gave way, rippling slightly with each step, and the closer he got to his room the more the tiles shook, starting to blur almost from the high movement, swirling and crashing like 2-D small waves. The tile shapes became amoebic and inter-webbed. He found his breath was strained and loud in his ears, and his dream body started to feel weak and fatigued the further he pushed down the hallway.

As he arrived at his door, there came a cool wind from further down and in its wispy grasp was a clutter of leaves. They danced down the hallway past Bryce, a slow but continuous stream of them flowing across the blurring floors, down to the atrium and through to the "right hallway" that he had forgone for the path he currently walked. A large bird, what he assumed was the same bird from the atrium, came coasting down the hallway as well. It was large and dark in color; bigger than the crows he occasionally saw cluttering trees and making their awful calls. It cawed as it blew by, a low kind of gurgling sound, and carried on down the hallway, watching him intently as it passed. Most of the leaves took the same path as the bird, though some came to rest on the floor, floating on the vibrating tiles. He wiped his brow as a cold sweat had overtaken him, and wanting to be out of the strange hallway, he reached for the handle and pushed the door open. Bryce stayed in the doorway as the leaves blew gently behind him.

He was looking at himself, in his bed lying quietly and looking out the window at the trees and the leaves and the moon. The floors here were a swirling black and white mass, shifting and flowing and shaking and melting, like oil and water the two whirled back and forth against each other. A shape rose from the floors, a soupy mass of black and white swirls. It thinned before it began to take a semi-human form, much taller than normal, oddly dressed, and quite unaware that Bryce was standing in the hallway door. The figure that had risen from the floor reached a long pale hand and rested it on the dream Bryce's shoulder. The thing was standing in a full-bodied dark robe that went down to its ankles, revealing equally dark shoes. Its hair looked quite unkempt and ragged, blackest black, knotted and greasy. Bryce immediately knew that he should not enter the room, that somehow, he was intruding on this creature.

The beast turned toward the doorway Bryce was standing in and flashed an overzealous smile, large pointed sharp teeth in an impossibly wide mouth beneath a pair of black eyes, its large pupils nearly enveloping the entire socket save a thin white perimeter. Bryce's heart slammed in his chest and he had to lean against the doorway to keep from collapsing from the wave of dizziness that came over him. Behind the beast, Bryce saw and locked eyes with himself, dream-Bryce. The dream boy sat forward in his bed and cleared his throat as if to speak, but the beast turned its gaze back to him in concern and dream-Bryce slumped back onto his pillow and exhaled slowly, assuming the bedridden position he had been in when the door was first opened. The hair on Bryce's neck stood up as the creature turned its head methodically back towards him, and Bryce quickly reached for the door handle, stepping back away from it and into the hallway. Their eyes met as Bryce's hand found the handle, causing his knees to buckle beneath him. Bryce thought his head might explode as he fought to avert his eyes. He leaned heavily on the door handle for support as he shifted his weight backwards, pulled his eyes from the creature with a turn, and sprinted back down the hall towards the atrium.

The floor whirled in front of him, a pulsing, mesmerizing display of black and white chaos. It threw his depth perception significantly and he nearly tripped with his first step as he tried to sprint. Bryce peeked backwards to see if he was being pursued but found that the doors, including the one he had just exited, had vanished from the hallway. He turned back but where he expected to come upon the atrium, he was surprised to see that the hallway dead-ended into a staircase up ahead. Bryce slowed slightly as he approached it, his brain crying out in confusion. He peered anxiously around to see if the creature was following him, but seeing nothing, he walked the last few steps to the base of the stairs, which he found went up to only the third floor. Bryce glanced back again to find the still empty hallway, but the watchful feeling remained, and he wished more and more that he would wake. He pinched his cheek but remained dreaming, sighed in frustration, and looked up the stairwell.

The cool wind blew down the hall, rushing by him and abruptly up the stairs, curving around the bend at the mid-level landing. Bryce followed the leaves and quickly reached the top, which emptied directly into a very short hallway with one room in front of him. The breeze blew the leaves by him and where they should have hit the door they instead passed through it, disappearing behind the surface as if it were an illusion. It was an ordinary room door except that on the wall near the door handle there was a bowling-ball-sized hole in the drywall. Taking another step closer, he also saw that the hole was burning along the edges, the way paper looks as it slowly smolders. What was odd was that it was not red embers, but a deep purple, almost black, glow. He held his hand near it to feel for warmth but instead found the opposite, a cold chill the nearer his hand came to the hole. He took a step back in bewilderment and again noticed the floor, though still vibrating, was doing so in unison as the black and white swirled in harmony, a kind of choreographed routine. It buzzed slowly, loudly in his ears, dancing gracefully in stark contrast to the chaos he had witnessed earlier.

He looked back to the stairwell for signs of the monster but found that the stairs had disappeared behind him, a solid cool grey hospital wall now standing where he had just come from. Again, he did his best to shrug off the strangeness and turned back towards the door. The feeling of being watched was still there but had changed its attitude. It was no longer as oppressive and uninviting as it had been all along, but was soothing now, welcoming, and Bryce rested his eyes to appreciate its calm nature. He opened them and reached for the door handle, as a leaf bounced off his hand and then passed through the door's solid surface in front of him. He twisted the handle and the floor hummed; he could feel it now through his feet, its sound grew to a buzzing crescendo, and a light shown through the cracks of the door. He pulled the door open hard, expecting the light to pour in around him like a rush of water.

He was sitting in his bed, in the dark of his room. Bryce looked around utterly raddled as he looked to his room's door, which was now flung open to the brightly lit hallway outside. He glanced around in a hurried panic, flung the sheets off his body, and jumped from his mattress. The cold linoleum floor met his feet, and he jumped back into bed in surprise. He had certainly been wearing his moccasins before but now his feet were bare, hanging from his bed above a clearly motionless floor.

Confused, Bryce reached for his phone and clicked the side button to check the time. 12:21 a.m. He certainly had been sleeping, and he knew he was dreaming, but he could not remember awakening. The dream itself was as clear as if he had been fully conscious: the atrium, seeing his dream-self, the one-way staircase, the door. He slid his feet back towards the floor, forgoing his moccasins for the chilly floor, and approached the hallway. He normally would shut his door before going to bed and even in the off chance he had forgotten, the nurses circle the halls regularly to check on the patients. By midnight, someone surely would have found him asleep and closed the door for him.

He poked his head out into the hallway, leaning onto the doorframe, and looked both ways. There were two nurses walking to his right and away from him, passing the familiar bulletin boards and hallway seating that he expected to see. He was assuredly awake now. Bryce shook his head and looked to the other side of the hallway to find more familiar scenes of the fire extinguisher that was posted near his room and a folded wheelchair next to one of the benches. Sighing, he pulled back from the doorway and tugged the handle to shut the door. A scratching sound below gave him pause as he stopped the door's motion and looked to the floor.

He swallowed hard. A leaf. There was a leaf caught between his door and the linoleum. Strange for it to be on his floor now, and without visitors this day, it was even less likely it came from outside. Bryce bent slowly to take it, half expecting the floors to start vibrating and swirling again. He gripped the stem and pulled it out slowly, twirling it between his fingers. Bryce noticed a black mark on one side of the leaf, an ink that was written and glistened beautifully in the light that fell through his door's window. The ink looked as if it still might not quite be dry on the leaf's surface. He was careful not to touch it as he examined the symbol of sorts, a strange-looking, almost-cursive mark that he had never seen before.

Bryce turned to walk back to his bed, kicking the door closed behind him, all while examining the strange symbol. He rotated the leaf trying to determine which way it was supposed to be read but could not make sense of it. He kicked his feet up on his bed as he turned on the nearby lamp and looked closer. Gently, Bryce pressed his thumb on the edge of the symbol and then checked for ink. A slightly black tread outlined his thumb print and the leaf showed a small smudge. He spun the leaf in his hands a few more times and to his surprise, now found the symbol was replaced with a drawing of a bird in flight. He spun the stem again and it was back to the strange symbol. Another spin and nothing happened. Bryce scratched his scalp and spun the leaf more and more but without change. He rubbed his eyes, assuming his brain was playing tricks on him and lying back into bed, transitioned seamlessly back to sleep.

10

WAIT AND PRAY

M ikel strapped the saddle tight before gently petting his horse's large muscular neck. He tossed the small pack over its back as well, just a day snack worth of food and a water skin for the road back to Eislark. Short and sweet was the road between the sister cities of Trillgrand and Eislark, with the Trillgrand capital far and away being considered the fairer of the two. Eislark had its own unique charm to it, a much larger version of a small quiet fishing village, built with the sand-brown stone that the ocean provided. Theirs was not an elegant lifestyle but a working one, and the Larks were all-around a bit harder than the Trills: harder working, harder drinking, harder fighting. Save for the prestigious Blue Hearts of Trillgrand, whose rank with a sword or spear rose above them all.

With all the fishing, they were always well stocked with provisions, and being the only city willing to do business with the Western Island, and even the Northerners on the rare occasions they sent a fleet so far down south, the city did quite well for itself. Their ports were full of trade ships, loaded with various trinkets and gold, spices, Western foods and clothing, weapons and armor, merchants, and thieves. But while Eislark was plain and quaint, Trillgrand was beautiful and bombastic. Clean white stone buildings with neat, blue trim windows and doorframes, all lined along the incredibly well-cobbled roads. The Trill generally had wealth, not to say that none lived in poverty, but any that had money did their best to show it. The finest craftsmen from all of Endland dreamed of opening up shop in Trillgrand, selling their fine clothing, silk dresses with matching hats and gloves, or shiny leather shoes and boots, jewelry, and impractical but flashy weapons and armor. If someone in Endland wore a piece of clothing that looked expensive, it probably came from Trillgrand and it probably was even more expensive than it looked.

Mikel, having concluded his meeting with the High Council, was doing all he could to exit the flashy city as quickly as possible now. His dreary garb, after having changed out of his scrubs from the other Realm, and gruff exterior did nothing but draw curious looks at best, reproachful ones at worst, though he did not mind any type of look he received from the women of Trill. Something about his swashbuckler facade drew curiosity from even the most sophisticated-looking women. But now was not the time for romancing or even acknowledging the looks with his one-sided smirks. He could do nothing more here for the Hunt, as upsetting as it was, and his friends were now alone. He was keen on returning to Lord Belmar in Eislark and updating him on the dire situation Endland would soon be in. Back against the wall, a familiar feeling for a former cutthroat, but this wasn't just his life in the balance. Eastern, Western, and Northern lands, all the free people of Endland, would soon know the truth of the matter. Janeph and Bartellom would either return empty-handed or not at all. And with the last Hunt a failure, the Chosen would be unequivocally lost from Endland. The Grim would find their way into Endland eventually; it would be a matter of when, not if. They would amass their forces in the shadows until they felt confident enough to strike at Endland's free people. War was coming.

He sighed and tied the last strap off to secure his horse before grabbing the reins and guiding it out of the stables and through the inner castle courtyard. Reaching the gates of the inner castle wall, he pulled up and prepared to mount for the ride home before a commotion from outside gave him pause. In a frenzy, Petravinos came storming down the road towards the castle gate, holding fast to his large hat as his horse continued at full tilt even as he approached the barrier. Mikel pulled his horse to the side of the inner gate as it lifted for the Councilor Supreme, barely clearing enough height for him to continue his rapid pace beneath it before he caught sight of Mikel and pulled hard on the reins.

"Mikel! I had hoped to catch you before your ride up the coast!" the old man called out as he circled his panting horse back towards him, adjusting the deep blue hat atop his white hair. Mikel gave a short respectful bow and took a few steps out from beneath the giant archway to meet him.

"Councilor Supreme! An honor to meet you, in the flesh this time. I did not know you were in the city when we spoke." They met on the pathway as Petravinos labored off of his horse. Mikel did his best to remain dutiful as the old man struggled to dismount until a stable hand ran up to hold the horse and assist. Petravinos spoke as he regained his footing in the soft dirt below. He pulled his staff from the saddlebag on his horse and handed the reins to the young stable hand who had helped him dismount, patting the young boy atop his head and waited a moment for him to walk ahead until he was out of earshot.

"I've only just arrived, and I am sure you wish to inform Lord Grekory of all that has happened, but if you have just a moment, any detail you could provide on the Chosen prospect may help Janeph and Bartellom identify them." Petravinos was walking back to the stable where Mikel had just left and turned to see if the Captain was following him. Mikel begrudgingly retreated with his own horse back down the path to the stables.

"I wish I had information, Councilor Supreme, but we had not been able to narrow our selection before I returned here for the ambush request. Even if I knew anything, I assume you have already sent the last of our spare stone with the message to Lady Janeph. What good would information do us now?"

"If there was information to send, we would find a way, you silly Lark!" Petravinos grumbled loudly and without hiding his irritation. "We must do what we can to assist this last effort!"

Mikel now grumbled, even more so than the wizard. "Down to Klane's Crypts with 'information'! I can assist! If we can 'find a way' then let us find a way to send me like I asked in our meeting!"

"Mikel, you should know the cost of sending a person. We could send a thousand letters before it would balance out, probably more. And you may not know the effect of removing that kind of quantity from a net, but it is substantial. It cannot be done." Mikel frowned and took a sharp breath as Petravinos planted his staff in the stone road with a frown of his own.

"What of the nets over the wilds!" Mikel continued, doing his best to express his anger without yelling. "Are they not already exposed? The Grim can most likely reach the Northern and Western Islands already, their nets were never as well-kept as ours. What would another hole above the Eastern Island do? What are the odds they even find it or utilize it?"

Petravinos said nothing as he began walking back towards the stables again, not waiting at all for Mikel. He followed the old man with irritation as he pulled his horse along behind him, catching up in a few short steps.

"Our net is all that separates us from a flood of beasts into our Realm. We've chipped away at the stone that upholds it and now all members of the Council relay various reports of oddities across Endland." Petravinos paused in speech and movement. "This, of course, is all classified, Mikel." He nodded in acceptance as Petravinos continued walking, whispering in a hushed voice.

"It is worse than you may know, Mikel. The men of the swamp have been seen again in Swilmagapan. Trees of Dawnwood stride through the forest. The orcs have been spotted all across the Trill Plains stretching beyond their agreed jurisdiction. Dim lights dance in the plains and lakes near Bol-Garot. Something wakes in the deep mines of Gritvand. Everywhere, oddities are being reported, and as their number increases, so does the people's fear." Petravinos hushed as a family and their donkey-drawn cart passed by. The two children being towed pointed toward the wizard in fascination as the old man cast a small ball of sparks above their head with a smile before continuing.

"If we open our nets any further than we already have, the Grim will assuredly find their way in. They may yet find their way regardless by nothing but sheer dumb luck; we have sacrificed much in the pursuit of Chosen and have left ourselves at the precarious edge of protection. All we can do now is hope that Janeph and Bartellom can do what all others have failed to do and return Chosen to us so that we may root out these reports and secure Endland once more."

They reached the stables and Petravinos looked around suspiciously. The stable hand that had taken his horse was now unloading the saddle but appeared inattentive, as did the nearest passersby who moved up and down the road from the inner gate. Petravinos moved in another step and lowered his voice even further.

"I am sorry, Mikel, but we cannot afford to send you. If this Hunt fails, Eislark will need its captain. Endland will need its champions. I fear dark times may be ahead of us." Mikel nodded surprised at the gloomy words, and looked away disheartened. Petravinos sighed and rested an old ringed hand upon the young man's shoulder. "Janeph and Bartellom are more than capable in battle. A Blue Heart of the highest rank and noble blood, and a Northern warrior of legendary lineage, dishonored or not." Mikel patted the wizard's shoulder briefly in return before he mounted his horse without a word. Mikel turned his horse to exit before he bent low over the horse's neck to address Petravinos.

"You've set them up for failure, Councilor Supreme. They will fall. They will fall and I must sit here doing nothing while it happens." He straightened upon his mount and gripped the reins. "You asked for information, how about this. Next time the fate of our Realm hangs in the balance, perhaps share things such as the availability of precious resources. Others might find it useful when planning the single most important operation in Endland's history."

"My young Captain, you know not the tribulations I have seen in my years. What I do, I do with intense measure and thought. Everything I have experienced goes into my decisions, and you would do well to remember that, and remember your place when speaking with a Council member."

His tone was short and agitated, far and away from the paternal tone he had taken to this point. Mikel bristled in frustration, but he gave another short semi-respectful bow before he spurred his horse with his heels and went out of the stables and down the road toward the gates, riding rapidly back to Eislark. Petravinos watched mournfully as Mikel disappeared beyond the gate before he moved to tend to his own horse.

11

THROUGH THE DOOR

ometime after he had fallen back asleep, a loud noise abruptly ripped Bryce out of his slumber. His eyes flashed open, adjusting to the darkness of his room as he continued to lie motionless with his senses on full alert, concentrating in order to discern what had made such a noise. With the lack of sensory input, he saw nothing but dull shadows and his ears started to ring lightly in the pure silence. After another minute, he concluded he had heard the noise in the last moments of another dream before waking. A second noise sat him upright. It was an impact of some kind; he thought he could feel the vibrations as something collided with something else, it echoed around and through his body.

He swung his feet to the floor, feeling for his moccasins with his toes and the desk light with his fingers. Finding the switch, he flipped it but it failed to illuminate. A few futile attempts of flipping it back and forth brought him a small sense of dread. He secured his soft slip-ons with his feet, and hopping out of bed, dropped to his hands and knees and followed his hand along the cord to check that the lamp was plugged in. It was, to his dismay. A bad bulb, he figured as he got back up and walked around his bed to the window, opening the blinds in hope of a clear moonlit night. There was some, but the night was young and the moon must have been on the opposite side of the building at this point in its cycle. It, coupled with the light from the window of his door, gave just enough illumination for him to make out the vague shapes around him. He traversed the darkness cautiously toward the light switch, shuffling his feet across the floor to avoid tripping on some unseen object. He peered out the door's window to the lit hallway as he flipped the light switch for the room.

The light switch behaved the same as his desk lamp had, doing nothing to alleviate the darkness. The hallway lights shining through the small window suddenly lost their shine as well, and with only the moon at his back, the hall was now darker than his room. Bryce's heart began to accelerate as a shot of adrenaline entered his bloodstream. Something was wrong. Even when a thunderstorm had knocked out their power during one of his episodes in the summer, generators had restored the electricity in a matter of seconds. Bryce and Johnny had even asked one of the nurses about it the next day out of curiosity. He had already been awake at least a minute and still he stood in darkness.

A third crash came, weird and unnerving as the first two, distinctly down the hallway to the left as again the ripples of the impact gave slight vibration through the structure. It felt as though the sound was sapped from the air and then released all at once back into the world. It made the hair on his neck stand on end and he quickly jumped back to his bed. He reached for his call button and jammed it repeatedly with his thumb as he pulled blankets over his head and did his best imitation of a loose pile of bedsheets. He formed a small hole in the blankets to keep an eye on the door, steadied his nerves with a deep breath, and waited in his laundry pile disguise for a nurse to come.

A few minutes passed before Bryce saw a shadow approach the door from his blanket periscope. Normally the nurses were incredibly prompt to call buttons but this time it was much delayed. The door cracked open, just as Bryce remembered that the call system was an electrical system. His call button had done nothing, just as the light switches had done nothing. The fact that someone was at his door was pure coincidence. His heart raced as a hunched shadow pushed the door open to its entirety, the door bumping into the stop against the wall with a soft thud. Bryce wished he had decided to wait in the bathroom or under his bed instead of on top of it in an exposed pile of blankets.

"Bryce, are you in here?" Came a soft whisper. It was a woman's voice, nervous and rattled, but somehow soothing and familiar. He still did not move from the blanket camouflage though; the small amount of moonlight coming through his window wasn't enough to identify the hunched form, which did not seem as familiar as the voice did.

"Bryce, are you here? It's Jan."

"Nurse Jan!" He sprung from his hiding spot in a flurry, sending the blankets in the air and clearly causing Jan quite a scare as she fell back against the doorframe. He ran towards her but stopped when she put a hand up towards him.

"Slowly please, Bryce." He slowed to a walk and again took in her hunched form. She certainly didn't look well, he could see now that he was closer. Her face expressed suppressed pain, even in the darkness that much was clear. He paused a foot or two from her.

"What's going on? Did you hear those noises? And where is the power? I thought the power—"

"Bryce, I need you to accept what I am about to tell you as the truth without another question. Can you do that?" Bryce paused but nodded slowly. "You and the other children are in danger." Bryce almost broke his silence after her first statement but bit his tongue to allow her to speak. "In danger from what is irrelevant at this point. You need to head to the third floor, get to the northern wing, last room in the hallway. Get there as fast as possible. The other kids and nurses should be heading there as well. Nurse Bart will meet you there, he is on the first floor now gathering the others. I'll gather everyone on this floor. Go now, and if you see any others, tell them to follow but do not linger long, you are all being pursued. Do you understand?" Her vulnerability and desperation shone brightly in this last question and actually made Bryce wince in concern.

"Yes, but what are you talking about? What's happening? Why would we go to the third floor if we're being chased? Shouldn't we just exit the building?" Another of the strange compressed sounds ripped through the air, cutting him off and causing Bryce to cover his ears in fear and disgust. Whatever it was, it was nothing he could even begin to assign to a possible cause.

"I cannot explain now, Bryce, but I will in due time if you are who we seek. Now please, you must go." He had never seen her in such an exasperated state and it frightened him a great deal. He complied nonetheless with a grim nod. Jan smirked painfully and rolled off the doorframe and into the hall, heading towards the source of the strange noises. Bryce started to run after her but stopped in the doorway at the sight of a small pool of dark liquid on the floor. He tapped a fingertip to the warm liquid and held it in the minimal moonlight to see the crimson sheen. His heart raced as he poked his head out of the doorway and looked in the direction she had run, but there was no sign of her.

No time to analyze, he thought as he turned right and sprinted towards Johnny's room, which was the first room on the third floor's north wing from the main stair. He whipped down the hallway towards the stairs as fast as he could in the darkness but the hall was a mess and made it difficult: flipped beds from the rooms, ceiling tiles broken and scattered on the floor, papers and carts turned over, posters and bulletin boards ripped and disheveled. He skidded to a stop in his moccasins next to a broken bench because mixed in the rumble was someone, huddled and immobile, sprawled in another pool of dark liquid. Bryce averted his eyes quickly, but the image was burned in his memory as he ran all the faster.

Bryce continued down the hall, and reaching the main stairs, gripped the near side handrail and allowed his momentum to sling his way up the first few steps. Another of the noises echoed up the stairs behind him, giving him a small comfort that whatever was making the sound was definitely below him and behind him now. As he reached the midpoint of the stairway and turned to continue up, he saw that the lights shone brightly on the top floor, as if whatever was happening below was a slow rising flood that hadn't quite reached the upper levels yet. Reaching the top of the stairs he blew through the first doorway and smashed into Johnny's room. He was met prompt-ly with a swift smack to his forehead as something struck him and hit the floor.

"Ow! Geez what the hell man?" Bryce yelled rubbing his head as he grabbed the door handle for stability.

"B-man, is that you?" A crouching Johnny stood from be-hind a small stack of pillows and blankets forming a plush bar-ricade atop his bed. "Holy crap, sorry! I didn't know what was going on so I armed myself for an intruder." Bryce bent down and picked up the object that had just cracked his head.

"So, to be clear, you threw the remote at me, expecting this light plastic to deliver a fatal blow? Or did you think that the remote might distract me into watching TV?"

"Shut up, man, I panicked! There is something weird going on so I grabbed the best weapon I could. Have you heard those noises? Like, what is that?" Bryce nodded, understanding his friends concern.

"I don't know but something is happening on the lower floors, something bad. I think Nurse Jan is hurt," he said holding up his bloodied fingertips. "And she told me to get up here and get to the end of the northern hall, third floor. Bart's going to meet us, and anyone else I see we're supposed to bring with us."

"What do you mean Jan's hurt? Why are your fingertips bleeding? What's going on man? Is this an elaborate joke? I told you you'd never be able to top my Christmas joking spree from last year, so don't even try. Plus, this isn't even funny." Another noise echoed through the air as the third-floor lights flickered, shutting down Johnny's accusations and shrinking the two of them as the sound reverberated through their bodies. Johnny's face was serious now.

"Alright, wherever we're supposed to go, let's go, B. But what about Zack? He's south wing. Did Nurse Jan say she was going to get them too?"

Bryce thought for a moment. "We'll go there first, south wing, then double-back here to the end of the hall like Jan said." Johnny grabbed his Converse from under his bed and started slipping them on, forgoing his fluffy slippers.

"Serious run mode shoes, I'm ready, let's roll."

They exited the room to the hall, Johnny still struggling to slip on one of his shoes as he hopped into the doorframe to stabilize and slide his foot into place. As Johnny struggled, Bryce ran across the hall and opened the doors to yell in at whoever was inside. Johnny followed suit with his shoe finally on and headed to the next room on the other side of the stairs but froze looking down to the midlevel landing.

"Uh, Bryce?" Bryce emerged with two children a few years younger than he behind him.

"What man? We've got to go!" He walked towards his friend but stopped next to him, the two younger kids staying back a few paces. A shadow was stretching up the stairwell floors and walls, but not in the form of a person. It was moving like it was alive itself, dark shadow tentacles grasping at the walls, deep and heavy, long strands of black groping for grip, pulling the rest of the darkness up with it. As it climbed, the light above the landing flickered, struggling against the living shadow's nearing presence. The terrible noise exploded up the stairwell, snapping the boys out of their trance and sending a wave of terror through their bodies; the source of whatever was making the impacts was clearly at the bottom of the stairs. And worse, the noise seemed to have triggered the shadow to move faster, for the tentacles flared wildly as if spurred by the noise.

All at once the group ran further south, opening the nearest doors and yelling at whoever was inside to follow them. The occupants of the nearest rooms began to exit as the boys continued to the next doors, with the newest members of their group following suit. After a few doors they had a small platoon of collectors, pulling everyone out of their rooms into the darkening hallway as they headed to the end of the hall. They reached Zack's room, the last room, into which the small army quickly filed in and slammed the door. Zack was sitting on his bed with a pint of ice cream in his hand and *The Price is Right* playing on his TV. He glanced over at the large group that had just invaded his room with pure confusion, still holding the last spoonful of what appeared to be cookies and cream in his mouth.

"Uh, hi, everyone." He glanced down at his mostly empty pint of ice cream and then back at the group. "Was there a party tonight that I didn't know about? I would have gotten a lot more ice cream if I knew. Johnny, did you forget to invite me to a party at my house again?"

"For real man? You're eating ice cream at a time like this?" Johnny was flabbergasted and also clearly jealous.

"At a time like what? It's always a good time for ice cream, Johnny boy," Zack said, smiling and digging his spoon in for another scoop. Johnny smacked the spoon out of his hand and it splattered against the window.

"Dude." It was all that Zack could say in mourning of his lost ice cream, looking to it as it slowly slid down the glass. Johnny's smile shined through his nerves, that impish grin of his, but quickly sobered as the lights flickered again.

"At a time like this," said Johnny, pointing to the lights. "Haven't you noticed? Something's going on man, and we're not sure what but we've got to get to the north wing ASAP. Nurse Jan told Bryce and he told me and I'm telling you because we couldn't leave your fat ass all alone in the south here. So, we're here and now it's time to go!"

"We're supposed to be going to the north wing? Then why are we here?" one of the kids from the group cried out.

"Shut your mouth when you're talking to me!" Johnny yelled at no one in particular. "You'd be snoozing in your bed if we hadn't come along so just zip it, alright?"

No one else spoke and Zack, normally one to question Johnny's stories, got up and put on his shoes without another word as the group hurriedly filed back out into the hallway. Bryce exited at the end of the group, just far enough back to hear Johnny whisper that Zack should bring another pint if he had it, to which Zack happily obliged. With the group out in the hall and Johnny and Zack spooning scoops of ice cream at the end of the line, Bryce started directing them back to the North wing.

"Let's go! North wing, last room!"

The group took off, sprinting down the flickering hallway in a mad panic as Bryce slowed to the back to bring up the group with his friends. They entered the atrium, rounding the circle to the north wing as groups from the east and west wings ran ahead of them. Another crash ripped through the hallway, echoing from the northern atrium stairwell they were fast approaching and causing some of the children to stop out of fear. Bryce kept them moving as did Johnny and Zack, spoons in their mouths and pints in their hands still. Bryce saw ahead that the shadow was starting to crawl off the stairs into the hall. It clung tightly to the walls, a two-dimensional being that was rising steadily, climbing upwards to put out the electric glow of the tubed lights above them. Bart and a group of children rushed up the stairs from where the sound had come from, Bart getting to the top and waving the kids to the north wing like a third base coach waving home the winning run. He saw Bryce's group approaching from the corner of his eye and turned as he waved the last of his group down the hall.

"Keep moving, last room in the hallway!" The large nurse yelled out in a booming voice. Bryce gave a thumbs-up from the back of the pack as their group of kids rushed past the stairwell.

"The south wing is clear!" Zack cried as the trio ran by him. Bart nodded as another crash rang so close and loud the boys felt the sound waves reverberate into their bodies and rattle their rib cages. Bryce felt a rush of cold move just behind him and turned back to see Bart fly backwards as a shadow slammed into him, a black ball of deep purple and ebony. Bart hit the floor as Bryce skidded to a stop while Johnny and Zack both dropped their ice cream and spoons in the shock of the impact. They staggered next to Bryce and turned to face the commotion as Bart sat up slowly.

From the stairwell came a creature, long hair, pale skin, curved elongated fingers. Bryce lost his breath. It was just as he had dreamed, the beast that had sat in his dream room. The creature climbed the stairs slowly, lurched forward on all fours with his sights set on Bart, who had almost regained his footing with the help of the wall.

"Stay back, beast!" he yelled with such a blaring voice that the creature did pause momentarily as the lights flickered again. Bryce glanced up to see the shadow tentacles reach the lights, which ultimately lost out as darkness consumed the hallway. Their eyes not quite adjusted in the strange purple glow from the shadows that now had consumed the walls, they saw the creature raise a pale hand as a deep black spot began to form in its palm. The boys backed up slowly, as poor Bart slid his back up the wall to stand fully before him. The black spot grew into a black and purple ball, sparking dark fizzles of energy as it grew to encompass its whole hand.

The monster released the energy as the sound, the evil awful crashing sound, sucked the world of noise for a split second and shook the hall, racking the boys to the point of collapse. A bright flash erupted from Bart's location, equally as bright as the dark of the black ball that had been shot at him. The light would have stung their eyes on a sunny day at noon, but in the darkness the sting was what Bryce had to imagine having a laser pointer shined at you felt like. It blinded the three of them as they rubbed their eyes in pain and tried to reopen them. Bryce managed to peek long enough to take in his surroundings and quickly thought he must have suffered some sort of vision damage.

Nurse Jan was standing in front of Bart, glowing white and clutching what appeared to be a large shield out front towards the monster. A fine black mist was evaporating off the shield as she pulled a small dagger from her waist, which was no longer the elastic band of scrubs but rather a brown leather belt that wrapped loosely over a long white and blue battle skirt, spattered with red blood. The red grew a darker shade at her left side where a break in her blue and white armor could be seen. Her left arm let the shield drop to the floor with a loud clang as it momentarily balanced on its edge.

"Nurse Jan?" Johnny whispered in awe.

All three, Bart, Jan, and the creature, looked at the boys in surprise. The beast grinned and Bryce turned to evacuate, grabbing his friends' shirtsleeves as he did. But as he stepped his arms were jerked back. He glanced toward his friends but they were motionless, like two anchors in the shadow water that they were now submerged in.

"Let's go guys, come on!" He tugged again looking back at Jan and Bart, both of whom were still looking towards the strange scene, unblinking and immobile. Bryce's epiphany came as the smooth voice of James came from behind him.

"Hello, Bryce, quite a crazy night you're having, is it not?" James walked up behind the boys from down the hall, placing his hands on each of their time-slowed shoulders.

"James! You've got to help them! That, that thing is attacking Jan and Bart and, and I think it's after us too!" Bryce had turned to point to the beast, but there was only a dark cloud where it had been, a shimmering shadow in the surrounding stillness. Bryce looked on in confusion as James bent down between the slowed friends to look at Bryce at eye level. Bryce turned and met his gaze but looked over his shoulder at the dark cloud that used to be the beast.

"Nothing is after you, Bryce. You're already dead."

Bryce opened his mouth to respond but could not find words, and closed it quickly. He searched for a hint of a joke but James did not allow it onto his pointed face, only offering a somber expression.

"I know this is hard Bryce, but it's time to go. You have to trust me. Your friends will be fine." James flashed his smile to try to ease him, the same one that had gotten him his Sir Creepsa-lot nickname. The wide and maniacal smile turned Bryce's gut in a way that was nothing like what he expected to feel from a gentle reassuring statement. He instinctually retreated from James, from both the smile and James's proposal to leave his friends behind.

"No way! I can't just leave them here with that, that mon-ster attacking them! Dead or not! And Jan is hurt, and Bart." Bryce's voice faded as he looked to the nurses. The blood on Jan's tunic ran from her ribs down to below her hip, contrast-ing against the white of the garment. The shield she had let drop was still falling forward now, looking like an impossi-bly large gold coin suspended in low gravity. Bart was up and leaning on the wall but was also clearly in pain. His shirt where the black-purple flame had hit him was discolored to match the projectile, and his chest beneath it was the same, but from bruising or the energy, Bryce could not say. James's smile dis-sipated slightly at the lack of attention, and he moved his face in front of Bryce's vision to reclaim it.

"Not to worry, dear boy. They are dead as well!" Bryce scrunched his eyes and rubbed his head with his hands as he tried to comprehend the news. "I'll take you first and be back for the others in a jiffy. But we haven't the time to argue, Bryce, we must go and we must go now." He said this as he stood from his lowered position and offered his hand. Bryce tried to formulate a counterargument but realizing the futility in it, he reluctantly nodded. James returned the nod and stood between the still immobile Zack and Johnny.

"Take my hand, child. A few words and we will be on our way." Bryce looked at his friends—both with ice cream on their faces still from trying to eat as they ran—and couldn't help a small smile despite the situation. Leave it to his friends to have a pint of ice cream while running for their lives. Well, dead lives.

"Wait a minute," Bryce said as he pulled his hand from James's and turned back to walk over to one of the half-eaten pints, dropping to a knee in front of it. James's smile evaporated and was replaced by a scowl with a voice to match his displeasure as he retracted his outstretched hand.

"This is no time for treats, boy! We've precious little time!" Bryce paid him no mind and dipped a finger in the container, pulling out a miniature scoop on his fingertip and ate it. He looked over out of the corner of his eyes toward Jan and Bart as his mind raced. He saw the shield, suspended in a slow-motion fall, three steps away, maybe four. Not as close as he wanted to be, but it would have to do.

"James, you've got to try this. It's hands down the best flavor out there if you ask me. Then we can go, just one bite for the road." He took another dip as James's scowl grew to a full frown. He took a step past Zack and Johnny towards the boy and stretched out his hand again. Bryce kept his eyes on Johnny, who's blinking motion had now become slightly more discernible as they started their closing motion. Time was speeding back up.

"Bryce Blooms, we must go now! There will be time for food later!"

"Oh, come on! *Live* a little! It's amazing!" He took another scoop as he extended the container towards James and took a quick glance to Johnny, whose eyes were closed and reopening now.

"Enough! We must go now!" James's voice bordered on desperation as he took another step towards Bryce, his anger showing through without restraint. "This form is—"

"Draining?" Bryce interrupted. James stood motionless; his face caught in angry surprise. "I find it odd, James, that you're here for me, for us, to guide us now that we're dead. Do you know why?" James's face was contorted and his eyes fierce, but there was panic in them as well. James unknowingly obliged to Bryce's desire and stepped towards the boy again, his hair becoming slightly unrulier, his fingers elongating. James was a fuming menace as Bryce stood now from his knee and picked up the pint container with him, finger-scooping another bite and nearly choking on it as he tried not to show his growing fear as the Creep took his true form. Another look to Johnny, showed that his hands were moving, reaching out towards where Bryce had been a few minutes ago. Bryce's own hands were moving, shaking slightly, but he did his best to conceal it and James was seemingly too angry to notice.

"How could I be in need of guidance," Bryce paused to take another bite of ice cream, swirling his finger to help melt the last of the pint that was left as James took another step, "if I'm able to pick up and enjoy some ice cream? Could it be because I am not actually dead?" The shadow where the Creep had been siphoned towards James as he morphed, a monster before him, his teeth long and sharp, cloaked in a sweeping black robe and nearly eight feet tall. His fingers were so long, twice that of a normal man, and incredibly pale with dark purple nails at their ends. His hair was shaggy and unkept, down to his shoulders and jet black to match his robes. Bryce could not help his fear now; the beast stood before him.

James jutted his right hand forward to grab the child just as Bryce tossed the ice cream towards him. He turned towards Jan, Bart, and the shield as he heard the impact of the frozen treat and the growl of the monster. The shield was falling quickly now, not quite full speed but still fast, as Bryce reached out for the handles. Another step and it was in his hands and with all his might, he ripped it off the ground onto his left arm and spun its golden decorated face back towards James, jumping into a ball to conceal as much of his body behind it as possible. The world went silent and then a crash from James sounded and Bryce felt the energy from the blast impact the shield, rippling through his arm and up to his shoulder and torso. With his feet off the ground, Bryce flew backwards like a cannonball and crashed into the wall near the stairwell. A dull pain in his ribs pulsed in his brain but he ignored it, rubbing them with his free hand. He poked his head out from behind the shield, smiling at the very real possibility that ice cream had just saved his life, and saw Jan and Bart circling past the Creep towards his friends.

James wiped the ice cream from his face as he lunged for the nurses, his long, curved fingers grasping their ankles as he flung them backwards like they were dolls. Bart hit the wall directly above Bryce and slid further down the hall toward the atrium and Jan did much the same on the opposite wall. Johnny and Zack, in their bewilderment, had still not moved as the Creep turned to face them.

Bryce stood quickly, pulling has hand from the shield's holster. He started spinning with all his strength like in an Olympic hammer throw and he tossed the shield toward James's back. It wasn't exactly straight or level as it left his hands, but it was on target just enough, connecting with James's right shoulder as the world lost sound again, spinning and staggering the monster forward onto one knee and outstretched hands. The black ball in his hand erupted into the tile floor, a web of cracks and splinters radiating from it as the strange black energy dissipated. The impact was close and strong enough to send both his friends backwards from the explosion and to send the beast spinning in the air. He recovered rather nimbly, landing on all fours and whirled his pale face back towards Bryce with a snarl.

"You're coming with me one way or another, boy!"

He stood and a thin dark sword lowered from the Creep's robe, or perhaps it came directly from the creature's flesh. The point came first, glistening even in the relative darkness of the hallway, reflecting the odd purple glow of the crawling wall shadows. The hilt slowly appeared behind the rest of the blade, forming in the creature's palm, his long fingers gripping it tightly. Bryce, realizing he had just thrown his only protection across the hallway, looked around desperately for an escape route. A crash came as Bryce dove forward to the floor in front of the stairs, a black projectile sending a shower of fine drywall debris onto him as it vaporized a hole in the wall corner.

Bryce looked up to see the Creep's hand extended towards him for another blast. He rolled right, away from the monster and bounced down the stairs like a human log as another blast evaporated part of the top stair. He stretched out his limbs to stop the roll and jumped to his feet quickly near the midpoint landing of the staircase, looking up to see the Creep already at the top of the stairs, leaping down with his black blade raised for a strike, eyes wide with his maniacal creeper smile baring his sharp fangs. Bryce braced for the impact, putting his hands up in a pitiful defense before a figure collided with the Creep, slamming into his back and into the wall well above Bryce's head.

Bart had tackled him midair, his arms wrapped around the beast's torso. He smashed the Creep against the wall, and the two were now grappling at the mid-stair landing. Bryce raced back up the stairs two at a time and peeked backwards to see Bart and James in what looked like a crocodile death roll at the landing, fists and elbows flying as each attempted to gain control of the other. The Creep's sword had been sent clanging down the lower-level stairs and was thankfully out of reach for the moment.

"B-man!" Zack yelled as Bryce moved from the brawl and towards his friends.

"No time kids, get to the room now!" Jan yelled as she slid her shield back onto her arm and jumped down the stairwell to join the fray. Bryce didn't miss a step and ran right between his friends as they patted him on the back and turned to follow. The group looked into a few of the rooms as they ran but saw no children to gather, although in the darkness they only had the faint moonlight shining through to do any sort of investigating.

"Bryce, what the hell happened back there?" Zack panted as they ran, "You were next to us and then you were in front getting blasted into a wall by that, thing."

"It's James," Bryce replied. "He slowed time again and tried to take me, said we had already died." Zack almost tripped at James's name.

"Wait what? We're dead? Was he going to help Jan and Bart fight that thing or did he run away?"

"No, man, James is that thing. I don't know what exactly it is, but if he's here to guide us somewhere, it can't be good. Who knows if we are even supposed to die? I think he was trying to convince everyone to just follow him blindly."

"He's that monster?" Johnny asked incredulously.

"Down!" came a yell from behind them. The boys glanced back to see one of James's purple orbs ripping down the hall. Half falling, half sliding to the ground, they hit the tiled floor hard as the ball whizzed by, narrowly missing one of Johnny's shoulders. It continued down the long hall until it exploded into a black and purple crater on the far wall. With a glance backwards they saw Bart swing a large hammer into the back of the beast's leg and leap to the beast's back, looking for a rear-naked choke, all while Jan gracefully dodged and parried the beast's black blade with her shield and dagger.

"Go!" yelled Bart as James reached back, covering the nurse's head with a massive pale hand, and flipped the large man over his shoulder. Without hesitation the kids jumped to their feet and ran again, continuing down the hall towards the last room, where the orb that had just been fired at them now smoldered on the drywall in purple flame. Bryce saw the room door and suddenly felt he may be back in his dream. The hole in the wall gave off its faint purple glow, pulsing and sizzling and emitting a small trail of smoke.

"I've seen that before," said Johnny, pointing to the odd smoldering hole in the wall before Bryce could remark on it. Zack and Bryce looked to him in surprise as Zack extended his hand to feel its aura.

"In a dream," Zack added. Bryce was floored at the news. "It was cold in the dream too."

"With the leaves? Did you see the leaves and the swirling floor?" Bryce yelled, speeding up slightly so as to open the door first.

"Floor yes, but no leaves in mine. But I saw Sir Creepsalot too," Johnny replied hastily as Bryce reached for the handle, hoping to feel the hum of energy as he had in what he was now thinking was more than a simple dream.

"No leaves in mine either, B-man," Zack supplemented as Bryce grasped the handle and ripped the door open. The boys burst through the door to the sounds of screaming children and a range of makeshift weapons being thrown at them. Another remote struck Bryce square in the forehead as he entered, and Zack took a toilet paper roll to the chest before the kids realized who had entered.

A million questions flew at them: what was happening, why did they get separated, where were the nurses. There were far fewer people than it seemed they had gathered, but their loud voices made up for the lack of population. Too many to hear and too many to answer, the boys tried to calm the group, raising their hands and yelling for quiet. Through the window, a series of blue and red flashes lit up the mostly dark room, giving a weak strobe light effect.

"Here's Johnny!" Johnny yelled, grinning as he looked to his friends for recognition. The children quieted a little but upon receiving no responses, he continued, "Now then . . . what we've got here is a failure to communicate."

Bryce intervened before he could go any further down a quote tangent, which he tended to do when speaking in front of crowds. He had once sat through a Johnny presentation in school on the solar system back in the fourth grade in which Johnny had spent half the time speaking like Harry Caray, and the other half quoting *Armageddon* and *Star Wars*. Somehow the kid managed a B-minus by offering next to no content and babbling like an idiot for five full minutes. But this wasn't the time for a Johnny rambling. In his dream opening the door was the final step. He didn't know what to do now that they had arrived.

"Listen up, everyone," Bryce started.

"No man!" Johnny interrupted, "That was a perfect opportunity for 'Listen up, this will only take a second!'" Bryce only shook his head with overzealous malcontent for his friend's lack of concern. "You blew it!" Johnny yelled before Zack covered his mouth so Bryce could speak, and Johnny held up four fingers for his quote streak as Zack continued to cover his mouth and restrain him. Bryce ignored him and spoke as loudly as he could without yelling to speak over the chattering of the others.

"Did Jan or Bart or anyone else say what we were supposed to do here?"

A million voices rose from the group at once, and Bryce had to hold up his hands again to try to calm the crowd. He looked around the room as their chatter died down.

"Ok, different approach," Bryce continued. "Show of hands, who was given *specific* instructions from Bart or Jan or another nurse on what to do *after* reaching this room?" No one's hand moved this time and the room stayed silent. Bryce looked to Johnny and Zack, all three shrugging when the door exploded open, flying off the hinges like a rectangular missile and clipping Bryce's left arm. Where Zack had stood, he was outside of the blast zone but he had jumped toward the projectile, using his body as a buffer between it and the kids huddled around Bryce's left. Zack was thrown back into the children, bowling them over, and one of the hinges whirled past Zack's head and buried itself in the comparatively soft drywall on the opposite wall. Bryce looked up from his knees, holding his left arm and looked to the children who had suffered Zack's big belly instead of the solid wood door. They all seemed OK, although Zack looked beyond dazed and most likely had suffered a concussion.

"Jumpin' Jehosaphat, Trigger!" came Johnny's shocked cry as he ran to help Zack and the others to their feet, apparently having avoided any contact with the blast or debris. Bryce turned around to face the doorway as those that had been spared from the blast quickly retreated from the open hallway. The pain burned through his left arm in blinding fury, and he knew immediately his forearm had been broken, shattered maybe. He breathed through the pain and tucked his arm close to his body.

From the darkness of the hallway in stepped James. Half human, half whatever the hell he was, the dust from the exploded drywall and door settled like snow on and around him. His fingers were still elongated and his black eyes searched calmly. It looked as if his pupils had nearly swallowed his iris and sclera whole. His one hand held the dark blade he had summoned, which he spun dexterously in his hand. And that signature Sir Creepsalot smile, bright white and gleaming like a torch in the night. He put his free hand in his robe pocket as he casually observed the devastation of the doorframe, kicking some drywall nonchalantly and flicking debris with the tip of his sword before addressing the crowd.

"Well, my dear children, it appears that this silly game of hide-and-go-seek is up! And what a game it was, I must admit!" James was speaking as an older playground bully would to his younger victims. A child near the door, dazed by the blast, had the misfortune of landing squarely in his sight. James looked to him curiously, turning his head to the side before he kicked him violently across the face, showering blood onto the wall and rendering him a blubbering mess. The child wiped his mouth and crawled away on the floor, the Creep licking his lips in sadistic satisfaction as he widened his smile, looking for the next nearest child to torture.

"You certainly did try to escape, didn't you? I am only here for a select few of you, there need not be such bloodshed. You know who you are, you've seen me just this night while you slept. Come forward and no more shall suffer!" Johnny was trying to help the child who had been kicked move away from the beast when a hard backhand sent Johnny skidding across the floor. The Creep was toying with them, like a cat who has caught a bug beneath its paw. He aligned his right foot above the next nearest child, aiming to stomp her poor head like a grape. He eyed the girl as he had the first child, assessing her intently.

"Ah, not this one either, there is no recognition in her pleading eyes. If you will not come forward, oh Chosen, then I will go child by child until I get what I've come here for!" He raised his foot for a solid stomp.

"Oh, come off it already, you big ass," Johnny cried out as he stood from the vicious hit he had taken and began walking back towards the beast. Bryce and the others looked to him in horror.

"Johnny, what the hell are you doing?" Zack sputtered through his bloody door-smashed teeth. Johnny ignored him, adjusting his glasses on his face, the frames bent and the arms uneven from James's blow.

"You don't scare us with your cheap Halloween costume crap! I've got a mask that looks just like yours at home that I wore for Halloween last year!" James's smile didn't falter in the slightest as he lowered his foot gently to the ground besides the child he had prepared to squash and strolled towards Johnny now, dragging his blade slowly behind him. Johnny stood tall, fists clenched at his sides and a brave glare on his face. If he was afraid, he certainly wasn't showing it.

"Is that so, Johnny Pragg? I doubt very much that anyone could copy this face. It would take a truly twisted individual to create a mask in my image." He showed his bright creepy smile wildly as if to emphasize his point, his mouth nearly swallowing his ears.

"You don't know what you're talking about, Jimmy-boy. I went as a smiling pile of poo emoji last year and I'm telling you, that mask I have is a spitting image of your stupid face. Ask Bryce, he saw it! I swear, if I didn't know any better, I'd say that you were wearing it right now!" Johnny's trademark smirk rose on his lips as he pushed his glasses up his nose and then quickly took them off. One of the lenses was gone, popped from its frame when James had sent Johnny flying. "And look at this! You broke my glasses! You're going to pay for these, man. Do you have any idea how much a pair of spectacles costs in this day and age? A smiling pile of poo just broke my glasses! My mom is never going to believe this!" Johnny was looking down at his glasses, examining them intently before putting them back on and smiling up at James with his cocky grin.

James's face had quite the opposite reaction, his scowl replacing the pearly white smile. Bryce and the others were dumbfounded. Bryce stood and stepped between Johnny and James momentarily before being swiped across the room with one of

James's elongated hands. Bryce crumpled to a ball in agony as his broken left arm slammed to the floor repeatedly with his roll across the tile. His vision tunneled as he swooned from the pain and his hearing was as if he had just fallen down a very deep hole. He focused hard, fighting back the blackout as he had so often during his odd dizzy spells and slowly worked to his hands and knees.

"You insolent child! You do not know to whom you speak! You should be cowering like a rodent before a serpent!" James's fury had only been partially taken out on Bryce. The rest would clearly be spent making an example of Johnny. James stepped forward as the boy stepped back, still smiling but fearful now. "Chosen or not, you will be taught a lesson! Bear witness, ingrates, disrespect will only yield pain!" James raised his hand to strike Johnny, not with a fist, but with the dark blade he wielded, which glinted in the dark purple hue of the shadows and the alternating red and blue from outside. Bryce tried to get up but face-planted as his broken left arm screamed and buckled under his posted weight.

"Bryce, Bryce, Bryce. What are you doing?" Bryce, using his right arm now, posted his upper body up and crouched low, resting on his toes. James, human James, was in front of him. Behind he could see Johnny in mid-defense, arms raised above his head shielding from a black shadowy mass that stood before him. "Your arm is broken; I would say in more than one spot from its misshapen look."

Bryce lifted his left arm away from his body. It pulsed angrily at the motion and he quickly pulled it back against his ribs.

"Yea, seems a little beat up," said Bryce, mirroring James's crouch as he gently rested his right fingertips to the floor.

"I am surprised to find two of you here, perhaps there are even more. But something about you in particular is interesting," James confessed. "It's rare for a mark to realize he's being hunted, let alone a mark who is a child." James glanced back to where Johnny was still bracing for a gruesome slashing. "So, I'll tell you what I'll do, Bryce. If you come with me right now, I will spare the others. Not only their lives tonight, but I will not pursue them ever again."

Bryce looked around to his friends and the other children, frozen in the monster's spell and cowering in huddles or behind what they could find. He sat backwards from the balls of his feet down to his butt with a thud, causing his arm to jolt in pain. Bryce grimaced and then brushed aside some debris with his good arm as he continued to look over the destruction James had caused, the splinters of wood and metal that lay strewn across the floor from the door explosion. He thought about how Jan and Bart had been battling him and how James had now reached the room with neither of them in sight. Bryce picked up a nearby piece of doorframe shrapnel that looked like something that could be used to stake a vampire before dropping it. He rested back away from the beast on his right hand, sitting now as if he might be watching TV.

"What happened to Jan and Bart? I don't see them." James's grin grew.

"They are incapacitated boy, just outside the doorway as a matter of fact. They will be quite a joy to interrogate later once I have secured you. But that fun will have to wait. It is time, Bryce, enough stalling. We are going now or I will weed out the Chosen amongst you."

Bryce looked to the doorway and thought he could make out two bodies, surrounded by an odd purple aura glowing lightly from the hallway. He closed his eyes, breathing deeply before opening them and looking to James.

"New terms. Jan and Bart go free, everyone else is free from pursuit until the end of time, and I go without a fight. That's the deal." James didn't flinch as he smiled unkindly.

"How about I relieve poor Johnny of his head and then I take you with me just the same. And once you're secured, I will take my sweet time during the interrogation of these protectors of yours," he motioned toward the doorway where the unmoving bodies of Jan and Bart lay. "Savoring every agonizing cry that they spew out. Even better," he said snapping his fingers. "I'll make sure you have a front row seat to all the fun! Oh, what a joy that would be! Yes, I think that would be the best way to do things." Bryce met his stare calmly and unfazed before responding.

"I don't think that's the route you want to take, James. Something about going willingly is of importance to you. Why else go through the charade of being a guide after we supposedly die? Why else trade an unknown number of targets for just me?" James's face dropped in surprise before quickly masking back to a scowl. But not quick enough that Bryce did not notice. "Release Jan and Bart. When I see them through that door we can leave and I will go willingly. The rest will not be pursued and we will be on our way. Do we have a deal?" James's gaze remained locked with Bryce's and it was all Bryce could do to keep his composure. Gambling with his friend's lives made his stomach flip, but everything he had observed pointed to some need for obedience in traveling with James. His stare continued and for a second Bryce feared he may have misjudged the situation before the Creep replied simply and angrily through gritted teeth, "Agreed."

James began muttering to himself with an enchanting cadence as Bryce glanced to Johnny. The slowness that James had used on the rest of the room was nearly over; Johnny was moving noticeably, ducking from the impending sword attack. From the doorway the faint purple glow had dissipated, and rolling slowly now, rocking forward to a sitting position were Jan and Bart, bloodied but clearly alive. Jan's eyes opened and blinked painfully, locking with Bryce who set his jaw with clenched teeth at the look.

"They are free, and now we must go!" James cried in unexpected desperation. He reached with his right hand for Bryce's broken arm, which Bryce quickly pulled away out of instinct, wincing in pain. James growled loudly and instead grabbed Bryce's left thigh before beginning to mutter to himself again. His hand was freezing. It felt as if it might be burning it was so cold, like snow caught between glove and hand. Bryce eyed the long hand for a moment before suddenly grabbing the nearby vampire stake shrapnel and plunging it through the back of the beast's wrist.

12

ENTER THE VOID

James howled in pain, snapping backwards and ripping his hand away. Bryce felt the shrapnel tear at his own leg, but he held on with his right hand as James jumped to his feet. The room suddenly became dark and grey, all around him the debris and children became fuzzy shadows, and he felt as though he had entered a freezer. Bryce's head pounded, a horrible time for his illness symptoms to manifest. James was making his way towards where Johnny was standing, or at least where Johnny had been; the room was void of all the children. It was only James and Bryce now. The dizziness and headache dissipated as suddenly as it had come, and he now found himself feeling whole in the strange dark vision, all while he hung onto the shrapnel like a fish on a line as James shook his hand in pain and anger.

The world around him quivered in black and grey shadows, as if the entire landscape had been covered in a living darkness. It was vaguely similar to the creeping shadows on the hospital walls but less ominous. Instead of a creeping purple aura, the images around him simply seemed absent of color. The world swayed with the Creep's steps as he careened towards a deep black negation where he had thought Johnny once stood. The very fabric of the three-dimensional space bent and waved with his motion, as wind would ripple a sail. And far away, within the background of the bleak landscape and beyond a patch of dark grey mist, was a castle of sorts, ruined and crumbling. And as his eyes rested upon it, he felt an unseen gaze meet his own for a split second before the Creep reached the deep black spot. The temperature rose and the colors returned as Bryce's grip slipped, and with a final whip from the beast, he was flung into the wall above Johnny, back into the real world. His back made contact first and he slunk to the floor in a heap as he again bumped his broken forearm while his leg bled from the unintentional self-inflicted stabbing. Johnny, alive and not shredded to pieces, looked over to Bryce and up at the beast, who was pulling the shrapnel from the back of his hand.

"What the hell just happened?" he yelled. "And why is your leg bleeding?" Bryce smiled at his friend before it melted to fear seeing the beast towering above them now, purple blood dripping from the shrapnel he had removed. He clenched it tightly, eyes fierce in a face of perturbation. His injured hand hung limp at his side.

"Impossible!" the beast cried seeing Bryce slumped on the ground bleeding. "You traveled with me?"

A golden flash smashed the back of the Creep's head as he summersaulted next to the two friends and crashed to the floor. Bryce saw Jan rushing in through the broken doorway. Her shield crashed to the ground in front of them with Bart right behind her, a large singlehanded battle hammer in hand. The beast leapt back over the boys towards Jan and Bart with its black blade drawn as Johnny slid over to Bryce who was somewhat propped up on his good arm.

"Seriously, what the hell is going on?" Johnny cried as he tried to stop the leg from leaking further, pressing Bryce's sweatpants into the jagged wound.

"I honestly don't know, but I'm glad you're alright. I didn't mean to cut myself but I thought taking away that hand might stop him from clawing your head off." Johnny shook his head as he pressed his hands onto his friend's leg with increased force. Some blood ran through his fingers, the cut seemingly deeper and longer than it looked on the surface.

"You're crazy man. I like you, but you're crazy."

"Plus he always uses his right hand to shoot that purple whatever-the-hell it is at us," Bryce said as he grimaced. "I figured attacking that might also stop him from being able to use it, you know?" Johnny looked over to the Creep in battle, noting only physical attacks being thrown and a lack of the goose bump inducing crashes they had heard earlier.

"You ain't called Eagle Eye for nothing, eh?" Johnny grinned, still pressing the leg as Zach's large hand pushed Johnny out of the way.

"You're doing it wrong; you need something else to soak up the blood!" Zack yelled, ripping off his crew neck to press it around Bryce leg. "And what the hell is this purple crap?" Zack asked looking at his hands and to Bryce's leg.

"It has to be that thing's blood," said Bryce. "I can feel it burning around the cut." Jan suddenly slid next to them, her stringy black hair full of sweat and blood and hanging over her eyes. The boys stared with uneasiness at the sight of their cheery nurse so battle worn and wounded.

"You must leave this place now, Bryce. We will be right behind you. Grip this tightly and do not let go. Then break the stone." She pulled a strange necklace from her robe pocket and slid it under Bryce's bleeding leg, small purple stones glittering even in the absence of light.

"What about Zack and Johnny?" Bryce asked, pulling the string out from beneath his leg. The boys still kept their pressure on Bryce's leg as they awkwardly listened to the conversation. Jan shook her head frantically.

"There is no time, Bryce, he seeks you."

"And them! We all saw him; we even all had the same dream!"

"Three of you?" she yelped. "This is only enough for one, maybe two with the spare stone." James landed on both feet directly above Jan with blade raised before a swing of Bart's hammer met the beast's knee, buckling it and causing him to roll away from the children. Bart had his hammer from the hallway but was also now wearing his own set of armor, much cruder looking than the shining and finely crafted pieces that Jan wore.

"No time!" Jan concluded aloud to both herself and the boys. "All three of you, grip it, break the stones, and do not let go!" Jan yelled as she jumped back into the fray with Bart. Bryce eyed the gold coin that hung from the end of the necklace, holding it between the three friends as the battle continued around them. It was magnificent looking, aside from the stones themselves, which were rough and crude but shimmered even as they held the necklace stationary, a purple spark fizzing within them. Along the length of the stones were strange symbols, nothing the boys recognized, except for a large one etched into the gold coin at the end. Bryce pulled the necklace toward him with his good hand and rubbed this thumb along the flawless grooves, following the shape of a crown and grain on one side and the strange symbol he had found painted on his mysterious leaf on the other side.

"I saw this symbol before," Bryce said still tracing the shape. "This is what I found on that leaf under my door after my dream."

"What are you talking about with this leaf, man?" asked Johnny quizzically.

Jan crashing next to them again broke their conversation. She slid on her back from whatever blow launched her but sat up quickly, grasping Bryce's hands around the necklace with her own before grabbing one of each of Johnny and Zack's hands and doing the same. Blood dripped from her knuckles as she pulled her hands from the necklace and her somber expression held them captivated over her physical condition.

"You must go now. Break a stone and do not let go. You must stay gripped to this; do you understand? Hold onto this as if your lives depended on it."

She stood suddenly as Bart cried out, the group looking over to see a short black blade sticking from his back as he fell to all fours. The Creep stood above him, ripping the blade out viciously and sending a sharp line of dark red along the floor and wall behind him. The beast's foot crushed Bart flat to his stomach, the blade now pointed to the back of his neck.

"Now, boys, do it now," Jan whispered. The Creep looked up to Jan as he pulled Bart's blond hair hard, ripping his head up and placing the blade beneath his throat. His sinister grin gleamed towards Jan and the boys as Bart tried to wiggle free in futility.

"A casualty of war, Lady Blue Heart, another soldier meets his end at the hands of the Grim. Your blood will be spilt next and the boys will be mine." He froze, the grin evaporating in an instant as his eyes met the necklace the boys now held. "No! You fool! You cannot send three with such a token; you'll send them to their doom!" He spoke as he moved, dropping Bart's head to the ground and sprinting toward them, his fury now replaced with desperation. Bart gripped James's ankle frailly with one hand, enough to trip him up and slow him a step.

"Now, boys, break it now!" Jan yelled. The three sat motionless as the Creep regained its balance and leapt towards them, Jan parrying his dark blade with her dagger and her entire body weight, redirecting the beast around them.

"Go!" she yelled, and with her right foot, she pivoted and kicked down against the necklace, smashing it hard against the floor and cracking a number of stones. She began to speak but her voice was sapped from the room like water down a drain as the spark of the strange stones connected and a crack formed slowly down their centers.

"*What?*" Bryce yelled but while his mouth moved, no words left his lips. Jan smiled woefully and raised a hand as if waving goodbye, a look he could not remember the jolly nurse ever displaying before. Coupled with his loss of hearing, her look put a pit in his stomach and he looked to his friends who all shared his horror. Johnny said something, or tried to, as his mouth moved silently just as Bryce's had. His frantic look said it all. The world turned around him, moving in sharp uneven frames, breaking into large pieces, then smaller, and still smaller it fractured. He swooned and swallowed hard but found he could not even hear the saliva go down this own throat and his heartbeat was vacant. He reached out to Jan but as close as she had been to smash the necklace, she was now an infinite distance away, stretching thin away from him. His palms began to sweat, then his whole body. Trying to blink, his eyes fought back, struggling to close against an unseen force.

Sweat poured profusely from him now as the broken pieces of the world around them began to melt, blurring and meshing together, the shapes of the somber waving Jan and despairing James, the other children around the edges of the room, the nearly incapacitated Bart, the wreckage of the blasted door; it all blended into one another, a horrible Monet forming before his eyes. The lone constant was the white light that radiated slowly from the stone, drowning out the blurred colors of the room, pulling them from existence, just as the sound had, slowly but steadily until the room was all but washed out, a white world fainted with black outlines of distorted shapes. The three could hardly see each other because the light was so complete, though it was not bright or painful—it was just bountiful and encompassing.

Bryce gripped the necklace hard but found that he could not perceive what was in his hands. He squeezed further but could not feel his fingers against his palm. He kicked the ground with the back of his heel, trying to feel the floor he sat on, any sort of sensory input. Where the ground should have stopped his leg, the washed-out floor gave way like thick mud and as he kicked a second time, the sensation of mud was gone, replaced by nothing, feeling as though he was only kicking air. His foot floated through where the ground had been and he felt he might flip upside down through the colorless world. Bryce held the necklace all the tighter, even without the sensory feedback. Even his broken arm lost its pain, and Bryce used it to feel where his face should have been, but his reach never made contact, an arm endlessly searching for his dissolved body which he was no longer sure he still had. Whatever Jan had done, it had invaded their senses and detached them from the world.

Then, all at once, everything that had been removed came rushing back. The colors and shapes of the room returned, exploding into their retinas and then increasing in vibrancy and energy at an exponential rate, pulsing and glowing bright in their minds. It was no longer serene white, but painfully colorful, erupting a lifetime of vivacity through their senses. Blinking offered no reprieve from the intensity as even the black of closed eyelids was colorful, resonating deep and heavy. Opened eyelids returned the flared scenery from before but the over-sensitivity was not restricted to sight alone. The noises of their heartbeats, the sweat dripping down their armpits, the squeez-ing of the muscles in their hands; all could be heard, drumming and grinding and straining, loudly in their ears. It all echoed around them, a swelling of separate sounds that were intermin-gled and individual at once. Every nerve ending in their bod-ies was on, blooming with input from all around them. Their bodies sung in sensory, walking the line of euphoria and agony as the smell of blood in the air from the battle, the taste of the dust, the cool of the linoleum all rushed around them, shaking the room with their sense. Bryce took a breath but felt his lungs might explode from the contact of air along his throat, and the noise of air rushing through his windpipe echoed deafeningly in his ears. Worse yet, his broken arm's pain had returned in amplified anguish as well, and he thought his mind might melt from the oversensory rush.

The room quickly left them, shrinking below their feet as the three boys rose upwards in the amplified state and melt-ed through the ceiling at an extreme speed. Bryce squeezed the jewelry with ferocious intensity. Johnny and Zack gripped it with both hands, just as hard as Bryce from their grimaced looks, as the trio's legs floated away from the necklace. Bryce held as tight as he could with his good arm, the pain in his bro-ken arm splintering in horrible magnified furry. Faint objects that were difficult to identify whirled past them as the colors and objects crashed and melded together. Arching his head to the right, Bryce tried to steer towards a new direction, tried to will himself to stop, but nothing happened.

Bryce's stomach lurched as they suddenly dropped, chang-ing directions from the feeling but visually the colors still swirled and pulsed the same as they had. He remembered being on Marge's brother's boat once and feeling a similar nausea. The trick, Uncle Slim had said, was to focus on the distant horizon or some other far-off, unmoving point to regain your equilib-rium. Bryce peeked around him, and past his friends who still held wildly to the necklace, but trying to find a horizon or any fixed spot was impossible. The world around them was melting too quickly and erratically. The transitioning of lights and darks and color swirls flashing and quaking was nonstop and without orientation; it was as beautiful as it was terrifying. A dot of light appeared ahead of them at the edge of the color swirl, the first static point they had seen since their takeoff. Bryce locked his eyes to it as it grew in size more and more rapidly as the colors and lights sped by even faster.

"Look!" came Johnny's voice, booming around them with their heightened senses. He pointed to the light but quickly regripped the necklace with both hands as the tension on their arms had suddenly increased with their speed. Bryce's grip became strained. Looking to his friends in fear, he felt his fingers on his one good hand begin to slip, the broken arm uselessly held close to his chest. Zack saw the look and reached towards Bryce as his grip gave fully, the force outward proving too much. Zack's hand glanced the hood of Bryce's sweatshirt and Bryce felt a short tug before his two friends were gone. Bryce suddenly felt the full effects of gravity as he whirled through the vortex of colors. He was falling in random directions, down, now up and to the left, now swirling. The direction of gravity was changing as the colors morphed around him, and he felt his consciousness slipping, feeling this may be what pilots and astronauts experience in high g-force. He concentrated hard, focused on nothing in particular, only on remaining conscious, but the forces proved too great. His vision tunneled, his thoughts faded, and he was lost to the vortex.

ACT 2
ARRIVAL

13

ALL FOR ONE

The light faded as he dove through it, grabbing nothing in his arms as he fell to his chest with a hard slam. James posted his lanky pale arms on the dusty floor, wincing as his wrist gave, before punching the floor hard with his good hand, two, three, four times as radial cracks ran through the surface. He glared towards Janeph now, his hatred whole and fully faced. Janeph said nothing but tried to meet his glare with equal intensity.

"You fool! You ignorant selfish fool! You've sent them to their deaths!" James cried, still on his hands and knees. Janeph smiled cheekily despite her wounds as Bartellom hobbled up beside her, clutching his shoulder, a limp arm hanging from his torso, clearly damaged where James had plunged his black blade. He looked to Janeph with despair equal to that of the beast. The children around them cowered against the walls still, in shock at what had just played out. James jumped to his feet and turned towards the pair as he held his bleeding wrist with his long pale fingers, trying to stem some of the purple blood that ran from it.

"That was them! The only potentials in this horrible Realm! And you've sent them to die to keep them from me!" Janeph nodded knowingly.

"Correct. But they will never have the unfortunate opportunity to be molded by you or the Grim King, or any of your horrid lot. And though they will never know it, their sacrifice will have saved Realms well beyond their own, including Endland." James looked to Bartellom and saw the shock that mirrored his own at Janeph's cold delivery. The beast broke his surprise with a snarl, clenching his good hand as his other went limp to his side.

"When I get to Endland, and I emphasize *when*, I will see to your death personally, Lady Janeph. Had I known it was you earlier, you'd already be dead! But not before all that you care for is destroyed in front of your very eyes. You will suffer like no other in Endland before I finally end you." He spoke confidently, the statement being fact in his mind. Janeph smiled all the more, accepting the challenge.

"Strong words for a traitorous Dawnish snake such as you, Jamesett," Bartellom retorted with malevolence, a small grin finding his lips. "Do not be so quick to think the death of a Blue Heart will be so easily had, nor entry to Endland for that matter. The free people of the world look for such incoming anomalies as you, even your cold elves of Dawnwood." Jamesett flashed his insidious smile, breaking him from his wrath momentarily.

"My, oh my, am I speaking with *the* Bonethorne Drifter? Of course, I must be, a normal barbarian would never leave his clan at the behest of the people of Endland. Plus, no other Endlander would hold such malice towards Dawnwood and her lovely people." His smile widened, peering over his high cheekbones as Bartellom's expression soured opposite the beast's. "And here I thought your simpleminded clan had run its course, lost from history but for tales that other clans tell their children in lessons of cowardice and gullibility." Bartellom's smirk vanished altogether, a red rage replacing it, consuming his expressions. A large neck vein bulged and he breathed deeply through flared nostrils.

"You pompous liar! I'll see your head caved!"

"Oh, but you had that opportunity just this night, dirty Bonethorne," Jamesett reminded the barbarian, "and it ended with my blade in your back and at your throat. And were it not for Janeph essentially murdering three poor children, you would have drowned in your own blood this night. Perhaps you need some more time in the war pits of Bol-Garot. Then again, you wouldn't be welcomed there, now would you? Not with that dishonorable clan name." Jamesett, deliciously satisfied with his stinging words, bowed strangely, arms out and bent at strange angles before he blew away in a wisp of smoke. "Until next time, Drifter."

Bartellom slammed his hammer hard into the ground, on what he must have wished was the Creep's skull, as he fell heavily to his knees, sweat and blood dripping from his face to the cool floor below him. Janeph gently placed a hand on his shoulder which was met by his snapping a short sharp look towards her before softening. He looked back down shaking his head to ward off his thoughts before reconnecting eye contact with her with a somber expression.

"Apologies, Lady Janeph. I've failed you. I've failed the Bonethorne name."

"It matters not, Bartellom," she said in but a whisper. "What's done is done. But I cannot believe that was Jamesett himself. If the scrolls are true, he's not been seen since the battle of Jornun. And suddenly he appears today to make an extraction, personally? Are the Grim as desperate as we are? They've made every extraction for years, so why send someone as legendary as Jamesett to retrieve Chosen?" She spoke half to herself and half to Bartellom as she gestured to him to stand. He obliged with some difficulty, his left arm hanging limp at his side

"If it is him, I will find him and bring that two-faced bastard's head to Bol-Garot as penance for my ancestor's mistakes, by Phont I will. I did not think vengeance could be had on that snake." Janeph nodded knowingly with a small smile of her own before sobering and looking around to assess the damage done while Bartellom shook off his vengeful thoughts and reached out to Janeph's shoulder.

"The children, Janeph. How could you send those children to their deaths? A necklace is enough for the transport of a single person. Even with adding some of the stones that Petravinos sent, sending even two would have most likely meant death! But sending all three? Lost forever in the void . . . ."

Janeph turned away from him and waved a hand over her shield, muttering under her breath as it began to fade from her forearm in a shower of soft sparks, and hiding the tears that welled in her eyes. She then turned back, avoiding eye contact, and walked out to the children who were now slowly gravitating towards them at the center of the room.

"We must have faith, Bartellom. Were any of them truly Chosen, they should stand a chance. Not all of them, no. But if even one makes it alive," her voice trailed as Bartellom blinked in slow surprise.

"Janeph, I cannot believe what I am hearing. You sound like Hulmar! *Maybe* one Chosen for the lives of two children? Life is not a bargaining chip to be bet with. Should they not emerge, they will spend an eternity in transit, lost forever in the space between! How can you be so nonchalant?" He looked to her, perplexed and disappointed, leaning awkwardly to his left as he tried to hold his arm to his body. Janeph sighed deeply and looked to the other children, bruised, covered in debris and thoroughly confused.

"We do much that is not fair to those we Hunt, Bartellom— much that is not fair to those caught between us and the Grim. But I can say Endland has never had a Hunt where we encountered more than one mark, let alone three such as this. If we can get one back home, just one, Endland's fortune may be changed. If there was another way, I would have pursued it. But we were losing that fight." She shook her head in self-correction. "We lost that fight. Jamesett, if that was him, is as skilled as the tales say. If the children were true Chosen and had been taken by him, the Grim King could have been in Endland before the first frost."

Bartellom averted his eyes in contemplation before he nodded with slight dissatisfaction and labored his hammer around his torso, strapping it to his back with a thud.

"I hear your words, Janeph. The action is disturbing, but your logic is true."

She sighed heavily before looking to the other children that had now gathered around them. Covered in drywall dust, door splinters, blood from the fight, and shrapnel, none seemed to have more than minor distresses. She watched them soberly in the still-flashing police lights before looking down.

"We must go, Bartellom. I cannot bear their looks."

Bartellom nodded and without a word they each pulled a thick leather pouch from their belts, wrapped tightly with crisscrossing strings. From the pouches they pulled necklaces similar to the one that had been given to the boys, along with a large white stone from Janeph's pouch. They each gripped their own necklaces in their hands as Janeph placed the white stone in the center of the room. She weakly smiled to the kids and stomped on the stone, cracking it with substantial force. A wave of light expanded rapidly past the children, through the walls, and out into the world. She watched it continue out the window for a moment and looked to the mesmerized children, caught in its magic. She wiped another tear from her eye and punched the large purple stone of her necklace to the ground while Bartellom flexed his stone tight in a massive palm. The gems cracked, and the world became white to them as they faded from the children's view amidst the rubble, leaving them alone in the mystifying magic.

14

CITY OF SAILS

———◇———

Zack looked to Bryce's blue hood, cut clean at the neck-line and held tightly in his clenched fingers. The trip they were on immediately stabilized as Bryce disappeared, like weight on a raft would be redistributed as it floated down a river. Were it not for the fact the he had just vanished in the whirling color insanity they were traveling in, the boys would have been relieved at the constancy their surroundings now emitted. The light spot they had been traveling towards was very near now and the speed at which the pair traveled began to slow, the colors swirling less, the sounds and other stimuli returning to a normal and tolerable level. They felt their feet float back beneath them, natural gravity returning, and as they passed through the light like a doorway, the necklace began to disintegrate in their hands.

Solid ground rose to meet their feet and they found them-selves standing in a brightly lit stone room, tall stained-glass windows pouring bountiful sunlight upon their faces. Sets of medieval armor were paired off in each corner, and on the one wall where there was not a stained-glass window stood a large wooden door instead. A set of torches framed the doorway, lit and burning unnecessarily in the sunlight-strewn room. Aside from the armor, they were alone.

"What. In the hell. Just happened." Johnny whispered as he spread his arms trying to maintain his balance. Zack said nothing, still grasping his friend's severed hood in his hands. "Zack, what just happened? What the hell did Jan do to us? And where the hell did B-man go?" Johnny said more forcefully, grabbing the hood from Zack and waving it in the air. Zack didn't move, even as Johnny forcefully brushed his face with the hooded cloth.

"I . . . I don't know. He was with us, I grabbed his hood, and then he was gone." The two stood in silence, first looking at the hood and then at their surroundings. Reddening sunlight encompassed them and brightened a beautiful circular stone mural which they stood on, a large white ship on a red sea. It was beautiful with an intense dedication to detail but all the floor was covered in a thin layer of dust. Most of the room in fact had dust covering it, and the only spots that seemed clean were the areas beneath the torches and where the doors swung open, small trails of clean swept by walking feet. The armor watched all, silent sentinels standing guard over the clearly seldom used space. Polished red and white metal, the armor looked mostly for decoration as opposed to combat.

"What room are we in? Is this some weird therapy room or something?" Johnny asked, looking across the dirty floor and out to the setting sun. "And wasn't it the middle of the night? How is the sun setting again?" Zack pulled his phone from his pocket to check the time, but what it read was ludicrous.

"J-man, you got your phone? Mine says it is 71 minutes past 2F."

"It says what now?" Zack showed him his screen, 2F:71. Johnny shook his head and fumbled around his pockets before pulling out his own phone. He tapped it repeatedly but was met with a black screen.

"Nothing Papa Bear, dead as a doornail, or so they say. I swore I was at like 90-percent when we left the room with B, it had been charging all night." He shook his head as he forcefully pushed it back into his pocket, frustrated. "What's going on, man?"

But before Zack could respond, they could hear a commotion on the other side of the door. Footsteps and voices approached. Johnny dropped the severed hood and started running immediately towards one of the sets of armor but before he could fully get behind it, the doors were pushed open, revealing a band of people led by a very short man, five-feet tall at most with a beard that he nearly stepped on as he shuffled his feet. He was dressed in a deep red robe, similar in color to the ship mural that they stood upon, and he carried with him a very peculiar walking stick, a full foot taller than he. The robe wrapped loosely over a thinner white shirt and both were tied at the waist with a thin, clean white rope, which emphasized the bottom of his small protruding gut.

Two men on each side of the short man wore dark red armor with white trim. As they approached, their hands were gripped tightly to their swords, still sheathed on their hips. Behind them stood a group of very inquisitive faces, each with a small book and a feathered quill in their hands. They all stayed a safe distance behind the short man and the guards that flanked him. Their dress was odd: flowing, single-colored shirts and plain pants, some loose from improper sizing while others, on the more sophisticated-looking individuals, looked loose and draping by design. Still others wore tight tunics, extending well beyond the waist and most were tied off with a belt or two. Their shoes were mostly mid-shin boots or short clogs, and not one of them wore shorts or sweatpants like the boys wore. Instead, they wore plain-colored, textured slacks, crude based on what the boys were used to seeing and wearing, and those with long shirts may not have been wearing pants at all.

Zack snatched up the hood and instinctually took a few steps back as the group approached. Johnny froze in place, half hidden behind one of the sets of armor in the back corner of the room. Zack and the group stood opposite each other with the floor mural laying between them before the long-bearded man at the front of the flock of people cleared his throat.

"Hello!" His voice was high pitched and he spoke as if the boys might be deaf. "I am Lopi Lidobol!" At this he bowed very low but all the while kept his eyes on Zack and glanced quickly at the ill-concealed Johnny. "May I ask your names?"

Zack could not tell if this was just how the man spoke or if he suspected he and Johnny might be hard of hearing. He said nothing as he eyed the guards, still gripping the swords tightly. He looked away quickly back to Lopi, who was smiling cautiously at him. Behind, the crowd seemed to be holding their breath now after writing constantly in their books since Lopi had started speaking. Behind him Johnny shuffled ever so slightly behind the armor, slowly but surely concealing his entire body. Lopi stood patiently for a few more moments, still smiling.

"Were you sent here using a necklace?" He was still yelling as he mimed with his free hand where a necklace might be worn around his neck. Zack nodded softly. Lopi clapped his hands quickly, resting his staff against his shoulder, as the group behind him went into a frenzy writing. "Was it given to you by Janeph?" he continued to ask, his excitement building.

Zack's face scrunched at the question and the guards took a step back, all except Lopi, who continued his optimistic smile as he leaned on his driftwood staff. Johnny was now all but behind the armor, having moved a millimeter per second since the conversation started.

"What is a Janeph?" Zack asked. Lopi jumped as he clapped again, the scribes behind nearly setting the parchment they wrote on ablaze they wrote with such fervor.

"You speak!" yelled Lopi. "Oh, what joy! This is a marvelous sign, I think! Are you having trouble hearing me?" He continued to yell at an unknowingly obnoxious volume.

"Um, no, you don't have to yell, I can hear just fine." Lopi clapped again, a cymbal-wielding monkey windup toy of excitement.

"Wonderful!" he exclaimed in a normal speaking voice, but even at a normal decibel, Lopi's voice was still quite high pitched. "This is stupendous! May I ask you for your name again?"

"Zack Kapule," he responded, and for some unbeknownst reason, attempted a slight bow towards the group. Johnny snickered from behind his armor hiding spot as Lopi stroked his long beard happily and bowed in return.

"Zack Kapule, it is wonderful to meet you." A large crash from the corner interrupted him, causing the small man to point his staff with unexpected quickness towards the source of the noise. The two escorting guards pulled their swords as well as they confronted Johnny, standing motionless behind a toppled armor set.

"No, it's OK, he's my friend!" Zack said taking a step between Johnny and the men. Lopi kept his staff pointed at Johnny and his eyes remained locked.

"Why was he moving so slowly and away from the rest of us? Such odd behavior is not a good sign, it may be a symptom of shifting sickness."

"Aw, you guys knew I was there?" Johnny said, disappointed and a little frightened with the weapons pointed at him.

"Oh my, he speaks as well!" Lopi straightened his staff and replanted it on the stone floor. The crowd behind let out audible gasps, writing and murmuring among each other. "Another peep and the lot of you can wait in the Great Hall!" Lopi said to the group sternly; most only partially listened, still murmuring in slightly quieter tones. "Now then, may I ask your name, friend of Zack?"

"May I ask just where the hell we are?" Johnny retorted, much to Zack's dismay. Lopi smiled, though his eyes did not, and nodded so quickly Zack thought his head might pop off his shoulders.

"Of course, of course, of course! You must have many questions! This is Eislark," he said, spreading his arms out wide in front of him, "the largest port city of the Eastern Isle and home to the finest shipbuilders in all of Endland!"

"Oh, Easter Island!" said Johnny. "This is where those big head statues are, in part of England, I guess. I always thought Easter Island was some exotic place. Who knew, eh, Zack?"

"Oh, do you mean the heads of the old kings?" Lopi interjected. "My, I am surprised Bartellom was so open with his heritage. You must have grown quite close with him?"

"Heads of the old kings? Bartellom? Does that sound like England, Zack? I never paid attention in geography. Or history," Johnny replied, scratching his head. Zack shook his head "no" in confusion.

"I think he said *Eastern* Island, not Easter Island, Johnny. And that is definitely not in England, but I don't know where we are now. I've never heard of Eislark."

"Ah, Johnny is his name?" Lopi asked, extending his hand as he beckoned for more input.

"Johnny Pragg, aka, the Joker, aka, Mr. J, aka, the best friend you never knew you were missing." He bowed ridiculously, flailing his arms wide like dangling wet noodles and shooting a quick grin to Zack as he did so. Lopi returned a standard bow before standing and clapping to himself.

"Johnny Pragg! Wonderful!" Lopi clapped again before he pointed to where he stood. "To be clear, this city we are in now is Eislark, which is on the Eastern Isle, which is part of Endland, though I am sure that sounds strange." Lopi stated very matter-of-factly as the scribes behind wrote frantically.

"See, Easter Island in England, Zack! And Eislark is a city there! Aren't you listening?"

"Johnny, are *you* listening? We're in Eislark, I think I can agree with that. But it is on the *Eastern* Isle, which is part of *Endland*." Johnny looked at his friend and then to Lopi and then back to Zack.

"Is that not what I just said?" Johnny asked both of them. Zack closed his eyes in annoyance and breathed deeply.

"Are you feeling dizzy, Zack Kapule? That can be a sign of the sickness as well," Lopi asked, concerned and slightly pointing his staff towards the boy. Zack shook his head.

"No, I just don't know where Eislark is, or *Eastern* Isle, or *Endland* for that matter." he said, looking to Johnny as he emphasized the locations.

"Same team, Zack, we're arguing nothing," Johnny retorted with arms open and shoulders shrugged. Zack half sighed and half growled.

"I'm just very confused is all. Where are we? And where is Bryce and Nurse Jan?"

"This will be confusing, Zack Kapule, but I will be sure to have a map brought to your quarters. Better yet, I will bring one while you're apprised of the current situation. Although your Hunt originated from Trillgrand, not here. So, I should not really be doing any explaining at all. But it's no matter, I shall provide you the information in Petravinos's stead! And the fact remains, *two* of you have arrived, and you are nearly beyond the sickness timeline!" he exclaimed to no one in particular. He then motioned behind him to the crowd as a very old man dressed in red garb similar to that of Lopi hobbled forward with some effort and extended a large hourglass before the group. It looked far too heavy for the elderly gentleman, but he was very committed to holding it out before him so all could see. Everyone watched in silence, including the boys, as the last grains of sand fell through the opening and settled in the bottom half. The old man smiled a semi-toothless grin, and Lopi jumped and clicked his heels like a leprechaun, clapping as he dropped his staff. One of the escorting guards very narrowly snatched it before it fell to the floor and handed it back to Lopi.

"What a joyous, momentous occasion! Perfectly intact with no signs of the sickness! The first non-Endlanders to make it here unaffected! Come, this way! I shall offer an explanation and then you must meet the lord of Eislark and the other lords and ladies at the feast. My, what luck that you should arrive on this night!" Lopi turned quickly before Zack or Johnny could get a word out, the sea of scribbling individuals parting before him as the two guards paired off and marched forward to escort the boys.

"Wait, we still don't know what the hell's going on! Is this the hospital? Are we doing some weird experimental treatment or something?" Zack cried out, though Lopi was already through the large wooden doors and into the hallway. Whether he was ignoring the questions or simply did not hear them was hard to say with the crowd all speaking among each other and gawking pointedly at the boys. The old toothless man was still grinning widely as he did a sort of jig with the hourglass as his partner, some clapping around him to cheer him on. Johnny raised his hand to speak before the nearest guard patted his back firmly towards the hallway, causing him to take a step.

"Go. Follow," he bellowed in a deep voice as he bumped Johnny again, causing him to take another step.

"Baby Ruth?" Johnny mocked back loud and slowly as he skipped away from the guards, causing Zack to giggle as he was quick to trail his friend. The boys followed where Lopi had gone through the crowd, the scribes writing and speaking. As they passed by, fragments of sentences caught their ears, mostly words like *small, impossible, children, chosen*. Neither knew what to make of any of it.

The crowd followed them out into the hallway, which was lined with tall rectangular windows as well as lovely decorations. Flowers hung along the top of the walls, freshly picked from the smell of them, while red banners adorned with the white ship hung between the windows, the same image as was on the mural they had stood on in the dusty room. The stone floor was incredibly smooth, light brown-grey in hue, with a small short red carpet covering the transition from hallway to room. Peeking out the windows on their left, the boys saw they were quite high up, and the corridor they walked rounded gently to a large castle looming ahead. Its cool brown stonework was lighter than the interior, sun bleached over the years no doubt, and stacked neatly down to a courtyard where people worked in and out of other smaller brown-stoned buildings, all thatched with long reeds or grass, browned to a darker shade than the stone they sat upon.

Armed guards stood at red and white flag posts on the ground and along a great rounded wall that surrounded the courtyard. Beyond the inner-castle wall stood a large town, houses and wooden buildings with ant-sized people riding ant-sized carts through the maze of streets that separated the structures. And as the houses sloped down gradually, they stopped at a wide half-moon bay of water. The buildings met the arched side of the water, running right up to the deep blue waves, while the flat side of the half-moon met tall cliffs, jutting out of the earth like a great row of ragged black teeth. Still further beyond the cliffs was an ocean or lake where large ships with white sails dotted the sunset waters like freckles on a shimmering face. All were sailing inland to a small opening in the cliff face that connected the outside waters to the bay.

"Papa Bear, where the hell are we? Camelot?" Johnny asked as both boys stood mesmerized. "We're in a freakin' castle! This ain't The Land, I know that much."

"I have no idea. We were in the hospital before. Was that necklace some kind of, like physical laughing gas?" The guards that were escorting them had stood patiently a few feet back as the scribes passed them but they now moved uncomfortably close, and the boys quickly resumed their walking. Another pair of armed guards stationed at what seemed to be the middle of hall looked grimly at the two as they whispered; the guards' hands finding their sword's hilts in caution. Johnny took a hop step closer to Lopi and the pack of people, with Zack close behind. Lopi was moving quite nimbly for having such short legs and had moved a good distance while they observed the landscape. They slipped their way through the crowd of people, who were all watching intently and writing frantically as they did so, until they came upon Lopi at the front of the pack.

"Mr. Lopi, is there a reason these guards don't like us?" Johnny asked quietly. "Like, were we transferred to a specialty hospital or something?" Lopi nodded understandingly.

"I know this must be very confusing for you two. I'm confused myself at your questions. I promise I will try to make this all clear, just a little further. Oh, and Mikel has arrived this morning! He will offer comfort as well, and I suspect Janeph and Bartellom will come in the next day or two. My, this is quite peculiar that you arrived here and not Trillgrand!" Lopi continued his disjointed conversation out loud. Zack and Johnny looked to each other in utter confusion.

"Does saying 'make it clear' mean something different? Because I don't have a clue who or what he's talking about," Johnny whispered to Zack, who bore a similar look of extreme puzzlement.

The group reached the end of the hallway and Lopi pushed open a large set of doors as they entered into an even larger hallway. They stood on a short balcony overlooking a staircase that wrapped downward along the four walls of the tower. A number of landings split the staircases as they worked their way downward, each with its own set of wooden doors, rooms, or hallways leading every which way from the large tower. At the bottom of the stairs, there was an open floor, tables and chairs lining it, and filled with a crowd of people. It was all illuminated by a great many torches and a roaring fireplace that appeared to take nearly an entire wall.

Lopi did not miss a step and quickly began to descend the stairs, nodding pleasantly to the people who passed by. Each of them nodded in return before resting their eyes on the boys, dressed in their earthly garb and undeniably sticking out compared to the tunics, robes, and dresses that everyone else wore. The boys tried smiling at the first few they saw but were only met with stares and whispers. They soon soon did their best to avoid making eye contact with anything but the back of Lopi's bobbing head. Red and white sashes and flowers covered the walls, intertwined with thin brown branches into living artwork that softened the rough stone edges of the castle. Each of the landings had a large round red carpet, adorned with the white ship, large sails reaching for a wind that would never propel them. Even with the vast space that the hall filled, the decorations around it provided a warm and intimate feeling.

After descending along the first staircase, Lopi took a turn at the first landing through a set of the wooden doors and into another hallway. Passing a few sets of rooms, he stopped abruptly in front of one, turned and stepped past the boys to address the scribes that followed him.

"The lot of you can wait in the Great Hall," Lopi announced to the group in his squeaky voice. "We can reconvene before the introduction to Lord Belmar. Boys, this way, if you would be so kind."

They were pushed forward by the guards that escorted them, as Lopi opened the door and gestured for them to enter. They obliged, mostly due the guards' hands pushing gently on their shoulders, and entered a large room full of bookshelves and a great many tables. The bookshelves were three times as tall as the boys, covering every inch of wall space save for the back, where there was an entirely windowed wall. It provided ample light for the room and allowed the setting sun to shine through. The tables that lay between the shelves had short candles upon them, unlit for the moment until they were needed. Above them there was an open ceiling revealing a second floor with even more shelves and tables. A staircase was in the back directly across from the door they now entered and was the only spot on the far wall that was not window. A handful of people sat sporadically at tables in the large room reading. Most remained oblivious to them but a few others' eyes lingered on the group before a stern "ah hem" from Lopi brought their attention back to their own books. Lopi gestured for the guards to go back to the hallway and after some angry whispers, they obliged, walking heavily out of the library in stomping protest.

"We will be right outside should you need us, Councilor Lidobol." Lopi said nothing and closed the door in the guards' faces with a click before turning and walking past the boys who, still taking in the vastness of the space, had not moved more than a few feet within the room. The short man proceeded to a nearby table, snapping his fingers above the unlit flame to produce a spark. The candle lit, and waving his hand over the other wicks, so too did the remaining candles including a lantern that he now picked up.

"Come, boys, have a seat, there is much to tell," Lopi said as he lifted the lantern to the shelves and began to look through the one nearest him. Both boys were trying to process the instant fire Lopi had produced before they slowly moved forward and sat at the opposite side of the table, watching silently as the strange old man searched the shelves. Lopi at last pulled a thick blue book from the shelf and dropped it heavily on the table opposite the boys. He thumbed through the first few pages before stopping and spinning the book so the boys could read.

"*Land to End: A Cartography of Endland.* This was first on my list of topics to discuss had one of our Eislark Hunts bore Chosen. So, seeing as you've somehow ended up in the wrong city, I'll take the liberty of explaining as if you had been meant to arrive here." He was giddy with excitement and spoke quickly, almost nervously. "Truthfully, we are not sure what is best to be discussed when meeting new Chosen, no city has ever had a Chosen survive the shifting! So, we've certainly never had a Hunt arrive in the wrong city! But we cannot wait for Trillgrand to arrive, and so I will handle this!" Johnny and Zack said nothing, blank faces staring back at Lopi before Zack looked to the book and nudged Johnny, pointing to the title at the top of the page.

"*Endland*, Johnny. I told you it wasn't England." Johnny leaned forward and studied the title carefully with a scowl.

"They must write their letters weird in England, like a 'd' is a 'g' and vice versa," Johnny retorted, leaning back in his chair with crossed arms. Zack shook his head smiling and slid his finger underneath the word *Endland* and to the word *Cartography*.

"So that's pronounced 'Englang' and that word is pronounced 'cartodraphy'? Could you define that word for me?" Johnny leaned forward again flabbergasted, eyeing both words back and forth a few times before leaning back in his chair again, recrossing his arms in dissatisfaction.

"I don't know man; they speak that weird British language over in England. It's got to be an accent thing."

"They speak English in England, Johnny. *Engl*ish in *Engl*and. And Mr. Lopi doesn't have an accent at all. So, explain that one?" Zack said triumphantly. It wasn't often he had Johnny on the ropes like this; he was slippery when it came to being wrong, somehow talking his way into a no-contest instead of being outrightly incorrect. Johnny annoyingly rolled his head back and blew a breath of air out, his lips bubbling audibly as he did so.

"I don't know, Zack! Lopi here was probably raised in the US before moving here to run this stupid library, and the writer of the book is just an idiot and doesn't know his alphabet." Zack only grinned. Johnny sat forward again now, leaning heavy on the table. "Alright, smarty pants, if we're not in England, then where exactly are we?"

"Well, as I said earlier, you are in Endland, more specifically the city of Eislark, as the map shows before you," Lopi said, deciding to cut the argument where it was before it digressed any further. Zack and Johnny leaned forward over the table as Lopi continued, pointing on the map. "This city is the largest port city of the Eastern Island and boasts the largest navy in Endland, though those tots of Cliffpoint may say differently. Don't be fooled, pirates are always fictionalizing their strength! Nevertheless, we also have our elite warriors, the Gull, that would go toe to toe with any western barbarian swine."

"Gull are the guys who followed us here? With the swords?" Johnny asked as he pushed his glasses up his nose, still looking at the map.

"Erm, no. Those were just soldiers. The Gull, Eislark's elite knights, are equipped with armor and must adhere to strict training to obtain their prestigious title. They man the critical halls and many of the key guard posts throughout our great city. Most of the largest cities in Endland boast their own form of elite forces, actually."

"So, this must be the capital of England, right Mr. Lopi, with the best Gull people and the biggest navy and stuff?" Johnny asked flipping the page as he looked for more clues to where they were.

"Well, no, Eislark is not the capital. All the cities of the Eastern Island acknowledge Trillgrand as the capital and Umbrin Sarn as our king." He was flustered at the question but moved quickly to change topics. "Although, those of the Western and Northern Islands view the Barbarian King Hulmar Da as the true ruler of Endland. There was a war a few short years ago between the East and the North-West alliance, well after the Aging. It was eventually agreed that we should go our separate ways, split the lands, and let each govern as they saw fit." Lopi moved Johnny's hand from the book as he spoke and turned a few pages to an illustration of the signing of the treaty. "Now, that conflict has not been of significant issue as of late. Though there are still political spats from time to time, the real threat to Endland has been in recent times the Grim King." He whispered the last part so low it was barely audible, his eyes saying very clearly the phrase frightened him.

"Who is that?" Zack asked touching the old book's pages as he soaked up the treaty image. "And where is this island in relation to like, Ohio?"

"I don't recognize that name. But if you are referencing your home, it wouldn't be listed here as we're not in your Realm anymore." Zack and Johnny looked to each other befuddled, both pulling their eyes from the book for the first time since Lopi placed it on the table. He crinkled the corners of his mouth in a thin-lipped grimace.

"I think it best that you first understand the Chosen," he started, feeling their uneasiness at his last comment. "You see the Chosen were individuals of extraordinary ability. Great warriors, somehow tied to the past and present. For some, it meant incredible strength, others intelligence, still others could manipulate elements, objects, or even people. Each was unique, though many did have overlapping traits."

"So, are you Chosen, Mr. Lopi?" asked Johnny pointedly. "I saw the magic trick you did with the candle."

"No, no, I am not Chosen." Lopi laughed as he spoke as is if the idea was quite ridiculous. "I am a wizard, with abilities similar to certain Chosen I suppose, but not Chosen. I do not possess the link to Chosen past, and I certainly do not possess any physical combat skills. You see, as a Wizard I am required to study constantly for even the most basic of spells. It requires a natural gift, but also practice and repetition and time and effort. The simple sparks you saw me create to light these few candles took months of practice as a child to master. More complex spells require even more time reading and practicing, years and years. The greatest wizards are always the oldest, as they've had the most time to study and refine their skills."

"Oh, so you're a wizard. Yea, that's not strange or anything. I'm a Chupacabra where I come from, and Zack here is one-sixteenth Bigfoot. But you must be a pretty good wizard, Mr. Lopi, I mean going bald and all, white beard to the floor and what not," Johnny said innocently. Zack ribbed him with an elbow as Lopi chuckled.

"Dude, you just called him old," Zack whispered, trying not to move his lips.

"Dude, he is old," Johnny replied, unvarnished and mocking.

"It is quite alright, I am old but I am also skilled, Johnny," Lopi replied gently waving his hands in the air to calm the boys. "But there are others far more skilled than I, and none more so than Petravinos Morgodello, the Councilor Supreme of our order and advisor to the king in Trillgrand. Petravinos was around for the Aging and has spent a great deal of time with spells of time, which has prolonged his life well beyond any wizard before him. He is truly one of the greatest to ever live."

"This is insane," Zack said, gobsmacked. "You're telling us you're actually a wizard?" He closed his eyes and rubbed his temples with the tips of his pointer and middle fingers. "Can you just send us home or something? Or wake us up? We don't belong here and I'd like to snap out of this."

"Agreed, Mr. Lopi. This was a pretty good dream and all, but it's getting a little boring now. It's time to wake up I think." Johnny added rather calmly, not at all as troubled as Zack was. Lopi smiled but his dolorous eyes did not match the rest of his face.

"That would be where you are wrong, Zack Kapule," Lopi responded unruffled. "You see boys, you *are* Chosen. You standing here is proof. You are the first we've seen in many, many years. And this is your home." Johnny straightened up with a twisted face.

"Wait, *we're* Chosen? So, like you mean we're warriors and we have powers? Oh man, don't end the dream, Mr. Lopi!" He jumped up before Lopi could respond, pushing his chair backwards as he did so and raising his arms, fists clenched. "I'm a freakin' superhero!" Zack pulled the one string of Johnny's hoodie so that the opposite side disappeared into its threaded hole.

"Well, if you do have powers, they aren't mind reading or future telling," Zack said, laughing as Johnny smacked Zack's hand swiftly. "I think you would have seen that coming."

"Johnny Pragg, please sit down, I must explain," Lopi said insistently, looking over to the other nearby tables in embarrassment. "There is much we do not know or understand about the Chosen. It was their law that Chosen would raise Chosen, leaving the rest of us blind to their trials, their training. Even the High Council of Wizards is unaware of their methods. Many speculate that is where the seeds of distrust were first sowed, the first in a great many conflicts between Chosen and commoners, but I digress. The point is, while this is surely strange, beyond strange, this is your true home. And you are destined to be here and to return Endland to its former greatness."

"I think you've definitely got the wrong guys," Zack said, pointing to Johnny, who was desperately trying to fish his hoodie string back into the open. Lopi smiled and shook his head side to side.

"I'll admit you are," he searched for words as Johnny struggled with his string, "less mature than I thought the Chosen would be."

Zack laughed quietly watching his friend, and Lopi continued. "But it is no matter. What we do know of the Chosen is that their abilities manifest with age. I am willing to bet you have already noticed the earliest signs of their arrival: headaches, dizziness, nausea."

"Whoa, wait, how did you know about that?" Zack cut him off. "Are you actually a doctor?"

"It's one of the few things we know of the Chosen. It was the first signs in children to distinguish those who were Chosen and those who were not. If a child displayed the signs, the Chosen masters would be notified and come asses them, and if they showed promise, they would be taken for training. Does your world not know how to identify these things?" Lopi asked skeptically.

"There are no Chosen in our world!" Zack rebutted in loud frustration. "I don't even understand what that is, just send us home!" Johnny took a break from restringing his hoodie to punch Zack hard in the shoulder. Zack recoiled and rubbed it in pain.

"Dude, what the hell was that for?"

"We're in a library, Zack, inside voices please," Johnny said with a smirk. "Don't be that guy." He returned to his hoodie as Zack fumed, still rubbing his shoulder.

"I know this is confusing, but you are essential to our survival, and the survival of a great many Realms. Strange and ancient beasts have re-emerged, sulking in the dark corners of our lands, beasts thought to have disappeared with the Grim King. Beasts that the Chosen would have rooted out in the Golden Age. Beasts that now roam unchecked."

"So, it's that grinning king or whatever causing the problems?" Johnny asked as he gave up on his hoodie string for the moment and walked to the other side of the table, looking through the shelf that Lopi had pulled the first book from. Johnny selected one, *Historical Facts of Endland and Her People*, and began flipping through it as if it were a comic book.

"The Grim King," Lopi corrected, turning in his chair to watch the child. "Most do not believe it is his doing. He has been banished since the Aging, a great many years ago. The

High Council suspects him though, well at least part of the High Council does. There is debate." He stopped abruptly, looking hastily to the other tables and making eye contact with a few individuals as they looked back to their books. Lopi cleared his throat uncomfortably. "The High Council has no opinion on the matter," he said loudly before shifting to a whisper for the boys to barely hear. "But many signs point to him."

"Is his actual name Grim King or is that just what you call him?" Zack chimed in. Lopi glanced to the nearby tables from the corners of his eyes again and still looking around, leaned in towards the boys. Johnny leaned over the table with his book as well, eager to not miss out on the secret.

"Kuor-Varz."

The boys did not reply. Johnny set his book down and resumed trying to pull his hoodie string out of its hole. Zack waited a few seconds for more information from Lopi, but when none came, he slid the book Johnny had brought over in front of him and began to look through its pages. Lopi stayed leaning forward, shocked at their lack of response.

"*Cooler-Wars*, doesn't sound so grim to me," Johnny said laughing to himself as he pulled the hidden string out of his hoodie triumphantly and sat in his chair again, working to even the two sides. "Why is he causing problems now? Was he on vacation or something?"

"*Kuor-Varz*," Lopi enunciated slowly and quietly, "is the single greatest threat our world has known, that all Realms have ever known. He was once Chosen before falling out with their order and beginning his own following, the Grim. There was a great battle over a century ago between the Grim and the Chosen, the end of which resulted in the banishment of Kuor-Varz and a number of his fellow Grim to the Medius Realm."

Lopi spun the *Historical Facts of Endland* book from Zack and thumbed through the pages before stopping at an illustration of a ghastly looking man sitting atop a twisted throne, and on the page's counterpart, a dark brooding dragon in a somewhat darker cave. He spun the book back towards both of them.

"Got it, *Corn-Farts* is a freaky looking dude," Johnny said, peering warily at the image in the book, "but I still don't see what any of this fairy tale stuff has to do with a couple of kids from Cleveland. I know dreams are illogical and all, but this one is a little over the top. And why not just get your own Chosen to do whatever it is they have to do?" Lopi cleared his throat uncomfortably.

"Well, boys, you see—"

"They are all gone, Johnny, weren't you listening? We're the first 'Chosen' to be here in a long time," Zack interrupted before Lopi could finish.

"I was listening but then I got distracted when *somebody* pulled my hoodie string halfway out of my sweatshirt."

"Yes, quite true, Zack," Lopi continued mournfully and ignoring Johnny. "In fact, you boys are the only Chosen there are. You see, we banished the Chosen after their fight with the Grim ended, very soon after the Grim King was sent away. They've been gone just as long as he has now. And so, your presence here is quite profound to some but also quite unsettling to others."

"Wait, so they beat the Grim dude and saved your butts, then you kicked them out of their own city? What the hell is your problem?" Johnny retorted as he flipped through the *Historical Facts* book on his own. Lopi looked abashed at the boys with a few nervous strokes of his beard.

"It was not immediately after, and it was not just from the city. They had to leave this world, this entire Realm. There was a vote among the rulers of Endland, and it was decided we did not want the Chosen's presence in our world. Their abilities had massive side effects following the final battle with the Grim King, if the writings are to be believed. A great deal of history from that time was lost; there was unrest among the people, riots and persecutions. There was a great deal of fear that the Chosen would rise against the commoners of Endland and claim the land as their own. Their powers were too great, and so they were forced to shift away, traveling to other Realms, some as groups, some on their own, banished from the land many had just died protecting." Lopi looked in the distance at nothing in particular, eyes focused well beyond the walls of the library as he softly rubbed his chin.

"There were a number who resisted, fought against their perceived injustice. They were eventually banished by force or eradicated." He paused again as he looked to the boys with a great deal of sadness in his eyes. "But now you are here! And not a moment too soon, for our expendable shifting stone has all but run out! The mining of the precious stone has run dry for quite some time." He paused again, looking warily to the others in the library. "But you will be instrumental in the potential retrieval of even more Chosen, and Petravinos will be most pleased upon his arrival!" He was giddy with excitement again as the boys continued to look through the two books Lopi had laid on the table.

"So, let me get this straight," Zack asked as he sat back in his chair shaking his head. "We're Chosen, whatever. We're not even on Earth anymore. And we're supposed to help a bunch of people who just basically kidnapped us, even though the last time Chosen people helped you, you kicked them out the second they finished the job?" Lopi's lips twisted in dissatisfaction but he nodded.

"I would not word it quite so, but for simplicity's sake, yes, that is correct."

"Well, I want to go home. My mom is going to flip her lid," Zack finished. "Plus, how would we help, even if we wanted to? If Chosen teach Chosen like you said, we won't be able to learn anything." Lopi opened his mouth to respond but then closed it as Zack sat back waiting for a response. Johnny's grin grew wider as the seconds of silence ticked on, and he gave Zack a supportive wink.

"Oh man, not so quick on your feet, are you, dream?" he questioned, pushing his glasses up his nose.

"Johnny, I don't think this is a dream, man. I don't get it at all, but I think this is real. We're not even on Earth."

"I promise Petravinos will help," Lopi finally responded. "He was around for the Aging and the banishment and is Endland's expert on Chosen. It is a fairly straight path to our sister city and capital of Trillgrand. He will be here soon enough."

"Wait, wait, wait. Didn't you just say that Age banish thing happened more than one hundred years ago? How could this

Petra guy be around for that and still be alive?" Zack accused sharply.

"He's the time wizard, you idiot. *Weren't you listening?*" Johnny mocked in his best Zack-voice. "He obviously time traveled or something."

"Not exactly 'time traveled' but more time extended. His magic has slowed his aging to that of a heavy syrup as opposed to free-flowing water, if that makes sense," Lopi corrected Johnny but smiled at their bickering. "But I think I've swamped your heads with enough information for now, please allow me to introduce you to the Lord of Eislark and the rest of the Eastern lords!"

"I'm with Zack," replied Johnny. "Just send us home or wake us up. Because if you think Zack's mom is going to flip, wait till you meet my mom. Plus, I'm not dressed to meet the king of England anyways." He stood from his chair and spread his arms from his sides to emphasize his lounging sweatpants outfit.

"Come, this way!" Lopi said, ignoring them. He had already flipped both books closed, scooped them up, dropped them onto the bookshelf, and he was halfway to the door. Zack stood next to Johnny and they looked to each other with intrigue and puzzlement at their predicament. Lopi briskly opened the door and exited the library out into the swarm of scribes that was still eagerly awaiting them, a school of fish waiting for their morsels of food. They had evidently ignored Lopi's request for them to wait elsewhere. Zack sighed deeply as he scratched the top of his head, and Johnny clapped him on the back with a heavy hand and smiled.

"Just relax man, it's only a dream!" Johnny said and followed the short old man out into the crowd. With another sigh, Zack reluctantly followed his friend.

"Off to meet the king of England," he mocked lightly.

15

NO REST FOR THE WEARY

The feeling of the floor beneath her feet made her feel safe enough to open her eyes. Bartellom stood before her, eyes still closed, a second behind in his travel, as they both got their bearings. The cool blue tapestries of Trillgrand lined the few areas that were not windows, which poured in the setting sunlight. They both took a moment to relax, Janeph kneeling lightly on the grass that they stood upon, and looked up to the glass ceiling that covered the room. Returning here never got old, and even now battled and bruised and with the unknown outcome of the Chosen, a smile found her lips in the serene, quiet tower.

They waited a minute for Petravinos to enter and greet them, but he did not appear. Janeph looked to Bartellom with a small wrinkle of concern before she stood and made for the doorway with Bartellom shortly behind her. They both had to look quite the sight, scuffed and bleeding, Bartellom's arm acting as a creek for the stream of blood that ran down his shoulder and dripped steadily from this hanging fingertips. It all contrasted strongly against the capital's pristine off-white and blue decorated hall-ways. They did get some curious looks from the folk in the main hall as they continued to march to Petravinos's chambers, but they paid them no mind. Down the stairs of the northwest tower towards the cellar room, they finally reached the doorway and with a pull, found the room to be empty. Stacks and stacks of books and scrolls, it was an immense chamber of tapped and untapped knowledge with a single large table on one side covered in many layers of melted wax and a small, rather uncomfortable-looking bed on the other wall. The rest was storage for the various readings, his personal library.

"Where in Phont's name is he?" Janeph asked incredulously as she entered the large room, looking side to side as if he would suddenly pop from underneath a pile of parchment. "Would he not have come greet us as we shifted home? I would have thought the arrival of the last Hunt would have him bouncing with anticipation!" Bartellom shrugged one massive shoulder as he wiped blood from his nose with his good arm.

"This has been the wildest Hunt I've ever been on, Janeph, and I was selected for a Hunt made exclusively of those Swilmagapan outcasts earlier this year. Petravinos not greeting us or even being in his chambers just adds to the insanity." Janeph turned and stormed past Bartellom back up the stairwell towards the main hall.

"Where to now?" Bartellom called from behind as he followed, laboring with his limp arm at his side like a heavy swinging pendulum.

"We go to the top, to the king. We must find the children," she called back as they worked through the hallways to the throne room.

"Janeph, we sent all three of them on a shifting string meant for one. Is it possible that none of them made it?" Bartellom asked innocently, wincing already at what her response would be. Janeph stopped and turned to face him abruptly, pointing a finger into his muscled chest. She may have punctured his armor if she pushed any harder.

"Until we hear from the king or Petravinos or someone of authority that no one has arrived, we shall refrain from discussing such scenarios. One had to make it. They had to." Her words were sharply whispered through clenched teeth. Bartellom took a step back nodding, but his face showed his lack of faith.

"Apologies, milady."

She turned away quickly and resumed walking down the hall without a response. They walked the rest of the way in agitated silence, back to the main hallway, and with a quick push past a pair of Blue Hearts, they were both within Trillgrand's throne room. The room was long, at least thrice as long as it was wide, with a row of tables running down either side of the room. The small windows that lined the long walls allowed veiled columns of rapidly fading light to shine through, small beacons illuminating the room in the young twilight. Above was another mostly glass ceiling, which in the daylight hours would allow for a bountiful sunlight to flood the space. Now in the coming dark, a series of torches were lit and hung on the walls between the small circular wall windows. There were a great many torches at the far end of the hall, set upon in sconces on the back wall every few feet, assisting the tall candelabras that lined the edge of the stairs leading up to the throne.

The pair had some difficulty reaching the back of the hall, having to work through a rather regal and elegantly dressed crowd. The men wore tight fitted collared shirts, frilling beneath their chins and similarly at their wrists and even out the bottom of their pants at their ankles; the women wore flowing dresses, draped perfectly to their frames, with lovely matching necklaces and rings. Janeph analyzed their feet self-consciously and found their finely crafted clogs were especially glowing compared to her dirty calloused boots, splattered with her own blood. She felt uncomfortable in the stately setting, but the crowd surely felt the same or even more so seeing her and Bartellom's rough appearance, and she did her best to hold that viewpoint in her mind as they brushed past them.

They approached the stairs, which were short and deep enough to take two steps before needing to step up again. Its shape was a horseshoe, with the legs of the shoe running along the left and right sides and the loop of it along the back wall with the throne centered atop it. Standing at the base, Janeph was eye level with the top-most landing; Bartellom, being taller, could see nearly to the back of the platform. She looked side to side, seeing the horseshoe's legs narrow so that two guards could just pass each other if they needed. On the tops of the stairs, both on the furthest to the right and left on the narrow upper landing, stood a Blue Heart, pale blue armor from chest to toe and with two short swords, one slung to each hip. They stood motionless, hands on nearside hilts, watching the crowd beneath the king with eyes hidden behind their white and golden helms. At their position before the king, they were surrounded on three sides with a height disadvantage; it was a mostly unnecessary precaution being in the castle of the capital, but still a smart and well-thought-out defense tactic.

To the left and right of the throne stood the king's advisors, Forde Kern for matters of the people, and Difon Bijal for matters of coin. And seated between them was King Umbrin Sarn, adorned in neat white clothing and a short cape, soft blue on the underside, and white with fine gold stitching to match his tunic on the outer side. His dark, well-kept hair was radiant against the white of his clothing. The golden wheat crown sat squarely on his temples, its gold matching the fine laced frills that adorned the edge of his tunic collar and end of his sleeves. The throne he sat upon matched the gold as well, solid plated with entwined wheat branch etchings making the body of it.

Breaching the front of the crowd, Janeph and Bartellom interrupted a pair of guests having some sort of conversation with the king, which Janeph did not notice or did not care to notice as she barged between them and knelt at the foot of the horseshoe staircase. King Sarn raised one eyebrow at the commotion, but when two hidden Blue Hearts stepped forward from behind the throne, he raised an open hand to pause them.

"My King, fortune unto thee."

"And unto thee, Lady Janeph." He eyed her curiously as Bartellom knelt heavily next to Janeph, the knuckles of his wounded arm grazing the marble floor and leaving a streak of blood. The pair that was speaking with the king backed away cautiously from the besieged pair as Janeph raised her head to address the king, smiling as best as she was able with her bruised and scuffed cheeks.

"You appear to be wounded," Umbrin continued mildly, "and I do not see any new faces accompanying you. Was the

Hunt unsuccessful, then?" Bartellom raised his head now with raised eyebrows and Janeph stood abruptly.

"None returned before us? Where is Petravinos? Why did he not meet us in the shifting tower?" she asked unsettlingly, a quiver in her voice. Her fists were clenched at her sides and Bartellom now stood next to her, both bracing for the news. Umbrin let out a short sarcastic chuckle and sat upright from his usual slouch. Janeph and Bartellom were not amused at the laugh and did their best to keep straight faces.

"I know not what that old hack does with his time." He looked around at the crowd with a demeaning glare and a sneer. "I've not agreed with these Hunts since their inception and now it seems I've been proven right in their futility. Two years of searching for nonsense and myths on the whims of a group of parlor trick performing fools. Deaths of hundreds of good men and the depletion and deterioration of Endland's shifting net, and for what?"

The crowd, light and cheerful as the pair had barged to the front, was now on edge, an awkward silence fully enveloping the room. Bartellom and Janeph said nothing, looking forward with glowering faces. Janeph had been playing this game her entire military career, and she knew Bartellom had similarly been jabbed with disparaging words for his own shortcomings. She had kept her tongue, always, and especially now at the stoop of their king, she would continue to do so. They looked upwards at the fit and trim man, his short dark beard a shadow around the narrow strip of arrogant and nearly always exposed white teeth. He leaned forward, his hands gripping the ends of his throne's chair loosely.

"Nothing to say of your worth during these Hunts? Nothing in defense of the men you've let die?" Janeph felt her lip curl slightly; an insult to her was one thing, but to the dead was entirely another. Umbrin saw it, his smile growing at the sign of Janeph's leaking aggression.

"What of the countless reports of Grim on our Hunts?" Bartellom bellowed loudly, sapping the smirk from Umbrin's face immediately. Janeph looked to him, pleading restraint with her eyes. Bartellom did not meet the look, consciously keeping his gaze away from her and locked on the king. He sat idle on his throne with pressed jaw and flared nostrils as the barrage continued.

"What of the abduction of countless individuals in the other Realms," Bartellom said, "seen firsthand by every respectable military man and woman from every great city of Endland? We sent three marks back, the first potentials of a Hunt in months, one of the few to ever send marks at all, and you berate us? If you do not believe—"

"Watch your tongue, Drifter! You forget your place!" Umbrin snapped, standing in front of the golden wheat throne. A small clearing of the throat caused Umbrin to look over to Forde on his left, who subtly gestured for calm with his open hands. Umbrin obliged and relaxed his demeanor, his shoulders slumping from their tense upright hold, and turning back to Bartellom and Janeph, he flashed a smile and let out a short curt laugh.

"I am aware of everything; I am your king! And I am most acutely aware of the of lack of results. Even if you did send three marks this night, they will just melt like the others, bodies failing under the weight of their new and exotic environment. We've nothing to show for two years of sacrifice!"

Breaking his train of thought, a young boy burst through the hall doors and scampered quickly through the crowd and next to Bartellom and Janeph, breathing heavily.

"What is this intrusion, boy? Can you not see the king gives council?" Forde said loudly, stepping forward from behind the throne in his golden robe. His bald head gleamed in the torchlight, glistening off of the oil that he always applied to his pristinely hairless scalp. He was not of age to be fully bald as he was, but he was not young either; a middle-aged man with lackluster genetics.

"Apologies, my King! Apologies, Sir Kern, urgent message!" the boy said, winded, nervous shrills amplifying his anxious prepubescent words. He held out a scroll that Forde was already walking down the stairs to retrieve. "It's just arrived and I was told to deliver it at once, so I started running—"

"Yes, yes, a lovely story. Hand it over," Forde snapped as he pulled the scroll from the boy's outstretched hand. He bowed low as Forde turned and returned up the stairs toward Umbrin.

"Fortune unto thee, my King," the boy said and turned to leave before Forde stopped him with a loud commanding voice, still walking up the stairs but never turning to look at him.

"Hold, boy! Our king may wish to respond to this message if it is indeed so urgent." Forde glanced back from the corners of his eyes and smirked as the boy turned back around and bowed again, keeping his eyes low. Janeph glanced over at him as he stepped back in line with her and Bartellom and then looked intently to the scroll that Forde now held. She saw the blue wax seal, a Trillgrand blue, but could not make the seal itself. Forde walked slowly back up to the throne and handed the scroll to Umbrin as he resumed his position a step behind the throne. Umbrin broke the seal and read silently. He leaned to the side of his throne towards Forde as he held the scroll out for him. Forde took it gingerly and read it himself as King Umbrin leaned forward in his throne and motioned for Bartellom and Janeph to come forward with a wave of his hand. The two started up the stairs and seeing them move, the boy looked up and stepped forward as well.

"Not you, boy, you can wait until we have a message to send," Umbrin said with authority. The boy stopped, took a step backwards, and stammered an inaudible apology before looking back to the floor with a tilted head. Janeph and Bartellom continued up the steps toward their king after a glance back towards the boy, and both bowed upon reaching the last step, Bartellom's consciously shallow. Umbrin spoke in a whisper, still leaning forward on the edge of his golden wheat throne.

"Well, it seems the Councilor Supreme is making a visit to Eislark to investigate a shifting anomaly. I cannot say when he set off however; he did not indicate a time of departure." The pair looked to each other with hope and then back to their King. Umbrin leaned back slightly, though still on the edge of his seat, and rubbed his short beard in contemplation, looking beyond the two as his ringed fingers ran over his long dark stubble. He refocused on the messenger.

"When was this letter received? Were you sleeping on the job and thereby neglected to pass this information to me?" The boy's eyes grew wide with fear as he began to shake his head rapidly.

"No, my King! A raven only just arrived! The letter master gave it to me right away and told me to run it to you as fast as I could!" His voice cracked more than once in his plea, and Umbrin studied him long with concentrated vision before he smiled warmly.

"Of course, my boy. Thank you for your honesty. Petravinos often sends his letters from the trail, he thinks it gives him a head start." He looked to Janeph and for the first time in their conversation, spoke without condemnation.

"You truly sent three marks?"

"We did, my King," Janeph replied without further detail. Umbrin again looked past them, focused on an invisible host as he rubbed his beard again, lost in his thoughts.

"Quite an accomplishment, if any actually turn out to live, which I doubt. Could they have arrived in Eislark instead of Trillgrand? Are the stones not bound to this city?" he questioned honestly of the pair. Janeph sighed, and Bartellom licked the front of his teeth behind his lips anxiously.

"Three were sent on one string, my King. The extra load may have thrown their shifting off."

"Three on one string of stones? Is that safe?" Umbrin asked, still genuinely without criticism. Janeph slowly shook her head "no."

"We encountered a powerful Grim, Jamesett of Fermlo, and were losing the fight. Quick decisions were made, and I am prepared to live with the consequences. It was all of them, or none of them," Janeph said after another sigh. Bartellom shifted his weight uneasily at the open admission of fault as Umbrin measured her words.

"The long since banished Jamesett arrived? And you were losing a fight to him? I doubt that very much. Not the great Lady Janeph of the Blue Hearts and the Bonethorne Drifter," he said, breaking from his genuine questioning to a disdainful mocking tone. Bartellom squeezed his good fist tight, Janeph swearing she could hear his muscles constrict. She kept her face unwavering, meeting the king's cheeky smile with an impassive stare. Umbrin continued as if the insult had never left his lips. "No matter. You are to follow Petravinos to Eislark; meet him on the road if you can. Speak with Lord Belmar about what they have found." He stopped and looked away, calculating. "Is tonight Eislark's summer harvest?" he asked aloud over his left shoulder.

"It is, my King, but we declined the invitation from Lord Belmar to govern the land. Had we known that Chosen may be arriving there this very night, we may have elected to attend," Forde chimed as he stepped forward to be even with the throne. His attempt at making light of the situation did not meet Umbrin well, his face cold and void of even a trace of a smile. Forde lowered his head awkwardly and stepped back to his position, out of the sight of Umbrin's vexed vision. The king turned back to Janeph and Bartellom, his eyes warming as they moved from where Forde had stood.

"No sense in crying over spilled wine, I suppose. You are to head to Eislark immediately. Yours is the last of Endland's Hunts and if one of your marks miraculously survived, it shall be Trillgrand's to command." He looked them over again, the viciousness of their wounds apparent up close. "Can you ride tonight?" he asked the pair. Janeph looked to Bartellom, masking her concern as best she was able, which was not very well.

"I am able, however, Bartellom may not be able."

"Bartellom is able," the brute corrected with a grunt. Umbrin looked to him with skepticism.

"Some food and a moment to assess our wounds would go a long way," Janeph added, pleading more with Bartellom than with Umbrin. The king nodded in acceptance with a small smile.

"Yes. Bartellom strong. Bartellom no feel pain. Bartellom get marks back for Trillgrand," Umbrin mocked in a deep slow voice, smiling hearing his own contemptuous words. It seemed it was all he could do to keep from laughing aloud at his own impersonation. Bartellom did not flinch, holding his clenched fist tightly to his side. Umbrin gave him a few seconds to respond, which he did not, before continuing in his normal speaking voice.

"You shall leave immediately. I shall ride tonight as well to meet with the people of Endland, conveniently gathered for Eislark's harvest. I will see you on the morrow, sometime before supper I suspect."

Umbrin waived his hand for the boy to come forward and for Forde to come beside the throne. The boy immediately obliged, tripping up the first step his legs ran so quickly, and Forde moved to grab a small table before coming forward. The people's advisor presented the king with a finely crafted wooden slab, upon which lay some parchment and a quill stuck into the surface. Umbrin wrote quickly on the makeshift table, rolled the scroll, and handed it to Forde as a young girl stepped from a room along the back wall with a blue wax candle. The wax was dripped carefully by Forde atop the rolled letter, and Umbrin promptly pressed one of his many rings into it to seal the note, leaving the crowned wheat impression. Forde extended it directly to the boy, who was waiting and watching anxiously besides Janeph.

"You are to have this flown to Petravinos immediately," said Forde. "He rides for Eislark; your master is to send his fastest bird. Go now."

"Fortune unto thee, my King!" the boy said, bowing deeply as he grasped the scroll and scuttled down the stairs, through the crowd, and out the door of the hall as fast as his legs would move him. Umbrin nodded approvingly at the boy's efforts before refocusing on Janeph and Bartellom.

"Take what provisions you need for your trip, but there is no time for treating your wounds. You leave immediately. I doubt there is a mark to be had, but if there is, you and Petravinos are to claim it for Trillgrand. I will dispel any qualms when I arrive. Ride well Drifter, sister. Fortune unto thee." Umbrin waved them away the instant the words left his lips and motioned for Forde to come forward. Bartellom bowed quickly and turned to walk down the stairs before Janeph could even start her bow.

"Do you not wish your king fortune, Drifter?" Forde called from behind him arrogantly. Bartellom paused on the first stair, and turned to address the man. The look in his eyes caused

Forde's confidence to evaporate. The Blue Hearts moved their hands from loose on their hilts to a full tight grip as they visibly tensed, the rageful aura compressed around the barbarian. Bartellom held his gaze before softening with a look to Janeph. Her heart raced at the tension, and she pleaded with him desperately with her eyes to diffuse the situation. Bartellom begrudgingly muttered through clenched teeth.

"Of course, Advisor Kern. Fortune unto thee, King."

He turned and continued on the stairs as Janeph, breathing a sigh of relief quietly to herself, bowed low. She eyed Forde as she rose from her bow, a cold hard look that was met with an equally cold stare from the man. He leered before leaning to whisper to Umbrin, never taking his eyes off her.

"Fortune, brother," she said.

She turned and left before she could see the rest of their whispering play out, picturing in her mind's eye a swift kick to the bald man's face as she chased after the lumbering Bartellom into the hallway.

16

HISTORY AND
THE HARVEST

———◇———

opi closed the Library door behind the boys as they all
made their way back through the crowd and toward the
large central tower. They continued down the staircase,
wrapping down until Lopi led them through another large set of
doors, these with ornate red and gold trim etched into the stone
frame. Fish, hooks, sun, boats, waves, and sails, all carved with
exquisite detail. The hallway beyond was lined with many of the
Gull Lopi had mentioned in their library lesson, large armored
knights, adorned in dark maroon armor, helm to boots, and a
tall pike in hand. The boys stared in fascination, but the knights
did not move or speak as the group continued past them. Only
a short hard tap of the pike's hilts to the floor as Lopi crossed
their vision gave the group any indication that they were being watched at all. The sound echoed in the hallway, following
them as they walked, and even with the setting sunlight filling
the space from the many windows, the sound gave the boys an
unnerving chill.

They approached another set of wooden doors, these too
with the gold and red intricacies etched in the doorframe, and
from beyond the doors there could be heard a great many voices,
laughter, and music. Lopi motioned towards the two Gull posted

in front, and following another stomp of their tall weapons to the floor, they opened the doors before them and the sounds and sights filled their senses.

A room as tall as five men was before them with four large candle chandeliers hanging down the center from the doorway to the opposite end. It was roughly square and to the left and right, nearly encompassing the entire wall, were monstrous windows, three on each side, letting the setting sun's light pour through their openings. The light touched the floor nearly to the far side of the room, stretching across the long tables that made parallel aisleways to the windows and that had a great deal of food and drink atop their clean wooden surfaces. Roasts of what looked to the boys to be chicken and lamb, bushels of fresh berries and fruits, loaves of bread stacked as tall as the seated guests, some sweet covered in frostings and others next to large plates of half-melted butter and jam spreads. Many sat and feasted on the banquet that was laid before them, washing the food down with wines and meads from the plentiful gourds that found table space between the food platters or from the large barrels near the sun-soaked windows.

A particularly rowdy table was drinking heavily from the largest of the barrels, stamped with crossing hammers being held by burley fists. The men and women all stood a head taller than the rest of the crowd and were significantly broader in the shoulders than the others. They had odd dress compared to the rest of the guests, mostly fur and animal compared to the clean woven shirts and gowns of the others. Some even stood without a shirt, hot from the celebration and the sun they stood in or perhaps warmed from the ale they were rapidly pouring and drinking. One huge man, larger even than the others that stood around the ale, was at the center of the group, laughing loudly and gulping his drink from a mug that matched his size. His drink ran down his red beard. Tufts of his ragged red hair extended from beneath a heavy looking dark metal helmet, fit snugly to the crown of his head.

The other nearby tables kept their distance, secluding the boisterous table to their own corner of the hall closest to the alcohol. Each of the tables at the front had their own central figure who had a crown-type piece sitting atop each of their heads as they conversed merrily with the party around them. A very short man with dark brown hair surrounded by other equally short men; a woman, tall and fair with beautiful blond hair; a somewhat rugged-looking man, with two hatchets tucked in his belt. They all sat near the far end of the room from the entryway, which ended with a small and short set of stairs and a large throne chair. The stairs created a rather minor height differential compared to the rest of the floor. Centered atop the throne sat a young man, far younger than the other figureheads; not a touch of grey could be seen in his hair. The wrinkles he showed were only where his cheeks and eyes creased while laughing, which he was doing quite a bit of at the moment.

Providing a joyous and upbeat tune that none seemed interested in listening to was a minstrel band; their soft horns, crude guitars, and tambourines filled the space that the many conversations did not. The scents of the food made the boys' mouths water instantly, their eyes growing nearly as wide as the windows that lined the room, and they subconsciously bobbed to the minstrels tune as they walked into the throne room, completely enthralled. It was a party unlike any they had seen before.

"Johnny, I think we *are* in Camelot!" Zack said as they took in the scenery. Johnny did not respond but his openmouthed grin matched Zack's giddiness. Lopi was not as enamored with the scenery as the boys were and was already making his way down the center table aisle beneath the great candle chandeliers. The armed guards that were escorting the boys now took an uncomfortably close step on either side of them, snapping the boys out of their trance, and they quickly refocused on the short man and moved to catch up.

As they approached the man on the throne, they could see the backing of the chair that he sat on was etched with decorative fish, water, boats, and paddles, similar to how the entryway framework was engraved. Prominently at the top and back was a ship's steering wheel, the grips of which extended beyond the top of the chair in a half circle. The whole throne was decorated in the red and white and gold that had littered the halls they walked, and the man sitting atop it matched the scheme. He wore a deep red tunic with gold, red, and white decorative pattern sewn into the fabric, fish and boats and waves intricately woven into the clothing with fascinating detail. His boots were laced with golden silk, and the crown he wore looked like it was made of intertwined fishing net and hooks, a contradictory combination of elegance and crudeness.

Behind him stood a set of Gull, the fully armored knights that had stomped their large pikes in the hallway, two directly behind the throne and one each on the far edges of the slightly elevated platform. A pair of chairs sat on either side of the throne, somewhat decorated in the fashion of the throne, but not with such grandeur as the central throne. One of these was occupied by another man, similarly dressed in dark red, but his clothing made him look more prepped for a trek on a trail than a feast. The color of his clothing was much deeper than the clothing of the man on the throne, so deep it bordered on purple, even black in the shadowy parts of the garb. A dark hood rested on his neck, pulled back and off his head for the party, and many small knives could be seen laid across the belts that clung tightly over his shoulder and to his chest. Beside his chair rested two scimitars, blades exposed to their surroundings and reflecting the dancing candlelight across their strangely dark metallic surfaces. The hilts were decorated as dark fish, mouths open exposing the sharp metal blades as if they were their tongues. Both men were laughing loudly with each other, drinking cheerily as they spoke.

The people that ate and drank at the tables caught sight of the strange procession lead by Lopi and quickly became silent watchers. There was a great deal of whispering, and some even joined the procession towards the front of the hall, falling in line with the group that had been writing since the boys' arrival. Like a wave, the silence shifted from the doorway towards the throne, and as they approached the first stair, the minstrels even stopped their song so the only sounds that could be heard were the murmurs from the crowd, the shuffling of feet, and the loud laughter of the two men atop their chairs. Suddenly realizing they were the only source of sound, they glanced around the quiet whispering room, both still chuckling softly.

Lopi reached the base of the stairs and stopped, bowing low, nearly half his beard now resting on the stone floor. The two guards that had been escorting the boys stepped from slightly to the side, to directly in front of the boys. Zack and Johnny nearly knocked heads as they both leaned toward the center to look between the guards' arms and over Lopi's balding head. They could make out the crowned man, wiping tears from his eyes from laughter, as the man in the dark red nodded in acknowledgment of Lopi.

"Master Lidobol!" started the crowned man. "You are late for the Festival! Perhaps the errant shifting was more than just a false call? Maybe someone actually arrived? A lost Endlander returning home?" His words were drenched in sarcasm, but the man to his right smiled wearily and sipped quickly from his mug to hide his forced features. Lopi genuinely smiled, his aged teeth showing beneath his bushy grey mustache.

"Lord Grekory Belmar, I bear wonderful, extraordinary news on this harvest day!" Lopi exclaimed loudly, taking full advantage of the unequivocal attention he currently held. "It was no false call! Shifters have arrived! But they are not of Endland! And they are alive, intact, coherent, and without any signs of the shifting sickness! This has been by far the longest any individual has ever fared, from any of Endland's previous Hunts!" Grekory, for the first time since the group had entered, stopped laughing and measured the short man with a keen gaze. He glanced toward the man on his right who was equally sober now, and the two exchanged skeptical looks.

"What are you saying, Lopi? Someone has arrived from outside Endland? We don't even have a Hunt out, how could we have unexpected guests? I pray you did not bring them here. It is an ugly scene when those not of Endland arrive," he stated boldly, trying to peek behind short man and the guards. "We must remove them before they disintegrate or burst to flame.

We have guests, Master Lidobol, and food nearby, and I do not wish for either to spoil at the sight of a man melting to a puddle." Johnny and Zack looked to each other frantically before quickly checking their hands and bodies for signs of deterioration. Someone from behind them dry heaved loudly. "See what I mean! You've upset my guests, Lopi!"

"My lord, I do not mean to get too far ahead of myself, but they are not of Endland and they are not deteriorating." He paused dramatically, looking coyly from side to side at the nearest tables, their crowned leaders peering with anticipated yearning. "Eislark may very well harbor the first Chosen Endland has seen in well over a century! The prophesies may be at hand!" Many gasps and whispers filled the room. The scribes unable to contain their emotions, joined in the commotion as they wrote frantically, everyone talking at once in a burst of commotion. Zack looked to Johnny confused and tried peeking out around the guards, getting an obscured view of the two seated men before a few of the crowd members stepped closer, causing the guards to brace themselves and push the boys even closer together. The crowned individuals all craned their necks for a look, the large red-haired man's head looming over the crowd, as Lord Belmar laughed lightly.

"Legends, Lopi!" the lord exclaimed over the clamor. "You speak of false legends, not prophecies. The Chosen nearly ruined Endland with their internal bickering. They're nothing but foul stories of second-class wizards who murdered thousands! I was reluctant to send any to aid in Petravinos's other worldly search; we should have kept our stone for Eislark and my men at their posts. Instead, they have bled for a misguided old wizard, facing Grim devils in strange lands!" He stood as he grabbed his goblet from his chair's armrest and took a mighty swig. Lopi, smiling far less enthusiastically now, started to speak before he was abruptly cut off. "My father's father never gave a damn for these stories, nor did my father, and nor do I! As it's been shown for many years, there are none that can handle the shifting but those born here in Endland! The Chosen either never existed or are gone! And so too are you! Take your tales and your 'Chosen' with you. I've a celebration to host."

"But, my liege, you do not understand! They speak! They walk and converse and have logic!"

"*They?*" asked the man in dark red curiously, looking to Grekory with increasing intrigue. "More than one, Lopi?" Grekory let out a loud sarcastic laugh at his counterpart's questioning.

"Oh, now there are more than one? Come now, Lopi, if you are going to have a bit of fun, at least make it convincing. Not only does Eislark boast the first Chosen but also the *second* Chosen?" He laughed loudly again as he sat back in his throne, a few of the nearby guests joining in. "No, I think not, Lopi. Enough of your foolery, more wine! More music! It is the summer harvest! It is a time for celebration!" There were many cheers from the crowd, and the minstrels now realigned to commence their music, the horns and guitar starting again.

"Lord Belmar, they are here, right here! They speak!" He bustled backwards and forced his way between the two guards, grabbing both Johnny's and Zack's arms and pulling them forward through the crowd. The man in dark red spit out his wine in a fit as he stood, coughing up what had not been expelled.

"Lopi, you fool, have you lost your mind?" yelled Grekory in anger, standing again with his goblet. "These are children, not Chosen! Plucked from the Shoreline Orphanage, no doubt! You've gone too far in this jest, and the absurdity has cost poor Mikel his drink! You there, another for the Lord of Swords!" Grekory beckoned to the nearest maid. Mikel shook his head as he caught his breath and halted the maid's arm.

"I am sorry, Lord Belmar, but I'm afraid this harvest night may end sober for me." Lord Belmar looked to his friend in muddle and disappointment. The boys' faces were alit with a mix of glee and confusion as they soaked in Micky's odd appearance. Zack thought he might run up and hug him at that very moment. His short scruff remained on his chin and his hair reached his shoulders now that it was not tucked away as it was in the hospital, but the rest of his dress was misplaced.

"I know these boys," he said at length, marveling at them with disbelieving eyes. Grekory looked inquisitively.

"What do you mean, Mikel? You've seen them at the orphanage?" The lord trailed off and shifted his dark brown eyes to the children. While certainly young, the boys could see his look was not inexperienced, not simply an heir made lord. And in the moment, they saw a great deal of concern cross the young lord's face. Zack couldn't help but wave shyly, and Johnny gave a peace sign accompanied with a cheesy smile. Lord Belmar blinked a few times before drinking heavily from his goblet.

Mikel winked openly to Lopi and the boys, leaning towards them and scrunching his one eye and most of his face in tactless, unsubtle fashion. The crowd gathered closer as the music had subsided once more, all working to get a look at the boys that stood before the throne. No one spoke, no one seemed to breathe, and Grekory did not move his gaze from the boys even as he drank, his concerned look morphing to fear. Lopi's broad smile returned as Mikel stepped down the stairs to look at them more intently and chuckled.

"But they are *not* Chosen," Mikel concluded. A great many puzzled looks crossed the faces of the guests, most lively was Lopi's and most unamused was Lord Grekory's. "I'm sorry, Lord Belmar, you must forgive me, but I cannot go any further with this ruse. Although I must admit, I did not think it would fool you. But I think it only fair to our guests that we reveal this hoax." He spoke loud and confidently, holding out his cup as the maid he had stopped now filled it. Lord Belmar leaned back from his slouched position with a small scowl and the faintest forced smirk.

"What hoax is this? Explain yourself."

Mikel laughed loudly and took another sip of wine from his cup. Lopi stood in disbelief, mouth open to counterargue but he could not find words.

"There was a great deal more we intended to play out, a marvelous script Master Lidobol put together. But I fear it will derail an already marvelous festival; these children are not Chosen."

Confused grumbles could be heard from the crowd, the crease in Grekory's forehead deepened, and Lopi began stammering to those closest to him.

"What is the meaning of this?" Lord Belmar bellowed from his throne.

"I'm sorry, Grek, I'm sorry. Let's hear it for our great wizard, huh? Mischievous as the best of them!" Mikel said, waving an arm towards the short wizard and clapping high above his head, an empty hand tapping with a soft thud on the chalice metal. A confused chorus of clapping slowly rounded the crowd following Mikel's lead as he laughed loudly again. Grekory, standing in front of his throne chair now, did not clap, and Mikel turned to him with a smile.

"Lord Belmar, forgive us. We meant no disrespect, but when the idea came about, I couldn't refuse. Lopi is quite the jester, I must say, as surprising as that may seem, and equally as bold to target his own Lord." Grekory said nothing as he sat slowly upon the throne chair and crossed his legs, leaning to one side again, and surveyed the room. The boys could feel the tension of the crowd around them, and Lopi swallowed as softly as he could in the dead silence. Mikel looked to his lord with a grin. Grekory observed the group for an uncomfortable number of seconds before laughing loud and heartily. Mikel's grin became a full smile before laughing and taking another swig of his wine. The crowd laughed as well, including Lopi, albeit with an extreme sense of nerves.

"Lopi, that is quite unlike you. To think Chosen have arrived, and better yet, Chosen children! And on the harvest of all days, I should have known!" Grekory laughed and wiped the corner of his eyes with the back of his hand. The crowd laughed as well, the uncomfortable air slowly dissipating as more caught on to the joke. "I bet these children really are from the Shoreline, aren't they? And here I had taken the bait and gotten myself into a frenzy!" Another hearty laugh as the majority of the crowd now joined; even Johnny laughed before Zack flicked his nose to snap him out of it.

"Master Lopi, please step forward!" Lord Grekory called out. Lopi obliged and shuffled to the base of the stairs. He gave another great bow as he had before, beard touching the floor, and took the few steps up to the throne as Grekory leaned in from his chair. Mikel took another sip of his wine as he stepped a near the pair.

"See to it that these children are well fed and dressed to-night," Lord Belmar said loudly, loud enough for the guests below him to hear plainly. "They are to be my personal guests for the evening for their performance in this unexpected ruse." Lopi began to argue but Grekory continued, now addressing the entire hall. "The harvest season begins, brethren, but there is even more to celebrate this year! For we now have Chosen here in Eislark! The first city to boast their ranks in nearly a hundred years!" He laughed sarcastically as some of the crowd raised their cups with a flippant yell and laughter. "And for being the mastermind behind this ploy, Master Lidobol shall be hence-forth known as the 'Chosen Jester.' Well earned, Lopi! A toast to the Chosen Jester! And to the new Chosen!" There were cheers as Lopi stood abruptly, caught off guard by his Lord's mocking praise. He gave a short bow to Grekory, who reciprocated, and then to the crowd who mirrored as well, all save Johnny and Zack who only watched the odd scene unfold. Grekory clapped Mikel's shoulder fondly as he returned to address the crowd.

"Tonight, we celebrate! Feast! Dance! Be merry! Fortune unto thee, people of Endland! And one more round of applause for Master Lidobol!" The whole crowd cheered this time, a very loud and happy ovation, and the minstrels took their chance to seize the energy, jumping right into song. Many of the mob who had been crowding those who they now believed to be ordinary or-phans, returned to their original tables or danced to the catchy tune between them. The hall boomed to life, breathed into the festival by the Eislark Lord, as conversation, song, and dance re-sumed among all the people. Grekory motioned for Mikel to take a step closer as he took his seat in the now roaring hall.

"What in Phont's name is going on here?" Lord Belmar asked harshly through a fake smile, raising his goblet to them. A maid ran over to Lopi and offered him a cup, which he took and sipped with the others in a faux toast.

"Grek, I apologize. We couldn't have all the Lords of End-land thinking Chosen had actually arrived here. But the truth is I met these boys on my Hunt with Lady Janeph and Bartellom Bonethorne. The fact is that they are actually here . . . ." Mikel looked to the boys as they awkwardly took a seat at one of the tables and looked eagerly at the plentiful food around them.

"Truly, Mikel?"

The captain nodded to his lord. Grekory did his best to keep his face cheerful, but he could not help a rough rub of his chin in frustration. He took a full gulp of his wine and wiped the corners of his mouth with the back of his sleeve.

"Lopi, you are to say nothing to anyone else about this, save the message you are about to write Petravinos and King Umbrin. I suspect Petravinos will wish to meet these children personally, this being a Trillgrand Hunt. He can make a final determination on their true nature. Mikel, the children shall have their fill here before entering their chambers. I want them in the Western Hall with a view of the bay, the Kings Quarters until Umbrin arrives. Lopi, they are to have fresh clothes and fire going when they arrive. They shall feel welcomed here in Eislark."

"Yes, my Lord. I will see that their rooms are prepared immediately. But if they are not Chosen, why such effort?" Lopi replied curiously, causing Grekory's brow to furl.

"You said they were Chosen, you dolt! And Mikel all but confirmed it! And assuming they are, they will remember what a pleasant stay they had on their first night in Eislark." Lopi's puzzled face cleared with an inching grin. "A memory we can perhaps use to our advantage in the future. And I agree with Mikel, the other lords cannot know yet, and certainly not the masses. Too many voices in their little Chosen ears, they won't know who to listen to. We must be the first to enter their good graces, understood?" Lopi nodded and with another low bow, skipped past the crowd and down the table aisles towards the doors.

"And I will emphasize again, Mikel, that we must shine brightly in the children's eyes. Eislark must be an ally of the Chosen, if that is truly what they are," Grekory said as he rubbed his chin slowly, studying them. Zack and Johnny were next to each other, sword fighting with chicken legs as they laughed together, the other guests watching and laughing as well. The lord's look gave Mikel an uneasy feeling but he kept his thoughts to himself.

"Of course, Grek. I will speak with them tonight, and when Petravinos arrives, we will already have a budding Eislarkian relationship with them." Grekory nodded and smiled. He waved his hand gently toward the wine servants, who quickly filled his cup again as he slouched in his throne.

"To the unexpected, I suppose," Grekory said faux-cheerful as he raised his cup towards Mikel. He met it with a clank and they both drank fully.

17

THE LOFTED LANDS

⬥

A sudden rush of air filled his lungs, his eyes burning in the red sun as they opened, disoriented and lost. Reaching out, there was the familiar touch of grass along his fingertips, and he rolled from his side to his back and attempted to reset his shocked diaphragm. He looked around bewildered, trying to remember where he was. Where he sat and a few feet around him, the grass was barren, dry and brown as if that area alone had felt the force of a full drought. The rest of the grass beyond the dry dead circle was tall and luscious, and it whipped slowly in the high winds as the setting sun stretched over the plain, giving the tops a golden hue over the otherwise green blades.

He managed a few deep breaths as his wind came back, and he rolled to his hands and knees, stretching his torso up to look past the tall grass. Where he sat was a small field, small enough to see the ends of it on all sides, filled with nothing but long knee-high green grass. He scratched his head and looked oddly at the dead yellow grass around him, a glint catching his eye from the reflection of something shiny, bouncing the sun brightly. Crawling towards it, he pulled it from the snarled grasses' grip. It was a gold coin, wheat stalks forming a crown on one side with the same strange symbol he had seen on his leaf engraved on the other, and it hung from the end of a crude rope necklace with cracked white stones set in it.

All at once, it came back to him, a floodgate of memories released. The hospital, James, the escape, Jan and Bart, the purple stones, and lastly, whatever had happened to him, Johnny, and Zack in that color vortex. He stood quickly, almost losing his balance in dizziness before crouching low to the ground again and dropping his head between his knees, half afraid he would suddenly be sucked back into the swirl of colors.

"Johnny? Zack?" He called out mildly to his feet, eyes still closed in his vertigo state. He remembered slipping from the necklace Jan had given them, pulling with him the piece with the coin as he fell. He remembered plummeting through nothing and everything, disoriented by the shifting gravity. And then it all went black. Bryce stood much slower this time and dusted some of the dead grass off his sweatpants and blue hoodie. He looked around a little more at the grass and closed his eyes, rubbing his face with his hands in dismay as the necklace dangled between his fingers.

He pulled his hands away and looked to them in confusion, both arms extended. He flexed his left elbow effortlessly. No pain, not even a little. He quickly checked his left leg where the cut had been. His sweatpants were torn where he remembered the shrapnel stabbing, and they were stained red and purple where his and James's blood had soaked in, but his skin was healed over, nothing but a dark purple bruise surrounding the location, a line where the metal had sliced him. He distinctly remembered the pain his arm had felt; he had nearly passed out from it as James had toyed with them. And yet here he was, arm flexing and leg healed over.

A large cloud came between the sun and the land, drawing his attention back to his surroundings. He continued to flex his arms as he took in the land, waiting for the pain to suddenly rush back. There were blue skies mostly, aside from a handful of giant white puffy clouds floating gently through the warm air. It was different than the cool crisp fall air they had at the hospital, like late summer instead of late fall. From where he stood in the clearing of dead grass, there did not appear to be a path through the open field in any direction, much to his disappointment. To the west, where the sun was midway through its descent from its high noon peak, the field looked like it sunk and then rose to a hill, though he could not see any landmarks beyond the hill's crest, trees dotting it as it fell and rose. To the south and the east, the field eventually ended in tall trees, the swaying grass halting just before the trunks' grips reached into the ground. The trees had small colorful blue fruits dotting their light purple leaves, which were unlike anything he had seen before. And north, still in the field but near the tree line, sat a shack atop a jut of land, too steep to be a hill but not tall enough to be a cliff.

Still clutching the coined necklace, he began to work his way towards the shack's base, leaving the dead yellow grass, feeling the warm sun-soaked blades on his hands as he went. Without a path he walked cautiously, unknowing as to what may be lurking out of sight, stepping as if he was in murky water or a dark room. The shack hill rose from the field before him as the tall grass gave way to short shrubs and rocky terrain. Bryce walked up close and surveyed the mound, trying to identify the best way up. It was certainly steeper than it appeared from his landing spot and was more of a gradual plateau than a hill, greater than 45 degrees slopes of loose stone and soil with sheer drop points scattered throughout, and maybe 30 feet up. He circled to the left and right a bit, hoping to see a trail of some kind or a rope system, but there was nothing save the steep sides.

With a sigh he took a step back and began to analyze the surface in front of him for the best approach. The short shrubs that had overtaken the grass were also growing sporadically in the side of the plateau, small and frail looking and no bigger than his head. He grabbed one that was low and nearby, tugging it lightly to test its strength. The plant held firm so he gave it a harder tug, causing its hold to give slightly. They weren't terribly strong but they might be used as an emergency stop if he started to slip.

With one last glance up the face of the mound, he began to climb. Leaning forward on all fours like a bear he crawled up the face, lightly grabbing the shrubs wherever possible or if he started losing his balance. It was slow and laborious as his feet slid backwards in the loose soil and stone and the plants gave way if he pulled too firmly. He continued to make climb until about halfway up when he hit a particularly loose patch of dirt, which slid rapidly under his feet and almost caused him to fall backwards. He quickly dropped to his knees to lower his center of gravity, but the soil just gave more, forming a miniature avalanche. Desperate, he reached for the nearest shrub to slow his slide. For a moment, Bryce thought that he had lucked out and grasped a deep-rooted plant on the plateau. But just before he could completely reverse his momentum, the plant uprooted, spraying a fine mist of fresh dirt and leaves into the air. He tumbled backwards down the face of the mound, rolling with the soil and stone he had loosed. A resounding thud echoed through his ribcage as he landed flat on his back at the base of the plateau. The last of the dirt and stone shower bounced down onto his chest and lap as he sat up slowly and glanced down at the shrub that had so nearly saved his climb. With a disgruntled sigh and a flick of the wrist, he tossed the uprooted plant over his shoulder.

"Now what do we have here?" came an old gruff voice from above. Bryce jumped to his feet in embarrassed surprise and glanced up, sending the dirt that had landed on him back into the air again. The stranger's voice matched his appearance. A man was standing at the top of the plateau with wispy grey shoulder-length hair that blended seamlessly into his knotted beard and rested on a plain brown robe. It looked like something an old hermit might wear, or a bathrobe from the '70s that someone just couldn't let go of. The stranger leaned forward on an old wooden staff, carved fairly crudely from what Bryce could tell, and which only added to his dilapidated image. He looked deeply at Bryce, causing him to shift uncomfortably under the old man's gaze. The two looked at each other, neither speaking, only observing the other.

"Um, hi, I'm Bryce. I seem to be a little lost."

"A little lost, indeed," the man interrupted. "How did you get up here?" Bryce looked to the man, perched well above him and scrunched his face.

"Do you mean how did I get down here? I don't rightfully know, sir."

"Sir, ha! My, I've not been called 'sir' in a good long while." The man did not move his gaze from Bryce, but he did smirk, and Bryce thought the frown on his forehead lessened ever so slightly. "But my question stands. How did you get on my island? And what is your business here?" Bryce cleared his throat, suddenly feeling incredibly nervous as the man's smirk had faded and his gaze had intensified with such fire and precision, he seemed to be looking right through him. He felt as though a hot pad had been placed on his face and chest as he stood under the man's look. Bryce cleared his throat again in an effort to regain his composure.

"Well, sir, I honestly don't know. You see I didn't even know I was on an island."

"You don't know how you got to the place you stand? Are you another one of those wandering Gritvanders? No, I reckon not, you certainly don't look like a dwarf. Or perhaps a lost Swilmagapan traveler, wandering to the point of nuisance and mischief? What are they, Swilmenese? Swillsons? Bah, whatever, they are annoying is what they are! Somehow or another they've managed their way up here on more than one occasion, and I've been forced to remove them. So, are ye a Swilly or what?" the man asked as he looked intently at the boy, and then answered his own question before Bryce a chance to speak. "No, no, you don't look quite odd enough to be from the swamps, certainly odd clothing though. Perhaps you are a Swiller refugee but something in my bones says otherwise. Ah, a poor Trillgrander then, is it?"

"Well—"

"No, no, couldn't be a Trillgrander, they'd not set foot in the West. Even the partial West, they'd trigger a revolution! The Swillys go as they please, but not a Trillgrander. Even if they did, they'd not come up here. Unless . . . a spy?" The old man accused and peered through slit eyes at Bryce, studying his demeanor intently. Bryce uncomfortably looked away and to the fruit-speckled trees on his right to escape the scrutiny.

"Nope. If you are, you're the worst spy I've ever seen. No backbone and dressed like a loon to boot. Perhaps loony enough to be from Swilmagapan after all?" The old man stroked his bearded chin in thought, his cool blue eyes analyzing intently. "Unless, that's what you'd want me to think. That'd be a brilliant move for a spy, wouldn't it? But a spy without knowing why he's come to where he stands? Unless . . . yes, another spy tactic. Playing the lost traveler card, eh boy?" Bryce's eyebrows were raised high at the conversation the man was having with himself. He waited a few seconds, expecting the man to continue and soon enough he was proven correct.

"Well, boy! Are you the best spy that has ever crossed paths with Walding Zarlorn? Or are you just a loon, lost in the Lofted Lands, unknowing to how you've come to where you are and what you're doing where you stand?"

"Well, um, Mr. Zarlorn—"

"Phont!" the old man yelled in panic. "How do you know my name!" The man was bent over angrily now and pointing his crude walking staff at the boy with one hand and waving a clenched fist with the other. Bryce perplexing scratched his head.

"You, uh, you just said it," Bryce replied quietly. The man gasped, and then covered his own mouth with his free hand, stomping the ground in frustration with his walking stick. He stomped in a little circle for good 15 seconds and were he not so clearly furious, Bryce might have laughed at the sight. He finally stopped and leaned back over the hill's edge towards Bryce.

"My, what a spy you are, boy. Quite good, I will admit, extracting that information. But if you do not tell me how you've come to stand here, I will be forced to smite you." The man smiled at the last part, as if envisioning poor Bryce in a pile of ashes.

"Wait, what? Smite me?" Bryce cried in surprise, taking a half step backwards. The old man only nodded, still smiling.

"OK, um. So, like I said, I'm Bryce. Bryce Blooms. I am from Cleveland, Ohio. I don't think we're still in Ohio, are we?" The man's gaze did not waver and he made no inclination that he intended to respond. "I don't know how that happened, but we've got to be south somewhere, right? It's noticeably warmer here. Are we still in the US?" Bryce prodded cautiously, but the man still did not move as he scratched his beard and breathed a long sigh.

"Master Bryce, I am afraid as good as you are at extracting information, you are equally as bad at providing a good backstory. I know it does not matter now, as you'll soon be blasted to oblivion, but if you intend to make someone believe in the place you came from, try using a *real* city in a *real* land." The man gripped his staff with both hands. "I am sorry, spy. But it is not time for anyone to know my whereabouts. Goodbye."

"No!" Bryce cried, closing his eyes and throwing his arms up in front of him in a futile attempt to stop whatever Walding was about to unleash. The necklace in his hand was ripped away, and Bryce quickly opened his eyes as he tried to reach for it. The old man promptly smacked Bryce square in the forehead with his staff, stumbling Bryce backwards a few steps. Walding was standing in front of him at the base of the hill with the necklace held in the sun, the gold coin shimmering in the warm orange of the sunset. Bryce rubbed his head.

"How did you do that? Did you jump down the hill?" Bryce asked, bewildered, as he checked his palm for any signs of blood from his forehead. The man snorted loudly.

"Jump?" he replied pointing behind him with his staff, never taking his eyes from the gold coin. "Do I look like I am of any age to be jumping off of ledges, Master Bryce?" Bryce cocked his head to one side to look behind Walding. A crude set of rocks lined the hill, messy, worn, and uneven, but clearly a set of stairs. Bryce opened his mouth to retort but Walding continued before he could speak up.

"How did you come by this token? Did you find this or was it given to you? Or perhaps it was taken?"

"It was part of a bigger necklace." said Bryce. "Jan gave it to us but it fell off as I was—I'm sorry, but were those stairs always there?" Bryce was still flabbergasted.

"It fell off as you traveled the Void?" the man asked, smiling and looking to Bryce from the corners of his eyes. Bryce's eyes widened.

"Is that what that color thing is called? Have you seen that? It's insane!" The man's smile widened to reveal a crooked set of teeth, although they were not as bad as one might expect given the rest of his outward appearance. He extended the token back towards Bryce, who took the necklace eagerly from the old man's hand.

"My dear boy, this token is that of Petravinos Morgodello, the greatest wizard in the last hundred years. Perhaps two hundred." He paused now, thinking. "Although Kinred Quem'oa was quite marvelous in her days, just before Petravinos entered the Council." He pondered as he stared off into the clouds. "Let's say one hundred for certain, two hundred is in question, but I could be convinced either way." Bryce only stared at Walding in puzzled amusement. "And I would make a presumption that the *Jan* you are speaking of may be Lady Janeph of the Blue Hearts. Quite good company indeed." Bryce, at a complete loss, could only look at the man. "Ah, of course," Walding continued, "you haven't the slightest clue as to whom or what I am speaking of, do you, Master Bryce?"

Bryce shook his head in response. "Did you say wizard?" he asked skeptically, scratching his head. Walding ignored him as he continued.

"Well, my boy, it seems you have a case of the shifts. My words, they call it the sickness or something dull. The shifts, now that's a name, isn't it? Memory loss is the prime symptom, as I am sure you remember." He paused. "Or perhaps you don't. Either way, if my presumption that Janeph was your company leader and being afforded such a prominent token from Petravinos, you are most certainly a Trillgrander," Walding said, pointing to the gold coin. "And a high ranking Trillgrander for that matter. My, they sure do recruit the Hunting parties young, you can't be more than 15 years! Perhaps you are the spy I had thought. Or perhaps not, I am quite unsure." He stopped again, looking over Bryce curiously. Bryce could not comment before Walding began speaking again. "But regardless, I will help you at least return to Trillgrand. If we act quickly, you won't remember any of our encounter and my name will be safe once more. Once your old memories return, these new ones will evaporate like water on the rocks! You are quite lucky to have this coin; I was about to lay you to waste! But a friend of Petravinos is a certainly a friend. He knows how to keep his secrets. Of this I have no doubt." Bryce took the slight pause in Walding's sentence to blurt out a response.

"Um, that would be great because I don't have a clue as to what you are talking about or what exactly is going on," Bryce retorted, running his hands through his hair sheepishly.

"Very good! Let us first start with a proper greeting before we try to refresh your memory. No harm once your memories return, they often overwrite the 'memory loss' portion that you are experiencing now. Strange, isn't it? You forget everything and remember only the recent until your memories return, then they replace the recent! So, we might as well be cordial, right, my boy? Although, you do already know my name, and I yours. Bah, no matter! Formality is best!" Walding extended his hand towards Bryce as he continued. It was steady and his grip was strong, much more so than Bryce had expected. "I am Walding Zarlorn, fortune unto thee." Bryce reciprocated pleasantly.

"Bryce Blooms. It is good to meet you."

"Now then," started Walding, "you must tell no one my name. Call me grandfather and nothing more until your memories return." Bryce laughed lightly but realizing he was not joking, quickly stopped. Walding took the short silence as acceptance and continued. "We should get you oriented to your surroundings. Do you know where we are or have any memories of where you came from?"

"Well, I don't know where we are, Mr. Zarlorn, er, grandpa, but I landed over that ways." Bryce turned around pointing to where he had landed as he spoke. "I only remember waking up. It wasn't far, I really wasn't walking too long before I got here." Bryce turned back around to empty air.

"This way, Bryce," came Walding's voice from above. Bryce glanced up and met Walding's eyes from atop the cliff at the peak of the steep staircase. "Up, boy, a sight such as this one will promptly restore your memories, I am quite certain." Walding called as he walked out of view.

"Are you like one of those crazy workout guys? Like eat, sleep, breathe fitness kind of thing?" Bryce asked, at a loss as he viewed the stairs and walked towards them. Walding's head popped back over the cliff's edge.

"Eating fitness is an impossibility. Sleeping fitness is utter nonsense. Breathing fitness would most certainly lead to asphyxiation if it could be inhaled. I do not think your line of questioning is valid, my boy."

His head popped back out of view as Bryce started up the stairs. Thirty-two uneven and tall steps later, Bryce reached the summit. It was too many steps for a man of Walding's age to get there as fast as he had, too fast for even a kid Bryce's age to do so at full sprint. He glanced back down the stairs again and then over to the shack that stood a few feet from the top of the stairs. It was worn and crudely constructed, the windows were small, like portholes in a boat, and the frames were uneven and appeared to be rotting. It looked like the old man had made the shack himself from scraps he had found around the nearby forest. Walding stood a little further beyond the shed looking out over the far side of the cliff, hunched lightly on his staff. He looked back to Bryce as he waved him over.

"This way, boy." Bryce walked toward him past the shed but approaching the edge of the cliff he, stopped abruptly. "Welcome to the Lofted Lands," said Walding without looking to him.

Before him lay the end of the field that he had awoken in, and now he could see beyond the hill that had obstructed his view, but it did not empty into a valley or stream. It ended abruptly, dropping off to nothing, a cliff face in the sky elevated high above a vast sea. Beyond their island was a series of land masses, floating in the sky hundreds of feet above the water. Some nearby islands were linked together, crude rope bridges joining them, like unfortunate flies caught in thin spider web strands. Some further off in the distance looked to have their own small shacks like Walding's, narrow trails of smoke rising from them. There were dozens of the islands, varying in heights above the water and in sizes but all clearly without any means of support below or above them. The island they stood on seemed to be the highest of the lands in terms of elevation, but it was hard to tell how much bigger or smaller it was than the others.

"How?" was all Bryce's aching mind could manage after a few moments of disbelief.

"No one knows for sure how the Lofted Lands came to be, Master Bryce. Legend says Phont himself created them, a sanctuary away from the busy and tiring world of Endland."

"But this is land! It's land! This is land!" he cried, stomping his foot to prove that what they stood on was in fact solid. "And it's just floating!" Walding laughed.

"Very good, boy, this is most certainly land. But a Trillgrander such as yourself has surely seen these from the coast of Eislark on a clear day such as today! Now you're just on top of them instead of below them. Well, that is assuming you have traveled to Eislark. But, it is so close to Trillgrand, you must have traveled there by this point in your life." Walding turned and pointed to the opposite side of the island to the east, where more of the logic-defying islands were strewn in the sky, and beyond to the horizon where a shoreline could be seen but little else, a minor protrusion from the otherwise smooth line of the water. "What Trillgrander hasn't seen the City of Sails, even one as young as you? It is quite the city, is it not? But even still, the Lofted Lands from above offers a far greater scene. Only a few have ever beheld such a view, boy. You are in rare company," he said, looking out to the floating lands in knowing appreciation. "Does any of this ring of familiarity?" Bryce could only shake his head.

"I'm sorry Mr., uh, grandpa, none of this is making any sense. Phont, Eislark, City of Sails, Trillgrander, floating islands!" he said, spreading his arms to again emphasize the strange slab of floating rock that they stood upon. "It's all nonsense." Walding scratched his head and scrunched his eyes as he took in the scenery.

"Odd, typically a few landmarks are all it takes to undo the shifts, and the memories are triggered like a rockslide. You certainly are exhibiting extreme memory loss. Do you feel ill otherwise? Feeling light-headed, or perhaps you feel like vomiting, or are you having any dizziness or body chills?"

"Not recently, but I have gone through all of those at some point. Recurring, actually. I've been sick quite a lot this last year," Bryce replied. Walding masked a growing grin, quickly replacing it with a scowl, not subtle enough to get by Bryce.

"When exactly did you exit the Void, Master Bryce?"

"Well, I am not really sure. You see, I sort of had a rough landing. I remember the colors and the sounds and—"

"The Void, my boy, the Void," Walding interrupted.

"Yea, the Void. I remember being in the Void and then I got separated and I think I passed out," Bryce replied thinking back. "Because the next thing I knew I woke up over in that patch of dead grass. I may have been here for minutes or hours. I really don't know." Walding looked on Bryce wide-eyed and the grin that had been masked was shining through more and more by the second. He regained his composure, returning to a grinning scowl, like when disciplining a child who is too cute to scold. His breathing was quick and short, and a tinge of disbelief was upon his face.

"Gramps, are you OK?" Bryce asked, concerned, and Walding nodded emphatically.

"Yes. Master Zarlorn, if you please, enough of this grandpa talk. Now then, can you show me exactly where you landed?" Walding asked gently, poorly masking excitement or nerves in his voice as he spoke, Bryce could not quite tell which.

"Um, yea sure." Bryce turned as he spoke, pointing to the far side of the island. He could make out the patch of dead yellow grass quite plainly from atop the hill. "Do you see the yellow patch there?" A hand on Bryce's shoulder came quickly as he was pushed toward the stairs.

"Oh my. Oh my, oh my! Phont, this can't be!" Walding cried to the open air as they descended the crude stairs, so quickly Bryce nearly fell twice. Walding kept his footing without issue as they hit the dirt and gravel at an impossible rate and paced briskly into the tall grass, Walding now leading after having forced Bryce down the stairs. They were upon the dead patch quickly, and Walding patrolled around the circle muttering to himself as Bryce stood at the edge of the green grass, watching. It was hard to tell if the man was frightened or jubilant as he mumbled quietly.

"Is this a special grass, Mr. Zarlorn? Is it sick? When I landed, did I crush it?" Bryce asked anxiously after a few minutes, fearing he may have inadvertently killed the plant. Walding continued to circle the patch and then quickly approached him, dropping his staff and grabbing Bryce by the shoulders with both hands. Disturbingly strong for his appearance, Bryce retreated as the old man's face was pressed close to his.

"Tell me, boy! Tell me truthfully! Did you do this? Did you draw this life?" Walding asked in loud hysteria. The spark in the old man's blue eyes gave Bryce the impression this was incredibly important, and it made the boy uneasy as he glanced again at the dead grass.

"What? No, no, I didn't do anything, honest! It was dead when I woke!" Bryce shrieked desperately. "I don't know what it looked like when I got here. I only remember the Void, or whatever." Walding released him abruptly and dropped to the grass on all fours, crawling around and feeling the dead grass in his hands.

"Impossible. Oh, my this is quite impossible! But here it is, all the same! How superbly strange!" Bryce stood motionless on the edge of the dead and living grass as Walding scoured the ground and talked aloud to himself.

"What is going on, Mr. Zarlorn? Is it the Trillgranders?" Bryce guessed, causing Walding to stop crawling and look to him incredulously.

"What? Trillgranders?" he replied tersely. "No, boy, this is something ominous and spectacular. Something that I have not seen in many, many years were it not my own doing." He trailed off and resumed feeling the grass. "Are you certain this is where you landed?" Bryce nodded assuredly.

"Yes, definitely. I woke up kind of right in the middle here and found the gold coin thing."

"And what of your state, boy. Were you well?" Walding asked as he grabbed his staff and approached Bryce again. The boy took a step or two back from Walding as he approached, causing him to slow as he recognized Bryce's startled nature. Walding cleared his throat to reset himself before he stopped his approach and from a safe distance asked in a calm voice.

"What was your state before and after?"

"My state? I mean, I had just blacked out."

"Yes, yes, you lost consciousness in the Void. And while you traveled it, what was your state? And then when you awoke, what was it then?" Walding snapped quickly, clearly not enjoying Bryce's slow delivery of details. Bryce could only look confused at the man, unsure of what he was asking. Walding stamped his staff to the ground impatiently, madness returning. "What was your state, boy! Were you tired, sick, hungry, injured, aching, anything that you were in the Void then but are not now?"

"Oh, yes!" Bryce cried out hurriedly, fearing the man might strike him or have a stroke from his frenzy. "I was kind of beat up, my arm was broken I think, or sprained at the very least. It definitely wasn't right. And my leg was cut, too, but it's not anymore." Bryce exclaimed as he held out his clearly normal arm to Walding but then blushed realizing how silly he sounded. "That must sound crazy, I know, but it was really hurting at the hospital."

"What incredible news! My boy, why did you not say you were Chosen? And where is Janeph? Were you separated? They are not here, did they perish in the Void? Even so, a successful Hunt is incredible news! Simply incredible!" Bryce shook his head at a loss, though he was mostly sure now that Walding was happy with the dead grass.

"Wait, Janeph? That's what Nurse Bart called Jan in their meeting!"—the name suddenly dawning on him—"I thought I recognized that! But I still don't really know what I was Chosen for, Mr. Zarlorn."

"Master Zarlorn, my boy."

"Right, Master Zarlorn. But if Jan and Janeph are the same, she was fighting that thing with Bart. And we were sent to, to the Void or whatever, and she and Bart were left behind and Zack and Johnny were right there with me in the Void, but I don't know where they are now." Walding stroked his beard as the boy spoke and continued to do so as he responded.

"Ah, so there truly were others? And Janeph attempted to send you all on a single String? My, what trouble she must have been in, you all could have been lost! Well, the others may yet be lost. Most likely lost, yes, quite unfortunate. Not a way for anyone to go, I hope you did not know them well. What was this thing you spoke of that Janeph battled?"

"What do you mean lost? We need to find them; are they on another island or something?"

"Seeing as you have the string of stones, I doubt they shall ever land. They will just traverse the void haphazardly in a whirling descent of infinite purgatory. Like I said, not a way for anyone to go. But the fight, boy, what of this fight from Lady Janeph and Bartellom?"

"Wait, what? Where exactly are we, and why aren't they coming here?"

"They're gone! Cascading through nothing and everything at once and forever! How much clearer can I be! Now, details on the combat!" Bryce visibly shook in frustration.

"He was a beast! Black hair and long nails and he could freeze time and teleport and all sorts of stuff! James was his name. He tried to convince me to go with him somewhere. But I realized what he was, and then he beat Jan and Bart to hell and nearly killed me and my friends! And now I'm in this place and now I don't even know where my friends are or where *I* am or what I was chosen for or how I got here or who the hell you are or if James is still after me. Geez, and if I'm not in the hospital, Marge is going to be worried sick. I'm going to be grounded for eternity! And now if I have another dizzy episode I don't even know where I am to even get help!" He felt his emotions swell up as he spoke and the lump in his throat blocked any more words from leaving his mouth. Red embarrassment rushed his cheeks, and he looked away quickly. Walding's expression softened as he restrained his own excited emotions and walked over, placing an old strong hand on his shoulder and bending slightly to speak to him at eye level.

"Jamesett? You were pursued by Jamesett?" he asked quietly and with pain in his eyes. Bryce shrugged, still swallowing his emotions as he kept his face turned away to hide the welling tears. "My boy, I apologize, it's just this moment is quite exhilarating. Being Hunted is no easy endeavor, especially without knowing anything about anything, as you do! And then to survive the Void and truly arrive in Endland, plus the loss of friends." He trailed off as he looked around at the grass again. "My, there is much you must learn, boy, there is much we must do and quickly! Come, let us have some tea, you can sit and rest as you tell me of your travels from the start of it and then we shall begin. But first let's allow you some time to center yourself."

Bryce nodded but felt the emotions still welling in his throat, the fear and anxiety rising in him as he thought of his friends being lost in the Void, of Jan and Bart being beat to a pulp by James, of his parents more than likely scrambling about the hospital looking for him at this very moment. His leg pulsed in pain, and he swooned backwards. Walding's strong hand planted on his shoulder kept him standing, but he felt the world slipping, and he felt anger, red and hot rise through him. The world blackened as his fists clenched with white knuckles.

"Boy, calm yourself! Breathe!" Walding's words came across him hollow as he felt the rage, squeezing his fist so that his own nails dug deep into his palms. His leg pulsed in pain as Walding's words echoed around him as if he had fallen into a deep cave. His sight blurred, dark swirls twirling on the corners of his vision as the sharp pain radiated up his leg and through his torso. Walding released his hand from Bryce's shoulder, dropped his staff, and clasped both hands at his navel as he looked intently at Bryce. The dark tunnels swallowed his vision and he again fell unconscious.

18

DINNER WITH THE CAPTAIN

———◇———

Scraps of food flew around the table, ravaged like a kill by a pack of wolves. Zack and Johnny ate everything they could get their hands on under the gleeful supervision of Lopi, who drank and laughed much with the nearby folk, bobbing between the tables where the guests sat to soak up as much of the pleasantries as he could. Most of the crowd had moved past caring about the children and now were quite focused on enjoying the food and drink that were distributed freely. A million questions had flooded them after Mikel's appraisal of their charlatan identities, but Lopi had been quick to cut them off. "Let them eat, let them rest!" he had yelled. "Another time, they can provide the hilarious details. In the meantime, I am more than willing to tell the story!" He was clearly getting quite a kick out of being so popular.

The boys still did not quite understand all that was happening but whether it was the enormity and jovial atmosphere of the feast or the rush of surviving their harrowing escape, both boys found themselves feeling incredibly alive, well, and hungry. And so, they ate the various foods: squash and soups, meats and cheeses, fresh fruit, some familiar, some not, and a great many pastry desserts. They also were passed large mugs of ale to wash it all down, much to the delight of Johnny, who had just grabbed his second mug. Zack was much more reserved with the drinking but made up for it in food, taking handfuls of every plate that was passed his way.

Lord Belmar and Mikel sat in their chairs still, the mob of people from the hall enjoying the joyous celebration. Some still spoke in hushed voices at the perimeters of the room, notably many of the more prestigious-looking individuals, their quiet conversations drowned out by the minstrels' music that had resumed. A few danced as before, but most ate or hounded Lopi to ask how it felt to pull off such foolery on the Lord of Eislark. The guards that had escorted the group now had assumed posts nearby where the boys sat to quell the small crowd. The pair upon the throne area watched the scene unfolding, Grekory slumped slightly to one side with his chin resting atop a loosely clenched fist. Mikel was more attentive but could not help notice the Lord's seemingly sour mood.

"What a day this harvest has been, Mikel. But less so from the festival and more from our new guests." Grek laughed lightly at his own shock. "Have Chosen really returned?" he muttered, chin never leaving his knuckles. Mikel shrugged at his Lord's question, playing with one of the small knives from his bandoleer, testing its edge gently along his fingers.

"It certainly seems that way, Grek. As sure as I sit before you, these boys were in the Realm that our party Hunted in." Grekory shifted his weight right to left, resting his chin from one clenched fist to the other as he adjusted in his chair and sighed.

"But how is that possible? I had thought only those of Endland could shift without side effects. And my father said Chosen were but a bunch of wishful wizards, self-inflating their importance by spreading impossible stories. Were they more than that? Was it all true?" Mikel again shrugged as he watched the boys and sheathed the knife he fiddled with. He took a swig of his wine, emptying the cup, before he addressed his Lord.

"It was years before our time and you know the history of that era is desultory at best, full of strange and curious tales. But what records we do have, if they are to be believed at all, seem to indicate the Chosen Order splintered, the Grim rose and turned against the civilized world, and there was widespread destruction. I cannot say these boys have the potential to impact history like those stories suggest, but I can tell you that they are not of Endland, and that in itself proves they are unique. If they truly are Chosen, they may become powerful and would undoubtedly play a part in the months and years to come. To make a good impression may go a long way, Grek. Chosen as enemies cannot bode well for Eislark or the free peoples of Endland." Mikel spoke to himself as much as to Grekory, a stream of consciousness to the open air. The Lord nodded with pressed lips in acknowledgment of the just assessment. He swigged his cup and motioned for a servant to top him off. A maid ran up immediately and filled his cup to the brim again.

"Well said, Mikel," Grekory said before taking another drink. "Best to error on the side of caution. The children's invitation as my personal guests will be extended indefinitely, for as long as they remain in Eislark. We will be the first city they remember and it shall be their greatest memory." He straightened abruptly, "Mikel, I would prefer your direct contact with this matter. As you have already won their affection, easing them into Eislark should prove a simple task."

"Of course, it would be my honor, Grek," Mikel bowed his head, "but as I sit and watch this mob of bystanders work to get a peek at them, I am afraid we may have started them off in a precarious situation. The lords in attendance are no fools, not even Lord Dern or Jalp are without skepticism. And the Keepers, Phont!" Mikel remembered suddenly, burying his forehead in his non-wine hand. "They've been writing nonstop since they entered the Great Hall! Lopi retrieved the children with those scribes in tow! It will not be long before stories begin to circulate, you know how the Keepers are. Every one of them will embellish the grandeur of their arrival and soon we will undoubtedly draw the jealous eyes of the other lords, or worse, the Grim. And certainly, King Umbrin. This was a Trillgrand Hunt; he will be seeking to collect what began as his."

"Always two steps ahead, Mikel," Grekory said a smile, "and I do not disagree with anything you've said. We've this night and perhaps the morrow before word gets out; we must keep them safe until then. The children are to be under your direct care or the Gull's watchful guard. In the morning we will convene with the children and discuss what their arrival means for Eislark and for Endland as a whole."

"Agreed, Grek. I'll see to it that they make it to their chambers and are under watchful guard."

"Thank you, my friend. Go to them, make sure they are having a good time at this feast."

Mikel stood and bowed low to his Lord and approached the crowd around the feasting children. Wiggling his way through the people, he eventually reached the opposite side of the boys' table; they were still shoveling food down their throats by the handful. Johnny gave Mikel an openmouthed smile as he took his seat across from them, half chewed food nearly spilling onto the table.

"Micky! You've got to try this chicken! I don't know what they put on it but holy crap is it delicious. Like the best chicken I think I've ever had. This is my third piece!" Zack yelled after a giant gulp of food.

"I 100-percent agree, it is fantastic!" Johnny popped in. Mikel laughed loudly as the two ate.

"Boys, believe it or not, that is not chicken that you are eating. The chicken is here," he said, pulling a large plate from further down the table in front of the boys. They both stopped chewing immediately and looked to Mikel, perturbed.

"This isn't a chicken leg?" asked Zack as he pointed to the half-eaten leg he was holding.

"My boy, many creatures have legs. You have legs, don't you? Why must that be a chicken leg?" Mikel replied coyly. Johnny dropped his food and started dry heaving, moving his plates away from him in a frenzy.

"Oh, oh no. I'm going to puke," he managed between convulsions. "Papa Bear, we're eating some guy's legs!" Zack looked to the leg in his hand in disgust and then to Mikel for confirmation. Mikel laughed all the louder.

"Johnny, come now! Do those look like some guy's legs?" Johnny stopped dry heaving and analyzed the leg he held in has hand for a moment. If possible, his eyes got even wider than they already were.

"Mother of God! It's a child's leg! It's way too small to be a full-grown guy's!" Johnny started dry heaving again as Zack began spitting out the half-chewed food onto the table. The crowd around them watched in confusion and a few took a step or two back from the children. The scribes wrote fanatically. "We're cannibals, Zack! And not just man-eating cannibals, we're kid-eating cannibals! That's got to be the worst kind of cannibal!" Johnny was a maniac, trying to stick his fingers down his throat to force himself to throw up. Mikel laughed uproariously.

"Boys, boys, it's not human at all. And it is certainly not a child's leg, Johnny. What kind of beasts do you think we are here in Eislark? What you are eating is flostram, a bird found in the lands between and around Eislark and Trillgrand." He looked around at the prying eyes of scribes and nobles alike. "You boys can cut the act; Lord Belmar was much amused with it but it is over now. Although if you still have material that you practiced for the ruse, I will allow it, if only for my own entertainment." The majority of the suspicious looks around them subsided and the surrounding crowd returned to their merriment, much to Mikel's satisfaction. "Now, as you know, flostram are much larger than chickens, and can even be ridden by those who've gained their trust, which is no easy feat. But more importantly, they are simply delectable."

"So, so we're not cannibals?" Johnny asked sheepishly, muffled as his fingers still were trying to force their way down his throat.

"No, Johnny, you are not. You may both enjoy the food without concern," Mikel touted gleefully. Johnny and Zack both grabbed their discarded half-eaten drumsticks and clinked them together before taking ferocious bites.

"Micky, can I ask a question?" Zack said between bites. Mikel snatched a fruit pastry from a nearby plate and popped it into his mouth before answering.

"Of course, Zack, I must imagine you have a great many questions. But to be certain, I do not think this the proper setting for such a conversation. Too many ears and eyes are upon us." He whispered this last bit as he leaned over the table to grab another pastry before lounging back in his seat to continue. "When you've both had your fill of the harvest spread, I shall escort you to your quarters. We may speak there at length." Zack nodded in acceptance as he refocused on chewing a particularly fatty piece of meat. Johnny took a large swig from his goblet, brushed his mouth with the back of his sleeve, and questioned regardless.

"So, what's the deal with all these people that are following us, Mick? They've been writing nonstop since they walked in with Lopi."

"As I said, we can talk at length later but the short answer is they are historians," Micky replied as he leaned back into his chair and swirled his wine in his cup. "They write for the king and for city libraries and for other cities' records. The Keepers, we call them. They are documenting this momentous day, a joyous occasion for all of the Eastern Island. The Eislarkian Summer Harvest Festival is well-renowned in all of Endland; this one is especially noteworthy considering your arrival." Johnny nodded in understanding as he chewed heavily before swallowing the food and washing it down with more ale.

"I can't blame them for wanting to come here. This harvest birthday whatever thing is awesome. So much food, I wish I wasn't dreaming." Zack looked to his friend with concern as Micky shifted his weight, smirked, and took a swig of his drink. Johnny picked up on the silence.

"What's wrong with you, guys? I mean we can still have fun even if I know it's a dream, right? I figured it out a while ago," he continued as he stood abruptly, pointing to a bowl of fluffy white goop that looked to be some sort of frosting, "What is that stuff there? Anything cannibalistic or am I good to go?"

Mikel smirked and shook his head, giving him the all clear. "Nothing here is cannibalistic, Johnny, I assure you. But I think I must clarify; this is no dream." Johnny paid him no attention as he jumped behind Zack and shuffled down the table to grab the bowl and then shuffled back into his original seat. Taking a heaping helping on the serving spoon and raising it high, he remained climbed atop his seat and asked loudly to the crowd. "Hey everyone! See if you can guess, what I am now." Zack was quick to intercept the spoon before it reached Johnny's mouth, standing with Johnny now as both the boys held the large spoon in tension. Lord Grekory looked on with a scowled face, and Micky watched the scene unfold without movement, filling his cup with more wine.

"Johnny, you're not dreaming! This is real! I thought we established that in the library," Zack growled trying to keep the scene from escalating any further. "We're going to get in trouble, quit it!" Johnny laughed loudly as he sat down, letting go of the spoon and grabbing his leg of flostram again before dipping the whole thing in large bowl of frosting. A few nearby party-goers watched in disgust as he took a mighty bite and smiled widely while chewing and talking.

"That's exactly what my dream would want me to think. 'You're not dreaming, it's all real.' You're not going to convince me. I'm not actually in a castle, at a festival in front of the lord of England and eating, uh, what was this again?" Johnny asked, pointing to the leg of meat he held.

"Flostram," Micky said, sipping his wine nonchalantly.

"Aha! Gotcha, that's not what you said last time!" Johnny yelled, smiling at what he perceived to be a well-executed trap as he elbowed Zack in the sides.

"Johnny, for the last time, we're not in England, we're in Endland," Zack said as he pushed his friends elbows away from him. "We've been through this. And flostram is exactly what he said last time."

"There you go again! You keep changing it. First, it's flossram, now it's flotsrum. Get your story straight guys, you're all over the place," Johnny replied as he continued to eat the drumstick.

"Johnny, if we're dreaming, why would you ask about the writers following us? If it's all a dream, then who cares?" Zack retorted. Johnny held up a finger as he chewed and swallowed a bite of his frosted flostram leg. Zack looked to Micky for help but he only shrugged as he grabbed another nearby pastry.

"An excellent question, dream person," came Johnny's reply. "I was curious what my brain would come up with on the fly. Turns out, my mind is pretty quick on its feet. I am now 95-percent convinced if inception was real, I would figure out my dream was under attack within a few minutes." Johnny never looked up from his food as he spoke but still grinned as their eyes were upon him.

"I think you may be confusing your reality with this one, Johnny," Mikel said as his expression grew more somber. "This is real. Janeph, Bartellom, and I came to the hospital looking for gifted individuals and clearly, they ended up identifying the two of you. You are here for a reason." Johnny and Zack both stopped eating as their smiles dissolved for the first time since arriving to the feast, the worry written plainly on their faces.

"You mean the *three* of us, Mr. Dream Micky," Johnny corrected. Micky shook his head in confusion.

"Three? No, I don't count, boys. I live here. It's just you two."

"You mean, Bryce isn't showing up?" Johnny asked gravely, as the boys put down their flostram legs.

"Bryce? No, he is no doubt back in your Realm. I know it is difficult as you three were all close, but if he were here, he would have arrived with you two."

"He must be here," Zack replied, agitated as a scowl grew on Johnny's face. "He grabbed the necklace same as us! He just let go sooner, that's all." Micky sat forward abruptly, spilling his wine on the table. Nearby partygoers pointed out how drunk the Lord of Swords must be to spill his own wine, and the boys recoiled from the sudden movement as Micky flipped his glass back to its standing position.

"You mean to tell me the three of you all traveled on the same necklace? And Bryce let go before you arrived here? What was Janeph thinking!" Micky said, exasperated as he sat back in his chair again and then forward again. "It's by Phont's will that the two of you even made it!"

"Well, I'm sure Bryce made it too, right? Where is he?" Johnny asked now. "And further, if you're part of my subconscious, wouldn't you know that Bryce traveled with us?" Micky and Zack shook their heads in disbelief and sat in silence, Zack rubbing his forehead in annoyance.

"Johnny, this is the first I am hearing of Bryce's travels. I thought it was just you two," Mikel said solemnly. Johnny's face dropped in horrific realization, looking to his hands as if he had now for the first time seen them. He glanced around the room at all the guests and the food in awe before locking eyes with Mikel again.

"Oh man! This is real?" He shoved back from the table as he looked all around him again in newfound wonder. "That's the actual king of England?" He cried out, pointing to Lord Belmar. "And those are real knights guarding him? And just where exactly is Bryce?" The Keepers gained interest again, picking up on the outburst as they moved closer to get a look and listen in on what was happening. Micky glanced around the table suspiciously before he smiled and requested more wine from the nearest servant.

"And this is why we limit children's wine intake everyone!" A few laughs from nearby met his as he took a sip from his freshly poured glass. "I think it's time to go, little orphans! Off to bed!" Lord Belmar stood with his wine goblet in hand as the music slowed. He cleared his throat loudly, and a wave of calm washed over the people of the hall.

"Sleep well, young pranksters! Sleep well! It is a night in Eislark that is well earned! Fortune unto thee!" He said in a loud boisterous voice. Those with drink in hand raised their glass high above their heads, a chorus of good fortune praised upon the group as Mikel bowed. The boys simply stood and watched the scene unfold.

"And then we will go find Bryce?" Zack whispered as Mikel stood from his bow, raised his drink, and took one last mighty gulp.

"Yes, we will discuss that as well," Mikel replied as he wiped his mouth with the back of his free hand and turned towards the doorway. Johnny begrudgingly stood with Zack as they both pocketed pastries and walked from the table. Micky was already cutting through the crowd as the boys followed, waving and exchanging pleasantries with the folks that they passed. Many laughed and joked with them, offering a clap on the back and congratulations on their trickery, all the friendliness fueled by the excess amounts of wine and ale that had been provided. Some Keepers tried to follow but Micky ensured their restriction, whispering to the Gull at the feast hall's exit as he passed them. They stepped loudly and forcefully in the Keepers' way just after the boys skipped past them. Johnny turned and gave a sarcastic curtsy to the now-barred scribes before turning and catching back up with the others.

The three of them returned to the large stair hallway and went back up the way they had originally come. The area was filled with people from the festival now as they had meandered away from the Great Hall, groups of oddly dressed individuals conversing together throughout the stairwell, drinking and laughing as servants walked around with fresh fruit and breads for their taking. They weaved through the crowd down a new hallway, winding through a series of doors and corridors before Mikel stopped in front of a set of eloquently decorated double doors. If the trim around the doorways to the Great Hall was intricate, this was doubly so. A white ship crashing over the seas, gold trim in the sails, and waves on a red background. The detail was exquisite and the gold paint shimmered in the nearby candlelight. A set of Gull stood just outside the doorframe, heavily armed with their tall pike in hand. Mikel approached them and gave a short bow before addressing them.

"These children will be staying the night in the king's chambers by Lord Grekory Belmar's orders. Your post is not required here, I'll stay with them this night. You may find yourselves in the central hall where your services will be more needed; Lord Belmar has been generous with the drinks again this summer harvest."

The guards both slammed their pikes to the floor as one of them grunted in acknowledgment. Mikel opened the doors to pass, but a servant came running up towards them before he had passed.

"Captain Mikel, urgent message for you, sir. Strange news from Bim's Gate." The guards stomped their pikes again as they straightened them to their upright position, resuming their position as Mikel unfurled the paper and quickly scanned, eyebrows raising higher on his forehead with each second.

"On second thought, you will be needed after all," Mikel said as he placed the rolled paper in a hidden pocket of his cloak and turned to look at the boys. "The Gull are the city's elite forces.

They will protect you at all costs." This was met with another pike slam as Micky nodded emphatically.

"Yea, Mr. Lopi told us about them. They're like a weird version of the royal guard!" Johnny cried out as he began dancing in front of the pair of guards, extending two pointer fingers dangerously close to touching the nearest Gull. Micky quickly pulled him back with two hands on his shoulders and gave a quick spin to address him face to face.

"I am not sure what you are talking about, Johnny, but these guards will have your hand at a minimum if you lay a finger on them. It is best to give them a wide berth." Johnny nodded, somewhat in shock before Mikel motioned for the door, both boys obliging and entering. Mikel followed behind and pulled the door closed before he moved to the far side windows, pulling the curtains closed and beckoning them away from the door.

"Listen, and listen carefully," he said, crouching low to speak to them. "You are to keep that door closed and locked unless I am on the other side. The Gull will change shifts periodically, but there will always be guards posted to protect you. Trust no one but I, perhaps not even Lord Belmar. Is that understood?"

"Is something wrong?" Zack asked, confused.

"I've received notice of something at the bay, something that I must attend to immediately."

"Can't the Gull guys go instead? I thought you were going to help us find Bryce," Johnny asked innocently.

"I'm sorry kid, there are certain laws that require my personal review. The High Council has these established in the Eastern Island's cities, and while this one is certainly one of the most obscure in my opinion, I am still required to go." Zack nodded begrudgingly with Johnny. "But that is beside the point. If you boys are what we think you are, then you are of extreme value to anyone who would wield you. You must remain in this room until I return."

"Wield us, what are we a weapon?" Zack asked jokingly with a gleeful smile.

"Yes. Or a shield. It depends on who is doing the wielding, I suppose," Mikel said, not at all joking. Zack's face dimmed and the smile faded as Mikel shook his head.

"I apologize, this is all confusing. What you need to know at this moment is that you are valuable. And valuable things tend to attract unwanted eyes, especially when Lopi announces your arrival to every Keeper and lord in Endland, the damn fool." He looked away disheartened before resuming. "Only open that door for me, understood?"

"But how will we know it's you?" Zack asked openly, Johnny nodding in agreement.

"We will have a pass phrase, only us three will know it." Mikel said after a moment of contemplation. Johnny perked up immediately.

"Oh cool! How about 'This herbal tea is delicious, Mr. Person, but you know I prefer nachos'?"

"What the hell does that mean, Johnny?" Zack replied in irritation, arms flailing up in the air the second Johnny finished his ridiculous phrase. "It's so stupid anyone who hears it will know it's not normal conversation. Do they even have nachos here? It needs to be subtle like 'my food had too much cinnamon.'"

"Anyone could say that, Zack. I'm pretty sure I heard four people say that at the party thing tonight!" Johnny retorted.

"You heard four different people say 'my food had too much cinnamon' tonight? Come on Johnny, be real."

"Did you try those red cake things! They had way too much cinnamon! People were basically coughing up red dust!"

"Enough!" Mikel whispered through clenched teeth. "The phrase shall be 'I've received word that your horses will arrive on the morrow, both grey coats as requested.'" The boys looked to each other and then to Mikel.

"Yeah, that will work," Zack said for both of them.

"Good. Doors stay shut for anyone and everyone. I will be back as quickly as I can." And with that Mikel turned, walked hurriedly to the door, and left the room with a slam.

19

THE WORN THORN

e noticed the gentle rocking first, slight sways in his stomach registered the familiar feeling. The smell came second to confirm what his inner ear sensed. Marge's brother, Uncle Slim, had a little 21-footer that they would take out on Lake Erie when it was calm enough to go fishing. Without opening his eyes, Bryce knew he was on a boat. He laid still, eyes closed, rolling gently in the darkness as he half slept, half rested, listening to the waves lap against the sides. Not much registered as he opened his eyes. He could only make out dark shadows and a dim light on the edges of what looked like a doorframe or roof hatch of some kind. He sat up slowly and felt his hair touch the roof of wherever he sat. With a roll he was on his hands and knees and began gingerly crawling the few feet towards the light of the door, the rough wood meeting his hands, old and worn from years on salty water.

With a quick push, the door opened to a freshly starlit sky, the last remnants of the day holding fast to the edge of the world like a nearly sleeping eyelid. Bracing himself on the sides of the hatch door as the waves sloshed the boat back and forth, Bryce poked his head from the door and saw the frame of a small barge, no more than 10 feet wide and maybe 15 long. The aged, coarse wood made him a little nervous as he looked out over the vast dark water in front of him, and the tattered sail that propelled them didn't help settle his uneasiness. Only the sea lay before him with moonlit highlights of the waves gliding from the back of the boat. They slowly died into calm water, and with the star's reflections on the distant surface, it almost appeared that the sky and sea flowed together save for the fading line of dusk light on the horizon.

"Well, well, he has awoken. And how is the boy feeling? Better after a short rest, I trust?" came Walding's voice. Bryce turned to respond, still popped like a gopher from the hatch door.

"I do feel a bit better. But I don't remember getting on a boat. What happened after I blacked out?" Bryce said to Walding's back. The man was on a raised platform in front of him at a steering helm but had not turned to address the boy. He appeared a giant from Bryce's perspective, the hatch door only a foot or so from where the old man stood.

"You said you were quite tired, nothing like a catnap to set you right. Odd phrase, catnap, isn't it? Cat's sleep for quite extended periods of time; you would think a catnap would be a long sleep, not a short sleep."

Bryce laughed as he lifted his torso and hopped out from the hatch door, sliding his knees onto the deck and closing the door behind him. He stepped out from behind the old man but lost his breath as he beheld the sights they sailed towards. Beyond the rolling waters they floated on, a large wall of earth rose before them, hundreds of feet tall with fires lit along the surface and along the top ridgeline, like a brighter continuation of the stars above. They moved towards a small opening in the rock's face, an alcove on the water in an otherwise insurmountable cliff. The rock sloped gradually from the opening, fires glowing brightly along the rising surface. At the lowest point on either side near the water the lights were more concentrated, and further beyond the rock wall he could make out a city, buildings and towers illuminated by the distant firelight.

"Eislark, City of Sails. In the morning, the sea will be dotted with boats in even greater numbers than the lights that illuminate it now. It is quite an exquisite spectacle, Master Bryce," Walding said as he turned his back to the city to address the boy. "But more importantly, would you say you are well now?"

Bryce shrugged. "Sort of, I guess. Just as confused now as I was on the floating rock though. How did we get down from there anyway?"

Walding measured him intently before replying. "Do you remember anything before waking here?"

Bryce thought back to the hut, the yellow grass, Walding pacing like a coffee addict, when a flash of red filled his vision, the color ringing loudly in his head and then was gone as quickly as it had appeared. He did his best not to flinch at the flash but was unsure how successful he was, Walding's eyes never wavering from Bryce.

"Not much aside from meeting and looking at the dead grass," he lied at length. Walding had not stopped gauging him since the questions began but finally broke his gaze as the waves picked up and rocked the boat forcefully. Bryce looked to the front of the boat to see they had moved closer to the opening of the earthen wall now as he could see further beyond it. The opening sloped from very wide at the top to very narrow as it met the water, wide enough for at most one large boat to pass through it. Their little craft would pass easily, but Bryce suspected that hidden rocks just beneath the water's surface may further restrict the entry point, given the jagged and unclean layout of the natural cliff surface surrounding it.

On either side of the opening just above sea level sat a pair of towering carvings built from the rock, progressing from human craftsmanship to natural rock face in a seamless blend. The night's dark concealed the higher portion of the carvings that the bonfires could not reveal, but the bottom portions were clearly the feet of a taller statue. Bridges extended from the lower landing that the feet stood upon, connecting and interconnecting with other landings and bridges that were also built into the cliff surface further away from the entry point. They intersected along the ridge as far as he could see, illuminated by torches or fire pits every so often. Some landings boasted small buildings with great bonfires lit atop their roofs, casting light on the waving flags and the men posted atop them who looked over the vast and darkening sea. As they neared the bottom portion of the carvings, a pair of guards exited from a doorway between the feet on both the left and right sides of the channel. They walked to the edges of the landings and yelled out to their boat as Walding continued to make way towards the opening.

"You there! The Bay of Bim is closed for the evening. What business you have must wait for morning," One of the guards on their left shouted. Walding paid him no mind as he continued his course.

"There are ports on the outer wall where you may dock for the night. Turn back or you will be boarded," Came a guard on the right. Bryce shuffled over to Walding and tugged his sleeve as they moved nearer the entryway.

"Mr. Zarlorn, aren't they talking to us? I don't think we can go through," Bryce pleaded as he looked closer at the carvings. The top of the bonfires slightly illuminated dark openings along what looked to be the waist of the carvings. He could make the faintest glint of metal inside, and a gust of wind pulled a flurry of sparks from the bonfires high into the openings where the metal was revealed to be on the top of a giant spear, loaded into an even larger ballista. The weapon flickered to life in the dim sparks before they burnt out and it was shrouded in darkness again. "Mr. Zarlorn?" Bryce whispered nervously as Walding glanced down to him and slowed the boat before addressing the guards.

"Good evening!" Walding yelled in a loud and strong voice. "Sincerest apologies! We were caught further out to sea than we anticipated as I took my grandson here," he said, clapping Bryce on his back, "on his first fishing trip and are now running behind for harvest. Could you not allow a grandfather and his grandson passage on this harvest night?"

"The Bay of Bim is closed," the guard on the left repeated. "You may seek shelter for the night at the ports on the outer wall."

"Ah, but the boy's mother will worry!" Walding said. "Surely you can understand the wrath of a worried mother. I shall never be allowed to take the boy out again if I don't get him back in his bed tonight!"

"You know the rules, citizen, especially at your age. None are permitted entry after dusk. There are ports along the outer wall. Turn around now or be boarded. I shall not say it again." The guard on the left had now reached a wooden rail nearest the water as he drew a small horn from his belt. Walding eyed him, expressionless, as another brisk wind blew around them, a cold chill running up Bryce's spine and even Walding seemed to shiver as it wrapped around them. Walding's fist clenched, white knuckles showing even in the darkness as he squeezed the sail's rope.

"Mr. Zarlorn, let's just stay on the wall or whatever," Bryce said as mildly as he could to diffuse the man.

"They know not to whom they speak. If they did, they would be pissing their fancy armored pants! They would allow us to pass, even were I with an armed fleet of war vessels bent on the destruction of this city!" He spoke plainly and loudly and in no way attempted to restrict his voice from carrying to the guards. The one on the right bumped his comrade in amusement and the one on the left snickered with his. None seemed terribly concerned with the vague threats of an old man on an even older fishing barge.

"Are you really so important?" Bryce asked, a bit confused.

"Of course, I am! Walding Zarlorn is a name known to all! I should tell them to whom they speak, but I am not sure we are ready for such hysteria, Master Bryce. It is best to keep our identity quiet until the time is right." Bryce shook his head as he could hear loud whispers from the guards.

"They don't know who I am, Mr. Zarlorn, but you just stated your name out loud again, loud enough for half the ocean to hear," he said calmly, trying to smile it off. Walding's face dropped as he glanced to see both sets of guards leaning over the rail to get a better look at him.

"Phont! I've spoken in two conversations this day and twice now I've stated my name!" he yelled in panic, somehow still unaware of his boisterous voice.

"Is that true, old man, are you really Walding Zarlorn?" The guard on the right asked in exaggerated wonder. Walding smiled and puffed his chest, but before he could answer, the one on the left continued, in genuine fascination.

"Hero of the Aging? Or mass murderer depending on who you talk to. Grandmaster of the Chosen, responsible for the banishment of Kuor-Varz?"

"Yea, the same Walding that was exiled from Endland 100 years ago for treason and has surely been dead for nearly as long?" one of the guards on the right continued before he dismissed himself from the conversation and quickly returned to the chamber beneath the carved feet. Two of the three remaining laughed, but one remained silent as Walding strangled the sail's rope in his wrinkled hands. Bryce looked curiously to them and to Walding.

"I'm sorry, but that is quite impossible," yelled the guard from across the way. "Walding Zarlorn is myth, as is Kuor-Varz and the Aging and that whole ridiculous story."

"That's not true! My great-grandfather fought at Jornun. He saw the Aging first hand, it's all true!" the quiet one on the left chimed, causing the other two to laugh all the louder. Walding whispered quietly under his breath as Bryce leaned over to him and spoke in a hushed tone.

"Are you the same Walding that they are talking about, Mr. Zarlorn?" Walding measured Bryce and the others who still laughed before whispering back.

"Of course not, boy, you think I'm over a century old? I'd be dead twice, perhaps thrice over! Zarlorn is a popular last name, you see. It was just a ploy, hoping these nitwits would let us through. They are not as dumb as they look!" He shifted to a loud voice again as he addressed the guards with his last insult. They were still yelling across the channel, debating as he continued. "Men of Eislark, we will dock outside the walls for the night and return at sunrise for entry. Though you must know, I will be sending the boy's mother to you when she comes for my head in the morn!"

They paid him little attention as he lowered the sails and used a long pole to push the barge backwards and out of the channel before they headed south down the coast. One of them seeing the turnaround called out to them.

"Have a good evening, Grandmaster Zarlorn! Pleasure to have met you!" The skeptics laughed again. Walding loosed the sail as they left the edge of the dangerous rocky entryway, and they rapidly gained speed, skimming across the water down the coast. A gust of wind caught them as they quickly put distance between the rock opening and their boat.

"Mr. Zarlorn, what's going on? Are you named after a celebrity or something?" Walding did not speak as they cruised along, the entryway falling from view behind a large jut of rock with many torches atop it that protruded from the dark sea water. The boat skimmed quietly down the coast for a short while longer before he responded to Bryce.

"Now is not the time, Master Bryce. For now, I must ask you to remain completely silent. No movement, no noise, understood?"

"Sure, but—"

"Hush now, I must concentrate." Bryce dropped his question and moved to the left edge of the boat and took a seat near a rope anchor, which he held tightly as he sat and dangled his feet from the edge. He looked forward toward the endless water and caught sight of a dock approaching, a series of torches tied to it on its furthest edge. They never slowed, passing by quickly as Bryce could now see many docks ahead extend into the water, most of which were strategically placed in the natural coves that the rock had made. Just beyond the docks there were small buildings, some carved into the rock and others constructed in the open, all of which were noticeably isolated from the rope bridge causeway that was strung well above them on the cliff. Another gust of wind blew strongly, and Bryce could make out the sound of music and laughter from the shore.

"Why don't we just stop at one of these, Mr. Zarlorn? They sound like they're having a party."

"Hush boy, what part of silence do you not understand?" Bryce pressed his lips in a sheepish silent apology, and Walding softened as he scratched his beard. "Besides, nothing good ever happens on the outer docks after dark. Cutthroats' and swindlers' haven, these are. You'd want nothing to do with them. Although on harvest nights they are truly a good time." In remembrance, he looked longingly towards the shores a short while before he refocused somberly on the waters ahead. "But that was years ago." And with that, he whipped the boat around back towards the entrance at full force. The boat tilted at such an angle that Bryce summersaulted backwards and had to flatten out on his belly to keep from rolling off.

"Mr. Zarlorn!" Bryce cried out.

"Silence!" Walding hissed back, not slowing in the least. Bryce glared in frustration and crawled back to the hatch door, opening it and dropping down so only his torso was above the deck again. The coved docks whirled by, the wind catching the sails at full force as they skimmed across the water. They were fast approaching the jutted rock that masked their view of the guard posts when Walding extended his hands toward it, releasing the helm much to Bryce's shock. Bryce bit his lip to refrain from asking what the hell he was doing as a thick fog rolled in from the sea like a tidal wave of clouds, 30 feet high at least, moving in quicker than they glided across the water. Walding did not slow as the fog began to envelop them, swallowing the boat moments before they rounded the large jut of rock that signaled the entryway. Even with the lack of visibility he did not slow and still kept both hands off the wheel. Bryce strained his eyes to locate anything ahead of them before he felt the boat curve towards the coast and looked back to Walding to find the old man's hands were still not gripping the wheel. Bryce nearly asked aloud how he was managing a handless turn when muffled voices could be heard ahead. Through the fog some light could be seen, murky and unclear but bright spots that he suspected were the guard posts, now surrounded in the dense fog. Walding did not slow at all but somehow continued his turn to make sure the barge was roughly centered between the lights.

"My, haven't ever seen the fog come in like that, have you? Quickest and thickest I've ever seen!" came a voice through the mist.

"I'm not sure I have either. Your bonfire looks to be a candle across the way it's so heavy!" another voice replied closer and to their right.

"Maybe it's Walding Zarlorn's doing!" a voice on the left joked as others laughed, now slightly behind them as they continued through the fog. Walding kept his course and speed, a small smirk rising on his face as his extended arms quivered. The surf through the opening was choppy but Bryce's fear had subsided; it was clear Walding was in control as he steered the barge, and as they crossed the threshold of the gate, the fog broke in front of them, though it remained just as thick behind, as if it had gotten stuck in the rocks of the entryway. A small thin wispy tail of fog followed them into the open bay as Walding lowered his hands and exhaled slowly.

The bay was massive, and the waters danced with vibrant colors, green and blue lights glowing beneath the water's surface. Bryce climbed from the hatch and looked out over the boat's edge to get a better look at the entrancing colorful sway of the lights, galaxies of colorful shimmers, pulsing on and off below him. Further off in the direction of the city, the colors in the water faded, the torchlights on the pier and shoreline drowning them out and replacing the blue and green with yellow and red reflections. The city wrapped nearly the whole bay, with the smallest buildings at the furthest edges and largest buildings just right of center from the entryway. The castle stood the tallest among the buildings, towers silhouetted against the starry sky and lighted in its windows throughout its dark face, making it look like reverse Swiss cheese.

"I've not seen the Bay of Bim in many years. It hasn't changed much, as magical as ever. Eislark has surely grown though." Bryce looked to Walding curiously for a second before he returned his vision to the scenery.

"What makes it glow like that? It's not actually magic, is it? Some sort of plankton or something?"

"No, no, not magic," Walding chuckled. "Truly marvelous though, isn't it? An old tale will tell you they are the moon's children, fallen from the sky. They retreat to the depths at sunlight, waiting for the darkness so they can arise to see their dear mother again. But I think the truth is, no one really understands why they do what they do. But this is the only place in all of Endland that you can see something like this. And I have certainly missed it." Walding finished as he looked out over the pulsing waters. Bryce turned to face him, pulling his eyes from the light show.

"But don't you live on those island things not far from here? I would think you could stop by and see them all the time," he questioned.

"They are not as close as they look, Master Blooms. But pay me no mind. Just an old man lost in his memories." He smiled as best he could, but Bryce saw the sadness in his eyes. He did not press him as they made their way across the bay, floating on the fluorescent blue and green water. Walding curved the boat to the right, this time with hands on the helm, away from the larger buildings and towards a much smaller and rougher grouping at the far edge of the sprawling city.

The wisp of fog followed them until they came upon a small dock with a makeshift fence built atop it and a single torch lit at its end. Walding slowed the barge with the large pole that he had used to turn the boat and tossed a rope onto one of the dock's hooks, pulling it taut as the deck creaked loudly from the strain of the boat's slowing momentum. The creaking got the attention of someone; just on the mainland at the end of the deck, a light illuminated from within a small shack that was not any bigger than boat they rode on.

"Speak nothing unless I say; hopefully I have the right dock," Walding muttered quickly as he walked towards the edge of the boat and pulled another hooked rope taut. Bryce nodded and stayed put in the hatch door, half retreated in his gopher hole. The light from the hut moved from the window to an open doorway, and a young lady carrying a single candle walked towards the dock. The candle cast heavy shadows on her face but she could not have been 20 years old, her curly blond hair bobbing as she made her way towards the barge. Walding braced his hands on the dock as he beckoned Bryce to do the same. He obliged and skipped across the rough floorboards to grab hold of the platform. Bryce could not believe the dock was standing; he thought if he squeezed hard enough, he would leave his fingers impressions in the soft rotting wood.

"Good evening," the lady said as she was close enough to converse without shouting. She gave a short curtsy near the halfway point of the dock. "I must apologize, unfortunately we have no rooms left in the inn. You may dock and stay on your boat for the evening for half rent. That is all we can offer." She spoke plainly and without emotion; she had clearly been addressing strangers at the dock on many occasions and did not seem uncomfortable in the slightest with the conversation.

"Good evening, my Lady," Walding bowed low, leaving Bryce to hold the boat himself. He tensed his arms before Walding resumed his grip on the old dock. "The patient wind brings calm illusions through the cragged sky. What of the past morrow's yet past?"

The woman's face grew in surprise above the candle she held, her calm demeanor dissolving like the fog that hung behind the barge. She looked down in remembrance before perking back up and slowly working through a strange reply.

"The past is but tomorrow's today and with it brings the specter of this present. All is now, as will be, as was." She curtsied again, as Bryce looked to both of them, perplexed. "Please, follow me." She picked up an old rope from the dock near her and walked a few paces closer as she spoke. A short toss down to Walding and he made quick work of tying off the barge completely. Bryce held the edge looking to him and back to the lady. Now closer, he could see she was much younger than he had first suspected as the candlelight flickered off her pale skin, melding with the moonlight and green-blue glow of the bay. She caught his eyes as he quickly looked back to Walding, a flush of embarrassment running up his face that he was grateful the night concealed.

Walding motioned for Bryce to climb the makeshift ladder between them as he stood from tying the knot. Bryce was quick to hop up it, feeling the rung of each soggy slab of wood bow beneath his weight. He jumped to the deck, Walding close behind him. The woman curtsied again and turned without a word, leading the way back down the short dock. Bryce waited for Walding as he labored up onto the wood and then walked side by side with Bryce.

"What exactly just happened? Do you know her?" Bryce whispered inconspicuously. The woman passed the small shack she had come from and continued up a narrow alley toward a cluster of buildings.

"You will know soon enough. I do not know her, but I do know her family, as proven by her response. We will speak at length in private when we reach the Worn Thorn. Given your arrival, we need to reassemble the Chosen allies. This is our first stop," Walding said as they too passed the shack at the end of the dock. The young woman had entered a large building up the road from the dock and from the opened door, welcoming light flooded the dirt road as a roar of voices and laughter filled the salty air. Bryce lagged back as Walding entered first, the warm air rushing from behind him onto his face as the smell and taste of stale beer and vomit assaulted his nose and tongue simultaneously.

Walding and the young woman curved right through the open room, filled with small tables that littered the floor, not all of which were standing upright. It was swamped with a rough-looking crowd, almost all of whom seemed to be on some level of modest to extreme inebriation. Those above the extreme level sat nearly asleep in a corner or sprawled on a table or the floor, and the smell of beer was concentrated nearest those particular individuals. The others nearest the drunks ignored them, walking around them as if they were furniture themselves. The bar at the back of the room opposite the door they entered was crowded with men and women atop bar stools, all clamoring with each other or the barkeep for the next round of booze. In the back-left corner was a singer and lute player, playing music that was nearly impossible to hear over the raucous crowd. And in the back-right corner next to the bar was a staircase going up to what Bryce suspected was the inn's rooms.

Walding sat at a table on the far-right wall, the young woman standing by, waiting for Bryce. Getting distracted by the surroundings, he briskly walked to catch up, dodging a stumbling buffoon who was having trouble multitasking standing and sipping from a glass. Bryce smiled to the young woman as he approached, doing his best not stare into her blue-green eyes, a less fluorescent view of the bay waters surrounded by a fair-skinned face. Bryce sat next to Walding as she motioned him to the table.

"Thanks," he said plainly with a quick smile. She curtsied with a dip of her head.

"I will return with the head of the household. Fortune unto thee." She turned quickly and walked towards the bar, dodging her own set of drunks as she did so. Bryce watched her discernibly until she disappeared through a wooden door behind the bar. Walding chuckled as he sat back in his creaky wooden chair and folded his hands on the poorly kept table. Bryce mimicked Walding, much to his displeasure as his hands plopped in a puddle of mystery liquid.

"So now can you finally tell me what exactly is going on here?" Bryce asked as he shook his hands out and wiped them on his pants. "Like, for instance, where are we and when am I going to go home?" he asked, looking out over the rough crowd. Walding kept his hands folded, and at first Bryce thought he might not have heard him over the noise. He blinked slowly once, twice, before responding, searching for words.

"Bryce Blooms, you are in the city of Eislark, the largest port city in all of Endland, and Endland is the Realm we are currently in. You were given a set of crystals which transported you here. It was strung along with a gold medallion, this medallion," he said as he pulled the coin from his waistband, the light of the candles reflecting off of it before he put it on the table and slid it across towards Bryce. It sloshed through the liquid on the table, and Bryce took it with a shake and examined it more closely as Walding continued. "I was holding onto it for safekeeping while you rested but this medallion is extremely rare and is a sign that Petravinos Morgodello has become extremely desperate, desperate enough for him to send a personal token and his own crystal to bring you here."

"Who the hell is that and why did he want me to come here?" Bryce asked as a man across the room stumbled into a group that promptly shoved him into a booth where he either was knocked unconscious or passed out from his consumption.

"No, no, not *here* specifically, my boy, here to Endland. And your arrival in Endland means that you are special. Special enough to bring me out of my hiding and back to the civilized world for the first time in many years. Petravinos brought you to Endland, but I have brought you to the Worn Thorn. We are here to awaken the knights."

Bryce looked up from the coin as Walding cupped his hands around Bryce's, concealing the coin and suspending the conversation due to a drunk, hooded man walking uncomfortably close to their table. He passed slowly, or more so stumbled slowly, as Bryce watched him bounce like a ping-pong ball between two groups of tables. Walding kept his hands folded and kept him in the corner of his eyes before he moved his hands, pushing the coin close to Bryce's chest. Bryce kept the coin tight to his body but still played with it, examining the pristine craftsmanship of the strange symbol that was etched into it.

"So, I'm either having severe side effects to a medication or I'm dreaming or I am actually in an alternate dimension." He placed the coin on the table with a frustrated slam, which Walding quickly concealed with his hands as Bryce buried his face in his own. "This is crazy! I woke up in a field on a floating island for God's sake! This whole thing is impossible."

"Everything we do is impossible!" Walding said rather loudly, opening his hands with the outburst before he cleared his throat and refolded them over the coin, glancing at the nearby patrons who were too drunk to take notice. "Bryce Blooms, the fact that you awoke *at all* is remarkable. And further, you were lucky enough to end up in the Lofted Lands, no less on my floating island, instead of the middle of the sea, where you without a doubt would have drowned. It is a stroke of improbable fortune. And what all of that means is that you are Chosen." He whispered the last part as he leaned forward toward Bryce.

Before he could respond, a large man walked up to their table, leaning on a thick heavy cane over the both of them. His dark leather overcoat concealed most of his clothing as it was draped over his shoulders, neither arm through the sleeves, using it as a sort of cape more than a coat. Heavy silver chains hung around his neck, dangling low on a plain white tunic, tucked into a thick belt with a large etched bird buckle. The boots he wore were fur, rugged and worn but looking quite warm, the fur tufts sticking out at the tops near his mid-shins and tightly laced to the top where his dark blue pants tucked in, equally as plain looking as his tunic. He took his small hat off, two sizes too small for his large head, and tucked it under his arm, revealing a partially bald top. The short white wisps of hair that he did have clung to his hat as he removed it before floating back to his head like spiderwebs that have been detached from their post. He cleared his throat and breathed in deeply before addressing them.

"Fortune unto thee, good sirs, welcome to the Worn Thorn. I am Geaspar Eltenbranch, owner of this fine establishment." Geaspar spoke in a deep voice with drawn out *s*'s, and after the few short sentences, he already appeared to be breathing laboriously. A nearby patron puked in the lull of conversation, before a bar hand promptly gripped him by his shoulders, stood him up, and threw him out the door. A great many cheers erupted, but Geaspar ignored the commotion and dabbed a thin layer of sweat from his brow with a dirty handkerchief pulled from his inner coat pocket.

"Fortune unto thee, Master Eltenbranch, please have a seat with us," Walding gestured. Geaspar bowed his head in respect but did not sit.

"Thank you, but I would prefer we speak in private. If you would please, let us make our way to my office in the cellar." He gestured towards the stairwell with a small smile. Walding gave pause before he nodded. He and Bryce rose from their seats and walked towards the stairs, Walding leading the way with Bryce close behind and Geaspar bringing up the rear. Where the stairs had been seen going up, as they had noticed when they entered the bar, there was also a set of stairs down to a dank looking cellar, the smell of which reminded Bryce of slightly stale bread and vegetables on the verge of the transition from ripe to rotten. They stepped on sturdy wood steps towards a single torch at the lower landing, Geaspar following behind them with heavy footsteps.

"If you would, to the right past the shelves is a room, go right on ahead, I am a bit slow," he cordially called from behind, lagging down just a few stairs. Walding and Bryce obliged, passing shelves of ale and mead, breads, pot and pans, pillows, blankets, wood, nails, and an assortment of vegetables and dried meats. The cool air was refreshing after the damp heat of the crowd upstairs, and their footsteps created dull echoes on the dingy and dust-covered wood floor. Bryce had thought at first that they walked upon dirt it was so decrepit and grime covered.

Walding pushed open the door on the far end of the storage cellar to find a well-lit room, with a long table down the middle, five chairs to a side, between the cracked stone walls. On the far wall hung a number of weapons, giant clubs and axes on fine mounts, each with small inscriptions below them. In the center of the far wall sat a smaller table and a very comfortable-looking and immense chair with parchment and quills spread about it. A large drawing hung centered behind the chair and between the weapons. Bryce walked in and saw it to be a sort of family tree, many names and relations listed, none of which he recognized, and all of which were handwritten with impeccable penmanship.

"Welcome to my office!" Geaspar called from the shelves as he leaned heavily on his cane and partially on the doorway. "Please have a seat anywhere at the table." Walding and Bryce again obliged to the man's request, taking a seat opposite each other at the end of the table nearest the door.

"Now then," Geaspar continued as he pulled the chair back at the end of the table, seating himself between the two. "I grew up in this inn and bar. My great-grandfather founded it 40 years before the Aging, my grandfather took it from him when he became a man, my father the same. I washed dishes from when I was old enough to reach the sink," he said with a light laugh, to which Bryce also smiled, "and I took over the business at the ripe age of 19. And now at 52, an old man, I am for the first time in my life hearing the phrase, 'The past morrow's past.' If my father's fathers can be trusted to keep accurate records, it is the first time since shortly after the Aging that those words have ever been muttered outside of repetition for remembrance. So, with all that said, may I please ask to whom in Phont's name do I speak." He paused as he caught his breath and cleared his throat. Bryce looked to Walding who sat with his hands folded, focused on Geaspar. Laughter and muffled conversations could be heard between the stomps of feet through the floorboards above them in their silence. No one said anything as Bryce returned his gaze to the large man. He leaned heavily on the table and wiped his brow again with the handkerchief.

"My young counterpart here is Bryce Blooms," Walding said without moving or taking his gaze from Geaspar.

"That name means nothing to me," Geaspar interrupted as he leaned back in his chair. "Should it?"

"No, I don't suppose so. Not yet, at least. One day it may, it's hard to say for certain right now. What may be meaningful to one man may be meaningless to another, and who can say the importance of a man's name in the future?" Walding replied as he began to converse with himself.

"I will say it again. The boy's name means nothing to me. What is your name, old man?" Geaspar replied with a hint of annoyance.

"If you were not interested in the boy's name, I doubt you'll be interested in mine. Why don't we just get down to business as to why I've come to you?" Walding said calmly, hands still clasped and resting on the table.

Geaspar stood in a flash. His leather trench coat fell to the floor as he pulled two steel daggers from his belt, both of which now pointed a half inch from both of their necks. His large coat had obscured his build but he was not as portly as Bryce had thought, he was in fact just a very large muscular man, albeit with a layer of plumpness around his waist. His white tunic sleeves were rolled to the elbows showing his forearms, easily as thick as Bryce's head, and they did not waver in the slightest as they held the heavy-looking metal blades. Bryce did not move; Geaspar had drawn so fast that he was not at all sure what was happening until the knife was at his neck. Walding did not move either, hands still folded and resting on the table, but fear did not seem to grip him as it did Bryce, much to the boy's surprise.

"The boy's name means nothing to anyone and you won't divulge yours," Geaspar continued quietly. "I need your name, old man, and if it is as worthless as the boy's, I will be personally extracting how you came by such a pass phrase to warrant a meeting with me. And my methods of extraction are about as pleasant as skinning a live dragon." Geaspar spoke slowly and emphatically to drive home the gravity of his words. "Now, what is your name?" Walding sighed heavily, still unafraid but very much annoyed. Bryce remained a statue, only his eyes moved as they darted between the two.

"Is the unpleasantry for the one doing the skinning or the dragon being skinned?" Walding asked calmly. Geaspar's scowl deepened and Walding rambled on. "Such an odd phrase that one. In both cases I suppose they are unpleasant. Perhaps that's the point? It's unpleasant either way you go. We were just talking about odd phrases, weren't we, Bryce? 'Cat nap,' Geaspar, is such a strange one." Geaspar pushed the knife into Walding's neck so that the point drew a drop of blood. Walding stopped speaking but did not retreat from the pressure on his throat.

"Your name. Last chance. You've worn my patience and that phrase is too valuable to be spoken by a commoner." Walding sighed again, annoyance replaced by frustration.

"I had thought that phrase was meant for safe passage by members of the Order, certainly enough to instill some trust in the speaker. But if you insist."

"I insist," Geaspar replied and did not waver as Walding breathed in deeply.

"Very well, Geaspar. This is not the time nor place for this reveal. But you speak with Walding Zarlorn," he said plainly as he kept his gaze with Geaspar. Geaspar threw his head back and laughed loudly, the blades never moving from their position. Bryce pulled back a small distance, shocked from the sudden laughter that Geaspar projected.

"What kind of fool do you take me for, old man? Walding Zarlorn fought in the Aging! He was banished publicly but a few months after that. And nearly ages later you expect me to believe the Lord of Storms has arrived at my Worn Thorn looking for help from little ol' me?" Geaspar laughed again just as loud as the first time. Walding still did not move, but Bryce began to sweat as he eyed the blade at his neck, trying to ease his vulnerable flesh away from the cold metal.

"That is correct, Geaspar. Is that not what the phrase is for, to ensure those of the Chosen Order that mutter it find good company?"

"I must apologize, know I do not take pleasure in doing this," Geaspar replied, ignoring Walding's question. "But I must know where you learned that pass phrase. And if you are truthful, I will make your death a quick one and the boy's here even quicker." Bryce felt his brow might now contain enough sweat on its surface to be able to water a small plant he was so nervous. Walding still did not move, hands folded as they were when they first sat at the long table.

"And I too must apologize, Geaspar; you are nothing like your great-grandfather Geardon, whom was certainly one of the best friends I have ever had. You hang his axe upon your wall; it is a memento of what you should strive to be," Walding said as he visibly resisted the urge to go off on a longer tangent and stayed on target, much to Bryce's surprise. "Instead, you lack faith at the most troubling of times! When I produce the phrase, a phrase meant for safe passage, and I am put on trial by the one whom keeping the phrase was bestowed upon! And I did not much care for the last trial I sat on. What I must do now, know that *I* do not take pleasure in doing," Walding replied coolly.

"Do not think yourself impressive, old man! Knowing the family lineage is as easy as bribing a Keeper with a good book," Geaspar replied, but his strong words did not match his eyes. Bryce saw he was put off by Walding's bold statement, and his knowledge of his family seemed to be the driving factor. Walding remained still before sitting rigid in his chair and shifting his folded hands, his thumbs sticking up as they touched at the tips and his pinkies following suit pointing down. The rest of his fingers remained clasped but had loosened so that his palms were very nearly flat on his chest, just below his sternum.

Geaspar smirked at the movements, but his eye twitched mildly. "Pretending to gather will not intimidate me," he yelled in a nervous voice. Walding breathed deeply through his nose and exhaled slowly before beginning his chant.

The balance, The guide, The channel
They gather
The life, The death, The journey
It matters
The burden, The struggle, The triumph
Emboldens
The power, The weakness, The soul
Is Chosen

The flames on the torches flickered dim as Walding finished, Geaspar's brow forming heavy beads of sweat upon it as his blades quivered gently in his hands. Bryce felt the blade press hot against his neck, as if they had been warmed near a fire, and then they were pulled away as Geaspar cried out. He dropped the blades and as the flat end landed on the back of Bryce's hand, he felt the white-hot singe of the metal on his flesh. He jumped back, clutching his hand in a mixture of surprise and pain, as Walding stood simultaneously, hands still folded in the strange manner with his palms tight to his chest. The blades clanged off the table, but before they fell completely, Walding extended his palms and the daggers were swept away by a sudden gust of wind blowing towards the doorway. The knives slammed into the door, points puncturing the wood as they wavered in the wind like tall grass in a storm. Geaspar was blown backwards and fell onto his hip as Walding stepped toward him, the wind still blowing, but now instead of horizontal, it shifted vertical and blew straight down on top of Geaspar, pinning him to the dirty planked floor, years of dust and debris being cleared to reveal the old decaying wood.

"Phont's ghost! It is you!" Geaspar yelled through the howling wind. But Walding did not relent, unblinking as the wind continued to hold the large man down.

"Geaspar Eltenbranch, you are quarreling with someone who has produced the pass phrase! And beyond that, you have attacked them openly and uprovoked, drawing their blood!" Walding bellowed, his voice amplified it seemed by the wind, howling and roaring around the room. "And when he informs you that he is Walding Zarlorn, you double down on this betrayal!"

"Mercy, Grandmaster! You came to me for a reason, do not let my foolishness foil what you have come to accomplish. I was merely vetting out an unknown contact! How was I to know you could live so long?" Geaspar pleaded. Walding's eyes were wild but he fully clasped his hands, returning his fingers to their normal fold as the winds subsided. He lowered his hands to his side and took his seat, breathing in a slow, long breath and exhaling just as slowly. Bryce still stood next to the table, holding the back of his left hand where a blister was already forming from the hot blade's contact. Geaspar sat up slowly from the floor, dirt and soot covering the back of his white tunic.

"Slippery as always, the Eltenbranch's, especially under duress," Walding said with a wry smile. "Perhaps you are more like Geardon than I thought." Geaspar returned a smile embarrassedly as he dusted himself off, still sitting on the floor. Walding motioned for both Bryce and Geaspar to take their seats as he looked up to the still bouncing floorboards; the commotion upstairs seemed to have drowned out the wild wind that Walding had summoned. Bryce rubbed the back of his hand as his eyes remained locked on Walding, wide and unblinking, and he obliged with the old man's request.

"Will you hear me now, Geaspar? Or would you prefer an interrogation?"

"Apologies, a thousand apologies, Grandmaster. I had no idea!" Walding raised his hand to stop the mournful blathering.

"It is done, Geaspar, no sense in worrying about it now. If we could, I have a serious proposition for you."

"Of course, Master Zarlorn, of course! By Phont, I always dreamed the Chosen would return one day!" Geaspar said as he stood and dusted off his pants and shirt with his hands, creating small clouds of filth around the table.

"Yes, my request is in regards to that. I have come to you because the time for the Chosen to rise again has come." Geaspar stopped dusting immediately. "And if that is to happen, we will need our knights to rise with us. Your great-grandfather recruited and organized the Stars in the Grim Age, and I would like you and the Eltenbranch name, the ancestor of Geardon, to do the same in this era and revive the Chosen under a New Order. What say you?" Geaspar blinked in honest surprise as he straightened his chair up from the floor.

"What an honor, Grandmaster." His face was lit with a flash of joy and benevolence but it quickly turned to uncertainty and confusion. "Truly it is. But the Chosen rising again? You of all people should know, you were the last of your kind, banished from Endland, and up until a minute ago I thought you long dead. One Chosen returning, even a Grandmaster, is not enough to revive a fallen Order." Geaspar spoke as he grabbed his cane and overcoat from the floor, eyeing his daggers in the door, and retook his seat at the table.

"I've never left Endland, Geaspar, which I am sure many will find as a betrayal of trust. So, I've not returned, just resurfaced I suppose. But that is beside the point," Walding said, waving his hands in front of him to ward off his unfocused thoughts. "I have seen the world devolve, from afar, but even so I have seen it, and a fork in the road lies ahead for Endland, neither path being particularly smooth. One ends in perhaps the end of the free people and one in a new age. And whether I am received jovially or acrimoniously, and again I do fear the latter will be our reality, I am here to bring forth that new age, and ensure it is as bright as can be. And the centerpiece for all of this, Master Eltenbranch, is not me, but young Master Bryce." Walding finished, plainly gesturing an open hand toward Bryce. Bryce's eyebrows raised in surprise as he sat up in his chair, suddenly forgetting the pain from the burn on his hand. Geaspar looked skeptically toward the boy with eyebrows raised just as high as he rubbed his sore hip.

"I'm not sure what the boy has to do with anything, but times have changed, Grandmaster. My father would tell me stories, passed down from before the Grim Age, when the Chosen were beloved by all, when even catching a glimpse of one in the streets gave you bragging rights to anyone who'd believe you. Phont, even in the thick of the Grim Age you were seen as the only real force between civilization and annihilation, grumblings of foul sorcery be damned. But the Chosen are cursed now by the commoners and the lords alike who believe you existed. Most think of you as nearly forgotten myths." He shifted his weight in his seat and cleared his throat in discomfort. "And what's further, I must agree that if you've truly never left, you'll be seen as a traitor if you resurface. Death awaits those who evade their sentences." Geaspar paused and looked to Walding for recognition of his gloomy declaration. Walding nodded after a moment but did not say anything in response aside from a quick glance to Bryce, who smiled lightly. Geaspar scratched his chin before continuing.

"Although, you are right about the times, they have been getting dark, Grandmaster, for some years now. And as it's darkened, I've searched and listened ever more intently to the lands for signs of the Chosen, as my fathers have before me, dating back to your exile. For years I've waited for a shimmer of a sign, for any glimmer of hope. But never has there been the faintest hint, not so much as an ill-gotten rumor from a dissolute traveler. And now you appear at my doorstep! So, I must ask, what has changed to pry you from hiding?" Walding kept his hands clasped and smiled at Geaspar as Bryce felt his heart flutter in nervous anxiety at his growing understanding of the gravity of the conversation.

"As you know, Kuor-Varz was banished from Endland." Geaspar squirmed in his chair at the name, a pucker crossing his face like he had eaten a sour grape as Walding looked warily at the closed door to the cellar. Bryce darted his eyes between the two in the awkward silence. "Are you certain we are alone, Geaspar?"

"Of course, guests are not permitted below, and I've instructed Lesara to keep an eye on the stairwells. No one will cross her, you've nothing to worry," Geaspar confirmed as he motioned generally back to where the staircase would be. "And could we not mention *his* name anymore? Bad luck, it is, just stick with Grim King, eh Grandmaster?" Walding nodded, still looking uncertainly up at the bar's floorboards now, the thick wood the only divider between them and the raucous strangers above, creaking lightly amid the muffled laughter and chatter.

"Very well. What I am telling you does not leave this room unless I agree to it first. It will not be spoken of unless in my presence. Understood?" Geaspar and Bryce both shook their heads slowly, a little taken aback by the stern tone Walding now spoke in. Walding cleared his throat in uneasiness and exhaled slowly before proceeding.

"As I said, I have seen the world slowly slip into shadow since Kuor-Varz's banishment. Foul creatures slither in the dark, beasts not heard of or seen since the first rise of the Grim. Small towns in the wilderness lock their doors well before sunset now, and it will not be long before the great cities of Endland start to do the same. The High Council of Endland has recognized it and organized the cities' Hunting parties to go out to the other Realms, using up what precious shifting stone Endland has left to do so. What they were searching for remained a mystery to me as I sat from afar, cursing them for being so foolish as to chip away at the stone that powers Endland's only means of protection. But I should know better than to question Petravinos Morgodello, for it all became clear when Bryce chanced a landing near my home." He smirked towards the boy despite the ominous tone of the conversation. A sheepish smile in return, despite Bryce's confusion, allowed the discussion to continue.

"How much the Council suspects is not clear, but I have heard the whispers of the Void. There is no doubt that powerful creatures have always lurked in the dark of Endland but none significant or calculating enough to organize this influx. Too much has happened in too short a time for it to be random chance. It is my opinion that the Grim King is speaking across Realms, from the Medius. Which is really quite incredible if it is him. Communication from a formless world was thought impossible. Can you fathom his reach if he is speaking through the Void?" He cut himself off, realizing a tangent was forming, and read his counterparts, waiting for their response. Bryce's eyes were glazed over in a stupefied but intrigued look while Geaspar had grown more and more pale as Walding spoke.

"Grandmaster, even if all of that is true, even if the Grim King is pulling the strings from the Medius, which I agree is quite impossible, what has changed now that you've come here?" Walding nodded knowingly at Geaspar's point.

"I believe the last vision of Grandmaster Dalma Vo may be at hand." Walding was focused now, and his scatterbrained aura had melted away to an intensive demeanor. It gave off a feeling of security, and even without knowing what was happening, Bryce found himself comfortable and wondering if he was seeing a ghost of Walding's past. As if he heard the boy's thoughts, Walding shifted his eyes from Geaspar to Bryce, with a strong and solid gaze.

"You have arrived here with purpose, young Master Bryce, of that I am quite sure, and not a second too soon. The lords and ladies of Endland have grown fat and docile in the waning years of the peace the Chosen brought from the Grim King's exile. Some even ignore the shadow that spreads, scoffing at the Council's wasting of their resources, most notably King Umbrin. And were Petravinos not such a prominent figurehead, I believe his push for the Hunting parties would have been brushed aside and forgotten. But as fate would have it, he was heard, the Hunt's began, and today, I believe, their efforts have borne fruit." Walding smiled again towards the boy as Geaspar glanced between the two before resting his eyes on Bryce, disbelief and giddy excitement fighting for placement of his facial muscles. He slammed both palms down hard on the table and let out a short hard laugh, standing from his chair in excitement.

"Phont's beard, do you mean to say this boy is Chosen!" He drummed his fingertips lightly on the table in enthusiasm as Walding laughed lightly.

"I believe he is," Walding replied, still smiling, looking upon him. Bryce did not know how to respond, so he elected for a handshake by extending his hand, to which Geaspar ardently accepted, placing two hands on Bryce's, two catcher's mitts that swallowed his hand and wrist whole, and shook vigorously. Bryce sat but Geaspar remained standing and looked upon him, assessing his stature.

"By Phont!" Geaspar finally managed in excitement. "Do you think this means the other rumors are true as well?"

"What other rumors?" Walding replied quickly, unfurling his hands for the first time since their conversation had started. Geaspar laughed loudly, finally sitting back in his chair.

"You've not heard? It's spread like wildfire here on the south shore, probably all over Eislark!" Geaspar interjected. Walding shook his head incredulously, waiting for further detail. "Well, I should first say that it has quickly been discredited, an elaborate hoax by Councilor Lidobol. But just this night there were rumors that two young Chosen arrived at the Roost!"

Walding and Bryce looked to each other giddily. "Whom did you hear this from? Rumors often beget some truth, if the source is at least somewhat credible," Walding asked his large friend as he leaned over the table, beating Bryce to the question.

"The Keepers had traveled to Eislark for the harvest festival when an incoming shifting occurred. An unexpected shifting, from what I was told, but they just happened to be in the right place at the right time and were permitted access to the shifting room in Eislark's tower."

"Hogwash, shifting rooms are sacred places, none save those with explicit permission are permitted entry." Walding crossed his arms in a visual barring of the idea, resting his elbows on the table.

"What if a councilor allowed them entry during the harvest festival tour of the Roost Castle?" Geaspar led with a knowing smile, causing Walding to wince as he held his arms crossed and closed his eyes heavily.

"Lopi Lidobol led the Keepers to investigate an unknown shifting arrival?" he continued, never opening his eyes. Bryce fidgeted his thumbs, frustrated and waiting to interject in the conversation. He could hardly muster the restraint to not over-take their long-winded dialogue.

"Aye, so I was told. I'm sure Lopi ran right to the tower the moment he realized a shifting had occurred. And what do Keepers do but stick their noses where they don't belong? Ol' Loopy led them right to it!"

"How do you know they're actually here and they didn't just make it up?" Bryce interrupted bluntly. He was steadfastly excited at the news, his leg twitching rapidly beneath the table as he attempted to keep his composure. Walding could not help a smirk as Geaspar stammered back, unprepared for the young boy's sharp retort.

"I don't know it's true for sure, but I've spoken with a very reliable source, young Chosen. Do you know Fron Poltis of Eislark? Head Keeper in our city, lives on the north side of the bay in the wealthy part of town?"

"North side of the bay, like San Francisco bay? Are we near Cali, Mr. Zarlorn?"

Geaspar, confused, looked to Walding as the old man shook his head and shrugged. Bryce was anxiously looking between the two men. His leg fidgeted ever quicker with anticipation.

"Remember, Geaspar, Bryce knows very little of our Realm and its people, he is not of Endland."

"Aye, of course!" cried Geaspar. "Such a strange feeling, explaining a world to someone who's never known it. Well, Fron is a Keeper, that is," he paused and thought, "he's sort of a member of a group of historians who chronicle the goings-on of Endland. Very prestigious, very powerful group the Keepers are. And there are many in town here for the harvest festival, as there usually are for such events where the lords convene." Bryce's fingers drummed impatiently on the table and his leg jittered rapidly. Geaspar noticed and redirected his story.

"Anyway, it just so happens that Fron frequents the Worn Thorn on days where he feels he has written something especially divine. Despite his current status, he grew up right here in south Eislark, which has a bit of a reputation for being on the rough side of things, eh? But he likes to come back to his slums to celebrate, away from his ritzy and judgmental neighbors. His words, not mine. We were surprised to see him tonight with the festival going on, but he said he had to leave to write an especially marvelous entry. He was even more giddy than usual, extra thirsty for a celebratory pint, which has turned into at least three by my count. Bragging halfway through his second mug, he said he had just witnessed the greatest event since the Trial of the Exiles, blabbering about how the tome he had written this night would be read and reread for the rest of Endland's history, the smug bastard. And once he started talking 'bout it, he couldn't stop." Geaspar paused for dramatic effect and to catch his breath, heavy shoulders swelling as he deeply breathed the stale cellar air. The others leaned forward in expectancy.

"He said Lopi allowed them into the shifting room, and when they got there, they came upon two boys, completely whole, coherent, and stable. They were dressed mighty strangely, looking overwhelmed and out of place, but unaffected by the shifting. They spoke a short while whilst the sands of the Time Keeper ran through until the last grain fell, and that was that. Two unexpected and unfamiliar children had arrived in Eislark's shifting room. They were taken to Lord Belmar for introductions, then Mikel and Lopi announced it was all a hoax, meant to rile the lord, who certainly was riled, according to Fron. But Fron wasn't buying it as a ruse, especially if it was allegedly staged by Lopi. Fron works rather closely with the wizard and he said jokes against the lord goes against his squeamish persona. So Fron waited till the party had picked up again before he slipped away to his chambers to write and then here to the Thorn to celebrate. 'Words never flooded the paper so easily,' he had boasted. He is no doubt half a drop away from the chuck bucket by now, but Fron is well respected in this town and most of the Eastern Island for his work as a Keeper, especially with his writings on the Belmar tragedy years ago. I'd bet my last copper he saw what he says."

"Two others! Did he mention their names?" Bryce burst, unable to contain his excitement any longer as he leaned into the table with most of his body weight.

"Yes, as a matter of fact he did mention them. Strange names though. Let me see," Geaspar hunched forward as he rubbed his brow with a large hand, massaging the names from memory to the forefront of his mind, "Choony and Jauke?"

"Johnny and Zack?" Bryce burst out again, his chair sliding away as his hand slipped from the table, and he nearly cracked his chin on the old wooden surface.

"Yes, by Phont, that was it! Strange names indeed. Hold now, how would you know such a thing?"

"Walding, those are my friends! They're here!" Bryce was standing, buzzing with excitement, ignoring Geapsar's inquiries. "They made it! Can we go see them?"

"By Phont, *three* Chosen in Eislark! What an incredible day this has turned out to be! But I would not expect to be heading to the Roost, young Chosen," Geaspar laughed the words as he leaned back into his wooden chair and crossed his muscled arms. "You don't just walk into the Lord of Eislark's keep and seek audience with his guests, especially ones that have arrived under such uncommon circumstances, and especially tonight. The harvest festival is a closed castle event. Lords and ladies from all of Endland need protecting, and that doesn't just mean more Gull, they will have members of their own guard as well. Too many strange happenings as of late to allow anyone through except those cordially invited."

"Well, then, what do we do? Can't we get an invite? I mean, we're Chosen, right, that should count for something." Walding stroked his beard, arms crossed still as he thought deeply. Bryce remained standing, his anxious energy walled off like water in a dam, his toes tapping rapidly.

"If Fron has been blabbing to the Thorn's audience, there are no doubt other Keepers who figured the same as he and went off to write their own tomes of the Chosen's arrival," Walding said. "Which means very soon it will be common knowledge, if the lords and ladies don't already know something strange is afoot. They will be vying to use the Chosen by this time tomorrow, mark my words. There are not many individuals with positions of authority that I would trust with Chosen, especially not young Grekory Belmar. A good lad, but too hotheaded to wield such power as the Chosen possess. And what's worse, as this knowledge goes to the public, it will undoubtedly reach the ears of the Grim King's spies. The only action I see is to find them and hopefully retrieve them."

"But Grandmaster, how?" Geaspar stammered.

"Geaspar Eltenbranch, the time for decisions is now. Are you with the Chosen, or are you not?" Geaspar breathed in and held it for a second before releasing and smiling.

"Aye, you know it is runs in my Eltenbranch blood. I am yours, Grandmaster, young Master Bryce. The Stars will be born anew, by Phont I swear it. All is now, as will be, as was."

"Very good, Geaspar. Please kneel."

He did not argue and dropped a heavy knee to the floor, bowing his head before the old man. Walding placed his own hands at his sternum again but no wind or flame manipulation ensued this time.

"Please present your right hand, Geaspar Eltenbranch, and recite your creed."

Evermore, past and future,
Our light must shine Pure
Be Humane, oh Star
And Benevolent
Be Merciful
And Compassionate
Be Brave
And Never cease
All is now, as will be, as was

Walding smiled and breathed deeply, gently took Geaspar's hand with his own, and exhaled, revealing a seven-pointed star on the back of his hand. Bryce gazed in wonder as what looked like a tattoo spun slowly on his skin, the black lines of the star turning gently before they faded, and his hand was clear again. Geaspar too was watching gleefully and smiled a great toothy grin at the sight.

"All is now, as will be, as was. Rise, General Eltenbranch. We head to the Roost."

20

FIRESIDE CONVERSATIONS

———◇———

The boys sat near the fireplace in a pair of overly cushioned chairs, watching the embers glow bright beneath the iron rack. The fire was roaring when Mikel had left them but that felt like ages ago. The candles that burned on the tables gave off more glow than the fire now, and even though someone had knocked and offered to stoke the coals and refuel the logs a few times, the boys had kept their word to Mikel and refused the offer, keeping anyone from entering their room. Zack had tried unsuccessfully to stoke the flames himself with a fire poker but aside from his movement, they had sat motionless the whole evening.

The surreality of the last 12 hours dominated their conversation, Johnny finally ceding that they were not in England, though Zack doubted his seriousness. Neither was accepting of what Lopi had told them to be true, but they also were unable to explain the situation they found themselves in. When it came to their families, it quickly became worrisome, and soon after, they both elected for silence, and sat and stared at the hypnotic sway of the embers' glow on the charred wood's surface, hoping to suddenly snap awake in the hospital. Johnny was sitting with at least three animal pelts wrapped tightly around him and over his head as if he was preparing for the next ice age. Zack was similarly sitting with a pelt. His was draped over his shoulders as he leaned forward towards the dying coals. The last bit of log that had held to the iron rack fell, breaking into a vibrant and short-lived glow before it rested hot orange with the other coals below.

"Well, so much for coming right back. Where do you think he went?" Johnny asked from his blanket mound. Zack shrugged, entranced by the glow.

"Who knows. I'm more annoyed that he locked us in a room without TV and without any phone chargers," Zack said, removing his phone from his pocket and tapping the dead screen for the millionth time. Johnny shifted in his seat, pulling both legs up onto the chair and beneath the blankets.

"Do you think we're going home tomorrow?" he asked with melancholy. Zack pulled his eyes from the fire to his friend. Johnny did not look to him though, he was back to the fire now, a longing in his eyes.

"We can ask Micky when he gets back. Which will hopefully be soon," Zack replied, as he stood with his shoulder-draped fur and moved to the nearest window. Without a response from Johnny, he continued as he pointed out the glass. "I bet he's over by that weird pointy building. Or maybe checking out that creepy looking fog over the water." Johnny hiked up his furs and walked to the window to look out as well. The pointed-roof building was one that was well-illuminated in the darkness. Most of the city could only be seen in spots, small torches scattered through the buildings that sprawled before them. And the sea that they had seen earlier was now to their left and glowing in neon green and blue hues before butting up against the wall of fog. The rest of the sky was uncannily clear, save a single cloud that glided gently past the moon.

"Nah, he's probably back at the festival thing, eating pastries like it's his job," Johnny laughed back.

"Or he ate too many and has been on the toilet this whole time," Zack said with a smile. Johnny laughed loudly, and then put his best "stern Micky face" on.

"'I'll be back as soon as I can. But my bowels are exploding so, honestly, it could be a while,'" he mocked as best he could.

The handle at their door clanged gently as someone attempted to open the door from outside, sapping their soft laughter from the room.

"It's locked," came a very muffled whisper from the far side of the door.

"We should pretend to be sleeping! No pass phrase means it's not Micky!" Johnny whispered as he tiptoed towards the large nearby bed. Zack nodded and followed before a loud and forceful knock stopped them in their tracks.

"Children, this is Lopi Lidobol, I greeted you at your arrival, do you remember?" The children said nothing but tiptoed another step towards the bed. Another swift knock on the door, more forceful than the first.

"Children, are you awake?" came the hallway voice. Zack looked to Johnny and scratched his forehead nervously.

"We wouldn't have slept through both of those, we've got to say something," he whispered as quietly as he could.

"You don't know that," Johnny whispered back as he slid up into the bed. "I'm a very heavy sleeper." Another knock that shook the door frame.

"Children, please, this is of utmost importance." The boys were now sitting in the giant bed, pretending to sleep as the voice became more forceful. There were whispers in the hall but nothing that could be deciphered.

"Come now, children, I'm sure that would have woken you, are you in there?" Zack looked to Johnny with an "I told you so" look.

"Who's there?"

Johnny tried to cover Zack's mouth with his hand, but Zack grabbed his fingers and bent them backwards, prompting Johnny to cover his own mouth with his other hand to prevent his cry of pain.

"Ah, you are awake! Splendid! Please, quickly let us in, there is much to discuss!"

"Can it wait till morning? It's the middle of the night," Zack replied, Johnny giving a thumbs-up in approval of the deflection as he massaged his bent fingers. More whispers from the hallway were heard.

"I am afraid not; this is of utmost importance. Won't you please allow this brief discussion?" The voice was sounding slightly desperate now.

"Is Micky with you?" Zack continued. Whispers again, still indiscernible. "It sounds like someone else is there." The whispering stopped abruptly, and Zack looked to Johnny with a skeptical look.

"No, it is just I, Lopi, do you not remember from earlier? Short with a long beard? And are you hearing things? Perhaps the shifting sickness has taken hold. I should come take a look at you two."

Johnny emphatically shook his head "no." "Micky said no one is to enter and that includes Lopi," he said quietly to his friend, still shaking his head. Zack nodded knowingly in agreement.

"I'm sorry," Zack said to the door, "but I'm really tired, with all the, um, shifting. So, let's talk in the morning." He shrugged to Johnny for approval, who gave him another approving thumbs-up. There was silence outside and the boys relaxed.

"Boys, I cannot stress enough the importance of this," came the pleading voice. "I had hoped to review this together but I understand Mikel's orders. Please, I've a letter I am slipping under the door. Read it quickly and then burn it, and we can discuss it through the door. But please, read quickly! This is terribly important and time is of the essence!"

A letter was promptly and forcefully slid beneath the thick wooden door, stopping as it hit the large rug a few feet away. Johnny sighed in annoyance and, wrapping himself in the largest of his pelts, slid out of bed and walked gingerly towards the letter. He bent down on one knee to grab it and then lowered his head to peek beneath the doorway. It was somewhat difficult to tell, but the torchlight from the hallway was brighter than their room, and it looked to illuminate many more than one set of feet outside their doorway. He saw a knee and a hand press to the floor and he quickly straightened and jumped back, realizing someone was about to check under their door just as he was. He landed softly on the rug and backpedaled closer to the fire as the voice called out again.

"Did you get the letter, children?" the voice cooed. Johnny pointed to Zack to speak as he tried to quietly break the wax seal on the envelope.

"Yes, I've got it here," Zack said, watching Johnny fiddle with the paper. "Opening it now."

"Excellent! Let us know when you've read and burned it, and we can speak."

"Are you sure we can't wait till the morning?"

"Quite sure, I think after reading this you'll see why we must talk now."

"Why don't we just talk about what's in the damn letter instead of reading it?" Zack whispered to Johnny with annoyance. But Johnny ignored him and focused on undoing the wax that sealed the finely folded parchment. Zack could see it was bent into a square, a more intricate fold than a basic half or third bend. Johnny popped the wax from the edge and began undoing the many folds. As he opened it fully, a shimmering dust fell from the note, causing Johnny to hold it up curiously at eye level and sneeze.

"Ah, you've opened it I hear," the voice sneered, dropping from Lopi's high-pitched notes to a much lower octave. "No sense in fighting it. The effects are beyond you."

Zack jumped on the mattress now in fear for his friend as Johnny waved him to stay back, sending more of the shimmering dust into the air. His eyes drooped and he stumbled forward onto the rug, losing his balance. His body limped and his arms hung low, shoulders slumped, as his knees buckled to the ground.

"Inconceivable," he managed before falling face-first onto the plush red rug between the cushioned chairs. Zack panicked. He could not go to Johnny, for fear of breathing in whatever dust had been in the envelope, and he could hear now the whispers from the hall were much louder as they worked on the door lock.

"Got 'em now, eh boss?" came a slimy voice. "Almost too easy with kids, eh?"

"Shut yer trap," came the first voice. "We've only got 'em if your source's information turns out to be true. Otherwise, we've only kidnapped a couple of orphans."

"It'll be your ass if we got swindled," came a third voice, sounding tired and somehow bored. "Do you have any idea how long we've been planning the harvest heist. And to use our Gull armor on a thing like this instead?"

"All worth it, eh, when these'uns turn out Chosen. All worth it. What luck we's have, eh? And she'll be pleased. She will be most pleased. All worth it," the slimy voice hissed. All the while the lock clicked lightly in its metal frame, a crude countdown to the children's demise. Zack slid as quietly as the could from the bed and began blowing out the candles around the room, circling around the rug cautiously. He was unsure how far the strange dust could have spread, and did his best to stay as close to the wall as he could. Facing the dim fireplace, he gripped and dragged the corner of the rug away from the dying coals, tugging Johnny and the two chairs with it. It barely moved a foot as he pulled the weight across the stone floor before a resounding click from the door froze him. Zack regripped and pulled again, another foot, so that Johnny was closer to the door than the fireplace before the chamber door swung open slowly, revealing an unconscious Johnny before the lock pickers. They stepped forward just off the rug looking at the unconscious boy.

"Is the other in a different room?" asked the older gruff voice, looking from side to side from his Gull helm. "Your guy said there would be two here."

Zack smiled from his shadowy hide, still grabbing the edge of the rug and breathing in a slow, silent breath. He then held his breath, fluffed the rug like a bedsheet, and sent a cloud of the mystery dust into the air and into the intruders' faces. They all cried out in surprise, the gruff-voiced Gull stumbling forward, shoving the only member of the trio not wearing armor and causing him to trip over Johnny, tumbling to the rug in a puff of dust. Zack stepped as far back as he could, plugging his nose and pressing his lips to keep the stuff away from his airway. The two standing Gull flailed their hands in the air as the one that had stumbled staggered to his knees and looked around until he found Zack, purple eyes glimmering malice towards the boy.

"Not all sleep, eh?" the creature snarled, standing to its feet as the others took notice of Zack. They took a step towards him as Zack futilely grabbed an extinguished candlestick for defense. If the two were Gull, they were not here to protect him.

"A smart one, eh? Not smart enough. We's wouldn't use such things without proper measures, eh?" Emphasizing the point, the purple-eyed one that had tripped clapped his hands sending a cloud of the dust into the air as he began snorting in deeply. The others chuckled and flanked him on either side as the trio now approached Zack. He unplugged his nose, his hands dropping in defeat at his sides, and dropped the candlestick as one of the Gull removed his helm, revealing an old man with a trim and tight speckled grey beard.

"Up for a trip, young Chosen?" the man asked, smiling cruelly, his voice sounding much older than he appeared. He blew a handful of the mystery powder from his palm towards Zack, who quickly tried to plug his nose and hold his breath again. The world grew black as his eyes melted shut, knees buckling as Johnny's had, and he drifted away before he could feel the floor hit his face.

21

ENTER THE ROOST

The group rushed through the city, Walding leading, darting and dodging people and crates as they made their way towards the castle from the southern shore. Geaspar labored so heavily it sounded as if his lungs might burst, but he kept closely behind Bryce as they followed the old man. The scenery slowly changed from the rundown and disheveled looking buildings and roads near the Worn Thorn to progressively more well-kept homes and shops. The grass between the bricks of the road lessened, the doors and windows were not broken or uneven in their frames, and the crowd walking among the bars became steadily less boisterous. Just outside the castle grounds, the homes grew significantly in stature, well painted in red and white, some with small stables or gardens nearby, and the castle loomed large ahead of it all. They neared the inner wall separating the city from the castle grounds and Walding slowed, holding up a hand to notify the two behind him.

They slipped into the shadows between a small fence and a closed trinket shop and peered out across the cobblestone road at the inner wall. A pair of Gull were on guard along the neat stone road, standing before a large iron barred gate that led inside the castle grounds. The gate had an iron ship etched to the front of it, reflecting the nearby torchlight that was hanging on either side of the entryway. With their angle it was impossible to see what lay beyond the gate. The road, aside from the guards, was mostly empty; the next nearest person was a drunk, very out of place in the evidently higher-class neighborhood, sitting in the same alleyway they hid in, passed out with a fresh bottle of something clasped between his unconscious hands. Some raucous laughter could be heard down the road, where a crowd appeared to have recently stumbled out of an inn based on their nonlinear walking pattern. They were close enough to hear they were conversing but far enough that they could not hear what was being said.

"We must find a way inside. Gull watch the gates in heavy numbers tonight and I don't see my knocking kindly and asking for entry going very well," Walding said to the others quietly. "Or maybe that would work. Honesty is the best policy, is it not? Although it is not really a policy, it's just a word really."

"Master Zarlorn," Geaspar interrupted before the single-point conversation could continue further, "if we're planning on taking the Chosen away from Lord Belmar, I don't think a formal greeting is the way to go. I doubt very much he will hand them over to a should-be-banished 'traitor.'"

Walding smirked shamefacedly. "Right. Another way in then."

Walding surveyed the road again and glanced upwards at the towers and bridgeways that connected the many buildings of the castle grounds before he slid back into the shadows and closed his eyes, clasping his hands at his midriff as he had in the Worn Thorn's cellar room.

"Geaspar, you'll need to call the guards to the gate. There are likely more concealed behind the wall. Bryce, you'll need to run to the wall and jump. Get to the shadows, I'll be close behind."

"Aye, I think I've got a way to get their attention. You and the boy will be nigh invisible. But jumping the wall, Grandmaster, is that possible?"

Bryce looked to both of them and then to the wall across the way, at least 15 feet high. "Mr. Zarlorn, you mean jump that wall? Right in front of us?"

"Trust an old man, would you both? Run and jump when I say, Master Bryce."

Bryce looked to Geaspar for reassuring logic; Geaspar shrugged away the impossibility of what was being asked.

"Go Geaspar, and pull them the other way," Walding instructed. With a nod Geaspar was off, grabbing the bottle from the unconscious drunk near them as he shuffled from the shadows towards the guard post down the cobblestoned road. He stumbled slowly as he began to sing in a boisterous tone, swigging heavily between verses.

Oh, down the road,
Oh, down the lane,
To beer and cheer and mead and puke!
For on we go, to find Phont's hold
And drink in his tavern again and again!

The drinks there be topped,
The drinks there be cold,
And e'er which way, the women, behold!
With company so near and booze aplenty
Tomorrow be damned, to this night I will hold!

Oh, down the road,
Oh, down the lane,
To beer and cheer and mead and puke!
For on we go, these words we crow
If ever we're sober, then send us to Klane!

His voice was off-key and obnoxiously off rhythm as he stumbled up to the gate. He hiccuped loudly following his final word, tripped unathletically on a displaced cobblestone brick, and braced himself firmly on the iron barred gate with a big meaty hand. The Gull quickly shoved him away, staring at him with the dead eyes of their metal helms. Geaspar quickly perked up at the sight and saluted with his bottle hand, spilling some of the liquid on his short hat.

"Salute! The Gull are here!" he yelled to no one as he licked the corner of his mouth to catch a spilled drop. Looking up to his hat and to his saluting bottle, he quickly switched it to his non-saluting hand, but not before taking a generous swing.

Still saluting, he began to yell loudly, "Ho hut ho har! The Gull of Eislark march near and far! Let's have a drink and have a dance, just you and me, now hold my bottle, I've got to pee!" He chortled to himself, bending over as he began to cough from the excessive laughter. Distant laughing could be heard from the drunks down the road and a few more 'Ho hut!' chants echoed and cheered him. The two Gull did not move.

"Aww come on! I've really got to piss," he smiled side-eyed, "Or is it perhaps you'd like to hold something else whilst I piss and I can hold me bottle myself, eh?" He howled again in laughter taking another healthy swig before aggressively throwing the bottle against the gate, nearly falling over from the force of the throw and laughing all the louder as it shattered. The gate opened immediately as four more guards stepped onto the streets, all six of them forming a semicircle around the still-laughing Geaspar.

"Ho! Unfortunately, I've just broken me bottle, so only one thing left to hold now!" He started to back away from the knights with his hands up, still laughing, moving step-by-step away from the nook that the others hid in.

"What gentlemen the Gull are, eh!" Geaspar yelled to the other drinkers down the road, still backing his way toward them. They cheered again for him, though some now moved back inside the inn after seeing the Gull on the move. Geaspar raised his hands in victory, laughing as he continued to faux-drunkenly backpedal and leading the Gull ever further from their post.

"Now, run and jump!" Walding whispered. Bryce looked to him and to the wall.

"But Mr. Zarlorn—"

"Now!"

Bryce shook his head in frustration before turning and sprinting towards the wall. He jumped early, thinking to land just in front of it instead of face-planting into it. As his feet left the stone, he saw the ground shrink beneath him, much to his surprise, and he barely cleared the top of the wall as he pulled his feet to his chest to avoid the sharp protrusions that lined the top of the stone structure. As soon as he cleared it, he felt gravity take hold again, pulling him down quickly before slowing at the last moment, allowing him to land gently behind a few barrels; his feet hit the ground as if he had jumped the last stair of a staircase, not a 15-foot barrier. He whirled around to verify the height of the wall was still as tall as it seemed on the other side. A shadow moved above him and he stepped closer to the wall to allow it to move past. Descending from above in the same manner as he had, Walding stepped down behind the barrels, just as gently.

"Come, your friends will either be in chains or living like kings. My guess is the latter—Lord Grekory's attempt at flattery. And given Umbrin has stayed in Trillgrand this harvest, the king's quarters is the best bet," Walding whispered as they slipped quietly closer to the main castle keep. Beyond the wall Geaspar could be heard trying to dissuade the guards from taking him in, sounding much more sober than he had just a minute ago. Bryce followed Walding around the corner from where they had landed, moving under a straw awning. The old man's hand pressed Bryce's face, squishing him against the building surface.

Two guards patrolling the open courtyard walked through an inner gate into the open area across the way from them, a torch being carried by each. As the guards neared them, Bryce saw where the torchlight should have illuminated them hiding in plain sight, the fires dimmed instead, siphoning away like a candle at the end of its wick and leaving the pair concealed in the dark beneath the overhang. The pair of guards walked by without a glance in their direction, though they did look curiously at the dull light of their torches for a moment, continuing past where Bryce and Walding had jumped the wall and through another archway which led to a different area of the courtyard. The light returned to their torches and their surrounding area as Walding continued to hug the wall. Bryce moved to ask Walding what had just happened, but the old man was already moving quickly across the open area and further into the castle keep.

Bryce followed as they scampered across the courtyard to the opposite side through the archway the patrolling guards had come from. The archway opened to a wide alleyway between two large portions of the castle and seemed to lead toward the stables based on the growing smell of quarantined animals. An open-faced roofed bridge extended above them a few stories up, which connected the two buildings they stood between. Walding pointed it out in silent instruction as they shuffled down the alley as quietly as they could. A door could be seen ahead on their left at the far end of the building, a single torch lit on the frame, but thankfully it was without a watchful guard. The alley they traveled dead-ended into another wider road, from which some light conversation could be heard, growing louder as the infiltrators continued. But Walding did not slow. He moved towards and stealthily opened the large door, the sounds of chatter growing louder as Bryce slipped inside close on his heels before Walding silently shut it. Shuffling armor was heard outside in the alley where they had been moments before. Bryce breathed deeply to try and calm his racing heart, but Walding was already moving.

Inside and directly ahead was a long hallway, and to their left was a set of spiraling stone stairs, the same color as the outside stone castle but decorated with hanging candles on the walls and red and white ribbon trim spiraling upwards at eye level. Walding made quick ascension up the stairs, Bryce following as if he were the old man's shadow. They passed one landing where two Gull stood looking down the second-floor hall, close enough where Bryce could have grabbed their weapons, and up to the third landing. This one was bare of guards and followed a similar pattern, with the hallway extending left and a doorway to the right.

Walding did not hesitate and creaked the door open, sliding out onto the bridge and motioning for Bryce to follow before closing the door lightly behind them. The walkway was barren except for the series of torches that lit both ends and a pair that stood at the midpoint. They made their way across it, being sure to stay crouched low to avoid detection from any wandering eyes below. A set of patrol guards could be heard passing below them, bickering about something that they could not quite make out, and Bryce couldn't help but peek and see the many pairs of torch-lit patrolmen wandering the grounds. Walding promptly rapped the back of his head, and Bryce embarrassedly ducked his head back and continued across the bridge.

At the far end, they slid into the shadows of the small alcove that the door sat in. The torches burned on the wall next to their heads, and the recess was just wide enough for their shoulders to be hidden. Walding grasped the ring of the handle, gesturing for Bryce to go first but before he could, the door was pushed open. Bryce saw Walding's eyes widen before the door blocked him from view. Again, the light was siphoned from the surrounding area, this time completely snuffing all the bridge torches, thin wisps of now dead fire floating in the evening air.

Bryce squinted his eyes, peeking out in horror as two Gull exited the building, carrying heavy-looking sacks and escorting a vile-looking elf with shimmering purple eyes and an off-putting scowl. The light from the torches in the hall had also been put out from what Bryce could tell, for he was still hidden in the shadows of the door recess while Walding was hidden behind the opened door. The Gull and the elf paused in the doorway. From the wrinkles that formed on the elf's forehead, the scowl seemed to be a common expression for the elf, etched deep like glacial grooves into rock. That is not to say that he appeared old, worn perhaps, but not old. And holding his equally tatty cloak together was a large dirty-looking broach, decorated with an eye that was both open and closed, the eyelid split vertical through the pupil to allow it to see and not see at the same time. The dinginess of the jewelry, which was a generous classification given the level of grime that covered the broach, matched the rest of the elf's garb; his thin over cloak was ripped and full of small holes. Bryce guessed they may have been the only clothes the elf had worn for years. Nothing about him seemed pleasant.

No one said anything, the lidless eyes of the Gull helms staring forward as Bryce's deep blue eyes watched the trio through squinted eyes, trying to conceal the whites of his eyeballs. To Bryce's surprise, the Gull marched forward, pulling the chained elf with a swift jerk on the binds around his wrists and closed the door without event. The elf snarled, first at the Gull and then at where Bryce stood in the darkness, as he passed. Bryce did his best to meet the elf's ferocity but found himself retreating, leaning back from him as he walked by. He thought the shadows concealed him in the darkness, but the elf's direct gaze said otherwise. The Gull continued across the bridge without acknowledging them any further and disappeared behind the door that Walding and Bryce had just come from. The light returned to the torches. Walding stepped from behind the door with his hands clasped near his chest and his face crunched in confusion, curiously watching the door that the Gull had left through. Bryce waited a moment to follow again, but Walding remained fixated.

"Mr. Walding," Bryce whispered as he peered over the walkway's edge, "we should keep going. I don't think they saw us." Walding looked back to Bryce still befuddled but nodded, grasped the handle, and followed Bryce quickly into the hallway. Walding took the lead again once inside, taking the hallway directly ahead of them from the doorway with rapid but silent footsteps. Avoiding a few patrols, the pair made their way deeper inside the castle, Bryce always a step behind the old man as he weaved his way through halls and side rooms with precise furtiveness. Another staircase upwards and a final left turn led them to a pair of double doors, which Walding cracked open slightly. On the other side were a pair of Gull, manned at the door that Walding had pried open. They were at the base of a large tower where a great many people seemed to be celebrating. A stairwell wrapped the large square structure, starting on their right, but how high it went was difficult to say with the door only partially opened. Walding held back Bryce near the edge of the doorway before he stepped back, holding out his palm for Bryce to see.

"We are here," he said, pointing to the base of his palm near his wrist, "and we need to get here, up one floor." He then pointed near where his fingers connected to his hand. "The stairs are immediately to our right. We must go up that flight to the corner, up another flight past a set of doors to the next corner, and then up again so we are opposite of where we are now. There are guards at the double doors, both where we are about to exit and where we must enter. There may be others on patrol as well further above us."

Bryce nodded, waiting for further instructions, looking attentively to Walding's open palm. Walding peeked through the crack in the door as the sounds of laughter and conversation floated through. Bryce peeked too and found a few groups of people standing around talking and drinking from large cups as others walked around with large serving slabs covered in delicious-looking foods. They both leaned back inside the hall.

"I will extinguish the flames and then we must rush up to the top as quickly as we can. The Gull will be on alert when it goes dark, so do your best to avoid them. Stay close behind me, and we should be alright. Any questions?" Bryce scrunched his face.

"What's with all the people here?"

Walding shook his head, annoyed.

"It is the harvest festival, remember? The lords and ladies of Endland have come to Eislark for their yearly celebration. But that is not what I meant, I meant do you have any questions on how to get to from where we are to where we are going in the manner I've just described?"

"If it's a party, and there are a million people from all over, why don't we just walk through and pretend to be guests?" Bryce said, laughing lightly. Walding opened his mouth to argue, then closed it and peeked through the crack again. He turned back, smiling.

"Alright, young Chosen. I suppose that will work. Follow me, say nothing unless you are repeating me." Bryce nodded, smiling back, and they walked into the large tower together. The Gull at the door did not say anything as they passed, Walding giving them a smile.

"Fortune, good Gull," Walding said cheerfully.

"Mmm, yes, fortune, good sir," Bryce repeated in an arrogant aristocratic voice. The Gull stomped their pikes but did nothing else. Walding turned to wink at Bryce as they continued towards the stairs, the pair nodding and granting fortune to the few guests who glanced their way; the guests were smiling gleefully to each other and whispering intently as they eyed the boy. Bryce thought at first their giddiness was a side effect of what he guessed was wine in their goblets, but something about the way their eyes lit up told him otherwise. A small wake of whispers followed them as they walked, as a boat glides through the water. They walked up the stairs and past the first set of Gull, a pair stationed outside the mid-floor landing, Bryce swallowing hard as the guests became more liberal with their comments. Chosen ... clothes ... strange— tidbits of gossip caught his ears and as Bryce thought they had passed the guards, one of them slammed their pike to the floor. The guests pulled some attention from Bryce, shocked by the loud bang to the stone floor. The Gull were moving from their post, slowly walking behind the pair now. Bryce shuffled up quickly besides Walding.

"Mr. Zarlorn, those knights are following us, I don't think a 'fortune' is going to fool them."

"Yes, I know. Keep walking, stay close." Walding replied without turning towards him, smiling to the curious guests as they continued up the stairs to the second corner. More of the partygoers had taken notice now, and as the pair turned to continue up the last set of stairs, the Gull behind them slammed their pikes in unison again. This time the guests seemed to understand something was wrong, their chatter and laughter being subdued by their curiosity at the Gull's be- havior. Bryce stutter-stepped at the noise, but seeing Walding continue his stride without hesitation, Bryce quickly contin- ued next to him.

He saw Walding clasp his hands together in the strange manner he had at the Worn Thorn, thumbs extended up, pinkies extended down, and palms tight to his body, resting just above his navel. They rose up the last set of steps, passing a group of cackling women, laughing obnoxiously and taking full advan- tage of their invitation to food and wine. This group was one of the few sets of individuals who was not watching Bryce, Wald- ing, or the Gull, too inebriated to hold attention on anything but their own conversation. Walding peeked over his shoulder to see the Gull behind them still, one lifting his face guard to address them. The Gull stationed at the hallway they wished to enter also made their way towards them now, Bryce taking another step closer to Walding as the knights worked to corral them. Walding breathed in deeply and then slowly exhaled.

A scream from behind them gave pause to the Gull's pursuit. Walding stopped now to turn and look, as did Bryce. One of the women from the group that they had passed was hanging over the edge of the stair rail, dangling in the center of the open tower like a leaf on a branch.

"Help, please someone!" she cried out as her friends did their best to help her up without spilling their own wine, one laughing so hard at her friend's predicament that she fell over, sitting ungracefully on her rump as her wine sloshed over the edge of its cup and onto the stone floor. Bryce turned to run back to help but was stopped by a stern clearing of the throat by Walding, who looked down to him and nodded towards their destination. The Gull that had been following the pair quickly ran over to assist, and the Gull at the top of the stairs ran past Walding and Bryce as well. Walding chuckled softly.

"Some just cannot handle their drinks, eh, boy?" Bryce looked to him concerned. Walding turned away from the ruckus and continued up the stairs quickly. He breathed deeply again as Bryce watched another woman from the group trip suddenly and stumble down the last few stairs, wine flying across the red rug that fit tightly to the stairs. Bryce was turned forcefully away from the scene with one of Walding's hands on his shoulder as he motioned with his head again to the hallway. He quickly re-clasped his hands as they ascended up the last few stairs and opened the doors just wide enough to slip between them and into the hallway. Walding unhooked his hands fully as the door closed, stretching and wiggling his fingers as if his grip had grown tired as they walked.

"Did you make that happen somehow, Mr. Zarlorn?" Bryce asked after they had walked a few steps beyond the door.

"I think that accident was purely influenced by her excessive consumption of wine, my boy," he replied with a smile, not turning to address him. Bryce did not return it, concern still on his face. Walding looked to him from the corner of his eyes and sighed. "She was never in any danger, my boy. I was holding most of her body weight myself. Once the Gull reached her, I let them take over, but I would not let her fall."

"You were holding her body weight? What, with your mind powers? Is that how I was able to jump the wall outside?" Bryce asked skeptically.

"Yes, similar to how you leapt over that stone wall, but not with 'mind powers,'" Walding alluded with a cool smile. Bryce remembered the feeling of almost floating over the 15-foot outer wall a few short minutes ago and dropped his skeptical look. "There is much that is possible as a Chosen, Master Bryce. The rules of the natural universe need not apply to you, if you so desire. But that is a lesson for another time, I think. We can speak on this when we have found your friends, which will be very soon now. The king's quarters are just around the bend here."

Bryce forgot his disbelief immediately and skipped next to Walding in excitement. They rounded a short corner and came upon a magnificent set of double doors, ornate and glistening gold trim reflecting the bountiful torchlight. Walding stopped and extended his arm to usher Bryce behind him. Bryce obliged anxiously and looked over Walding's arm to see what gave Walding pause. Nothing seemed out of the ordinary aside from both of the doors being slightly ajar. The sound of doors closing heavily behind them moved Walding again, as footsteps could be heard coming down the hallway towards them.

"Quickly into the room," he whispered. "But behind me. Something is not right."

Walding pushed opened the door just enough to squeeze through as Bryce followed closely, and then closed it softly behind him, gently with both hands to minimize any noise it might create. He quickly turned and grabbed Bryce by his shoulders to prevent him from entering the room further. They both stood with their backs against the door in the almost complete dark as the shuffling of armor was heard distant, but getting closer. A fire had been going at some point, but it was mostly dead embers now, giving off a very faint orange glow to a pair of chairs sitting on a rug. The rest of the room was shadow and moonlight, dim outlines of a messy bed and a few small tables, but no people. Walding walked the perimeter of the room to his left to one of the tables with a plate of half-eaten food and a knocked over candleholder upon it. He reached out with his palm towards the candle, feeling for warmth, before he picked it up and tilted it to the side until a thin bead of molten wax dripped off the top and onto the table surface. He looked around the room again in confusion.

"These have just been put out but none rest in the bed," Walding whispered aloud. "I cannot think of another guest besides King Sarn himself who would be admitted to these chambers, aside from your prospective Chosen friends." Bryce rubbed his eyes sleepily and yawned.

"Yea, I guess that makes sense. Are they at the festival thing still?"

"Perhaps. But no guards at an open door to the king's quarters is another peculiarity. Even without anyone staying in this room it is watched to reassure nothing can be done while it is unoccupied. The fact that we could sneak into this room so easily says something is amiss." He yawned loudly as he finished his last sentence, the words melding with his drawn-out exhale. Bryce again nodded with drooping eyes.

"Well, let's go check the party or something. I might fall asleep standing up if we stay here any longer." Bryce turned to walk towards the door and tripped on the edge of the rug, which was heaped near where they stood. He stepped heavily onto the soft surface to catch his balance and a small cloud of shimmering dust puffed up around his ankle. Walding braced him on the shoulders and pushed him hard towards the doorway, Bryce stumbling another step across the rug as small clouds of the dust followed his feet.

"Hold your breath and stay away from the dust! Back into the hallway, now!" Walding said loudly. Bryce turned and looked to him with eyes half open and slack-jawed, but he obliged and sleepily opened the door with a pull as his cheeks puffed with air. He entered the bright hallway face-to-face with two Gull, walking on patrol towards him, and immediately expelled the air from his mouth in shock. Outside of the room, Bryce felt his body awaken, whether from the lights or the jump in heart rate from seeing the guards, he did not know. He heard Walding's

footsteps behind him in the doorway and reacted, pulling the
door mostly closed to keep the old man from entering the hall
himself.

"Hi there!" he cried out to the guards. "Any chance I can go
back and get some more food! Me and my buddy are starving
here!" The Gull approached him slowly and looked to each other, stopping a few feet from him as he leaned back against the
door. They both shook their heads "no" as one of them pointed
towards the room. The other looked side to side in the hallway
and down the other winding path.

"Well, can you grab some for us then? Please, just a little
food?" Bryce begged as best he could without sounding frightened. The guard that was looking around stepped forward and
lifted the face guard of his helm as he bent at the waist to address Bryce at eye level, revealing a large block head, scarred
and battered. His nose looked to have been broken at least once
and his forehead was permanently scowling, dark lines etched
into his tan skin.

"Where are your guards?" he asked in a deep, slow voice.
Bryce shrugged innocently.

"I don't know, aren't they supposed to be watching me, not
the other way around?" He attempted to joke mildly with a
cheesy grin. The Gull did not so much as twitch at the boy, keeping the same stoic unwavering stare. Bryce swallowed hard and
audibly as the Gull breathed heavily out of his flared nostrils.

"Bring out your friend," he said at last. The other Gull stood
by motionless, watching the pair. Bryce swallowed again.

"Well, you see, he's afraid of you guys so that's why I'm asking, and not him. If we could just get some food, we could go
back to bed."

"He should be afraid," the Gull replied coldly. "Bring him
out."

Bryce thought hard, mind racing.

"Well, you can go get him if you want, but I'm telling you he is
terrified of you guys. He's probably going to cry and then you'll
have a real mess on your hands. Plus, on top of all that, we will
still be hungry." Bryce heard a scuffle from behind the door and

a smile crossed the thick man's face, the first look that was not outright glowering. He stood straight, lowered his face guard and slammed his pike. His partner did the same and they both marched towards the door, pushing it quickly as they entered. Bryce waited outside in nervous anticipation, hoping Walding had found a safe hiding spot. He smiled, remembering the way the lights had been doused around them as they snuck through the castle grounds; of course, he had found a good hiding spot. Soon after they entered he heard a heavy thud followed by another and the sound of metal clanging metal. The door opened after a few seconds and Walding stepped back out of the room into the hallway, very sleepy-looking, but otherwise OK, and quickly closed the door behind him.

"Brilliant, Master Bryce. Simply brilliant," he said with a broad smile. "You are quite perceptive, and quite lucky they did not realize you were not the right child." Bryce gave an overexaggerated and sheepish smile.

"Yea, I was really hoping they hadn't met Zack and Johnny yet. That could have been bad. But what exactly is in that room, some sort of sleeping powder?" Walding nodded as he looked back to the door and sighed, rubbing his eyes to awaken before stroking his short scraggly beard in contemplation before responding.

"Yes, and with it being in their room, I now fear the worst. I fear they have been taken."

"Taken where?"

"Impossible to say, really. The festival has collected every lord and lady from across Endland. Any one of them could have taken a risk in extracting them for their own gain. And if the information from Geaspar is true, and the Keepers have already started blabbering about a potential arrival of Chosen, then we must also consider those whom operate in the shadows of Eislark know that they have arrived as well. Grim, Everseen, Black Hands, some random dolt who's hoping for a king's ransom. Phont only knows now."

"Can't you like, magic them back here or something? With your hand thingy?" Bryce asked in desperation as he folded his hands to best mimic the way Walding had done, wiggling his thumbs wildly. Walding let out a short, concise chuckle.

"That is not how it works, my boy. I wish it were so, but no. Such a gift was not bestowed upon me."

"Well, how do you know? Did you even try?" he said, still fiddling with his hands. Walding calmed him as he took Bryce's hands and adjusted his fingers, moving them so the tips of Bryce's thumbs touched and pointed up and his pinkies pointed down.

"I basically had it right," Bryce said looking to his hands, trying to memorize the feel. "Kind of a weird setup, you know?"

"Yes, but it must be held tight to your body, right at the bottom of your ribs here." Walding pushed Bryce's hands to his own chest gently. The moment he did so, Bryce went limp on his feet, eyes hazed and distant, as his lips parted slightly. Walding felt his hands pressured back by an unseen force and quickly fought his arms back to Bryce's shoulders.

"Bryce!"

22

GATHERED

The moment his open palms touched his body the world grew dark, and he found himself in the same castle hallway but now it was cold and dank, shadows dripping from the walls like honey from a spoon. The smell was not sweet though; musty and foul it stunned his lungs and nose with its odor. He saw Walding become a grey and blurry blob, muffled cries coming from him like he was being smothered with a pillow. He felt his leg pulse in a strangely satisfying pain as he listened intently, focusing on the incomprehensible mumbles coming from what he still assumed was Walding. It was eerily similar to what he had seen when he had stabbed the creep back in the hospital, and thinking about the encounter gave him a paranoid tingly feeling on his skin.

"Walding?" Bryce called out to the blob. There was a rush around him, the world shifting in a grey and black mass before his eyes. It stopped as suddenly as it had started, and Bryce saw a young blond man, kneeling before a crowd as they pelted him with stones and debris. Bryce tried to move his hands from his chest, but they were glued, locked tight to his body as if by unseen chains. A group of men and women around him were chanting loudly as a disc wobbled above the man's head before crashing down on top of him. Another rush of black and grey and he was standing over the man still, but gone were the people and the castle, and instead the man was sitting in an open field with soft tears running down his cheeks. The man stood slowly as a sharp gust of wind whipped by him, severing the chains that bound his hands to his side.

"Walding?" Bryce cried out again, louder and more frantic. Another mirage of grey and black, and now he saw Walding in the hallway they had just stood in, clearly this time, grabbing Bryce by the shoulders and shaking him rapidly. He could make out the faint echoes of his voice now, calling Bryce's name in his old, waned tone. Bryce felt himself pulled to his shadow body as his leg again pulsed in a comforting ache. He took a step towards his body and stopped, looking around quickly.

"Zack, Johnny!" he yelled to the shadow world. The shadows swallowed him in their swarm before stopping abruptly on a dirt road. Three hooded people walked silently ahead of him, one with a sack over their shoulder and another pulling a cart as the third led the trio with a torch. Bryce looked curiously to the group and along the dirt path in both directions. Ahead, the road wound slowly into a forest where another group of people had just emerged on horseback, trotting slowly towards him. Small huts and cottages dotted the bleak-colored countryside on either side of the road, fields of grain and vegetables stretched between the living spaces. Behind him stood a city, a great wall surrounding it with a few castle towers protruding over the tops of the wall. Even with the shadows Bryce recognized it as Eislark, the distinct steep sloping roofs atop the tallest towers gave away the castle identity instantly. He looked back to the trio still confused.

"Zack, Johnny!" he called again. He morphed through the world, but only a few feet, to close the distance that the group had walked away from him. Bryce watched them walk a few more steps and shivered in the cold of the shadows. He walked a few steps behind them, looking side to side for any sign of his friends. A sack atop the cart that the tallest of the mystery people dragged shifted as it ran over a bump in the road and out popped a pair of arms, bound together, and a head, glasses glinting on a boy's face. Johnny was gagged by a piece of cloth, which he promptly pulled out of his mouth as he surveyed the landscape.

"Bryce!" came Walding's voice loud and booming but distant through the clouds. The man leading the group hesitated and turned around, looking curiously to the air. Bryce saw his purple eyes and the strange eye broach, half open with a vertical eyelid. The elf turned back and continued walking away from the city, catching up the few steps to the others.

"Ah, Bryce is his name, is it?" a voice cooed softly from behind him. Unlike Walding's, this one was clear and directional, but as Bryce turned to see the source, he saw only the farmer's fields and the small houses. He shuddered, but this time not from the cold. A pair of eyes, at least twice as tall as Bryce, opened among the plants, as if a picture of the landscape had been taken and was now plastered on a giant face. No other features could be seen, only the eyes, huge and bloodshot, and they provided the only color the world offered thus far, a vibrant intense green against red veins. A wicked grin appeared below them, opening in the field as the eyes had, formed to a hidden figure, showing its large, decrepit yellow rotting teeth. The eyes blinked eyelids of pictured vegetation and scanned the area as Bryce averted his eyes in fear, up to the sky. The face formed in the clouds now, same as it had in the fields, as if the cloud imagery were someone's skin. The huge face looked intently, searching for him, Bryce was sure of it. The boy looked around frantically for a way out of the shadows, globs of the darkness dripping from the cart and trees and grass, a flowing world of glum, all with the otherworldly face scouring from above.

"Walding!" he yelled as he transported back to the castle, the eyes seeing him for a moment before he was in the hallway where Walding was still holding Bryce, shaking his shoulders frantically trying to wake him. Bryce ran towards his body as his leg swooned in pain, and he attempted to shoulder check himself, diving forward hard. He felt the contact and fell hard to the floor, his hands unclasping as he sucked in air rapidly, hyperventilating on the floor of a brightly lit and colorful hallway. Walding knelt beside him in dismay, worry laid plain on his old wrinkled face.

"My boy, what happened? Are you alright?"

Bryce breathed heavily but nodded, trying to catch breath he did not know he had lost. "I saw you!" he finally managed. "Or I think it was you. Were you ever chained up and then smashed by a floating plate?" Walding's face locked and his eyes told it all. Bryce continued before he could answer. "And I saw Johnny and Zack! Well, at least Johnny! They are on a road outside the city by a bunch of farmland. That elf and two others have them! Wow, I just said 'that elf.' Do elves even exist?" He remembered the face and shuddered visibly at the thought. "And I saw something else. Something or someone in the fields." Walding's face was aglow with fascination and anxiety as he moved to help Bryce to his feet.

"Remarkable, without even as much as an explanation you've tapped your abilities. And of course, elves exist, but what elf do you mean? Were they walking together? I don't recall introducing you to any elf. Were they at the Worn Thorn? Quickly, someone will have surely heard my yelling to you. Or perhaps elf means something else to you than it does to me?" His questions came as quickly as Bryce could process them.

"Johnny was in a bag on a cart being pulled by the tall guy, and I'm guessing Zack was in the other bag that the elf was carrying," Bryce replied, unable to focus on the other quick-hitting questions. He clenched a fist in frustration and sudden realization, "Those guards were carrying two bags! That was Zack and Johnny! We were right there!"

"What guards? We've passed many to this point." He thought on it for a moment. "Do you mean on the pass between buildings?" Walding said as he offered to help Bryce up. Bryce nodded and accepted Walding's extended hand, grasping it and pulling himself up before wincing and falling back to the floor as his leg gave out. He sat up, holding his thigh with both hands, his fingertips digging into his skin with a painful grimace as his leg locked out straight. Walding knelt again and opened the tear in Bryce's pant leg slightly. Dark black veins radiated from where Bryce had thought the gash from stabbing Jamesett had healed. Instead, there was a dark center where the shrapnel had punctured him and plum-colored lines radiating from it, which seemed to give off a faint dark glow. Walding pulled back the tear to its fullest and found that they stretched down to the top of his kneecap and up a few inches to his upper thigh. Walding looked to him gravely.

"Is that infected?" Bryce asked modestly before shaking off the thought. "Whatever, we've got to get Zack and Johnny, they had them in bags! The guards we hid from on our way in. They were escorting an elf on that open bridge, the ones that nearly saw us at the doorway. He had purple eyes, I've never seen eyes like that, and that weird eye pin." Bryce asserted as he extended his hand for another pull. Walding hesitantly obliged, gingerly lifting him with both hands this time and stabilizing as much of Bryce's weight as he could. Bryce stood pat for a moment before Walding offered his walking staff to Bryce and helped steer him further down the hall.

"Describe the pin you saw." Walding demanded tersely as a set of doors behind them were heard opening with heavy footsteps following. Bryce looked back at the sound before Walding snapped his fingers to regain his attention, squaring him face-to-face with a pull on his arm.

"The pin boy, describe this pin you saw!"

"It was an eye, but it was half open. But like not normal half open, the eyelid was split up and down. So, the left half was an eyelid, but the right side was the actual eye." He held his fingers vertical in front of his own eye to offer a visual, pointing left and right as he spoke. Walding closed his eyes in an extended thoughtful blink and then pulled him again down the walkway as they labored around a bend into a wider hall with multiple windows on the one side that overlooked the city and the bay. The opposite side was lit with many torches but was void of doorways or additional passageways. It seemed to be a type of observation deck, and a couple could be seen at the furthest window from them, arms wrapped around each other as they looked out over the illuminated town.

"The Undreaming do not pull such bold heists, but that eye is unmistakable. How did they move so quickly? They shouldn't be this organized. Has she returned? Has her power grown to see such future events?" Walding spoke with himself as they reached the end of the hall, past the couple, and rounded the

corner to find a pair of Gull approaching. Walding quickly turned them around back to the windowed hall, the couple
turning to express their displeasure at the commotion behind
them. Walding and Bryce nearly reached the other hall when
another pair of Gull rounded the far side, accompanied by a
handsome-looking man, two scimitars on his hips, looking
rather panicked. Walding quickly turned them around again to
go look out the windows.

"Micky?" Bryce asked aloud, seeing the man down the hall.
Walding straightened at Bryce's recognition and pulled a swift
tug on Bryce's arm to stop them.

"You know this man?"

"Yea! It's Micky!" Bryce cried out, pulling his arm free from
Walding's grip. Mikel jogged the short distance down the hallway to meet them, an enormous smile upon his face as he
opened his arms in welcoming joy.

"Bryce? By Phont, is that you?" Mikel ran forward and gave
him a hug as a father would to his son, Bryce doing his best to
keep his balance on his one good leg. Walding looked to the pair
in utter confusion.

"How is it you are here?" Mikel continued, pulling back and
squatting slightly, holding both Bryce's shoulders as he addressed him. "When only Johnny and Zack arrived, I feared you
had been lost."

"How are _you_ here?" Bryce responded, laughing lightly. "And
what's with the swords?"

Mikel laughed but was promptly interrupted by a throat
clearing by Walding, who watched the pair while fidgeting with
his staff.

"I apologize, but if you care for this boy and the others, we've
no time for pleasantries. Johnny and Zack are in danger, they've
been kidnapped, taken by the Undreamers."

"Whoa, slow down, partner," Mikel said, standing fully to
address the old man. "Undreamers aren't often in the business
of kidnapping and haven't been a significant threat for years,
decades perhaps. I don't know where the boys are, or what's
come over their guards," he eyed the ragged-looking old man

curiously, "Or who *you* are. But I doubt it has anything to do with the Undreamers."

"We've no time! They have been taken and are walking outside the city near a field! They must be recovered!"

"Yeah, I saw them, at least Johnny. They were on this dirt path heading towards some woods, next to a big like, wheat field or something," Bryce said confidently. "We've got to go now!"

Mikel studied them both, flabbergasted at the strange story. "What kind of odd night is this? Chosen here, Chosen evidently at the Bim's Gate, Undreamers in the Roost?" Bryce and Walding did not flinch. Mikel breathed a deep breath and turned to the guards that had been accompanying them, who stomped their pikes loudly in recognition.

"Please take both of them to—"

"The infirmary," Walding interrupted. "The boy has a condition on his leg; it requires the Court Wizard's immediate attention, Captain."

Mikel craned his neck back towards them and cocked his head as he looked from the old man to Bryce. The boy did his best to stand straight but it was a poor showing, and Mikel saw the lean in the boy's gait rather plainly now that he was looking for it. He again looked to Walding, studying him intently.

"Right, the infirmary," Mikel said as he turned back to the Gull. "They are not to leave your sight. Grab the next two Gull you see and bring them with you as well. If the boys were taken from the royal chambers, there may yet be others in the Roost. Be vigilant and do not let anyone enter, save Councilor Lopi."

The Gull stomped their pikes in acceptance, one leaning over and offering a metal-clad hand as support for the boy. Bryce eyed the Gull cautiously, remembering the off-putting guard now fast asleep on the royal chamber's floor, before he accepted the help and hobbled down the hallway back the way they came. Walding hesitated a moment and turned toward Mikel once more, observing the captain intensely. Mikel straightened, uncomfortable under the peculiar and investigative look he was receiving.

"Captain Mikel, do be careful in pursuing the Undreamers, they possess curious abilities. In any confrontation, be sure your ring is on hand, and do not remove it under any circumstances."

Before Mikel could find the words to respond, the old man turned and continued with the guards and Bryce. Mikel watched him for a moment before he turned to the opposite direction.He slowly rotated the thin and worn bronze ring on his middle finger and glanced back over his shoulder at the curious old man. It was not at all flashy and it blended rather uniformly with Mikel's lightly tanned skin; it was a difficult piece of jewelry to notice if you didn't know it was being worn to begin with. He eyed it a moment longer before running towards the Southern Gate with all haste.

———

23

A QUIET ESCAPE

The cool dawn dew was beginning its collection on the dirt road, the battered blades of grass that survived on the edges of the worn path showing small beads of water upon them. The sun had not risen yet, another hour or so off, but its light could be seen fighting the dark to the east, the otherwise black sky giving way to a mild purple. A few of the brightest stars still shined through the remaining night, but they were quickly fading as the sun took hold of the day. The group's footsteps were quick along the damp muddy road, but not hurried, shuffling as best they could outside the city gates and into the countryside. The tallest of them walked on the right side, furthest from the coming sunrise, and pulled a small cart just big enough for the large bag that sat upon it. In the middle was the shortest, hunched forward carrying a sack over one shoulder and clearly having some trouble with it. The last walked on the far left and a step or two in front of the others, unburdened save for a torch that guided them. They walked silently, all with hoods drawn from worn overcoats, moving forward in the mostly dark landscape. The tallest of them turned to look back to the city gates they had left, a few hundred feet behind them now.

"Don't ye be looking back, Awnsel. Nothing more suspicious than a dawn-time traveler looking back to the guards they've just passed," the man on the left said gruffly. Awnsel adjusted his look to the cart and attempted to show he was only adjusting his grip and not looking to the wall. The old-sounding man spit to the road disapprovingly.

"I'll feel much better when we're off this road. I can feel their eyes upon us," Awnsel said as an excuse as he lurched the cart forward over the uneven road.

"Yes, off the road would be much safer, eh? Let's get into the woods here Varn, let's get into the shadows, eh?" the middle one said as he again hiked the sack over his shoulder with some effort. "Out of their eyes, eh, and then to her. We will be rich as King Umbrin himself!" He shifted the sack again on his shoulder, leaning forward at a steep angle to do so. Varn let out a single sarcastic laugh as he shook his head.

"I think you just want to be able to drag that bag without looking like you're spoiling our traded goods. You'll have to manage further from the Eislarkian eyes, Dawl, before we can skip off into the woods," Varn replied plainly. "What kind of fools would drag a cart off the main road and into the woods? Suspicious fools, that's who." Dawl looked to him with a sneer, his purple eyes glinting in the little light that was available.

"Well at least let's have a switch, eh Awnsel? This'un is a heavy one, eh," Dawl beseeched his counterpart. Awnsel laughed shortly now, flexing a large arm as he pulled the cart with one hand.

"Sorry Dawl, you couldn't handle this cart neither. This here is a man's work. Cart pulling ain't for weak little moon elves," he laughed in response.

Dawl walked closer, bumping his hip into Awnsel's as he snarled, "Why don't ye put that cart down and we will see who's the weak one, eh?" Awnsel pulled back his hood, revealing a great many scars on his bald dark-toned skin and eyed him like an older brother to his younger.

"I don't see that ending well for you, *eh*," he mocked with a stern face, leaning his tall body over the average-sized elf.

"Both of ye, shut yer damn mouths and walk. We've no time for pissing contests, not with her waiting on us and not with them behind us. We've got to keep moving," Varn interjected with unexpected viciousness.

"If it's so urgent, why are we walking so slowly?" Awnsel asked, tugging the cart through a particularly muddy portion of road. Varn spit and wiped his mouth with the back of a leather-gloved hand as he glared at Awnsel. He trudged forward with the cart a few steps before catching Varn's surly eyes. He raised his eyebrows, waiting for an answer from the older man.

"To avoid suspicion, you dolt! I've just said so! And even more so, when the Chosen are found missing from their chambers this morning, what will the lord of Eislark do?" Awnsel and Dawl looked to each other trying to find the trick in his question.

"Maybe send out Eislark's best trackers? Maybe send out Mikel himself to find them and bring them back?" Varn led in a horribly condescending tone. "And if they see a set of tracks hop off the King's Road just outside the walls of the city, wouldn't a logical tracker assume a set of kidnappers might do such a thing to avoid travelers and get to their location as quickly as they could?" Dawl smiled a horrible smile, his teeth were cracked and plaque-stricken while Awnsel nodded with an approving head bob.

"Smart boss, very smart, eh."

"The longer we stay on the main road, the more sets of tracks they'll have to follow, and taking the long way will further throw them off," Awnsel added in as Varn spit again, this time approvingly.

"Precisely. So quit yer bitchin' till we're off the King's Road and then ye can take 'em outta the bags and drag 'em by their toes for all I care. But for now, shut it, and walk."

They trudged silently for a short while, only the creaking cart and the wet grip of mud on boots and wheels was heard. The bag on the cart shifted as they hit a divot and a hand popped from the opening. It slowly pried the crudely fastened rope hold apart, and none of the three seemed to notice as a young boy's head popped out far enough to see his surroundings. He fumbled gently in the bag for a moment before pulling out a set of broken glasses and placed them onto the bridge of his nose as he gained his bearings. He turned cautiously and watched the group, their backs silhouetted against the torch that Varn carried, casting wild shadows to the ground. Small sets of houses could be seen out in the fields as well, all dark still with their masters sleeping silently within them, thin trails of smoke rising from their chimneys, like steam over fresh-cooked broccoli. The only other light was the slowly growing dawn, still far off, and a very dim light coming from a thicket of trees in the middle of a large field some distance from the road, a campfire of some sort, with a slim trail of smoke gliding from the grouping, matching the smoke rising from homes.

Johnny looked in the direction the cart was being pulled and saw nothing but more fields which eventually gave way to a large swath of trees, as thick and bountiful as the farm vegetation that surrounded them now. The looks of a small group had just emerged from the forest, walking the same well-worn trail with their own torchlight. The path was straight and open, enough room for both sets of travelers to easily pass by.

"Phont above and Klane below. What's a caravan doing on the King's Road at this hour," Varn moaned, seeing the small group walking towards them. "Traders do not oft travel the night through the Narrow Woods, we should have had a smooth and uneventful ride to the trees." He adjusted his leather chest piece at the neck uncomfortably before scratching his thin grey beard. "Once we reach the forest, we'll hop the trail. Say nothing to these passersby. We're almost outta this," Varn hissed quietly, "and keep your eyes down Dawl, your cursed purple peepers are too easy to recognize for even the simplest man." Dawl snarled but nodded before stopping suddenly and turning his head to the side as if listening to something. Johnny quickly slipped his head into the sack as Dawl turned back towards the city, where small fires could still be seen atop the wall with tiny guards patrolling.

"Dawl, you dolt, keep walking!" Varn said sternly, spitting again to add to the growing moisture collecting on the ground.

"You didn't hear that, eh?" Dawl asked, ignoring Varn for the moment.

"Walk, you dog!" Varn yelled loudly. Dawl hesitated another moment, eyes probing the landscape for the sound, before obliging and catching up a few steps with the others. Varn eyed him with a brutal stare and Dawl met it with equal ferocity. The bag he was carrying suddenly flinched on Dawl's back and both the men's visages swapped to fright.

"No time to wait, eh, boss, this'uns waking already," Dawl said in a panic. Varn looked to the travelers approaching in the distance and back to the bag, which was motionless now. Awnsel stopped the cart silently next to them and left it as he joined in observing the bag. It moved as if on cue, and emitted a dreary groan. Awnsel rubbed his bald head beneath his hood in agitation and Varn spit ferociously.

"Do we have any more powder?" Awnsel asked anxiously. "Just drop a dash in there until we're past these folks and in the Narrow Woods?"

"Out, eh, used it all in the letter to make sure they'd fall asleep," Dawl replied, panicked.

"Look here," Varn stated boldly, attempting to take control of the situation by speaking loudly about it, "We will say it's some sort of livestock. A large pig or something. And that's only if they ask about it, ya hear? Otherwise, ye keep yer yap shut and just walk on by." Awnsel and Dawl nodded quickly. "What about the other one, Awnsel? Is he waking?" Varn continued, looking beyond his tall companion as Awnsel and Dawl turned to check as well. Johnny's sheepish grin met the three; the boy was all but one leg out of the bag as he froze to look at them. With hands still bound, he slowly slid his last leg from the bag, perhaps hoping they would not notice his movement. Varn spit again and took a step forward to address him.

"Think carefully, boy, about your next move." Johnny blew a kiss with his bound hands, jumped from the cart, and took off into the tall crops towards the nearest tree thicket. Dawl and Awnsel looked to Varn in horror. Varn promptly punched both their shoulders.

"Get 'em!"

Awnsel sprinted after him, leaping atop the cart and over it in a fluid athletic motion. Dawl was right behind him as he dropped the wriggling bag from his shoulder and stepped up onto the dirty wood's surface.

"Hold!" cried Varn. Dawl turned to scold him for being so indecisive when an arrow struck the cart where Dawl would have been had he taken another step. Awnsel skidded to a stop at the edge of the plants that Johnny had run through, finding the cart with an arrow buried deep into its wood. All three looked to the Eislark wall, where the arrow must have come from given the angle and distance traveled.

"Now what, eh, boss?" Dawl asked panicked. Varn picked up the sack that Dawl had dropped.

"We've still got one, make for the woods!"

24

TRAVELERS ON
THE ROAD

———◇———

The trees cast a fuller darkness over the path they rode, masking the moonlight from roots and divots that had nearly tossed them from their mounts a few times on the short journey. They had set a brisk pace from Trillgrand, riding quickly just as the sun had set, and had not let up but for a short break near a small tributary of the Mythes River to allow their steeds a drink and a well-deserved breather. At a slow pace, Eislark could be made in a day, leaving with the sun rising and arriving sometime after the high moon early the next morning. Most travelers would ride hard through the morning, stopping periodically and for a midday break before easing the ride through the afternoon and arriving just after dusk. Bartellom and Janeph hoped to cut that time further, catching up to the Councilor Supreme in the process, and be able to speak to Lord Belmar about the Chosen sometime in the early morning.

They rode silently, Janeph offering one "Are you alright?" to the wounded Bartellom, who simply grunted at such an insulting inquiry and pressed his horse harder, accelerating away from her. After that Janeph simply watched her companion as they rode, waiting for a sign that the damage he had sustained fighting Jamesett had reached a critical point. But it never came, a testament to his people's strength, and they rode on through the night, Janeph taking the lead through overgrown shortcuts that bore a straighter path through the trees than the standard winding forest road. She had spent many days playing in the trees of the Narrow Woods as a child, as well as traveling between cities while she visited Eislark with her parents, and had learned much of the land separating them in those years, back before the sister cities had drifted apart.

As they emerged from an overgrown path back to the main road, they saw a lone rider ahead moving at a steady trot. A light bobbed along near him, casting shadows as it moved, revealing the rider to be wearing a large hat. Janeph and Bartellom raced to catch up to whom they knew must be Petravinos.

"Councilor Supreme!" Janeph called as they reached within shouting distance. The old man's head whipped quickly to see who called him, the ball of light fading in an instant as he pulled his steed to a stop.

"Who goes there?" came the old familiar voice. "Not too close before I know to whom I speak."

"Janeph Sarn, of Trillgrand, and Bartellom Bonethorne, at your service, Councilor," Janeph called out as they approached and slowed to a trot.

"Why, my Lady! What has happened? I received word from our king that you were riding to meet me but that was all that was said. Please, details!" he exclaimed, riding back to meet them as he conjured a new ball of light. His white and light blue robe looked two sizes too big, as it always had since he had been ennobled into the wizard's order and was of exquisite craftsmanship compared to his worn and frayed blue hat. A loose belt wrapped his shoulder, where his dark oak staff was strapped securely to his person. He turned his horse on the path to wait for them to catch up.

"We had hoped you could tell us," Bartellom replied. "We returned to find you missing from your chambers and the marks we sent never arrived."

Petravinos scratched his bulbous nose in agitation with an old wrinkled hand as the three now rode together towards Eislark at a quick trot.

"*Marks*. As in, more than one?" he asked in fascination.

"Three to be exact," Janeph replied hastily, "but none have arrived in Trillgrand and we now fear the worst." Petravinos nodded understandingly but kept his smile. It was clear he knew something that the others did not. "Have they arrived in Eislark instead? Is that why you ride?" Janeph continued, picking up on his still somewhat optimistic look.

"I've unique instruments from my many years of study, my Lady, and they have indicated that a strange anomaly has occurred in Eislark this night; something has certainly arrived. Although, the stones from your Hunt were bound to Trillgrand, so the chances these are your marks is not likely."

Janeph looked embarrassedly to Petravinos. "Forgive me Councilor, but in the circumstances, we were forced to send all three on a single shifting string. We attached the spare stones you sent us for additional power, but . . . " His face sobered as he sighed, again scratching his nose in apprehension.

"I see. In that case it is unlikely then that this anomaly is anything extraordinary. And even had they arrived, at this point they have most likely perished. None survive more than a few minutes, before being overcome by our Realm."

The trio rode silently through the trees, which were growing increasingly thin as they neared the edge of the Narrow Woods. Petravinos dimmed his conjured light as the faint glow of dawn could be seen in the east to their right. The trees gave way fully to open fields and farmland, the final stretch to the Southern Gate of Eislark. It was a vast bland swath of land, small tufts of trees and clusters of tiny houses broke the monotonous rolling plains of corn, wheat, and berries. They were the only ones on the road, save a small band of travelers down the road heading their way.

"What if one survives?" Bartellom asked naively. "What happens then? I've been on a few Hunts and never bothered to ask what should happen if we ever extracted one."

Petravinos's smile returned, warm and distant, clearly imagining what a feeling of joy and splendor that would be. "They would have the chance to work with the High Council to restore the balance that has slowly been tipped out of our favor," he spoke to Bartellom directly before turning back to the road. "It has grown dark in Endland, and they would be a light in these times."

An outburst from the travelers ahead caught the group's attention, as one of the members riding their cart seemed to take off into the vegetation next to the road. Two others began pursuit before stopping abruptly, a small thud echoing from the cart. They were still far from the commotion as the three stood speaking on the road, their muffled and indistinctive voices barely reaching their ears. The fourth was nowhere to be seen, lost in the field they had sprinted into.

"Odd," Bartellom said nonchalantly. "I would have sworn that was an arrow strike, that distinctive thud of metal to wood."

Janeph laughed at him, to which Bartellom snorted in contempt. Petravinos was focused on the group ahead, still conversing on something as one grabbed a large bag that had been dropped.

"Not everything must be a sound of battle, Bartellom."

Ahead, the group sprung into the field, bag over the shoulder of one of them, but on the opposite side of the road of where the first member of their party had run. The cart they were pulling was left idle in the middle of the road, with Petravinos watching intently, a curious furrow forming on his brow as Janeph and Bartellom bickered quietly about the sound they had heard. A horn blew from the wall of Eislark, harsh and high pitched, snapping all their attention forward in surprise.

"We ride!" Petravinos cried as he spurred his horse into a gallop. "Eislark's horn does not sound without just cause!" Bartellom and Janeph were caught off guard but spurred their steeds as well, working to catch up to the old wizard.

"I will pursue the three to the right, Janeph, you are with me. Bartellom, to the left after the one."

"Why do we pursue them? We know nothing of them!" Janeph called out from behind.

"A shifting anomaly, odd behavior on the road before dawn, a splitting of their party, an arrow if Bartellom's ears can be trusted, and a warning horn from Eislark's nearest gate. Coincidence breeds causation. Something is afoot." Janeph looked to Bartellom in steadfast surprise at the barrage of logic and couldn't help but smile, the big man returning it. "We meet at the cart in the road. Fortune unto thee!" Petravinos yelled over the thundering hooves and veered off the road a good 50 yards from the cart.

"Aye!" Bartellom cried, veering left as Janeph veered right with Petravinos in silent acceptance. Ahead, the gates to Eislark opened as a number of horsemen exited the city. It was difficult for Bartellom to ascertain their number from the distance, but it was more than their rank of three without a doubt. He hoped they would follow Janeph and Petravinos; he could handle a one-on-one, but they were already outnumbered. To his delight, the horsemen had already veered towards Janeph and Vinos, bringing a smile to the barbarian as he rode.

Bartellom slowed as he reached the cart's location, hopping from his horse before it had fully stopped and landing with a wet thud in the thin layer of mud that coated the road. His wounds ached from the impact as he grimaced and looked to the crops. The cornfield that they had seen the one member flee into was thick and sowed in tight, close enough where his broad shoulders could easily touch stalks of parallel rows, but even so, it was clear where the runner's path led, seeing the bent and broken stalks of the individual's distinct trail. He scanned the ground quickly for signs of a boot print, and soon found one. It was a small shoe print, perhaps a dwarf or halfling, or a young man, and it had an odd pattern shown clearly on the impression in the mud, a distinct pattern of lines as opposed to the flat print of standard boots. It would be an easy track.

25

A LONG SHOT

The Southern Gate was not terribly far from the observation deck Mikel had left, but he knew Grek would need to know what to say to the people if the horn blew. He ran quickly, dodging guests as he weaved through the halls and back towards the feast. He stopped at a pair of Gull near the exit of the large tower staircase and looked to them both, breathing deeply to catch his breath.

"One of you, to the Southern Gate, gather riders and notify the scouts to keep an eye for any that have left for Trillgrand in the last half hour. We will ride and intercept any on the road. Go now, I will sound the horn."

The one Gull, smaller and presumably nimbler, looked to the larger guard before stomping his pike and taking off down the stairs to the lower portion of the tower. Mikel nodded to the other and resumed his sprint toward Lord Grekory's chambers. Up the stairs, through the halls, sprinting as fast as he could until he rounded a corner towards his Lord's door, the Gull guarding his room slamming their pikes with his approach. He slowed to a jog the closer he got before smiling as he tried to slow his breathing. The Gull opened the door gently for him, and Mikel entered to surprisingly find Lord Belmar still awake, standing in his nightshirt in front of an open balcony overlooking the city and the bay. He turned at the sound of the door and smiled curiously.

"Mikel! I had thought sweet sleep had stolen you from the festival early! What of the Gull's reports at Bim's Gate, has something happened on the outer wall? And have you spoken with the children? What do they think of our fair city?" He walked from the balcony to a small table that had glasses, a pitcher, and a large plate of fruits and pastries that had been taken from the festival.

"Apologies, my Lord, but I've no time for drinks. The report at the Bay of Bim was odd; an old Chosen name from the past was evidently used to attempt entry after sunset, followed by a single small boat gaining entry through an other-worldly fog. But it may have all been a distraction." He leaned closely, "The Chosen children have been taken, I am off at once." Lord Belmar coughed up the wine he had just drank and wiped his clean-shaven and alcohol-drenched chin.

"Taken? By whom?" he asked angrily, slamming his cup to the small table, sending a few loose grapes to the stone floor. Mikel opened his hands in a plea for restraint, which the lord somewhat obliged, though his body remained tense.

"I do not know, but I must go now. If you hear the horn, it is because we have located the enemies and there could be more within the Roost. The lords and ladies must know to take precautions."

"You mean to sound the alarm? Our guests will go into a panic! There will be chaos!"

"My Lord, there is no time! The children, the Chosen, may be lost! We will deal with the other lords and ladies but I must go!" He bowed, cutting off any rebuttal from Grekory, and left the room immediately.

"Bring them back, Mikel! By any means necessary!"

Weaving through the halls that he could no doubt traverse blindfolded from his years spent within them, he burst open the door to the outer wall and ran down its open walkway as quickly as he could, dodging the large bonfires, torches, and guards as he went. He made it to the stairs of the Southern Gate's lookout post and, glancing over the road, he could make out one set of travelers, slowly walking away from the city. He looked back inside the walls to see the riders had all but assembled before the gate's doors. He waved below to them, all raising their pikes back in reply as he jumped the stairs to the lookout precipice two at a time.

"Your long bow," he asked breathlessly to one of the two Gull on lookout at the elevated post. The Gull obliged without a word, handing the long bow slung over his shoulder to the captain. "Open the gates, blow the horn. We've enemies on the road," he said as he eyed the distance. The Gull stomped his foot heavily and ran away towards the opposite set of stairs to return to the main wall walkway.

Mikel stepped forward, surveying the travelers, who had stopped and were huddled together next to their cart. He pulled an arrow from the massive stationary quiver at the center of the lookout, one of hundreds, and knocked it while the other Gull watched silently. Pulling back on the string he eyed them and adjusted his shot left to right to account for the wind off the sea as he did his best to steady his strained breath. From the cart the travelers carried, someone jumped off and ran into the crops in a commotion. He angled his shot up for proper trajectory, breathed in and held it, and loosed the arrow as the satisfying twang of the string echoed. The rest of the travelers scrambled, one moving over the cart as the other prepared to do the same before halting suddenly. The thud of the arrow into the cart could be heard from their post, Mikel smiling at his shot.

"By Phont, Captain, nice shot!" The Gull couldn't contain his glee and moved to knock his own arrow.

"A good shot would have found its mark, but I'll take it." The travelers of the road took off, opposite where the first member of their party had fled to the fields, as the bay's horn blew loudly from further down the wall where the guard had run off to. Mikel leaned the bow against the waist-high wall as he quickly ran down the stairs the way he had come, calling over his shoulder, "No more arrows, they've something precious to Eislark. We will take them on the ground." The doors began to open as he leaned over the wall to call to the prepping Gull below.

"By order of Lord Belmar, you are to retrieve the two orphans whom have been stolen from Eislark. Bring them back alive, by any means necessary! Ride swiftly, Gull, strike like the tide upon the rock." They all raised their pikes into the air and cried loudly before spurring their horses forward out of the gate and onto the road. Mikel was nearing the bottom of the stairs as they left, calling out to a pair of Gull that had helped gather the horses for the others.

"Prepare one more horse for your Captain, would you?" he called calmly, his breath now steady once more, to which they quickly scrambled back towards the stable to retrieve one. Mikel waited for them, looking out the gate as his riders veered to the left, moving to intercept the unknown group who had fled to the woods. He fiddled with his bronze ring as he watched, still wondering what the old man could have meant about his sentimental token, a harsh memory of his steep rise to where he now stood. The Gull behind him broke his train of thought as they ushered a saddled horse forward for him.

"Captain, your horse."

Mikel nodded with a cocksure smile and mounted the beast gracefully. "Gather more riders, meet us in the woods. Backup is always welcome. Be quick, we know not with whom we are dealing and I do not intend to let our Lord down." They stomped their feet and were off to grab more men as Mikel turned to ride off down the road, swift as he could, to save the boys.

26

POWERFUL WORDS

Bartellom charged in, pulling his hammer from his back with his good arm to help usher his way through the crops, tracking the prints that he could find and following the destruction of the plants where he could not. The pattern zig-zagged: over two rows, back three more, changing directions and angles, but always there was a distinct boot print where the runner had planted to change direction. The prints worked generally towards a group of trees, and as Bartellom continued to track, he realized that was exactly where the tracks were leading. He slowed and stopped just outside the dense clearing of trees, too thick to see through to the other side. It was a small patch, a few hundred trees amid the fields, likely allowed to grow as it was in an effort to attract and trap small game. He listened intently on the edge of the woods and hearing nothing, entered silently, years of hunting in practice as he stepped without a sound. The trees became tighter and more difficult to traverse before he heard voices arguing quietly among each other just a short distance from the edge of the crops.

"Let's eat 'im. I haven't had human flesh in so long," a sniveling guttural voice said quietly.

"We're not 'upposed to do nothin to brings the guards' attentions to us! We're 'upposed to investigate, that's it! We cant's just eat 'im!" a deeper, authoritative voice replied.

"We cant's let 'im go neither, he'll tell abouts us. Then the humans will know we was 'ere. So, what's we goin' do?" A third crotchety old voice said. Bartellom could tell from their harsh sounds they must be orcs and finding them this close to the city was quite alarming. They were to be confined to the wilds between the Lord's domain; this close to the city was a serious infraction on the delicate and often forgotten peace they shared with Eislark and Trillgrand. Ahead, he could see the light of a fire. Peering around a thick tree confirmed three orcs standing in a small clearing around a boy who was bound by the hands and sitting on the ground in the center of them. Bartellom nearly blew his cover over the excitement of seeing Johnny, quickly ducking behind a large tree to steady his breath; the boy had survived the shifting!

Two of the orc's backs were mostly to him, the third was standing so that, if he was observant, he was looking nearly directly at Bartellom. He could surprise and conquer two easily, even with the one looking his direction, but Johnny would be a hostage; one would grab the boy before he could slay the others and then things would get very messy. Waiting for the one facing him to move was his best bet. He peered from behind the tree, hoping his opportunity would come sooner than later. Their bickering was growing louder now as the poor boy sat wide-eyed beneath the quibbling beasts.

"Fine, we eats 'im. But bones and all, we mustn't leave any clues for those Eislark Gulls," the one with the deepest voice said, "and then we's get out of here! Eislark cant's be taken, we's seen enough to knows that."

The two others snorted in wild satisfaction as Johnny tried to slide out of the circle. The one who declared they eat stepped a muddy rotting boot on his chest and pinned him to the root rampant dirt. Bartellom leaned his hammer against the tree and pulled a long knife from his belt with his one good arm, gripping the blade between a massive thumb and forefinger. If an opportunity would not arise organically, he would have to create one himself.

"Now hang on just a second, fellas," Johnny said from the ground, head partially beneath the leaves of a bush, hands bound at his chest just above the orc's foot. "You haven't even talked to me about this yet. I think I should have a say, you know, being the subject of eating. And I don't think you want to be eating me, if I'm being completely honest." The orcs laughed wickedly, jagged teeth chattering as Johnny laughed awkwardly with them.

"The boy wants to talk, Blark, and he don'ts want to be eaten," one said in his high shrill voice to the orc who had Johnny pinned. "What's a pity, poor stupid human." All three had their crude knives drawn now as the third elderly looking orc leaned over his counterpart's boot, his sharp jagged teeth but a few inches from Johnny's nose.

"And why's wouldn't we eat such a delicious-looking morsel?" he asked sarcastically.

"Well," Johnny replied, pushing his busted glasses up his nose, "I am kind of a big deal." He smiled as best he could with the orc still a few inches from him. "People know me." His smile was true, but his eyes clearly showed his fear, even Bartellom could see it from where he was. The orc looked to the others with a toothy grin as they all snickered, and Johnny cleared his throat to regain his composure.

"You see, I am a chooser," he said to the orc who had him restrained. They looked to each other, lost but still smiling at the boy's ruse.

"Chooser, silly boy? Whats will you be choosing? Whats part we should eat first?" the shrill-voiced orc asked, laughing again as he circled next to Blark to address the boy. They all laughed together as Bartellom waited patiently in the shadows; the shrill-voiced orc was in an even better position for attack being so near Blark, but the older one still was facing the barbarian rather directly.

"Damn, not chooser. Sorry guys, sorry. I'm just so nervous, you know?" Johnny joked with a heavy gulp. "I meant I'm a Chosen." Blark's smile faded, but the other two laughed in a low tone that made Johnny shrivel and pull away as much as he could with the boot upon him, trying to hide further under the leaves of the low-hanging bush near his head. The old orc moved next to Blark and threw his arm around his shoulder, laughing. Bartellom smiled at their new arrangement, eyeing his throw.

"We don't wants to be messing with Chosen, mates," Blark said with concern.

"Chosen's don't exist no more! He's just a meal!" the old orc bellowed as he shook Blark with his arm still draped around his companion. The high-pitched orc now leaned over the boy with his blade drawn, dropping to a knee for the kill.

"This'uns a smart one, pretendin' to be a Chosen. But Chosen's been gone a long, long time. Would be lovelies if he's was Chosen, but he's only food now," he said, putting his knife to Johnny's neck. Blark howled suddenly, arching his back and dropping his knife as his foot lifted from the boy. He fell to his knees as Johnny scooted back another foot from them, the shrill orc looking to his companion in confusion. The old orc traced the knife's trajectory back to where it was thrown to find the brunt of Bartellom's hammer upon his face, the barbarian having charged the group. Black blood sprayed as the orc's skull cracked beneath the blow. His body buckled to its knees in a heap as the barbarian pulled his hammer forcefully, spinning backwards with a pivot and swung downwards towards the shrill-voiced orc now. The orc did his best to dodge, still being on the ground, taking a glancing blow to his shoulder that caused him to snarl in pain, even with only one of Bartellom's mighty arms doing the work. The orc rolled with the blow and regained his feet with a defiant screech before turning and running from the clearing and into the trees.

Bartellom took a step to pursue but thought better of it as he turned to secure Johnny and deal with Blark first. He walked over to the writhing orc, still trying to pull the blade from his upper back as he wriggled on his side. Bartellom placed one foot on the orc's hip and leaning his hammer against his own leg, placed his good hand on the hilt of the knife. It had easily sunk half the blade's length into Blark's muscular frame.

"Tell me, orc, what are you doing so close to the Eislark border? And how did you come by a child such as this?"

Blark growled defiantly, not looking to his interrogator and instead focusing on the boy with a look that bore incredible sorrow. Johnny scooted back another foot on his butt as he sat and watched.

"Just out for a walk with me boys," he replied mockingly, "and this'uns came burstin' in, ruining our lovelies morning." Bartellom looked away dissatisfied and glanced to Johnny with a wince as he twisted the knife mildly. Blark squirmed and growled in intense pain, and Johnny mirrored Bartellom's wince at the sight. The barbarian held him firmly with his heavy boot, keeping him stuck to the ground but his eyes appeared sad and apologetic, looking every bit in pain as the orc he stood over.

"Come now, I take no pleasure in this. But this child is precious, and you and your 'boys' are much too close to the city. It's a treaty breach and a death sentence to be sure. So, what are you doing outside Eislark? There must be a reason."

Blark spit black blood and breathed a rattled and defeated sigh. "Yous wouldn't believes me, even if I told yous." Blark sneered again, defiant but in a whisper, but Johnny's attention was pulled from the scene as he caught the glint of a pair of yellow eyes watching from behind Bartellom and Blark. To Johnny's surprise the shrill-voiced orc leapt from the thicket he hid in, two daggers drawn to Bartellom's back, an easy target for the nimble orc.

"Stop!" cried Johnny, reaching with futility toward Bartellom's assassin, exposing himself from the bush. The small fire beside him doused in an instant, and the bush and smallest saplings near where Johnny sat grew black as if they had been charred. All the grass around him yellowed and decayed as the barbarian turned, pulling the dagger from Blark's back. He squared to meet the unexpected blow, driving the dagger deep into the beast's chest as he spun to face him. But he held no weight as the blade made its puncture, and letting go of the knife, the orc stayed suspended in the air, hovering a foot away from him, daggers pointed now just inches from his chest in a last futile stab. The orc's eyes moved rapidly in their sockets, looking to Bartellom, Blark, and Johnny in panic-stricken wonder. It was the only part of him that moved as his body hung in the cool dawn air, dangling by a nonexistent string like a piñata beneath the trees. The orc gurgled black blood from his mouth before his eyes darkened, body still suspended in the air. Bartellom gripped the hilt and removed the knife quickly, afraid what levitated the orc might migrate to him. It did not, and after a few moments the new corpse collapsed to the ground. Blark and Bartellom both looked to Johnny in disbelief. Johnny's mouth was agape with the faintest hint of a grin on his lips.

"Did I do that?" he said in a nasally tone as he pushed his glasses up his nose with his still-bound hands.

27

BAD BLOOD

———◆———

Walding paced back and forth at the foot of Bryce's bed as the two guards that had found them stood nearby, watching intently. They had been whisked to the infirmary wing of the castle at Walding's request, and truly the black veins emanating from Bryce's wound were all the convincing anyone needed. What Bryce could not discern was if Walding's anxious striding was out of concern for Johnny and Zack, the vision that Bryce had achieved, or the wound that he bore. And with the guards so near, he felt rather uncomfortable asking Walding outright and drawing unwanted attention.

A short man with a bald head and a very long beard burst through the doors, accompanied by two Gull close behind him. They pointed towards the boy, not that the man needed any direction as Bryce and Walding were the only non-Gull in the room.

"What have we here, what has happened? I was told there was dark magic afoot?" The short man said in a high shrill voice. Walding waved him over as Bryce pulled open the cut in his sweatpants to reveal the pulsing black veins.

"Phont above and Klane below! Who did this to you?" the old man squealed, having scuttled over to Bryce's bedside to get a closer look.

"Well, uh, Mr. Doctor, I accidentally did this to myself."

"Please, Councilor Lopi, is there anything that you can do for him? It is beyond my skills," Walding pleaded, as Lopi looked to the old man for the first time since entering the room and then back to Bryce's leg. The Councilor hovered his hands over Bryce's leg, feeling an icy chill emanate from the veins.

"It is an obvious infection, from what exactly I cannot say, but it will continue to spread if it is not treated. You say you did this to yourself, young man? If you want your life saved, I will need you to honestly tell me what you were doing to cause this. If you are not truthful, it will lead me down the wrong treatment path and you may die."

Bryce blinked and swallowed hard, feeling the gravity of the situation settle upon his chest, making his breaths short and heavy. He looked to Walding for guidance, worry written plainly on both their faces.

"It is alright, my boy. Tell the councilor the truth, he needs to know it to help you," Walding said as he offered a reassuring smile over top of his obvious concern. "But let me be clear, Councilor Lopi, that this cannot leave this room and it would be best if these guards were not present to hear it." Lopi squinted his eyes in analysis, deciding if he could trust the pair before he waved the Gull away from the bed.

"To the end of the room with you, I will let you know if you are needed," he said to the Gull, to which they slammed their pikes and promptly walked toward the door.

"Go on, my boy," Walding said as calmly as he could.

"Well, I'm not from here. I'm from Cleveland, a different planet or whatever."

"Different Realm," corrected Walding quickly.

"Right, a different Realm. But this thing was after me and my friends, this big beast of a thing, named James."

"Jamesett," Walding corrected again but addressed the name more to Lopi than to Bryce. Lopi's beard twitched and he swallowed hard as Bryce continued.

"It was after us, and it was beating the hell out of Jan and Bart, it may have even killed them, I'm really not sure. But I bargained with him to leave them alone and they kind of woke up, but then he was going to take me away so I stabbed his hand with this piece of metal. Oh, yea, when James was chasing us, he kind of blew up this door and scraps of it went all over and that's what I used to stab him, this broken door piece. But I also accidentally stabbed myself in the leg here," he said, pointing to the icy black veins. "And then he started freaking out and the world went all dark and cold, but then it went back to normal, and he threw me across the room but I could feel my leg burning already. So, I think it's an infection from the piece of door or something."

Lopi was expressionless, color faded from his face, and he blinked far more than was a normal rate as he processed the information. He then began to laugh lightly, chuckling as he looked into the distance. Walding scratched the back of his head as he curiously watched the councilor, and Bryce found himself out of breath after nervously rambling through the story.

"This is a joke, right? Was this Mikel's doing, or perhaps Lord Grekory's? Some retaliation for my display last night?" Lopi finally questioned, still half laughing.

"This is not a joke," Walding said plainly and without hesitation. "The boy needs help. In my unprofessional opinion, he was infected with blood, Grim blood, from Jamesett of Fermlo himself. It is a serious infection, and it will only get worse without your help."

"Then this boy," Lopi looked to Bryce, mystified, "by Phont, this boy is Chosen as well? A *third* Chosen?"

"You met Johnny and Zack?" Bryce questioned with rapid onset excitement, sitting forward from the bed he sat upon.

"Why yes, just last evening! And you know them, evidently!" He clapped his hands very quickly, his excitement growing as much as Bryce's, but then he soured suddenly.

"Did you say he was tainted with the blood of Jamesett? The Snake of Dawnwood?"

"I believe so, if the boy speaks the truth, which I think he does. He seems quite the honest young lad, does he not?" Walding replied, but before he could extend his conversational tangent, a horn resounded outside the castle. Lopi glanced out the nearest window to try to see what was happening, stepping toward the head of Bryce's bed. He looked over a courtyard which was now full of bustling guards and Gull, moving quickly toward the Southern Gate beneath torchlight and the slowly coming dawn.

"By Phont, what is happening?"

"Councilor Lopi, the boy needs your help," Walding pleaded, intercepting Lopi's thoughts on the horn and returning him to the matter at hand. "A Chosen sits before you, in need of a healer, and there is none so renowned as you." Lopi pulled away from the window and eyed the man as he measured him and then to Bryce, who's feet were anxiously twitching back and forth, colliding his shoes together at the big toe.

Silently, frantically, Lopi ran to a large series of shelves and cabinets on the far side of the room, opposite the doorway. On a thick wooden slab, he began piling bottles and ingredients from the shelves, searching and scanning, opening doors and closing them, doubling back to shelves he had already searched to select an additional item. He was in a frenzy. After a minute, he returned with a mountain of vials and components to Bryce's bed, resting it beside the wounded leg.

"These ingredients are some of the rarest in Endland, you are lucky we have them here. I keep an excellent stock. But do not think that Lord Grekory will forget these were used without his consent, his pantries laid bare." Walding cleared his throat loudly and in annoyance, snapping Lopi into focus. "Right, it matters not, to save a Chosen all must be made available! We must extract the blood, as much of it as we can and as quickly as possible. Grim blood is vile, and it will corrupt without question. The longer it is in your body, the more hold Jamesett will gain. Luckily it is away from your heart and mind, but it is a matter of time before it spreads," Lopi said as he placed a large metal bowl on Bryce's bed between his blanketed feet and started adding ingredients.

"Extract? Like with a needle?" Bryce asked with fear in his eyes. "Isn't there like some medicine I can take instead?"

"Grim blood is foreign to the body, child," Lopi said as he poured a sweet-smelling liquid into the bowl and began to mash the leaves and roots that he had already added into a thick paste. "It will not dissipate on its own. I fear it may always be with you now, but we can save you from being overtaken at the least."

"Overtaken?" Bryce was far gone from his excitement on hearing of Johnny and Zack and was rapidly approaching panic. Walding rested an old hand on his shoulder reassuringly as Lopi placed a thick folded blanket beneath Bryce's infected thigh.

"Do not fear, young one. This solution will concentrate the blood to one location, pulling the infection to the cut in order for us to remove it." He scooped a small spoonful of the dark green, thick liquid from the metal bowl and readied it above the boy's leg. "At that time, we will make the incision. The pain will be intense, and Jamesett will realize what we are doing and will have an opportunity to resist us. If we are lucky, he is unaware that you are infected, and we will have the element of surprise. Fight him back, I will extract as much blood as I can."

"Fight him back? With what?"

"This will not be a physical fight, my boy," Walding said with much needed calm. "Find a happy memory in your thoughts. Remember it, grasp the feeling, and do not let Jamesett have it. He will be deceitful, lying, and manipulative. Do not trust him, do not succumb. It will only be a short minute while Lopi cuts and extracts, but it will feel much longer for you."

Before Bryce could protest, Lopi plopped the paste onto the darkest concentration of black veins and smeared it around with the back of the spoon, covering a large area of his leg. It felt sticky like peanut butter, but it was more runny, and the juice that the thicker paste excreted was quickly running down the sides of his leg and onto the blankets that Lopi had placed. Lopi continued to smear the relish-colored ointment back and forth along where the cut had been, and to Bryce's amazement, the location of the cut became more and more clear, as if time had been reversed and he was un-healing, a jagged raised portion of his skin becoming increasingly pronounced with each lap of the spoon. Similarly, the black veins were slowly retreating to their source, pulling back to the raised skin where the shrapnel had cut him and collecting beneath it. Lopi, still smearing the spoon around, gripped a small short knife with his other hand from the slab of ingredients, about the size of a butter knife but with a shorter blade.

"Are you ready?" Lopi asked. Bryce nodded with clenched teeth. Lopi lifted the spoon away and began to cut along the raised skin. Bryce grimaced as thick black liquid oozed out of the cut, thicker even than the paste Lopi had applied. It seemed to be reacting with the solution that had been smeared on him, becoming more watery and turning a normal-looking red color. Lopi continued along the black line and Bryce squeezed his eyelids in pain as the long scar was slowly reopened. When he opened his eyes again, he found himself alone on the bed, the room dark, and Lopi and Walding gone. The only thing that was constant was his bed and the growing, throbbing pain in his leg.

"Bryce Blooms, hello again, dear boy. I've been expecting you for some time now." the salesman voice of James called from around him. Bryce, still grimacing, cursed under his breath; so much for the element of surprise.

"Go away," Bryce said boldly as he felt the cut of Lopi's knife tear further along his leg, watching the invisible blade work down the raised scar as even here more of the black ooze seeped out of his wound.

"Oh, ho. Is the little Chosen afraid of me? What a shame that the first genuine prospect is little more than a coward."

Bryce said nothing, concentrating on not crying out from the pain in his leg. It had been slowly intensifying the further Lopi cut and the more the black blood oozed from him, building with each ounce spilled.

"And this old fool thinks he can extract my blood? Tell me, did Lopi tell you how many people he has extracted Grim blood from?"

"It doesn't matter," Bryce said through his teeth, his jaw never opening as he spoke.

"Oh, but it does. Because the answer is zero. He's never done this, only read about it. The Grim are from another time entirely. You're his first patient." Bryce felt a wave of fear rise in him but did his best to quell it internally. It subsided, but not completely, a remnant of it lingering in his gut.

"Ah, there it is. *Fear.*"

Bryce was surprised that the Creep could sense such a thing and again felt the wave, a rising tide inside of him that was becoming increasingly difficult to control. He breathed in slowly before Lopi cut again, causing him to lose his air in an involuntary exhale, and now he felt anxiety rise as well. Again, it went down as he concentrated on it, but more stuck with him than before, building within his chest now.

"Just let it overtake you, boy. Let your mind wander."

Bryce almost did for a second, hypnotized by the soothing voice. But he closed his eyes and concentrated on his friends, thinking hard on them, their adventures and mischief through the years. It was the first thing he thought of when Walding had suggested a happy memory.

"Ah, but they abandoned you. Let you go as you traveled the Void. And left you alone in an unknown world."

The words were strangely haunting, and even though he recognized what Jamesett was trying to do, his ability to calm his fear was hampered by the ever-growing feeling of a loss of control. He searched his mind for memories but could not focus, breathing heavily as he felt another rip of skin in his leg that sent the pain to an unbearable level.

"You are mine."

He felt the darkness around him close in and his anxiety peaked, swallowing him whole as he clasped his hands tightly to his chest and extended his pinky and thumb. The darkness faded, replaced by cold dripping shadows, and to Bryce's steadfast surprise and relief, the pain and fear vanished. He opened his eyes and found he was standing next to his bed, beside his shadow self, and at the foot of his bed, sitting next to his feet, was the Creep. He had a wild and surprised look upon his beastly pale face, wide-open black eyes watching in disbelief.

"Impossible," Jamesett managed in manic shock.

Bryce jumped into his shadow self as Jamesett lunged for him, making contact with his body just before Jamesett's long fingers could reach him. With a flash he was returned to the regular world, Lopi wiping away the red blood from his leg while Walding dabbed the boy's head with a wet cloth. He was sweating, cold and heavy, and from every pore in his body considering the damp feeling on his clothes. Bryce leaned forward and looked down to find the black veins nearly gone, small dark strings extending no more than an inch from the long and fresh cut, a vast improvement from their reaching his kneecap just a few minutes ago. Lopi wrapped a clean bandage tightly around his thigh concealing the wound and tapped a hand gently upon it.

"Rest, boy, rest. You've done well, it's over now, just rest," Lopi said proudly as he gathered the ingredients on the slab and took the mess back to the cabinets. Walding was watching Bryce with more concern than the wizard and leaned close as Lopi walked away.

"What happened when you gathered yourself, my boy? It was only for a second at the end and then you returned to us," Walding whispered as he dabbed Bryce's sweating forehead.

"Gathered?"

"Yes, gathered! With your hands! When you focus your abilities. We are lucky it did not backfire. Gathering during such magic can be very dangerous."

"Oh, that. It was the only thing I could think to do; I felt like I was losing my mind. And as soon as I did it, Jamesett was there, I saw him. He tried to reach for me but I jumped back into my body first."

"What's that now, child?" Lopi asked, wiping his hands down with a clean rag as he approached the bed. Walding shook his head subtly towards Bryce.

"Nothing, Mr. Lopi, just saying how hard that was."

"Yes, and you did marvelously. Drawing such blood is never easy, especially when it is from a being as powerful as Jamesett. At least that is what the scrolls say. I am still mostly in disbelief it was truly him, but why don't you rest. I'll be just outside with," he paused and worked to identify Walding. "Oh my, in all this excitement, I never got your name, sir." Lopi bowed remorsefully toward Walding.

"Just a servant of Captain Mikel's, Councilor. He trusted me to bring the boy here and told me of the infection before he ran to the Southern Gate," Walding lied smoothly, handing the sweat-dabbed rag to Lopi as Bryce laid back in his bed. Lopi smiled as he took the rag and turned back to the cabinets looking for a place to drop it.

"Yes, I need to head that way now and see what exactly is going on. I trust you will stay with the Chosen until Mikel's return? The Gull will be here as well."

"Yes, of course, Councilor."

"Very good. Rest, young Chosen, I will come check on you in a few hours."

Bryce gave a thumbs-up as Lopi turned to leave, stopping at the infirmary door to speak with the Gull momentarily before exiting. The Gull did not move from their post at the door, and Walding took the opportunity.

"You say you saw Jamesett? Truly saw him?"

"Yea, I only heard him until I, uh, gathered. Then there he was, sitting next to me and looking super surprised." Walding breathed in slowly and exhaled even slower as his eyes darted side to side minimally, weighing unseen options in his mind. He rested a hand on Bryce's shoulder and looked intently upon him, his old blue eyes twinkling behind the weathered face.

"I must ask you not to gather again until I say it is safe. It seems Jamesett has taken a liking to you, and he may try to use your gift against you. So, no more until further notice, alright?" Bryce shrugged and leaned back into his pillow with his hands behind his head.

"Yea, sure. No problem."

"Good, now rest. You've done well today, my boy."

28

THE NIGHTMOTHER

Petravinos did not leave his horse as they approached the crops, instead picking a lane between the plant rows and riding through them. Janeph followed suit, entering a row of her own a few strides behind him and to his right. The leaves of the corn husks whipped their faces, Janeph doing her best to keep an eye on Petravinos through the plants and also look for the mystery travelers who had taken off ahead of them. She worried for a moment for Bartellom going on his own, but he was more than capable of tracking a single individual and even with one arm, he would handle most in combat. She exhaled deeply to relieve her stress as the crops gave way to unkept vegetation and, just beyond that, the edge of the Narrow Woods. Petravinos did not hesitate, riding out from the crops and into the dense shrubs towards the forest. There was no path from the crops to the trees, but it was clear where those they pursued had run. They followed the matted grass and foliage to the edge of the forest where Petravinos hopped from his horse as best he could for an old man, and he called back to her.

"I am no tracker, but I think it is safe to say they've entered the trees here," he said with a sly and excited grin.

"Agreed," Janeph said as she too dismounted and looked to the woods, "but they've taken us from our mounts and we now pursue blindly into the trees. If I were to ambush, it would be near here."

"We do not know whom we pursue, but I doubt they would set an ambush so close to the city they are fleeing. Far too close— any reinforcements would quickly overwhelm them," Petravinos said as he used his dark oak staff to brush the low ground bushes away and step between the outermost trees into the woods. Janeph followed, glancing back to see the Eislarkian cavalry that had come from the city gates riding up behind them from the rows of corn. She waved them over as she too entered the woods.

It was not overly dense on the outskirts, sparsely spaced trees with small saplings and bushes that could be easily swayed one way or the other. But as easy as it had been to track through the matted foliage outside the trees, it was equally as difficult now. Petravinos leading without any tracking skills did not help, and Janeph quickly caught up with him to offer her opinion on their direction. Behind, the Gull of Eislark were heard dismounting their horses and clamoring into the woods to back them up. Janeph bent low near a partially broken branch as Petravinos looked around quizzically, peering into the thicker parts of the forest that lay ahead of them. The Gull reached them as Janeph stood, and pointed deeper into the forest.

"They came this way," she said, "but whom exactly are we pursuing?"

"*We* are pursuing kidnappers. *You* are interfering," One of the Gull responded bluntly. He and the others approached the pair through the trees as Petravinos adjusted his oversized hat and looked upon them, pulling the aged brim as he leaned on his staff with a smile. A small group stayed in the field atop their horses, looking back to the gates for additional forces.

"I wouldn't say we are interfering, would you, Lady Janeph? I would say we might even be leading this rescue," Petravinos said with a wink and a tip of his large hat as he walked in the direction Janeph had pointed. "So whom has been kidnapped that we are now pursuing?" he called over his shoulder. The guards seemed to recognize to whom they spoke now, for they quickly abandoned their discourteous tone for a far cheerier and compliant one.

"Two children, they are very important to Lord Belmar," the same Gull said as he followed the Councilor Supreme and Janeph through the brush. "We must find them and return them."

"Lord Belmar has no children," Janeph balked. "I think it is safe to say he dislikes them in general. What makes these children so special that he would send Gull after them?"

"And to make thieves kidnap them?" Petravinos added from ahead of the group.

"I do not know, Captain Mikel gave the orders, but he seemed rather enthusiastic himself," the Gull replied as they walked deeper into the woods. "I expect he will be here shortly."

Janeph's heart fluttered in restrained hope. "Are these children boys or girls?" she asked bluntly.

"I believe it is two boys, orphans brought to the Roost by Lopi and Mikel."

"Orphans at the Roost? Has Mikel turned out so well for the Belmars that they now host street urchins regularly?" Petravinos stopped to participate in the conversation now, as Janeph swallowed her excitement.

"The story going through the ranks is they were posing as Chosen as a joke on our Lord, Lopi's doing evidently, and Mikel his coconspirator."

"Lopi having a go at Lord Belmar? That seems quite out of character for that timid man." Petravinos chuckled softly, though he looked to Janeph with equally hopeful eyes.

"It's the rumor among the men, so more than likely it is all a lie. But here we are, fetching children in the woods."

Janeph felt the hope rush fully through her, as well as a great deal of sadness at the mention of only two children. But it could not be coincidence; Petravinos investigating a shifting anomaly the day that they sent their marks to Endland and while Lopi and Mikel pulled a prank involving Chosen. She walked a few feet behind Petravinos, who had resumed his trek into the trees, and was pushing aside a small sapling. She was nearly even with him but paused as she noticed the scenery around her was darkening, but not from cloud coverage above. The canopy of the trees was thick enough that most sunlight did not reach them as it was. This was something else entirely. Ahead of Petravinos, the world was quickly burning bleak, as if someone had turned on a reverse lantern, casting darkness instead of light onto the world. Janeph took another couple of steps through the rough undergrowth until she was next to Petravinos, the world shrouding slightly with each step. She took a step backwards, and the world lightened. Another forward, and the darkness grew again. Petravinos experimented on his own, leaning his torso forward and backwards at the hips.

"What magic is this?" Janeph whispered as she stepped next to the old man, both peering ahead into the strange darkness. Petravinos looked around at the phenomenon before resting his eyes on Janeph and smiled somewhat gleefully.

"I can honestly say that I haven't the slightest idea."

Janeph was taken aback by the odd smile and even more so by his proclamation. He had lived three lifetimes with his magic and even he found their current environment a new experience. The prognosis frightened her.

"You haven't the *slightest* idea?" Janeph repeated in caution. Petravinos nodded in correction, still smiling.

"Well, I suppose I have a *slight* idea. I could venture a guess, but it would be only that," he said, stepping forward again. "How exciting is this?" he yelled out to the trees in exhilaration with arms stretched wide before him as he summoned an orb of light.

Janeph walked forward to follow him, pulling one of her long daggers from her belt as she spotted a series of broken branches alongside a set of multiple shallow boot prints. A lucky find in the lush green forest, but she would take it; they were on the trail. They followed the signs as the color slowly faded to shades of grey and black, the Gull marching silently behind them as Janeph now took the lead, the small ball of light from Petravinos bobbing around her. She tracked as quickly and silently as she could, stepping deeper into the woods and into the mysterious achromatic darkness. Soon they could only see a few feet in front of them before the surrounding dark snuffed out the rest of the world, even with the glow of the magic orb.

A row of thick trees came into view. Janeph, walking with her hands extended, very nearly felt the trees before she saw them. Tracking was nearly impossible now, as Petravinos commanded the orb low to the ground for her as the others huddled close in the oppressive dark, scanning what little they could see guardedly. Miraculously, she found another set of prints besides them, luckier for her even than the first set she had found at the woods' edge. They began following them, leading them parallel to the massive thick trunks, wide enough that three men would struggle to link arms around them, and arranged in almost a wall with their trunks so close together, no more than a foot apart. She thought it very strange that such massive trees could survive in such a confined way; the leaves were hidden in the darkness, but with their spacing, the branches of each tree would be fighting for sunlight to grow. In her years as a child playing in the woods, she could not recall such an odd arrangement.

A strange grey light shone faintly in the openings between the trees the further they followed the tracks, offering a very limited illumination that was a welcome reprieve from the pitch darkness. Peering between the trunks, Petravinos silently alerted the group to a single lantern, shining alone in a grassy clearing beyond the trees. Soon the prints led to an opening in the tree wall, offering a clear look at the source of the grey light. The prints walked into the grassy patch of forest in the center of the tree wall, towards the black-flamed lantern that sat in the middle of the strangely open area. It lay upon a knotted rotting stump, surrounded by a few circles of stones and small mushrooms on the forest floor. They expanded wider and wider from the stump center before they ran into the tree wall, which had a diameter roughly equal to their seven-member party if they were extended hand to hand. And despite the wide size, the entire interior perimeter of the tree walls was illuminated in the odd grey shimmer, offering a great deal more visibility compared to the foot or two that Petravinos's orb offered. With all of that, the most peculiar thing that Janeph noticed was the lack of sound from the forest. It was still vibrant and alive even in the strange oppressive darkness during their tracking, but sound had now gone way of the colors, disappearing from their senses.

"Something is wrong," Janeph whispered from the entrance to Petravinos. "The tracks go this way, but there is nothing here, it is walled off by the trees."

"Perhaps an illusion? Meant to throw us off?" Petravinos replied as he looked to the black lantern. "I agree though, something is off."

"Have we lost the trail?" asked one of the Gull as he stepped forward towards the pair.

"It leads this way," Janeph said, pointing towards the eerie lantern, "but it is a dead end. The trees close off any route but this entrance."

"If the tracks go this way, then we go this way," the Gull said plainly and walked past them into the clearing.

"We shouldn't, this is black magic," one of the Gull from the back of the party said, "When the black flame is seen, as day and night trade each other—"

"Quiet with your superstitious nonsense! We've been given orders. We follow the tracks."

The other Gull followed suit, ignoring the warning from the cautious Gull, as did Janeph and Petravinos after a moment of hesitation. Each step grew stranger, the walls of trees that surrounded them appeared to stretch further and further away the closer they got to the black-flamed candle, but its odd grey light still reached the tree trunk surfaces, illuminating a continuously widening area. And as they entered the circles of stones and mushrooms, some sound returned, but not of the forest. There were strange whispers, hardly audible voices around them speaking in an unknown tongue. The tree walls seemed impossibly far away, twofold the distance they had been at the entrance, but the Gull pressed on, unaware or uncaring. When the first Gull got within a few feet of the lantern, its light began to fade, taking with it the view of the tree walls as they were engulfed in the eerie black landscape. It continued to do so until it only offered a few feet of grey light in any direction, and the only thing that could be seen was the lantern upon its rotting stump and the innermost ring of mushrooms and stones that circled it.

"This was a mistake," Petravinos said grimly as the group subconsciously gravitated towards each other, circling their backs around the strange black-flamed lantern.

"What have you brought me, my child?" A woman's voice caressed their ears like the wind upon the leaves, gentle and chilling as the cool dawn air, rising above the other whispering voices that floated like mist around them. Janeph froze, feeling the hair on her arms and neck rise immediately, listening intently and hoping her ears were playing tricks. The party all did the same, none moving, waiting and listening carefully in the blackened world.

"An offering, eh, for you, my mother," a man's voice said without any of the silk that the first voice possessed. This one was harsh and ill-spoken compared to the completeness and pronunciation of the woman's voice. Petravinos looked back towards the guards and Janeph, a look of wonder and concern fighting for prominence in his features. The voices came from all around them, a source being impossible to discern as the Gull readied themselves, pikes drawn. Janeph's spine tingled up to her neck as the black flame withdrew further, casting more of the world into the eerie darkness. The party took another step closer together, closer to the dimming grey light of the candle.

"You spoil me, my child. This offering is . . . ." There was a pause and a sniff, the sound of one smelling a bouquet of flowers, " . . . *Rich* with power. And something else entirely," another sniff, floating around them indiscernibly. "Something I have not sensed in ages: *Chosen*."

Petravinos nearly fell over at the words. He looked to Janeph, eyes wild in excitement despite the unknown predicament they found themselves in. Janeph's adrenaline was pumping far too high to think too long on the meaning of the woman's words, but it meant it was all but certain at least one of the boys had survived the shifting.

"Yes, mother, yes. But there are those that would keep this offering from you, eh. We are pursued," the wretched voice replied with a hiss.

Janeph felt the group tense, collectively holding their breath in hopes that perhaps they were not the pursuers the harsh voice spoke of. The flame flickered, somehow casting their dark shadows unto the even darker world, betraying them.

"Yes. Yes, I can feel them," the smooth voice said, as Janeph could feel eyes upon her, searching and resting upon their company. There was another sniff, echoing around them. "Oh my, they are *rich* as well. What fantastically delectable children they would make; won't you fetch them for me, my child?"

The group could *hear* an inhuman smile, and collectively their skin crawled, goosebumps covering their bodies. Janeph looked around with a shiver and saw that Petravinos's intrigued smile had transformed into a straight-faced grimace. The Gull looked around into the dark and grey world through their unblinking helms anxiously, checking back to the others with rapid and nervous frequency as the grey light faded a little more and closed in around them.

"Of course, mother. May we have your blessing?"

"Yes, my child, yes."

The black flame of the lantern flickered again and the shadows deepened, encompassing them almost fully as the hushed whispers around them, still speaking unknown words to this point, now joined in unison. The soft chanting was like the wind, gently pressing their ears, a chorus of unseen spectres echoing around them.

In the darkness of the day
Across the land and sea and sky
Comes the children seeking play
From whom their mother needs reply

Beware her smooth and dire voice
It chills the bones whom sit and stay
And steals away the better choice
To begone at once without delay

Those who don't may see the flame
Of lightless dark and opaque grey

Yield or fight is all the same
Her children siphon them away

So when the black flame is seen
As day and night trade each other
Prepare, for from dusky sheen
Lo! She comes, death, the Nightmother

"By Phont, the Nightmother?" Petravinos whispered, barely audible to himself, his breath stolen by the fear in the air. His questioning put the company at the brink of panic.

"Mother takes care of her children. Won't you take care of your mother?" the voice cooed around them.

"Yes, mother," the voice said, but for the first time it did not echo from all around them. Janeph turned to its source and saw a pair of purple eyes open in the darkness before one of the Gull nearest her. She reached a hand in futility as the Gull too turned to face it, but it was over before it began. A blade flashed and a warm spray filled the air as the Gull's throat spilled onto the forest floor. He dropped to his knees nearly lifeless as the two nearest Gull stepped forward and lunged with their pikes towards the hidden attacker. The eyes closed in the darkness and where the pikes should have met flesh, they met emptiness. Janeph heard the swing of a sword through air as one Gull's head rolled from his shoulders and the other was run through, a sword erupting through his chest armor and out his back. Two more pairs of white eyes emerged on the edge of the darkness in front of the collapsing guards.

A rush of wind and light flared by Janeph towards the defeated Gull, staggering her as it whizzed by. The eyes in the darkness vanished, the wind and light whirling past and continuing beyond into the black scenery. It went well past where the wall of trees had been; the darkness carried it indefinitely as the magic grew smaller and smaller before disappearing into a speck. Petravinos stepped up besides Janeph with his staff gripped tightly, and Janeph pulled her second dagger. The two remaining Gull circled up with them, all four now standing back-to-back so they could survey all directions. Petravinos summoned a second glowing orb of light in the center of their formation as they scanned with strained eyes into the bleak lightless world around them. The second orb's light was hardly noticeable, casting another inch of suppressed light onto the forest floor.

"*That* one," the silky voice called out. "The wizard. Bring him, he is *delicious.*"

The Gull shifted a step towards Petravinos, just as a pair of white eyes appeared in front of Janeph. She touched her right blade to her left forearm, flat side so not to cut, and muttered quickly, "Lend your light." Sparks flew from her forearm, golden and hot they burst in every direction, the first color they had seen since entering the darkness. Her shield appeared on her left arm and produced a stronger light ahead of them, a focused lantern extending into a cone roughly 10 feet before the darkness overtook it. And in its light, it clearly showed ahead of them an older man with a scraggly short beard and a long sword in hand, glittering red with blood in the golden light. His face was caught in disbelief at his reveal, and he stepped back to find the darkness, spitting to the floor angrily.

"*Procaste!*"

Petravinos acted too quickly, pointing his staff to him as he called out in a thunderous voice. The older scraggly man, in mid-stride, froze with one leg reaching forward, locked in place. One of the Gull charged him, pike ahead of him for impalement as Petravinos concentrated with his staff held steady on the frozen assailant. Janeph stepped forward too, keeping the shield pointed towards the man and giving the Gull a clear image of his target. She caught a glimmer of purple to her left and rolled, feeling the wind of a blade rush above her head and through her dark hair. She rose to her feet from her roll, aiming the beam of light from her shield towards the scraggly man, but it only illuminated the Gull, pike extended in the air in a thrusting lunge that never met its mark.

"I've lost him in the darkness!" cried Petravinos, readying his staff again as he scanned wildly. Janeph quickly rotated the shield where her attacker had been, but found only the open forest floor. A guttural gurgling pulled her attention back towards Petravinos, where the Gull nearest him knelt on the fringe of the darkness, a long sword plunged down, deep into the crook of his neck and through his torso. The sword pulled out swiftly and retreated into the darkness, dark crimson showering the grass as it flung from the blade. The Gull held steady on his knees, blood leaking from his wound before he fell forward.

"Illumos Grandiose!"

A wave of light radiated out from Petravinos, traveling outward in all directions. It continued to expand, the Councilor Supreme concentrating with eyes closed and a sweat forming upon his brow as Janeph and the last living Gull searched for any signs of the attacker. The darkness was still complete beyond where the light touched, and they saw nothing within the illuminated forest that the spell revealed. It continued outwards before slowing down and reaching its limit, showing a huge open swath of grass that preposterously never reached the wall of trees; the clearing that was once seven men wide was at least five times that now, the rings of the rocks and mushrooms radiating outward ever further from the lantern in gigantic circles in a seemingly endless field.

"This is madness, I've illuminated entire cities with this spell and with barely half the effort I'm putting into it now!" Petravinos called through gritted teeth. His staff was planted in the ground with both hands and he quivered under the strain. Janeph and the last Gull moved towards the wizard, circling around the black-flamed lantern.

"Take out the source," Petravinos said laboriously. "Remove the lantern and perhaps this will dissipate."

The Gull did not need to be told twice and he reached for the twisted handle of the lantern door. His hand quivered an inch from the surface as he grunted with his strength to will his arm forward. It did not budge, repelled by an unseen force. Angrily, he pulled his hand, gripped his weapon, and swung his pike down with full force at the lantern atop the black stump. There was a flash and the sound of metal bending and snapping and as the light cleared, the lantern was revealed still atop the stump, unmoved. The Gull checked his pike to find the end of the blade cut cleanly, severed by the force of its contact, and he threw it to the floor in disgust as he pulled a short dagger from his boot and readied another blow.

"The flame will not be extinguished by anyone but her children," the silky voice mocked from the darkness around them, still slowly encroaching on the fading illumination spell. "You are *mine*." The darkness had overtaken Petravinos's spell to the point that the Gull's pike, had it not been severed, would reach the darkness threshold if extended fully. Petravinos shook mightily under the strain of the oppressive dark and eyed Janeph with worry.

"I cannot hold this much longer," he muttered painstakingly, "When it fails—"

He stopped abruptly as he crumpled to the floor, the light dissipating from the ending of his spell, the darkness rushing back to fill the space, leaving only the dim glow of grey light that the lantern emitted. A pair of purple eyes opened before Janeph and before she could react, the Gull leapt over her shoulder, dagger pointing down for a blow like a hammer to a nail. The eyes disappeared and the Gull swung at air and with the miss, he backed up rapidly to the little light that the party was circled around. A blade plunged from the darkness towards the Gull's throat, a killing strike with uncanny accuracy. Janeph parried for the unprepared Gull, swinging down with her dagger to redirect the blade to the Gull's chest armor, and simultaneously shone her shield in the attacker's direction. The blade glanced off the Gull's chest plate without consequence as the purple-eyed elf man retreated deeper into the darkness, dipping out of the shield's golden light and disappearing from view.

Two more blades flashed behind Janeph and the Gull, both aimed for the still-seated Petravinos. He quickly extended both arms, dropping his staff, as the blades approached and slowed to a crawl. He scooted back from his spot on the grassy floor, working back to his feet well out of reach of the blades as they resumed their speed and swung wide of their mark. The Gull and Janeph turned to counterattack but held off seeing nothing but the snuffed-out world around them. Petravinos grabbed his staff from the grass as the unknown female's voice cackled wickedly. The three regrouped again in a tight formation around the gnarled stump and lantern, heads swiveling in anticipation.

"These ones are especially succulent, aren't they, my children?" her voice asked with intrigue. The sounds of laughter rumbled from the darkness, answering the mother's rhetorical question in a noxious chorus. Clashing swords interrupted their venomous cackling, the woman's laugh sapped of its dominance. Janeph shined her light in the direction of the sounds as a sword clanged to the grassy ground before their feet, red with blood, followed by a stumbling boy with hands bound. The boy tripped over his own feet from an invisible shove that launched him from the darkness, rolling once and stopping on his side in front of Janeph. The Gull stepped towards him as he rolled with dagger in hand but stopped seeing his bound hands and his young age. Petravinos similarly readied his staff but relaxed as the boy sat up and looked to Jan.

"Zack?" Janeph asked cautiously as she bent low to look upon him.

"Nurse Jan?" he asked, fully confused. Mikel stepped from the darkness quickly, parrying a blade from behind him as he rolled past the party towards the lantern.

"Having a little trouble, milady?" he said with a smile, twirling his scimitars with ease.

"How in Phont's name did you find us?" Janeph asked incredulously. Another attack came from the front, the sound of the sword slicing through the air, which Mikel stepped towards and parried nonchalantly and countered with a front kick into the unseen darkness. There was a heavy sound of contact and a body landing solidly on the floor as Mikel laughed at the feeble attack.

"What's happened that so many men have fallen?" he questioned more seriously, seeing the Gull in the grass.

"This lantern, Captain, something about it has stolen the light from here," Janeph said frantically. "We've been on the defensive since the start and without any means to counter!"

He glanced around skeptically before he sheathed one of his scimitars, gripped the hinged lantern door, opened, and stabbed the top of the candle with his other sword. It bit clean through the soft wax just below the flame and as he retracted his blade, the flame of the candle came with it, leaving the lantern lightless. He quickly swung downward, cleaning his sword of the wax and wick onto the forest floor, and with a boot stomp, extinguished the black flame. Two blades came from the darkness, a purple-eyed elf and the old scraggly man behind them, aimed for Mikel's leather-armored chest.

Both were caught by an unbound Zack, blades in his bare hands as if he was catching a stick that a toddler had swung at him. The force should have removed both Zack's thumbs clean off and continued through his arms, but instead they were met with a thud in the crooks of his palms. Zack looked to his attackers, the whites of his eyes having overtaken his pupils, and as the darkness dissolved around them, so too did the attackers and their blades evaporate. The swords turned to mist and passed harmlessly through Zack's grip before disappearing entirely as the boy swooned and sat hard. He was partially caught by the Gull and Jan and was laid down where he stood on a large stretch of yellow grass.

"What power this boy has! And you!" the silky female voice said in surprise, her voice fading, distant with each word as sniffing could be heard around Mikel. "I had thought I knew all my children, but you?" The sounds of the nasal interrogation faded, and the light and color of the forest returned fully. The wall of trees that the party had been enclosed in evaporated as well, and they were standing in an ordinary clearing, ordinary trees, some small and others large, growing as best they could in among the grass and shrubs. There was actually quite a bit of dawn sunlight that shone through the canopy where they stood, and the only thing that was out of the ordinary was the black and twisted stump and the lantern that sat upon it. That and the dead grass and weeds that surrounded Zack, a short strip that extended from where he had lain bound on the ground to where he had protected Mikel.

"What in Phont's name just happened?" Petravinos asked, bewildered.

ACT 3
THE NEW ORDER

ENDLAND'S LORDS
AND LADIES

———◇———

The air in the hall was the biggest difference from the night before. The festival was jovial, everyone was there to eat and drink as much as they could, and the room was filled with the smells and sounds of a night comprised of mostly bliss. It was an excellent celebration with excellent people. But in one setting and rising of the sun, everything had changed. The same excellent people were in attendance but gone was the cheery and predominantly harmonious reciprocity between them. In its place was a skeptical and irritated hall, filled with men and women who only could speculate on half-truths from the night's proceedings. Between the Chosen children "hoax" and the Eislarkian horn being sounded in the early morning, they had taken the little they did know and twisted it into paranoid rumors, foreboding scenarios where unknown individuals were contriving unknown goals. For most found that Lord Belmar's ruse with fake Chosen to be ill-timed and out of character for the otherwise sensitive and bland lord. Humor was certainly not what he was known for, but rather a lack thereof, even when done in good taste and especially when done at his expense. And slowly throughout the morning the rumors of the kidnapping of the very same children had spread at the breakfast feast, further fueling suspicious substance to the rumors.

Some had heard that Petravinos had arrived in the morning's twilight, and others that not only he, but Lady Janeph Sarn and the Bonethorne Drifter had arrived as well, both of whom were members of an ongoing Trillgrand Hunt. There were rumblings of a *third* child, quite like the other two, with their strange dress and mannerisms, currently occupying the Eislark's infirmary wing and under heavy guard. The name of a long-dead Chosen was floating around the Eislarkian guards from a strange encounter on the water at Bim's Gate in the waning hours of the harvest night, though most of that hearsay was in jest. But more serious rumors also floated among the Gull, of four dead men lost to an unseen and otherworldly ritual and of orcs found prowling outside the city walls, one of whom was now thought to sit in the Eislarkian dungeon. The longer the breakfast went on, the more the rumors spread and morphed, expanding from three Chosen to a dozen, of Phont himself making an appearance at the bay's gate, and of an entire Trillgrand army mobilizing to secure the children. And the more the rumors grew, the less the lords and ladies were inclined to leave Eislark. Soon they had all clamored for an explanation of the oddities that had occurred that harvest night, demanding answers from Lord Belmar and Eislark. The young Lord begrudgingly informed the leaders that King Umbrin Sarn would be arriving around the midday to address the people on all their questions, which only fueled their speculation further and made Lord Belmar even more agitated.

When King Sarn finally did arrive, the aura of Eislark's Great Hall was clouded with tense and uneasy energy. The doors opened as two Blue Heart guards entered, another two behind them, and then King Sarn, adorned in a golden tunic, laced frills of pale blue puffed beneath his clenched jaw and tucked into his low-cut shirt, black chest hair billowing out the top like rain clouds amidst the blue skies. He was as put together as ever, even more so as he walked in front of his sister, Lady Janeph, who looked to have not slept the night and was walking with a slight bend to one side, hunched as she stepped down the center aisle. Her hair was not washed but had been attempted to be brushed. Black strands still twisted haphazardly from her scalp overtop the single braid that she wore. The light-colored plate armor she wore was dazzling white and sparkling blue but was scuffed in a few locations and had a dark dried bloodstain on the side that she leaned towards.

She walked slightly behind Forde Kern, his well-oiled bald head gleaming atop his all-blue robe ensemble. Bartellom was behind Janeph and did not appear to be in much better shape, but he walked with a toughness down the center aisle, especially when passing those of Bol-Garot. The largest of the guests, the barbarians, towered over the procession, drinking heavily despite the early hour. Jalp Dolhrant, adorned in what appeared to be the same exact fur clothing he had worn at the previous night's festival, spit on the stone floor just in front of Bart as the group walked by, promoting a chorus of low laughter from the other Garotians and a split-second pause from the Drifter before he continued without a word to the barbarian lord. King Sarn turned at the slight commotion but did not address the situation further.

Jalp and those that had traveled from Bol-Garot sat furthest from the raised throne, though only by a table length, and opposite Dern Dolthos of Swilmagapan, a curious-looking elf with one ear cut low, the hair around it shaved tight to his head as if to display the scarred appendage. The rest of his hair was long and an odd brown that glittered momentarily if the light caught it right, a dominant feature among the typically nomadic moon elves, as was his faint blue skin. But he was no nomad, he was the voice of the outcasts that the swamp claimed, the Lord of Swilmagapan. Even so, his clothing and style was benign, an off-yellow robe-like tunic with a wide green belt tightly wrapped around his thin waist. The Swill that sat around him were not only elves, but men, dwarves, a gnome, his half-giant personal bodyguard, Twop, and the notoriously shady but respected member of the High Council of Wizards, Polton Slint. A cast of misfits of those that society shunned or those that lost their way. None of their traveling party spoke as the king passed, many averting their eyes, save Dern, who acknowledged their king with a courteous nod and a smile. Umbrin either did not see or did not care to see and walked by without so much as a half nod. Dern still smiled, nonetheless.

The first set of tables, closer to the Eislarkian throne, were all filled by the less outsider representatives of Endland. Gritvand's hardened dwarf lord, Frilminn Warplod, sat stoically at the corner table of the aisleway, dressed in the full black and orange armor of his ancestors. It was hued with the glowing orange stones of the Southern Spine Mountains but its stylish look did not lead anyone to believe it could not take a hit; the armor was as finely crafted as anything in Endland, as was most of Gritvand's works. His long black beard showed small swirls of grey in it, matching the age of his wrinkling eyes, as wrinkled as one would expect of a lord burdened with running the largest mining operation in Endland. Easily half of any metal that anyone owned came from Gritvand and the expansive tunnels beneath the mountains to the south.

Beside him sat a small company of six dwarves, all equally armor clad but none as stoic. They could afford the jolly nature that their lord could not, and they took advantage. Gritvand boasted as many famous travelers and storytellers as it did blacksmiths, dwarves who set out to explore as much of Endland as possible, both above and below the surface. The six were drinking heavily at the midday meal and were undoubtedly giddy at the idea that they could be the first of Gritvand to tell the tale of Eislark and the new Chosen, if the rumor did in fact turn out to be true.

The next table over, still a front row view of the throne but away from the aisle, was the company from Dawnwood, appearing aloof and inconsolably bored. They wore rather elegant apparel, too fine for travel clothes, and perhaps that was the point. They often exaggerated their opulence to the point of annoyance when they were among anyone not from Dawnwood. The golden tree on the heavy purple backdrop was displayed proudly upon jewelry and light armor alike, all fitting trim and tight to their slender but toned elfin bodies. Most wore purple save for their lady, Clasari Blaidal, who wore a fine silver dress, which just hung above the floor when she stood and covered her arms halfway down her forearms before fraying into the dark purple of their emblem. She also wore a unique headpiece, a simple silver crown which came to a downward point that ended in a small golden leaf pendant centered on her forehead. The crown weaved between her light blond and braided hair and rested gently upon her fair, almost white, skin. Her small company sat around her, drinking their post-meal wine and talking quietly with little mingling among the tables around them.

At the other side of the aisle at the corner sat the lady of Verir, Sydnus Rethered, and her men, dressed quite the opposite of Dawnwood's company. Verir was known for its hard labor society and their clothing matched. A dark blue river ran across their chests if you asked a Verinite, though to anyone with sense it was really just a blue sash that hung from shoulder to hip and was the crudest form of a city logo in Endland. Their castle hall was much more decorated, but in terms of apparel, it was lackluster to say the least. It was very clearly not a priority for Lady Sydnus though, for she was far from a pretty woman and found no pleasure in playing dress-up. Instead, she had forged Verir into the most industrious city of Endland for anything involving manual labor innovations for farming, logging, herding, or hunting. Their machinery and gear were second to none and were it not for nature's bountiful blessings of grain upon the grand Trill Plains outside the capital, Verir would boast the most well-kept provisions on the continent.

Lastly represented was the city of Cliffpoint. Lord Xod Trintek and his sailors were from the southernmost point of the Western Island, the only city away from the mainland that lived by the Eastern Island rule. A rough bunch, their clothes, even their fine clothes, smelled of salt, sweat, and fish. Xod was well-dressed, regardless of the smell, fit in a fine copper-hued captain's coat and a leather skull cap that hid what little hair remained atop his head. He wore a heavy-looking chain around his neck which held an even heavier-looking medallion, engraved with the copper water droplet of their lands. The men and women that had accompanied him wore similarly dreary-colored garb, copper and black and brown on every shirt, pant, and shoe. They gave the appearance of a group that had seriously enjoyed their stay the night before and were dealing with the consequences of that enjoyment still at the afternoon hours now. One man held a wooden bucket between his knees, wiping his mustache clean of the stink of his own puke as he stared his mess in the face. The king did his best to ignore the Copper Drops, grateful perhaps that they were not nearest the aisle, and waited patiently at the foot of the stairs before the Eislark throne.

From the lone back hall behind the throne entered Petravinos, Lord Belmar, Lopi, and Captain Mikel. Lord Belmar was especially well-dressed, a tight red shirt with white trim around the seams and a pair of slacks, cape, and boots to match. Lopi matched the color scheme with his robes while Mikel wore his usual black-maroon leather garb, and similarly Petravinos in his oversized blue robes with his large worn straw hat. They met Umbrin at the stairs and all four bowed in unison before Lord Belmar made his way down the steps and extended his hands.

"My King, welcome to Eislark." Grekory and Umbrin clasped hands and shook enthusiastically. "I trust your trip went smoothly last night?"

"Yes, quite well, thank you, Lord Belmar," Umbrin said as they together climbed the steps to the throne. Lord Belmar motioned toward his Eislarkian throne, to which King Umbrin obliged with a smile and a half nod. The rest of the group took their seats atop the landing to the side of the king, Lord Belmar directly to the king's right, Mikel beside him, and Petravinos and Janeph on his left. Advisor Kern stood just behind the king's throne and Lopi stood awkwardly at the back doorway after Petravinos took his seat, before electing to stand between the Councilor Supreme and Lady Janeph. Bartellom never ventured up the stairs and instead sat at the corner of the Verir table, the men sliding away and cautiously offering him a mug of beer, which he humbly accepted with a smile. The man from Cliffpoint at the table next to them puked in his personal wooden bucket, perhaps taking of whiff of the alcohol, as the rest of the Drops laughed quietly at his misfortune.

"People of Endland," Umbrin started, interrupting the guffaws, leaning forward in the chair as he spoke. "I have come to

Eislark this day, riding through the night, to celebrate a potentially momentous day in Endland's history. I know not all here believe in what Petravinos and the High Council have deemed a necessary toll on our treasury and on our lives." Grumbles from the Garotians and those of Dawnwood came at their backhanded mention; they knew who they were, and they certainly had no issue voicing their displeasure with Vinos's obsession with the Chosen. "But today we may see the fruit of this tiresome labor. Today, perhaps, we will look upon the Chosen once more!" He looked over the people as they held their breath in anticipation and then addressed Lord Belmar directly, leaning one forearm on the throne's armrest and crossings his legs as he spoke.

"Lord Grekory, can you shed some light on what has transpired this last day?"

The request clearly caught Grekory off guard, having just settled into a slouch as their King spoke. He abruptly sat forward and cleared his throat awkwardly. "Of course, my King! Of course!" He cleared his throat again, louder with a fist before his mouth. "Lords and Ladies of Endland, as you undoubtedly saw at the harvest festival feast last night, we had some unexpected guests join us in the middle of our wonderful celebration."

"You mean the 'orphan pranksters'?" Jalp called out unapologetically and with enough sarcasm to fill one of the large barrels of beer they had drank the previous night. There were some annoyed chuckles from the crowd as Umbrin waved his hands to calm the noise and motioned for Grekory to continue. He cleared his throat a third time.

"Yes, as it turns out I was given some faulty information and I was not certain what was happening—"

"You were not certain what was happening? In your own city? That cannot be right, is it?" Umbrin interrupted coldly, waiting with a raised faux-surprise brow for a response. The corner of Grekory's mouth twitched slightly, but the rest of his posture remained statuesque, his eyes screaming silently at the king. Grek breathed deeply one breath through his nose, eyes still fiery, before replying directly to Umbrin.

"We have not had a Hunting Party start their journey from Eislark in some time. So, the news of new arrivals did not seem logical. I spoke at length with my trusted council, and we decided it best to keep things calm until it could be determined what was going on."

"Yes, it is as our Lord says, my King!" Lopi pipped from beside Petravinos, looking as awkward and out of place as ever.

"Or perhaps you intended to keep these supposed Chosen for Eislark," Lord Xod of Cliffpoint interjected before Umbrin could, his heavy sailor drawl dripping from every syllable. "Too closely bound are ye to Trillgrand, you the ugly wench of the two. Perhaps now ye mean to be wearing the makeup?" There was murmuring, mostly in opposition to the statements, but some in support, mainly those of Xod's crew.

"Not likely, Lord Xod," the Swill wizard Polton Slint replied. "What Lord Belmar states is true, Eislark has not launched a Hunt from their borders in many months, and he would not be so bold as to attempt thievery from the King himself. Even so, in the event there are actual Chosen in Endland, they should not be kept exclusively to the city that boasted the Hunt, Trillgrand or not." Many in the crowd applauded softly at his words. "The scrolls I have had the privilege of reading tell of the power of the Chosen, of their ability to do great things. And of their ability to do terrible things. They cannot be owned by a single city; it would throw off the balance of power that Endland currently enjoys." Lord Dern looked to his wizard crossed, but Mikel beat him to any retort.

"Owned, Polton? The Chosen are not animals, they are not Endland's slaves to be whisked across the continent to do our bidding. These are but children, and they must be treated as such, cared for and nurtured before being cut loose to protect us. Give them freedom, something to fight for, not servitude."

"If they are Chosen, they must be made to assist us," Umbrin said. "Just think of the possibilities. If what Polton and the Council say is true, we could be on the precipice of a second Golden Age. We could end the Northern and Western threats in weeks, perhaps days, eradicate them entirely!" There was some upset grumbling, mostly from Jalp and the other barbarians.

Disagree or not, those not of the East were still very much related to them and their ancestors. "And I suppose I should not be saying 'if' anymore, correct, Mikel?" Umbrin continued. "Did you not see these children on your Hunt with my dear sister and the brute? And if you did, and if they are here, then they must be Chosen, correct?" The Garotians and Jalp objected to Bartellom's minor reference with hearty huffs as Umbrin finished his last question to Petravinos, turning from Grekory to look to the wizard. The old man nodded reassuringly under his large hat.

"It is as you say, my King. To survive a shifting from outside Endland, to be alive and well here and now, they must be Chosen."

"Wonderful, let's assume they are Chosen then," Polton said with unbridled skepticism. "How can such power be controlled? Who among us can teach Chosen how to be Chosen? And furthermore, where in Endland will they reside while undergoing their teaching?"

"That is where I can come into play," Petravinos said from his chair. "I am the foremost expert on Chosen in all of Endland. Every scroll that is known to us, every scrap piece of parchment that has ever been run across, I own or have read at length. I've explored their Order as much as anyone alive, and I believe I can teach them what is required of them."

"Then it's settled. The Chosen will return to Trillgrand with Petravinos until the time that they are ready to defend us," Forde said from behind Umbrin's seat, pressing for closure on the subject.

"Now wait just a minute, there are problems in our lands at this very moment," Lady Sydnus of Verir said openly and boldly, using her husky frame to project her voice. "I don't have time to wait for their training, they are needed now! Our loggers have gone missing in Mobord Forest. My men speak of something lurking in the trees. They only work in the brightest of daylight and only on the very edges of the woods. How long until the Chosen are able to defend us against these mysteries?"

Lord Frilminn stepped forward slightly in the aisle with a stomp of his black boots. "Aye, we've trouble in Gritvand as well. Our deepest mines can no longer safely be worked in. The men say the shadows come to life. None have gone missing as yet, thank Phont, and condolences to you, Lady Sydnus, for the loss of your men. But this shadow, its presence works on our minds, gnawing at us, it causes disorientation and confusion. We've no time to wait around for this to grow and spread, we need action now." He took another step, becoming slightly more animated as he leaned his axe against his torso and punched one black armored hand into another. "That is what we were promised! Our resources, our soldiers, and our commitment to the Hunts—and we would find a Chosen to aid us. It's been two years of growing uncertainty, and now that we may finally have them, we must wait again? For how long? What encompasses training of Chosen? Will it be another two years?" The stoic dwarf spoke with a charisma and charm that was quite remarkable for the oft gruff dwarves, further augmented by his grave delivery. Many of the crowd nodded and mumbled in agreement as he stepped back into his dwarfish ranks.

"If I am being honest, they are needed here as well. I saw it firsthand," Lady Janeph said from her chair. "As did you, Councilor Supreme. Darkness stirs in the Narrow Woods, and Bartellom also met an orcish scouting troop just outside Eislark." There were some crossed looks towards Umbrin and Grekory at the news of the orcs, Grekory squirming mildly in his chair. "But even given these pressing problems, and I've no doubt what you say is plaguing your lands is true, these new Chosen are not ready to be our redeemers, nor are they ready to be our protectors from an orcish war party or whatever it was we encountered in the woods. We cannot simply toss them into the unknown and expect them to relieve us of these issues."

"All of these stories do not bode well for Endland, and I understand the desire for immediate results." Bartellom stood from the Verir table and addressed the crowd. "But we must not spoil this, there is no second chance. They are our only Chosen."

"What do you mean these are our only Chosen?" Lady Clasari asked pompously. "If something were to happen, we will simply go find more. Now that we've successfully extracted two, the process should come much easier, no?"

"The spare shifting stone is run dry," answered Bartellom.

"Do not address this pile of human feces," Jalp spit to Clasari, before Bartellom could elaborate. "He's not fit to address anyone here, save maybe the pigs running about in their pen." The Garotians banged their chests and punched the tables in united raucous approval.

"Order, Jalp," Umbrin said with suppressed amusement. "Your differences will not be decided now, though I certainly do not appreciate his leaking sensitive information, but I suppose it's already out now. We've expended the last of our free shifting stone to bring these boys here. Their Hunt was the last of Endland." Silence filled the room at the unexpected news as he looked to the brute with disdain. Bartellom looked to the crowd meekly, clearly unaware that the news of limited shifting stone had been secretive. "But do not worry, people of Endland, for we no longer need shifting stone! After years of effort and sacrifice, it appears we once again can say confidently that Chosen walk among us! Endland will soon see another prosperous age!"

The cheerful news brought some applause, but there was a damper on the mood, most notably from the Dawnwood table who still appeared quite bored with the conversation, and from Bol-Garot, who were drinking regardless but with skepticism written plainly in their posture. Umbrin waved as several servants came forward and handed out mugs and cups to those that sat upon the raised platform with him, except Lopi who was skipped over accidentally. Umbrin raised his glass to continue his address, smiling to the crowd in an attempt to win back some excitement.

"My King, before we toast, perhaps we should invite Endland's newest members so that we might all judge for ourselves these potential Chosen?" Lord Grekory asked as Umbrin shot him a sharp look.

"Do not interrupt the king, Lord Grekory," Umbrin said with a look that would dent a shield. He paused and waited, feeling the room collectively rise in anxiety and watching as small beads of sweat formed on Grekory's forehead. Just as the Lord began to reply, Umbrin cut him off, smiling wryly. "But yes, I suppose now is as good a time as any for us to introduce these 'Chosen.' Hopefully your Eislarkian manners have not rubbed off on them in their short stay here."

"Yes," the elfin Lady Clasari called out in agreement. "Let us see those that would throw our world into disarray."

"Let us see those that would save us," corrected Sydnus with a snarky roar and narrow eyes aimed at the beautiful elfin queen.

"Bring them forth!" Umbrin said with moderate excitement as he opened his arms to the people. Mikel snapped his fingers twice from his chair, smiling disarmingly to Lord Grekory, whose face was nearly as red as the Eislarkian crest. A pair of Gull at the Hall doors in the back of the room promptly tugged on the handles and swung open the heavy doors as the entirety of Endland watched intently.

30

PREPARE FOR
THE WORST

———◇———

ryce and Walding walked quietly down the hallway, Bryce
limping on a wooden crutch with his recently siphoned
leg still woefully weak. Walding watched him from the
corner of his eyes, arms clasped together loosely at his waistline
beneath his worn over cloak. The four Gull that escorted them
did not slow their pace for the crutching boy, and he was struggling slightly to stay in the center of the square formation the
guards walked in.

"I'm fine," Bryce said, noticing Walding's concerned looks.
"Whatever Mr. Lopi did sort of numbed it a little."

"It does not look like it is numbed. They should have just let
you rest, there is no need to drag a wounded child around the
castle on one leg, especially without telling us where we are going. You would think Lopi or Mikel would have escorted one such
as you personally instead of leaving us to their dogs!" Walding
called ahead loudly and with excessive annoyance to the two
Gull leading them. They did not respond, which furthered his
irritation and he let out an exaggerated huff to voice it.

"Well, it's fine," Bryce said, and gave a fake grin and a
thumbs-up with his non-crutched hand to back it up.

"Does your thumb hurt too?" Walding asked, dismayed. "You showed it to Lopi when he left as well."

"What? No, it's fine."

"Why then did you show it to me?"

"You don't know what a thumbs-up is?"

Walding scoured his mind at the question. "No. Does it mean your leg hurts?"

Bryce laughed, shaking his head. "No, it's like a symbol for 'OK.' So, like, you could ask me how I'm feeling, and I could give you a thumbs-up and you would know I was good. Or a thumbs-down if I am not good. Get it?" Walding nodded slowly as he spoke.

"I see, so it is similar to an ear pull?"

"A what?"

"Pulling your ear means you accept a proposed trade, it's quite common among the people of Endland. Sticking your finger in your ear means the opposite. It actually originated among the old street traders of Pilanthi, a universal language for any who entered the small town before it expanded to the rest of the land."

"Huh, you learn something new every day. Is Pilanthi where you're from?" Bryce said as they rounded another corner into the wide tower with the stairways that they had infiltrated the night before.

"Yes, it is where I grew up before leaving for my new Chosen life." His words were distant, and Bryce saw his eyes glazed over in remembrance before realigning with reality. "But I suppose you do learn something new most days, although I would not say every day. Suppose you simply sat in your hut all day, what then would you learn?" Bryce began to explain it was a saying, but instead just smiled and nodded in agreement. "Although, if you sat in your hut, perhaps you would learn a lesson in patience? Or of the side effects caused by sitting on one's ass all day. Perhaps learning something every day is realistic after all." He grew silent and scowled in deep thought as they labored down the stairs. Soon the echoes of another conversation came over them, distant but getting louder as they continued forward.

" . . . honestly the coolest thing I've ever done. Like frozen, in the air, floating. It was insane!" an impish voice drifted to their ears. Bryce craned his head towards the sound, picking up on the familiar tone as Walding continued to brood upon the concept of learning daily.

"Dude, that's nuts but wait, I've got one too. I caught a sword with my bare-freaking-hands, well two swords I guess, one in each, and it didn't even leave a mark! Look!"

"What? You caught a sword with your hand? Man, we really are like superheroes, this is crazy!"

"Children, this way," a strong voice said as a set of doors could be heard opening. Bryce quickened his pace towards the sounds, brushing next to their Gull escorts before being promptly shoved backwards by their strong hands. He looked to the Gull angrily but returned to a half step behind them, just out of reach of a shove if they tried it. They rounded a corner with the Gull to see a set of large double doors closing, the frame of which was intricately decorated in the red and white theme that they had seen throughout the castle. Their escort stopped in front of it as a large amount of clapping and cheering could be heard from beyond the doors.

"Phont, that sounds like a lot of people," Walding said, stroking his beard thoughtfully.

"Did you hear them?" Bryce asked excitedly, turning back to Walding, crutching quickly over to him. The old man shook his head, befuddled.

"Yes, that is why I said it is a lot of people. You see, only a large number of people can make that much noise when clapping, my boy. Do people not clap in crowds where you come from?"

"What? No, not the crowd, before that! It was them! I swear it was them! Zack and Johnny!"

"Your friends? The other Chosen?" Walding was now equally as excited as Bryce, bending over to look him in the face with wide blue eyes. "Then Mikel was successful in retrieving them! And despite their being taken by the Nightmother, that is rather impressive. But with that many people in the Hall to see them . . . ." Walding grew silent and began to pace between their escorting guards anxiously a few times before bending low towards the boy again.

"Listen here. It is the harvest festival, which means the lords and ladies of Endland are in this city and more than likely the king of the Eastern Island himself, all of whom are beyond these doors. We will soon be introduced to them all, which means that my intentions to keep all of you hidden is being erased as we speak. Phont, Lopi and Mikel will know I am no servant of Eislark." He was talking faster with each passing word, his eyes widening with growing realization, and he stood quickly in surprise. "My presence will also be revealed to Endland."

"That's OK, right?" Bryce questioned slowly, trying to bring his tempo back to a normal cadence. Walding bent at the waist again to address him eye to eye.

"No, it is not. I am not well liked in Endland." Bryce cocked his head in skeptical doubt, as Walding continued, "You see, when the world discovers you, they will seek to build you up and every path will be made clear for you. You three will be gods among men, so long as you stay in their good graces. But I am afraid I've since fallen from that path, and when they discover that I am still here, things may get . . . confrontational."

"But you're Chosen too, aren't you?" A Gull turned curiously to look at the pair, but Bryce paid him no mind. "Whatever happened, they won't hold it against you, right? I mean, I wouldn't be here if not for you. I'd still be stuck on that stupid floating island, or stuck at the gate on a boat, or arrested at the castle, or covered in weird black veins," Bryce said, worried, his eyes saddening as Walding drooped his head and sighed and met Bryce's gaze with a heartbroken stare.

"My boy, I have done some horrible things in my past that the world despises me for. I was never to return here, but I could not leave the world I love unprotected. So, I watched from a distance, waiting and listening in case I was needed. Your arrival signifies that time is now, and it means my time is at an end. You will have Geaspar at your disposal, who will be of great assistance to you. But I will not be allowed to guide you any further I am afraid. They will have my head at the end of a noose or atop a pike, and justly so given my actions." Bryce searched the old man's face for signs of a joke, but his somber face did not show any hint.

"This way," The Gull said as he and his counterpart began to open the doors.

"I know we just met, Mr. Zarlorn, but you don't seem like much of a bad guy to me," Bryce said confidently. "And Geaspar certainly seemed to like you once he actually knew who you were. So, who cares what happened before? You're the only one who seems to know what's going on around here."

"Let's go," the Gull behind them interrupted, standing awkwardly close to usher the two into the doorway.

"Whatever happens, remember, you must not gather, it is best not to push your body. My fate is my own. My choices have led me here. The life, the death, the journey is all at hand."

"I've got you, Mr. Zarlorn," Bryce said as he leaned on his crutch, pulled his earlobe, and gave a thumbs-up before he crutched into the room. Walding worriedly shook his head in protest, but Bryce was already entering through the doorway into the Great Hall.

———

31

OUTLAW IMPROBABLE

After a moment, a pair of Gull entered, followed by two young boys and a final set of Gull behind them. The crowds clapped and cheered loudly at first but it deadened the further the boys walked down the aisle. Johnny was waving as if he were royalty and gave some finger-guns to a large Garotian who had hooked him up with a mug of beer the night before, while Zack did his best to hide his swiftly blushing face. The large barbarian, clad in an even-larger bear fur, only stared at Johnny in disbelief.

"These are truly them?" the large Garotian said in a booming voice, louder and deeper even than Jalp's. "I had thought they might be a diversion for the *real* Chosen."

"Wow, man," Johnny said as he mean-mugged the burly man, raising his arms out wide in protest. "I'm nobody's diversion. I'm my own man, I created myself!" He flexed his thin scrimpy arms with a goofy smile.

"Come now, the Garotian is right. This is another ill-advised prank from Lopi, right?" Forde Kern said from behind Umbrin. "Where are the real Chosen?"

"These are really them," Mikel said, embarrassed, rubbing his forehead and covering his eyes from his chair, "and I think it must be evident to all that they very clearly need guidance and training before being asked to do anything of significance

329

for Endland." The crowd nodded among themselves, watching the two boys, thoroughly unimpressed. "But nonetheless, they are here and they are Chosen!" He stood and clapped loudly as a few crowd members joined, but most remained silent given the underwhelming visual, notably the king and the rest of the group atop the throne area. "But there is more still, where is the other!" He called to the back and snapped his fingers again. Janeph was shaken from her smile toward the boys as Mikel gave a quick wink. Umbrin looked most annoyed.

"What other? What is the meaning of this?" He snarled, but the Gull at the back were already opening the double doors with a heavy pull, as all eyes shifted with the sound. An even-less impressive small boy entered the hall, crutching along in a pair of torn pants and a bandaged leg, followed by another man, as old as the boy was young, who looked just as ragged in an old brown ripped cloak. Janeph stood from her chair, and Bartellom did similarly from his bench alongside the travelers from Verir, while Zack and Johnny turned and sprinted towards their hobbled friend, skipping high in excitement. They were stopped abruptly by armored Gull hands, who caught their arms just below the shoulder and held them loosely in place.

"B-man!" Zack said loudly behind the Gull's restraint. Bryce was still hobbling quick as he could across the tan stone floor while the old man observed the trio with an odd smile. The Gull escorting Bryce stopped him from reaching the others, a small chasm between the friends. The separation caused all three boys to frown at the stoic knights before returning their gaze to each other in elation.

"You guys are actually here!" Bryce said as he fist-bumped Zack and then Johnny over the Guards hands, dodging their iron gauntlets to do so. Janeph ran down the stairs as Mikel approached in a more controlled manner, meeting a smiling Bartellom in the aisle with a clap on the large man's shoulder. Bartellom grimaced and moved away sharply as Mikel apologetically smiled and clapped the other shoulder instead. The guards that had led Johnny and Zack into the hall stepped in front of Janeph to prevent her from approaching further.

"If you do not move, I will move you myself," Janeph said with a tough stare. There was some chuckling among the crowd, but the guards stepped to the side after Mikel waved them off. The friends each threw an arm around Bryce's shoulders as the guards separated, and Janeph bent low to hug them all. She pulled away and looked them over with a surprisingly sad look, and the tears that welled in her eyes were now questionably for sorrow as much for joy.

"I thought I had doomed you, Bryce. I hope you can understand why I did what I did." She whispered softly, "Please forgive me."

"Um, no problem," Bryce said, sheepishly eyeing her armor more closely now that he was not fleeing Jamesett. "But I don't really know what you think you did, I'm fine. Lopi patched me up good in his sick room. And these two seem just dandy."

"By the way, in case you didn't know, we might be in England," Johnny said informally to Bryce. "That, or you're just a figment of my dream. I'm leaning England, but still not really sure which one at this point if I'm being honest."

"You've got problems, man. For the millionth time, we are not in England, and we are not dreaming," Zack corrected as he threw his arms up in frustration, while Janeph snickered, stood and stepped back from the trio, wiping her eyes. "We're in *Endland*, and this is real life. Not that it makes it any less weird, but it's reality."

"Alright, whatever man. Also, B, we're in a castle," Johnny continued. "Also, also, we don't know if we can get home. Also, also, also, we met a wizard, and we have superpowers. Also, also, also—"

"My King, Lords and Ladies of Endland, may I formally present the three new Chosen of Endland!" Mikel interrupted before Johnny cascaded any further. The trio of Hunters clapped loudly, Bartellom banging his chest with his good arm, but most of the crowd only watched in disbelief. Johnny was quickly soaking up what was given with waves and blown kisses, while Zack and Bryce waved with significantly less enthusiasm. Petravinos had descended the stair and was making his way towards them now smiling ear to ear with unrelenting excitement, clapping the whole time he walked towards them.

"Chosen! Actual Chosen!" He walked forward and pinched a tuft of Zack's flowing hair. "I cannot believe you are actually here! You've done it, Lady Janeph, you've done it! We must start their training, there isn't a moment to lose!" He wrapped an arm around the lady in celebration, as he noticed Walding for perhaps the first time. "My, oh my, and who is this here? Is this their caretaker in the castle? I think we can relieve him of his duties now, Captain Mikel, don't you?"

"Not before recognizing this man's service to Eislark; he was paramount in ensuring these boys stand here before you. I would not have been able to track them so quickly were it not for him," Mikel said, leading the king for some sort of acknowledgment. Umbrin sighed in boredom. "Although, I never quite got your name, sir."

Lopi laughed from the throne stand, "Come now Mikel, I know it's been a rather eventful day, but surely you would recognize your own servant?"

"I don't know him, I thought he was one of yours. Why else would he insist on bringing the boy to the infirmary for care?"

The air in the hall shifted to unpleasant as Mikel and Lopi both gazed upon Walding. Umbrin was visibly growing impatient and irritated at the ongoing nonsense, and the crowd around the tables curiously looked to the old tattered-looking man, who remained motionless, hands clasped beneath his cloak.

"Please, for Phont's sake, state your name, servant," Umbrin said as he rubbed his forehead with an open hand, eyes cast aside in open detest. "Let us recognize you so that we can move onto the important matters at hand." Walding said nothing as he looked around at the crowd, analyzing the people, before Bryce nudged him elbow to elbow.

"What, my boy?" He said aloud and not at all at a whisper. Umbrin raised his face to the sky with a loud and labored sigh.

"Too late, you've lost your chance. Begone, fool, you've served your purpose. Now then, let's decide the best method for handling these children, shall we?" Umbrin waved a hand towards Walding, and the two Gull closest to him grabbed him abruptly by the armpits, much to the old man's surprise. Bryce was a little nervous but smiled and gave a thumbs-up to Walding, knowing a natural escape had been made for the old man. The guards escorting him moved easily towards the main doorway.

"Uh, so that guy is who exactly?" Johnny whispered to Bryce, arm still around his neck.

"I'll tell you later, but it's good that he's getting out of here now."

"The question still remains," Lord Xod asked loudly. "How do we proceed with these 'ere so-called Chosen? I care not for ghost stories. I'm more concerned with the *real* threats out there; orcs are roaming outside Eislark. How long till they decide to make another pass at the capital? Or until they restore their alliance with the sea people? They've both been quiet for far too long if ye ask me."

"If the Nightmother has returned, orcs and nymphs are the least of your problems; she is as real a threat as there is," Walding said aloud as he neared the door with his Gull escort. The lords and ladies looked dumbfounded but Petravinos's interest piqued, and he unwrapped his arm from Janeph's shoulder and took an inquisitive step towards the man.

"The Nightmother, you say? And why would a commoner like you think such a creature exists?" Walding looked over his shoulder toward the wizard, surprised, and then quickly to the Gull on his right.

"Did I speak aloud just now, sir Gull? I could have sworn I thought that instead of speaking it." The Gull said nothing but gave an emphatic single nod. Walding winced as Petravinos motioned for the Gull to turn him around to the rest of the crowd, which the guards promptly did.

"Do you intend to answer the Councilor Supreme's question, or do you intend to convince us you did not speak?" Polton Slint questioned him from his place alongside the Swillmagapan table to a series of laughs from the people. Polton did not join them; he was quite serious.

"I intend to figure how I spoke what I thought without thinking to speak it. Have you ever had that happen? Where you think you're thinking but find your thinking is speaking? Quite an odd phenomenon, isn't it?"

"Can't say I've had that happen in all my years," Petravinos said as Polton chuckled at the man's steadfast moronic antics. "But you've still not answered my question."

"Ah, yes, apologies," Walding quickly answered and tried to turn back to the door, but the Gull held him steady towards the gathered people.

Petravinos waited for more of a response but when none came after a few moments and the giggles began through the crowd, he looked incredulously back towards Polton, whose face was equally dumbfounded.

"Who is this man?" Petravinos asked agitatedly, arms open as he turned and called out to the crowd, looking specifically to Mikel and Master Lopi. None responded, most still snickering at the boldness and apparent idiocy of the old peasant. Janeph leaned closely towards Bryce to ask the same question, but he instead hobbled over a few steps and whispered as best he could to Petravinos.

"He's really not always like this, he's been really helpful to me since I got here. And I think he might be able to get us back home." Petravinos turned back towards Bryce and laughed loudly.

"Helpful? Get you home? I am sorry, boy, but you must have this man confused with someone of ability, or perhaps more importantly, a fully functioning mind."

"Bryce Blooms, his name is Bryce Blooms," Walding called from the doorway. Petravinos composed himself well, but the man was clearly starting to irritate him.

"First of all, Bryce, you belong here in Endland. Going 'home' is not an option."

"Wait, what?" Bryce looked to Janeph who averted her eyes, and he quickly snapped his eyes back to Petravinos. Johnny and Zack scowled with Bryce.

"It is the burden of the Chosen," Petravinos continued. "Endland is your home now, and it is your duty to defend it. This world is the linchpin that tethers the other Realms together. Your abilities must be utilized here, or your world, all worlds, may fall into disarray. But more importantly, this man is incapable of securing his own thoughts within his mind, let alone lending aid to others. Whatever you think he can help with, I can assure you that I am far more capable. You'll find no greater expert in the ways of the Chosen than I."

"My, the years have certainly brought you as much knowledge as they have misplaced pride," Walding said aloud, still perhaps unaware that he was speaking aloud. Bryce moved to interject, but Walding only paused a moment before continuing. "I remember the Petravinos who was ever humbled by his unbridled lack of knowledge. The wizard who knew that his prowess was embarrassingly minute when compared to the universe's vast reservoirs of untapped enlightenment. What has happened to you, my old friend?" Walding asked innocuously. Petravinos's face grew red with embarrassment and he gripped his light wooden-colored staff and bellowed, magically amplifying his voice so that it filled the room as thunder across the sky:

"You are nothing, peasant! A meaningless fleck in a cosmos of benign debris, slaving in a castle where you will die and be buried in a servant's grave! Your burden is light and your tasks meaningless! My knowledge alone has shaped Endland and the Realms beyond the Void more than you could possibly imagine!"

Walding broke his vision from Petravinos and looked away for a moment in deep thought, as if he had been slapped viciously across the face, sobering his honest eyes. The amplification of Petravinos's voice may have also had a physical element, a magical and invisible strike to the old hermit. But when Walding raised his gaze to meet the wizard's again, he straightened his spine, pressed his shoulders back, and grew a full three inches in stature from what all had assumed was just his hunched posture, bowed forward from years of gravity slowly pulling down. And as they had been when infiltrating the Roost, Bryce saw the clarity in Walding's old eyes break through the clouded inner cobwebs that swirled about his mind. Walding stepped forward and looked up to the king and around to the lords and ladies, who all watched as they too felt the transformation that was taking place before them.

"I know far more than you think, Petravinos Morgodello. But clearly you have lost sight of what is important. I had not intended for this to be revealed in this manner. Truthfully, I had not intended for this to be revealed at all. When I saw you were here, I had honestly wished it would be you who acted on the Chosen's behalf. But I am afraid I must take that role given your pompous state of mind, oh Councilor Supreme. I am sorry to say that I am more needed than I had thought. They must be trained, and I must do it."

None spoke. Umbrin Sarn sat upright in his chair, looking in grave concern at the power this man was conveying over his people. Johnny's eyes were wide with fascinated admiration and Zack's grin matched the feeling, their anxiety of home forgotten. Bryce smiled nervously seeing what he thought must be the Walding of yesteryear, the one that Geaspar had feared so unequivocally at the Worn Thorn. Petravinos's eyes were narrowed, searching the old man for recognition through every wrinkle of his mind and before Walding continued, he seemed to have found it, for his furrowed brow released and his lips parted with impossible realization.

"You lords and ladies mean to debate who will train these Chosen. Where they will live, how they will grow, and what you will teach them of Endland. What you truthfully contend is how their power will be distributed to you and when you will each get to wield it." He paused, perhaps for effect, perhaps to see if there were any objections to his accusation. None came. "But we are not soldiers in your armies! We are not pawns of the sovereign! We are Chosen! And we do not take orders from any in Endland! The burden, the struggle, the triumph, emboldens!" He closed his eyes and breathed deeply and reopened them, alight with passion, and looked directly to Petravinos. "You say I am nothing! You say I have shaped nothing and that I will die as nothing! But it is *I* who has shaped more than *you* know. I am the last remnant of the Golden Age that you all so desperately cling to, sucking the last drops of milk from the teat I provided! For I am the Last Chosen of the Old Order, the Prophet of Pilanthi, the conqueror of Kuor-Varz. I am the Lord of Storms and Grandmaster of the Chosen Order. I am Walding Zarlorn!"

The room was stunned. Had his words not been so forceful, so eloquently delivered, they may have laughed at the outlandish proclamation. But they were profound, and they rang true in the now-silent hall. The rumors of Walding Zarlorn being denied entry through Bim's Gate the night prior were still in the back of their minds as well, and all it took was one look to the Councilor Supreme, the only living man to have seen the banishment of the Chosen firsthand, and they would be convinced of the strange man's words. For Petravinos looked to have seen a ghost, and in essence he had. His mouth was still agape, a pale white flush had taken his normally red and cheery face, and his wide brown eyes told the story. This was *actually* Walding Zarlorn. One of the handful of Chosen still known by the commoners through legends and folk songs, Walding the prophet, and Walding the fool. Umbrin was standing now at the edge of the stairs, angry with Walding's bravado, as he stared calculatingly and sipped his wine. Bryce looked around quickly, remembering what Walding had said in the hall and fearing spears may suddenly be thrown his way or a noose drop from the ceiling and wring his neck immediately.

"Impossible!" Petravinos cried out, snapping from his stupor. "This is impossible! You were banished! I saw you banished, disappear before my very eyes!"

"It is I, my old friend," Walding said soundly and with a touch of sadness. "Though perhaps former friend is more appropriate. I wish I could have told you. But it was for the best that I remained hidden and I am truly sorry for deceiving you." Petravinos's unhappy eyes scowled as Walding offered a weak smile in hopeful reconciliation.

"Walding Zarlorn, the Lord of Storms," commanded Umbrin, snapping and pointing to the old man as the Gull responded, pikes now pointing towards him. Bryce moved towards Walding in protest but was held back by Janeph's strong grip on his upper arm. "You were to be banished from Endland for all eternity, never to set foot on our lands again. Why should I not have you killed where you stand?"

"Because you need me. I am the only hope for Chosen to truly return to Endland."

Umbrin laughed in the otherwise silent hall as he finished his wine and approached the odd man, walking down the short steps to the aisleway. The people, all standing to look at the Chosen master, watched intently as Umbrin crossed his arms, one hand massaging his beard in pretentious thought.

"'I need you,' you say? I can't see why. I've the Councilor Supreme to train the Chosen. I've a united Endland to fight orcs, sea people, and the shadows that draw from the darkness as of late, if you believe that nonsense. And in a short time, I'll have three young Chosen to defend us. What need have I of an old, murderous, exile-breaking fool?" The eyes of the room moved to Walding, like watching a slow-moving tennis match, waiting for the return swing.

"The Councilor Supreme does not know the first thing in training Chosen. I have trained dozens, hundreds perhaps, in my years as Grandmaster. I do not need scrolls and research to know how best to train them. The information resides in me the same as my bones. And while your united armies would do well against the threats of this world, as misguided as that conflict may be, they will not fare as well against the darkness. Especially Kuor-Varz."

Umbrin, taking the man's words trivially to this point, stopped at the Grim King's mention. Johnny and Zack bounced on their toes at the name, recognizing something in this strange world for the first time but clearly giving the wrong kind of reaction. All others present reacted in a similar manner to Umbrin, straightening abruptly with curled lips as if smelling a stiff drink. Some audibly gasped at the name.

"We do not say that name," Umbrin whispered. "A bad omen to utter it, especially within a city. Phont himself would hesitate to speak it! He is gone forever, you sent him yourself!"

Walding shrugged. "You are correct, but that was a long time ago now. Do not think that this growing darkness is mere coincidence. The Grim King seeks a return from the Medius, to finish what he started here, to spread throughout the Infinite Realms. I have felt his power grow from beyond and I am quite sure he is actively trying to return."

"The darkness is always fluctuating; it has nothing to do with the Grim King. A return is impossible, he is bound to the Medius," Petravinos pipped in a hurried voice.

"You are blinded, my old friend, if that is what you truly believe," Walding said plainly as Umbrin continued forward and was now just beyond the Gull whom held their pointed pikes toward the Grandmaster. Janeph and her Hunting Party watched their king, as she motioned Zack and Johnny close. Janeph knew her brother well. The look in Umbrin's eye was the same as it always was when he had found his maneuver in the political game that he so loved playing.

"You reveal yourself to us, the same day that Chosen arrive again in Endland," Umbrin said, clasping his hands behind his back as he began to walk back and forth between the aisle, his stage upon which he would perform. "Curious, is it not? While we have descended further into darkness over the last years, by your own estimation, you did nothing. While the cities of Endland spoke of obscure phantoms and vile creatures in the wilds, of the disappearing countrymen of Endland, you did nothing. While orcs raided our cities and villages, and the nymphs our boats and vessels, murdering and plundering, you did nothing. You've done nothing for more than 100 years! But, now that Chosen have arrived, now you make yourself known to the world, blabbering of demonic ghosts of the past and the universe's impending doom. You come in demanding that instead of fulfilling my duty as king and upholding your punishment, a just punishment as decided by our predecessors, I should instead pardon you? And not only pardon you, but also entrust our new Chosen to you for personal training? Because, conveniently, you are certain that the Grim King is planning an escape from an inescapable world, and you are the only one capable of training the new Chosen adequately to stop him. Does all that sound right?"

Walding hesitated as he analyzed the statements. "Yes, that sounds right, although the Medius is not entirely inescapable." Umbrin faltered as he paced, surprised at the open admission to what he was sure was a damning argument. He quickly regained his composure and smirked a thin line of white teeth.

"It would seem to me then, that this Grandmaster has lain in wait for his opportune moment to extract his revenge upon us. To steal away the only hope we have of combating the terrors and to use these young Chosen against us! To build his New Order in his vengeful image and regain his lost status through Chosen warfare!" Grumbles of agreement rolled around the lords and ladies as they eyed the old man suspiciously, some placing a cautious hand upon their weapons while the Gull took a half step closer toward Walding. Umbrin stopped his pacing and snapped for more wine as he set his jaw in a standoffish glare and smiled confidently. Walding stepped forward towards the King, unaffected by his words or by the tight fan of weapons that the Gull pointed at him.

"King Sarn, I can understand your concern," he began as he took another half step so that the blade of the nearest pike was within but an inch of his chest, just above his clasped hands. "I have not been merely on extended vacation; I have felt the subtle presence of Kuor-Varz since before my banishment, an impossible feeling, but there all the same. And it's grown since then. We've all seen the signs as of late, especially the High Council. His influence is slithering through our lands like the roots of a weed. The attacks in the mines of Gritvand's southern expanse, the woodland beasts in the forest of Verir, the man of the swamp lurking in Swilmagapan, orcs and goblins on the move through the Trill plains, stirring of the ogres in the Mild Mountains, Jornun's ghosts rambling throughout the Realm, well beyond the city's ruins, the Nightmother just this morning outside of Eislark. You think these mere coincidences? The Grim King seeks to gather his forces and return to Endland, and I fear he is closer to that reality than we think."

"Preposterous!" Polton Slint cried. "The Grim King is gone and has been for a century and nary a whisper of his name has been heard. Evil comes and goes like the tide, and while the waters are rising in this age, they shall recede with time." He seemed to be convincing himself as much as the audience, emotionally delivering his words with unrestrained anxiety.

"Time is not enough, Councilor Slint. Good men and women and their efforts are all that can deliver us from this dark hour we find ourselves in. Do not think time alone will solve this, that wishing this away will simply give the Grim King reason to abandon his vision for an Endland, for a universe, under his rule. And if you truly think this is but the natural rise and fall of good and evil, why then did you and the rest of the High Council initiate the Hunts to find and return Chosen to Endland?" Walding looked around for an answer, which no one was prepared to deliver. Polton shrunk at the pointed delivery that Walding had calmly spoken. Even Petravinos stood quietly as the people chatted among themselves.

"All of these have one answer," Walding continued, "because you have sensed it as I have, admittedly or in denial, that it is the Grim King's orchestration of these forces. He gathers his generals, his armies of the dark, and he intends to use them in his return, though I cannot say how or when. But he is coming." The people muttered more in contemplation, uneasy words filling the air. The boys soaked in the discussion like children watching cartoons, while Umbrin scanned the nodding people in a mild panic; he was quickly losing the room.

"But we've still time to act before we reach a tipping point," Walding continued. "I alone cannot repel Endland's evil, but with these additional Chosen, we stand a chance. This New Order of Chosen must be trained for the coming battle. And it is a matter of *when* not *if* this conflict will come to a head, of this I am quite sure. Will the good people of Endland support this New Order and stand against the coming darkness? Or will we continue to pretend all is well until it swallows us whole?"

"I ain't working on nothin' or going nowhere with no Walding Zarlorn—and neither are me men," Xod said assertively as he crossed his excessively hairy arms atop his small gut. "The Grim King's but a myth, as I've said since the start of dis'ere moronic Hunting. Ghost stories for the lil'uns to keep 'em in line. I'll crush any evil that eyes Cliffpoint myself. And while the rest of you lot may believe these'uns are special, I for one, do not. Nor does I believe this man sayin' he's an actual Chosen is anytin' but an ol' fool."

"Lord Xod speaks poorly but wisely," Clasari said in back-handed support. "The Chosen are gone; these children are just what they appear, children, and this man has lost his mind, brave or delusional as he may be to confront us with such a preposterous story. The Grim King is gone, and these Hunts have been nothing but a waste of time and resources." The rest of the room remained silent, and the longer it stayed that way, the wider Umbrin's grin became, beaming to the Councilor Supreme. Petravinos did not meet his jeering eyes and instead scanned the remaining lords and ladies in disappointment.

"If no man will offer their sword, then perhaps a woman will do," Janeph said at length, slamming her fist to her breast plate and striking Umbrin's smile in an instant, replacing it with a dangerous glower. "Wherever you must go, whatever you must do, I offer my services to the New Order."

"As do I," Bartellom called, still outside the Gull perimeter, somewhat near Umbrin and Mikel. The Garotians all roared boisterously before Jalp was able to call loudest above them.

"Bol-Garot will not send so much as a bag of dead rats to aid any party where that filth walks among them!"

"And we will not need you! A true barbarian already accompanies them!"

Jalp pulled his axe from the table he sat at, chugged his mead, spilling at least half upon his braided brown beard, and stepped forward on the other side of the Gull perimeter.

"You sound like you need an axe between your eyes, you filthy Bonethorne! It's high time to put an end to your worthless clan!"

"I've been on a Hunt for weeks, returning battle worn and wounded, rode through the night to be here, battled orcs this morning, and I've still the strength to smash your skull, you false lord!" Bartellom pulled his hammer with one hand, the other slung tight to his chest in wounded rest. The Gull now turned their attention away from Walding and looked outward to the two barbarians, Mikel doing his best to restrain Bartellom as the Blue Hearts ushered Umbrin backwards toward the throne. Lord Grekory whistled as more Gull entered from the hallway in rapid organization, surrounding Jalp with more pointed pikes.

The rest of the crowd sat back and watched; it was best to let barbarian matters be settled barbarically if at all possible.

"That is quite enough!" Umbrin cried out from atop his throne and behind his guards as his cup was filled with still more wine. "You can sort out your squabble on your own time, but not here and not now! The Drifter is free to waste his life as he sees fit, no one here cares what becomes of him. But Lady Janeph would do wise to reconsider her position and to remember her voice does not speak for Trillgrand or their people." Janeph did not turn to see Umbrin's eyes dagger her as Bartellom lowered his hammer to his back again. Mikel relaxed slightly next to him, as did Jalp as he sat heavily at the Garotian table and grabbed another cup of mead. Their pair of eyes did not leave one another, the fire between them raging silently.

"Bol-Garot, Dawnwood, and Cliffpoint have voiced their refusal for these Chosen," Petravinos said aloud as cooler heads prevailed. "The Bonethorne Drifter and Lady Janeph would continue their walk with them as individuals. What of Eislark, Gritvand, Verir, and Swilmagapan? Have they an opinion to cast in this discussion?"

"Hold now, Councilor Supreme," Umbrin called, surprised. "It sounds as if you are actually considering allowing this fool to live—and train our Chosen."

"That is because I am," Petravinos said quickly. Umbrin looked to those who had just voiced opposition, looking for support before he settled and sat in his chair with a shrug and a sip of wine.

"I will remind the Councilor that he does not have final say in such matters. The king will need a majority of the free people's agreement to allow such a thing to occur," Umbrin said, articulating each syllable with heated irritation. Frilminn tapped his hammer lightly to the stone floor and began speaking assuredly amidst the tension, Umbrin's head whipping to see the dwarfish lord take a step into the aisleway. "We would happily support their company if they would venture to Gritvand to investigate our southern expanse's mines. And if they should prove helpful, perhaps the companionship could continue beyond our borders."

"Aye, Verir would like to see their work before committing any men to their cause. Results beget rewards. For now, we would offer cautious support to this New Order," Lady Sydnus said in a calculated manner.

"And we would be most honored to host such peculiar individuals in Swilmagapan. I would suspect you'd find yourselves most comfortable amidst our people," Dern said with a short bow, to the very evident displeasure of his Councilor Polton. The king looked to each of the accepting leaders in extreme annoyance and then to the silent Grekory. The young lord sat forward, but Umbrin spoke before he could, timing his words to leave his lips just before the Eislarkian lord could speak.

"Eislark will continue to offer their hospitality until this amalgam of misfits departs, but I am afraid their efforts to their cause will end there," Umbrin said confidently from his seat as Grekory was forced to pause, mouth open as he held his speech. "Orcs were outside these very walls and one rests within the prison cells as we speak, so I am told. It would be wise to hold attention here."

"Surely one man could be spared," Mikel said lightly to Umbrin and Petravinos both, smiling to disarm the king. Grekory seethed atop his chair at the blatant overstepping of Umbrin's power.

"If you are referring to yourself, Captain, surely one man could not be spared," Umbrin replied coldly. Mikel looked to Grekory puzzled.

"My Lord, this—"

"Is exactly what Eislark needs, I agree, Captain." Umbrin cut off again, looking back to Grekory with an annoyingly large smile. "Strong leadership is required from the Eislarkian lord at this time of turbulence. It is settled, Eislark will not be supporting the new Chosen given such immediate threats outside its borders. Do you not agree, Lord Grekory?" Umbrin asked rhetorically, leaning forward in his chair and looking to the lord on his right. Grekory's eyes were embers, longing to ignite Umbrin aflame, and he licked his teeth beneath his lips in frustrated restraint. Umbrin leaned back as no answer came and sipped his wine in victory.

"I do not agree, my King," Grekory said firmly and with a fake smile. "Orcs or not, Endland is greater than a single city. We will deal with the threats, but we will also support this New Order and their exiled master. It cannot be coincidence that these new Chosen happened to arrive in our city. Eislark was part of this Hunt at its inception and Eislark will be part of the Chosen's future." Umbrin leaned forward again and for a moment it was unclear if he would allow Grek to live he eyed him so fiercely; it seemed he might strangle him right there on his own throne. But he soon smiled assertively and turned his attention to the rest of those gathered.

"And Trillgrand will, unfortunately, be unable to send aid. So that splits the room, four cities in favor and four against."

"My King, there is still Suthore to consider, who is not present for the festival," Petravinos reminded Umbrin gently.

"What poor judgment on their part, they've chosen not to attend and so they've forfeited their right to speak. And in that case Endland is split, and it must come to the king's decision." He looked smugly at Walding, and those leaders that openly supported the venture, and cracked his neck, twisting his chin upwards to both sides before settling deeper into his chair and slurping his chalice.

"There will be no New Order as long as this traitor walks among them. He has betrayed the trust of Endland and is in direct violation of the punishment handed down by Endland's ancestors." The Blue Hearts had moved down the short stairs and among the Gull as he spoke, and the troop of knights turned attention towards Walding now that the barbarian squabble had subsided. The old man stood his ground, hands held in one another beneath his long, worn sleeves, as he looked to the guards without visible concern. Umbrin stood from the throne and smiled his white teeth to the outcast.

"Walding Zarlorn, for that is whom you claim to be, you are hereby sentenced to death, by decree of the King of Endland, for violation of your banishment at the hands of my great-grandfather, Lobran Sarn, and the High Council of the first age of Umbrin." Two guards moved behind Walding, each gripping an arm as the rest of the guards' weapons were drawn and aimed towards him. "The Chosen belong to Trillgrand; they will be trained there under my guidance until I deem them ready for duty."

"You can't do that!" Bryce called out wildly, trying to crutch toward the old man as Janeph held him steady. Walding smiled to the boy, ignoring the weapons drawn against him.

"The burden, the struggle, the triumph, emboldens, my boy."

"What the hell does that mean?" Bryce retorted in frustration.

"If the new Chosen wish to be among their murderous counterpart then let them! They can have a front row seat to his end!" Umbrin called out laughing, his cocksure smile and pompous posture taking charge as he sat back into the Eislark throne with a backhanded wave of disinterest.

"This is not the proper course! You'll ruin everything we've done! Everything we've worked for!" Petravinos cried out in protest as the hall fell into chaos.

"Quiet yourself, *we've* worked for nothing. This Chosen insanity was always your idea and now it's resurrected a traitorous enemy, standing here in the flesh! I will uphold my family's decision from all those years ago!" Umbrin yelled back. "Take the children away or let them watch, it matters not. This execution begins now!" The Gull pressed their blades to Walding's chest as Bryce tried desperately to wiggle free from Janeph's restraint. The lords and ladies looked among each other, some in amusement, some in open detest.

"No!" Petravinos yelled with exuberant force. "It is the Council's duty to advise in Endland's best interests, and so I must advise against this. Killing a Chosen master at this time, even one as notorious and quite honestly deserving as Walding Zarlorn, is a preposterous discourse. Walding must go free and he must be able to train them under our supervision! We can discuss how and where but we must trust there is enough repentance in his old Chosen heart that he will act justly toward Endland and its people."

"I'll not be spoken to as a child, Councilor Supreme! Kill him and any that would prevent his death!" Umbrin yelled manically as his humor gave way to frustration. Bryce burst free from Janeph's grip with an abrupt shrug of his arm and stepped towards Walding, moving his hands together and towards his chest, trying to align his pinkies and thumbs while maintaining his balance on his one good leg.

"No, my boy!" Walding desperately yelled. He moved to stop Bryce, but his arms were held tight by the guards behind him and multiple pikes were promptly pressed to his chest and torso, piercing his old worn tunic. He closed his eyes and jerked his arms forward with all his strength as he clasped his hands, pinkies touching and pointing down, thumbs up, the rest of his fingers interlocked. It was done far quicker than Bryce could manage, quicker than even the Gull and Blue Hearts could recognize, years of muscle memory at play, and Walding quickly pulled his palms to his chest. A blast of air pulsed around his body, knocking the weapons a few inches away and out of his clothing as the windows on the far sides of the room shattered. A wild wind whipped through the crowd and swept Bryce from his feet before his fingers could interlace. He landed flat on his back in a stupor. The sky outside, a sunny day with soft summer clouds, was quickly becoming grey as thunder rolled ominously around the hall.

"Kill him!" Umbrin cried out hysterically, losing his aloof demeanor as lightning crashed outside the windows and thunder echoed as if it had clapped directly over the gathered people. The Gull around Walding lunged their weapons at their king's command, but not before Walding forced the wind around him upwards, knocking the pikes towards the ceiling with the strong gust. They formed a metal tepee as the pike blades clanged safely above his head. A large bolt of lightning flashed outside, blasting a hole through the ceiling that crashed to the floor just next to the hall doors and left black and smoking scorch upon the light brown stone.

"The next bolt will find its mark!" Walding warned loudly beneath the metal blades of his attackers. Umbrin said nothing as the Gull and Blue Hearts retracted their weapons and readied a second strike. The wind blew around him a second time, this time lifting him upwards and off of the ground, his tattered brown cloak billowing in the intense force. The blades again missed as they were thrust at chest level, now beneath his levitated feet. Lightning burst through the ceiling and connected with the interlocked pikes below him, blasting the guards that wielded them backwards from the shock. Walding lowered upon the charred and warped metal weapons as he looked to the dazed Gull and Blue Hearts, all of whom slowly sat up. The storm cleared slightly, thunder booming in the distance, a warning of what may yet be called upon. Petravinos, Lopi, and Polton all had staffs in hand but only watched him as he stood in his original place atop the sizzling heap of fried blades.

The king had dropped his glass in the stormy commotion, spilling wine across the sandy brown stone. It dripped down the stairs as he walked from behind the Eislarkian throne from which he had taken cover, peering to the old man with disdain. Petravinos, Lopi, and Polton now lowered their staffs as the wind died down, and it swept calmly back towards the shattered windows, moving the broken glass into neat piles a few feet from the openings. Bryce sat up from the ground, Zack watched with a blank look as he processed the commotion, and Johnny punched the air in adrenaline-rushed action approval.

"It is as Councilor Petravinos says," Walding continued somberly. "Now is not the time for this. I can assure you when the threat is gone, I will fulfill my original sentence. But for the time being, Endland needs me. The New Order must be assumed with these three at the helm, and I must be allowed to train them properly by the Chosen code. I will take them and train as we did in the Golden Age and, in short order, Endland will have its new Chosen warriors."

Umbrin was beside himself with anger. "You've attacked me directly and now you expect me to just let you go? You expect to walk out with the new Chosen under your guidance? I do not think so, you treacherous monster! You do not have Trillgrand's support, and therefore you do not have Endland's support. Take a look, good people of Endland, see this vicious demonstration of the reckless power these individuals possess! Walding Zarlorn has made himself known for but a few minutes and behold the destruction he has caused!" He pointed to the gaping holes in the ceiling, smoldering from the lightning that had ripped through it, and the windows at the edge of the room, where a warm breeze now blew. "And now he seeks to train three more in the same manner! Is this what Endland needs? Support this treason at your own peril, but do not doubt your king when I say that the bodies will begin to mount if he walks free. Any who aid him invites death to their doorstep!"

"Is this the best way, my King?" Dern asked quietly. "To act with such vitriol in front of our newest Endlanders?"

"He is a treasonous murderer! It was already ruled upon years ago! What other way is there?" Umbrin cried incredulously.

"Perhaps one could be found if all were involved," Frilminn countered cautiously, addressing more of the crowd than directly to the king.

"A dwarf without conviction; it be a sad day for Gritvand this day," Xod mocked disappointedly.

"Says the cutthroat," Lady Sydnus sneered. "Watch whom you insult, pirate. Frilminn only seeks proper justice."

"Which was already decided ages ago, as our king has said," Lady Clasari replied coldly, not even turning to address the lady of Verir.

"Circumstances have changed, Lady Clasari. What was decided in the past may not be best in the present," Lord Grekory said with calm and grace. Jalp very quickly erased his attempt for restraint as he gripped his axe and stood atop his bench.

"So much blabbering! I know a way to solve this right here and now! Last one standing decides what action to take!"

"Your king has already spoken! There should be no argument beyond that!" Umbrin cried angrily.

"My King, good people, I think it best to discuss this at length. And perhaps to allow Suthore's opinion to be heard? You are our king, but this is quite an unprecedented situation, and it would be wise to hear the people's opinions," Petravinos said as he turned to Walding with pleading eyes. "Can we ask that you move to Eislark's holding chambers until we have had time to decide the best recourse? And that you not prove us trusting Endlanders wrong by being a menace to this fair city? It would be as short as our stint in Jornun's cells, if you recall all those years ago."

"Of course, my old friend," Walding replied without a moment of hesitation. "I've no ill will towards anyone here, but the stakes could not be higher. Please, lords and ladies, as you make this decision, please know that I only have Endland's best interests in my heart."

"This is preposterous! We've all just been openly attacked by an exile and now we must decide if we should enforce a sentence on an already convicted man?" Umbrin was steaming and had stopped making attempts to drink wine for the first time since his arrival. The king breathed sharply through his nose with a semi-snort as none responded to his tirade. "Fine. The outlaw will be placed in the dungeon immediately. In fact, place them all the in dungeon, we can't be too safe. The guests will remain here, and the lords and ladies shall convene in Eislark's Council Circle." He paused to read the room's confusion. "Do not mistake this momentary mercy for absolution. This man is no friend of Endland. I expect this discussion will be swift and its results beyond contestation."

"Of course, my King. I think we are all in agreement with this recourse and the finality of the outcome, whatever it may be," Petravinos said with a short bow. Walding matched with his own bow as Umbrin searched the room for the faintest hint of verbal opposition for which to unleash another outburst, but in finding none, he promptly turned his back to the crowd and left down the hallway behind the throne, the Blue Hearts following closely.

"See to it that this lot is placed in the dungeons, Captain," Grekory called to Mikel as he followed down the hall with Lopi close behind him.

"Yes, my Lord. We will await your decision," Mikel replied to him as the pike-less Gull recircled around Walding for escort. Grekory acknowledged the reply with a brief wave above his head before he disappeared in the hallway followed by the other lords and ladies. The rest of the guests watched the parade intently before shifting their eyes to the mysterious Chosen and the outlaw, their faces ranging from fascination to disgust. It made Bryce uneasy, and he looked back to Walding with an uncertain smile.

"Nothing to fear, my boy. We will be out of here in no time," Walding stated with a more assured smile. "Well, in some time. Not no time exactly. Even the simplest of tasks require *some* small sliver of time, don't you agree?" Bryce laughed and nodded and took strange comfort in the odd man's demeanor as the multitude of Gull took positions alongside them and the boys.

"If it's alright, Mikel, I'd like to go with them as well," Janeph said, stepping with Zack and Johnny into the escort line.

"Of course, milady, it is your Hunt after all," Mikel said with a short bow. "And I don't suppose Bartellom intends to sit here with the rest of the guests?"

"I truthfully wouldn't mind another ale, but I am not sure alcohol and a room full of unsupervised Garotians is the best place for me," he joked as the others noted the agitated glares coming from the barbarian table.

"Agreed," Mikel laughed. "It will be a full escort indeed. This way everyone, off to the dungeons with ye!" he joked as he thrust a finger in Johnny's face in jest. The boys all laughed as the Gull began their movement out of the hall, the entire Hunting Party and Walding in tow.

32

ODD ALLIANCE

——◇——

He could hear the commotion from the stairwell, a clamoring of quite a few people, and listened intently for the sounds of his brethren. But the voices were high pitched and jovial, and he quickly ruled out any chance of a rescue. It was probably for the best; if others were captured, they might be inclined to talk. He would not.

The torchlight of the passing group began to further illuminate the dim hallway outside the small bars on his cellar door, and he peered as best he could through them. The shackles that bound his wrists to the wall were made for a man and were slightly lower than would allow him to stand full height, forcing him into an odd and uncomfortable half-slouched stance. But even so, Blark could very clearly see the tall blond man who had killed his companions, Sha and Foll, and he could hear the voice of the human boy they had nearly eaten. He snarled under his breath but before he could hurl an insult at them, more clamoring came from the stairwell.

"Captain Mikel!" a young girl's voice called out.

"Yes, young one, I am here."

"I've only been told to give you this."

Blark strained to see out the bars that were only open in the top quarter of the door, but could see nothing. The soft pitter-patter of the girl's footsteps back up the stairs echoed until they faded away.

"Hey, that's another one of those coins!" a young boy exclaimed excitedly, though it was not the one that Blark recognized. "That's super rare, right, Mr. Zarlorn?"

Blark gulped. Everyone knew the name of Zarlorn. He had thought the boy in the woods to be bluffing, but given how Sha had suspended in the air, and now the name of Zarlorn, perhaps the Chosen were indeed returning. The hope in his belly churned uneasily with consciously contained enthusiasm. It was a feeling he had not felt, perhaps ever in his life.

"Oh, is it chocolate? I love chocolate coins, I call dibs!" the familiar boy's voice replied.

"No, young one," an old voice replied. "It is the mark of the Councilor Supreme."

"Has he sent word on the Council's decision already? My brother is determined and oozes charisma, but even he could not have convinced the room so quickly." The woman's voice was strong and well-spoken, and Blark strained his neck again for a glimpse but was unable to see anything or anyone aside from the back of the blond barbarian's head. The sound of the parchment unrolling could be heard and Blark waited in anxiety, which surprised him greatly. Human dealings never gave him such interest.

"Petravinos wants the Chosen to leave. Including Walding," the captain said very quietly after a moment. "He says we cannot risk Umbrin undoing the efforts to bring Chosen here. We must escape. And he apologizes for being unable to directly help, but if he left the Councilor Circle, he would be the first suspect. He must maintain his position to guide Umbrin towards reason."

"Well then, he does mean us well. He did mention our jailing at Jornun, I thought that odd," the old voice said aloud.

"What is a Jornun?" a third boy's voice asked innocently.

"It is a very old city, dear boy. We were captured in Jornun as young men, many years ago, and without any justification I might add, but we never made it to the cellars. We managed to disarm our escorts and had to run out of the city still bound. We roamed the countryside with the chains around our wrists for days before we found a smith willing to unhinge us. So, the jailing in Jornun never truly happened, as he intends this jailing to never happen."

"Well then, let's go! With Micky leading, that should be easy, right?" the first boy's voice asked.

"I wish it were so, Bryce. But if I travel with you, there will be consequences. Umbrin would label me a traitor, and given my advisory role to Grek, the lord would suffer, and therefore Eislark would suffer. Umbrin is always looking for ways to undermine Eislark, and an act of treason such as aiding a formerly banished and convicted criminal's escape would all but seal my Lord's fate. Even without me accompanying you, Eislark will most likely suffer, but I cannot abandon this city. I want to do what is best for you boys, but Eislark needs stability as well. I fear I cannot simply escort you out, I'll need just cause for being left behind," the captain spoke apologetically.

"Then by force," the barbarian said. "We stage an escape, rough you up, Mick, beat some guards, and make it appear we've overpowered you. With a Chosen Grandmaster on our side, an escape is not an absurd outcome. And with your persuasive street-charm, you can convince the king it truly happened. Although you are correct that your reputation may take a hit, but Eislark should be spared Umbrin's wrath at your expense."

Blark's mind was racing. A Chosen Grandmaster. An impossible thought but perhaps Walding Zarlorn was truly outside his cell!

"My reputation means little, Eislark and Lord Grekory is what matters. The Belmars gave me new life, I can pay them back this day without regret if I must. But with a forceful escape, you will put the entire city into lockdown. We can stage it here, no problem. But the next set of guards you see beyond this dungeon, they will not so easily allow your passage. Beyond the dungeon here, you must go quietly."

"How are we supposed to do that?" the voice of the boy they had captured said. "If it was just me, I'd go ninja mode and be out lickety-split. But Bryce has got a bummed leg and there are like 50 of us in this group, so it would be pretty impossible to sneak out, wouldn't it?"

"There are 6 of us, 50 is not even close," the old man corrected with little emotion.

"I know that, gramps, that's why I said *like* 50. Saying *like* gives me some leeway."

"So, saying *like* gives you plus or minus 44 people of leeway? Is it that hard for you to count to 6?" the one boy asked with heavy sarcasm.

"Yes, Zack, everyone knows that *like* is a numerical fudge factor. It's first grade, man. Sometimes I wonder how you've made it this far in life."

"Enough, we're running out of time. They debate as we speak and their decision will more than likely not favor us," the woman interrupted. "We stage it here and then we walk out normally. My status has weight behind it, and without the Council's decision formalized yet, no one will be searching for us."

"Lady Janeph, as my actions would affect Grek, so too would yours affect your king brother," the captain replied. "Umbrin will be pushing for Master Zarlorn's execution and for the boys to be trained by Petravinos personally, no doubt within Trillgrand's walls. You'll be aiding a convicted murderer escape, and you'll be accused of kidnapping the boys. What's left of your title to Trillgrand would be revoked at the very least. Umbrin could not allow such insubordination is his own family. He would make an example of you to show his strength. You would be an outlaw, Janeph, everyone here would be."

There was a pause but from the words and tone that she eventually spoke, Blark could only imagine the woman was smiling. "I understand what it would mean."

"Very well, and I don't think there will be much change for you Bartellom, no offense."

The blond man snorted a short laugh. "I've lived my life essentially as an outlaw. This will simply be a formal title change. But it is too bad that we won't have a true street rat leading us, Mick. We could use someone who knows how to avoid detection and is as well-connected as you."

Blark saw the captain smile meekly as the large blond man moved slightly and unblocked the barred window. "I wish I could, my friend. But I can offer a captain's opinion on the next days if this escape goes well. The moment Umbrin's meeting ends and they fetch for you, the world will know you've gone rogue. Trillgrand's army is vast and the king's reach is wide. He will have the backing of the lords and ladies given your escape, and he will inform his army to begin searching the land while Eislark will undoubtedly be called upon to ensure the waterways are locked down, which Grekory will need to honor given the embarrassment of your escaping from his own city. And in back channels you can believe the king will have a black-market price on your heads. The reward for the return of the children will be immense, every bounty hunter from here to the Wastes will be looking for you. I just don't see how this doesn't end with Master Zarlorn, and most likely Janeph and Bart, at the end of a noose or run through on some back road or in the middle of the wilderness in not more than a day or two."

"You saw the room was split as well as I, Captain. Even with the king's command, there are those who would sympathize with, even approve of the New Order. Not to mention that Geaspar has been instructed to begin recruiting the Stars. We will have allies; we need only to escape these walls and the immediate area to allow them to be gathered."

"Is this'uns really the Walding Zarlorn of legends? The true prophet of Philanti?" Blark barked from his cell.

The hallway became deathly quiet before Walding replied, "Who am I speaking with?" Bartellom's head turned with surprise to see the orc beyond the door bars, but he was quickly moved out of the way and in popped an old ragged-looking man's inquisitive face. "Ah, master orc, it seems you've been eavesdropping on us, have you?"

"If it's really you, then I must asks something of you."

"We're not interested," Bartellom said gruffly from beyond the door. Blark snarled but kept his eyes upon Walding.

"Let's hear the young orc," Walding said with a hint of intrigue, ignoring the barbarian.

"We've little time for this, Master Zarlorn, orcs can't be trusted," Mikel pleaded.

"Yea, sorry, gramps, that dude was going to eat me if ol' Bart hadn't found me. Literally like five more minutes and they'd have been eating a Johnny sandwich. Plus, Bart straight up smashed one of his buddies' faces in, like hardcore messed that dude up, and then stabbed the other guy after I froze him."

Walding seemed rather surprised and smiled gleefully as he turned away from the door to address the boy. "My, you froze him? A Chosen with ice abilities is not something I've seen in many, many years. How did it happen? What were you doing exactly?"

"Um, well, it wasn't really ice. But the point of that, and my main concern was, ya know, him eating me."

Walding blushed and bopped his own forehead with an open palm. "Yes, of course, we can talk more on your abilities once we've escaped. Now then, is this true, young orc? Did you intend to eat this Chosen boy? And you, Bartellom, you took his companions' lives?"

Blark growled in embarrassment and quickly looked away as Bartellom rubbed his chin with a massive hand nervously. "Yes, we was goings to eats 'im. But we's didn't know he was Chosen. We thoughts he was just a runt abouts to spoil our hiding spot."

"Instead, you were found by Bart and captured."

"After he killed me mates."

"You were going to eat him!" Bartellom interrupted with a punch to the wall outside his cell. "Something tells me you weren't in the mood to do any negotiating. And you've not said what you were doing so close to Eislark in the first place!" Even in the dim torchlight Blark could see the red in Bart's face behind Walding, and he couldn't help but smile at the brute's outburst.

"Please, you must go now," Mikel begged, pulling Walding's attention away from the door. Walding nodded and turned away from the barred door without another glance. Blark panicked, banging his chains against the wall rapidly to regain his attention.

"I musts return to Kuldraz!"

Walding's head poked back through the dungeon door in an instant. "For what reason must you return? And I must ask: are outsiders now welcome in the home of the orcs? It was strictly forbidden in my time for any but an orc to enter, but I've always wanted to visit such a famous stronghold."

"It might be even more forbidden now," Janeph said in disfavor. "None even know where it is."

"I musts go back or Eislark wills be attacked! But if I cans get home, I cans stop them, stop them all!"

"And why in Phont's name would we trust an orc who was just about to murder a child and who was illegally trespassing on Eislarkian soil? Who's to say you wouldn't be providing intel so that you and your brethren could carry out the attack?" Bartellom asked pointedly, poking his head to the side of Walding's so he could get a glare at the orc. Blark surprisingly did not snarl but instead straightened and puffed his chest as much as he could, given his bindings. He looked to Bartellom but settled on Walding who was watching curiously.

"The darkness, it pleads with us to join's him, be his first armies of the shadow and raid the human cities," he looked away in thought before reaching Bartellom's cold eyes. "We was scouting for a raid on Eislark, it's true, to see if we's could manage it for the darkness. But the city is tough and fortified, you's humans are smarts in buildings and weapons. We's would fall like water on rock against that city, no ways. I already knew, buts I came so's I could tell father elder without doubt. It's not possible and now we can tells the darkness to go to Klane with their calls to us. We's orcs want no part of the darkness, it only leads to death. But it's smart, cunning, it eats at our's thoughts, pulling us to do what it asks us, chewing the good away whisper by whisper."

Mikel fumed in the hallway. "Spying for a raid on Eislark, you've just openly confessed to conspiring to break our treaty! And who exactly is contacting you to request these dark actions?"

"Please, it was only to prove we's couldn't do it! We were never to be spotted and we's be outs of Eislark and we's would tell the darkness away, prepare to fights it. No one's was ever supposed to be knowing we was there, you's must believe me! If I don't get back, they wills come for me! There will be blood, the darkness will get what it wants in the end!" Blark said as his voice cracked and he lowered his head in defeat and embarrassment. "You's humans wouldn't care, why would you's. It will be a slaughter and you's will be rid of us orcs."

"The Grim King's influence is strong, strong even for orcs. He squashes hope, douses the light, leaves you scrambling until he alone can provide a way out," Walding said aloud to the group as he watched the dejected orc. "What is your name, orc? You mentioned father elder, are you of a prominent tribe?"

Blark breathed short breaths through his nose and looked forward with tears welled in his eyes. "Me's name is Blark." He paused again, then said, "Blark Uth-nun." Mikel, Janeph, and Bartellom reeled at the name, but Walding was unfazed.

"And have the Uth-nun's the will to fight the Grim King? Has your people the will to sacrifice everything to freely bathe in the light?"

"We's hate the darkness, always nagging, always prodding, always searching, stabbing, digging. But we's always fight it. Uth-nun's never not fight."

Walding smiled and breathed a slow exhale. "Then you must return to Kuldraz, so that you may fight and prevent the attack on Eislark." Blark lifted his dejected face to the door, alight with sad hope. He could not see the human's faces, but he imagined their distrusting looks must be fierce. But his eyes never left the Grandmaster as he whispered quietly to Walding.

"The Uth-nuns will forever be in your debt."

"Master Zarlorn, please be reasonable," Mikel said pleadingly with forced calm; what Walding was considering very clearly did not sit well with the captain. "Orcs are notoriously dishonest. You cannot believe them, especially an Uth-nun. His blood line is responsible for the sacking of countless villages, centuries of war and murder across the Trill Plains, before the Grim King even rose to power. Releasing him is treason and trusting him is a death wish. I beg you to think this through, Grandmaster, think of the children, think of Eislark and her people."

"This orc was going to kill one of them!" Bartellom bellowed much more forcibly than Mikel had argued. "He would have killed me if given the chance, his companion very nearly did were it not for Johnny! They are a murderous race, hungry for power and strength alone, they will turn upon us the second they find themselves at the advantage." Walding turned quickly and for as cheerful as he had just been speaking to the orc, his expression now was doubly angry. He stepped forward toward them with bold posture, causing the men and the rest of the party to retreat.

"Have you forgotten your history? How many orcs died at Jornun battling the same enemy we prepare to fight now? Yet you choose to paint them as beasts, unthinking murderous creatures!"

"Orcs fought alongside humans at Jornun?" Janeph asked innocently.

"By Phont, has history been so lost? Of course they did! All the clans did, that was in fact the first time the clans united. Uth-nuns and Cedz and Maq-ogsels and all of the lesser clans! Any who were willing to fight Kuor-Varz were allies, and that is where we find ourselves now; we must not alienate ourselves with blind hatred! There is but one enemy to Endland and if we are not united against him, then we will all of us fall. Weak and self-serving are the people in this age of Endland, grown soft from years of prosperous peace. We need united strength, and yet you do not hear the cry of a new ally! Chosen and the Stars do not turn their backs upon children of the light!"

The party was in silent and slightly frightened wonderment before Mikel stepped to the nearest Gull and demanded he open the door. Bartellom clenched his jaw to stop himself from objecting as the Gull opened the prison door without question and unbound the orc's chains. Blark walked through the cell door behind the Gull and was free and among the party after a minute. Bartellom watched him cautiously, as did Blark to him. The two were nearly eye to eye, Blark only slightly shorter than the barbarian and far leaner, but still quite a large and muscular being. Walding interrupted the stare down with a loud and deliberate clearing of his throat.

"Blark, I must make myself abundantly clear," Walding said, pulling the orc's yellow eyes away from Bartellom as he shrugged his back with a wince given his deep stab wound. "If this is in any way a ruse that will bring pain to Endland or the New Chosen and its companions, as Phont as my witness, I will smite you in a crackling rift of electrical mayhem that will leave nothing but the remnants of burnt ash and smoke where you once stood."

Blark nodded in a frightened stupor and fell to both knees before the Grandmaster, utterly surprising the others.

"Master Zarlorn, Uth-nuns speaks of you in the highest regard. Our people tell stories of the Chosen and yours's many deeds. You's have my word, I's will fight the Grim King with you's if you's will fight him with me," he looked to Bartellom side-eyed, but somewhat less aggressively than he had just a few seconds ago and with a surprising tint of remorse. "Any who's ally with your New Chosens, who's allies with Master Zarlorn, is a friend of the orcs. Uth-nun word is Uth-nun blood, to break it is to spill it."

He raked his fingers across the back of his left forearm, sharp nails digging and leaving behind warm red trails, which he presented to a nodding Walding. The boys squirmed at the sight, but the others watched silently without reaction. The orc stood and offered his arm for all to see.

"Blood bonds are powerful things," Bartellom said gruffly, "but you won't buy my trust in a simple blood ritual." Blark's nostrils flared in dissatisfaction but he did nothing more.

"Yes, Bartellom, trust will be earned. And I've no doubt Blark will need to grow to trust *you* given what happened to his companions at your hands. But we've wasted enough time here. For now, we must move." He turned to Mikel with a sad smile, "Captain, you are a brave man for releasing him as you did and for your upcoming part in convincing the lords and ladies we escaped. This will all fall on your shoulders; I thank you for your efforts and may we see you again down Phont's path. And be mindful of your ring if things turn ill for you, it shall provide clarity in the darkest of shadows. You've an unkind past that will undoubtedly be trailing you now given the Nightmother's return. Be safe and fortune unto thee." They shook hands before Janeph intercepted and gave him a hug, followed by Bartellom, who gave them both an even bigger hug between his single massive unslung arm.

"Keep this world afloat from your side, we'll do the same from ours," Janeph said softly. "And if possible, keep my brother from causing us too much trouble."

"Yea, try not to drink too much while we're away either. I'm sure we will all need some when next we meet," Bartellom joked with a deep laugh. The boys now lined up around him as Bart and Janeph invited them in for even more hugs.

"We will be expecting a feast like the one last night next time we're here, Micky ol' boy," Johnny said with a smile.

"Yea, more Flostram!" Zack added gleefully.

"I'd just go for a normal day back in the hospital at this point, and I never thought I'd miss that place. But a feast sounds pretty good too," Bryce laughed as the rest joined in. Mikel bent slightly to address them.

"Look out for each other. I know this is all so crazy, but remember to be kids occasionally, alright? You've got some good folks watching over you, so you can afford a little mischief," he whispered the last part as he gave them all a hug before pulling away with a subtle wink and addressing the rest of the group. "Now go, get out of here, I'll handle your 'escape.' Fastest way out is through the south wing, you'll go right through the laundry yard, so you should be able to grab some clothing for your trip if you're sly enough. Janeph, lead the way, you've still as much authority as anyone until the meeting ends and you're labeled a traitor. And Blark," he looked warily towards the orc, "find something to cover your face, even Janeph's status will not dissuade guards from arresting an orc in their city. Get out of Eislark and get out fast. Fortune unto thee, New Chosen."

With a last fist bump from each of the boys, the party exited the cellars and ran up the stairs, following Janeph as Mikel began discussing the escape story with his trusted Gull. Blark smiled kindly to Mikel but it did not compare to Walding's, which stretched across his happy face ear to ear.

———————

FALLOUT

opi had shuffled over to Grekory and when the doors had finally shut, the Eislarkian Lord took his crown from his head and threw it with all his might across the empty room, and it clanging noisily atop the stone floor and into one of the perimeter tables. He had intentionally delayed his exit from the relatively small Council Circle so that Umbrin and the others would be clear and unable to do any eavesdropping. Only the idle tables, the hanging banners of the Endland cities, and Lopi remained as Grek unwound; he only had a brief few minutes before he would be noticed missing from the Great Hall.

"What kind of fool is our king!" he complained aloud, releasing what had been brewing during the entire court session. "He entertains the formation of a Chosen coalition with the outlaw at the helm for the better part of the afternoon as the Council and lords debate before shutting down the vote, declaring a kingly decision, and dealing death and chains for all but the children and his own sister. And even she now must be banished! He could have saved us all time and simply voiced his nonsensical verdict while the Chosen lot stood before us! His mind was clearly made up before we even began the discussion!"

Grekory's hands shook with pent adrenaline as he did his best to control his flooding emotions. Lopi nodded in agreement but spoke much quieter as he moved near the agitated young lord.

"He is acting foolishly, to be sure. And those children, they'll be like dogs, pulled to do their duty before returning to their Trillgrand cages. It is a horrible situation. But what can we do now?"

"All he had to do was allow this Walding to train the boys under supervision and all could have been avoided! Bring the Council in to supervise, one Chosen against the Council is surely in Endland's favor should the outlaw decide to lash out. Instead, he runs this land with his arrogance and emotion, seeking to etch his name into history one absurd decision at a time. The damn fool will be the end of us!"

"Phont's peace upon you, my Lord. Perhaps I can speak with Petravinos and see if he can dissuade our king."

"We've all had our chance to dissuade him just now but failed, including Petravinos!" Grek bellowed as he smacked his semi-full goblet from the small table it sat upon. "He listens to no one, not even his knowledgeable councilor, while he deliberately downplays all other opinions, especially that of Eislark, making a mockery of my title at every available opportunity! And I've grown tired of it! How I wish to tell him so!"

He stood and stormed across the hall, reaching to retrieve his crown from the floor but muffed the grab and instead fumbled it further from him. He kicked a nearby chair frustratedly, kicked the crown still further from him, and moved towards the main doors without it.

"My Lord, you must tread carefully. You've already openly challenged the king by voting in favor of the Chosen and Master Walding. The Sarns are dangerous to cross, especially so Umbrin. You must exercise patience, young lord," Lopi said as he shuffled towards the crown and picked it up gingerly, dusting it with his red robe sleeve. Grekory turned quickly towards the Councilor, red-faced and vibrating in the anger he was still emanating.

"And now, of all people, the Council's fool preaches to me. How low am I in Endland's hierarchy!" He snatched the crown from Lopi's presenting palms and stormed towards the doors to return to the main hall, gripping the handles tightly before turning and calling over his shoulder in somewhat more control, "See to it that Mikel and the new prisoners are brought to us immediately so that we can get this over with."

"Of course, my Lord."

A loud knock caused Grekory to remove his hands from the handles quickly. "Yes, yes, I am on my way, just a moment with my Council." He pulled open the doors with a quick tug but instead of finding a servant or guards, a bloodied and beaten Mikel stumbled through the doorway, falling forward to a panic-striken Grekory. The lord unenthusiastically caught the captain, eyeing the blood from his lip that very nearly wiped along his fine tunic.

"They're gone, Grek. Walding, he," Mikel shook his head in embarrassment and exhaustion.

"What's happened, Mikel?" Grekory cried as he pressed on Mikel's shoulders and balanced the captain back on his own two feet.

"I beseeched his patience, but he said his fate could not be decided here and now, that what they must do could not wait. We tried to slow him, but he is skilled beyond anything I've seen. Rendered the entire lot of us unconscious. They've gone, and I know not where."

"Gone? Who's gone? Walding? What of the Chosen children?" Grek was back to his full-blown panic attack.

"Aye, the lot of them."

"By Phont, this is terrible! What will the king say?" Lopi said, now joining Grekory is his panic-stricken tone, which caused the old short man's voice to travel even higher than usual.

"And unfortunately, that is not all," Mikel said as he wiped the blood that was running from his nose with the back of his leathered sleeve. "The orc that Bartellom had captured is also missing. Seems our battle with Walding jarred his binds and cell loose, and he took their escape to create his own."

Grekory's face was appalled and terror-striken, Lopi matching in dismayed fashion. "Lost in my own castle. By Phont, Umbrin will have my head! And we've orcs outside our walls without any information to their intentions! All because our king attempted to execute a man whom he did not fully respect or understand and then insisted on dawdling about with us before making his own decision anyway!" His face lightened at the thought, which caught both Mikel and Lopi off guard. "He's forced the last Chosen, as well as the newly arrived Chosen, away from us, all on the very same day. Come, we must inform him of these delicious circumstances."

"My Lord, the blame is mine. I should have been more careful, brought more men, reasoned with the man, something. To openly accuse Umbrin of this fault does no good for Eislark or for Endland."

Grekory brushed past Mikel in the doorway and placed a re-affirming hand atop his shoulder.

"This lays at the feet of the king, my friend. And the lords and ladies will know of his failings here and now. He will not drive us any further into Klane's eager hands."

He continued on without another word, Lopi quickly scrambling behind him, nearly bumping Mikel over he moved so sporadically. The captain sighed heavily before he too followed, down the short hall and onto the throne platform in the Great Hall. The king was seated again as he had been just a short while earlier, and he turned with a face of annoyance as Grek and the others made their way toward him.

"I was beginning to think you had gone to fetch the Chosen yourself, Lord Grekory. But seeing as you don't have them, what in Phont's name were you doing? Are the Chosen on their way? I would very much like to be done with this and be out of this saltwater town."

Grek bowed and sighed as he straightened, standing beside his own chair on the king's right side. "My King, I've just been informed of some terrible news. While debating the outcome of the Chosen, they have evidently taken their fates into their own hands and fled Eislark. We know not where they've gone."

Umbrin set his short-bearded jaw, and his eyes shifted from a playful, if not antagonistic sheen, to an icy glare as the murmurs of the hall began to rise. "Do you mean to say that the murdering Walding Zarlorn has disappeared from your city and took with him our newly received saviors?" He looked to Petravinos, who was still processing what Grek had revealed, "All your hard work, Councilor Supreme, and now you've given to a lunatic three new disciples with which to destroy us!"

"My King," Grek began.

"I'll not hear another word from you, you incompetent excuse for a lord! Who was responsible for their escort and security to the dungeon?"

Mikel stepped forward from behind the chair and bowed low to Umbrin. "Forgive me, my King. I underestimated the old man. Chosen abilities are something I am not accustomed to."

"Never trust a street urchin," Umbrin said sharply. "And yet as noble as a gesture as that is, it was a rhetorical question. The blame lies with Lord Grekory. And he shall be punished for it."

"I believe you are mischaracterizing the Eislarkians, my King," Petravinos interjected with much-needed calm. "Mikel has been a trusted and loyal subject for many years. Long gone are his youthful days of lawlessness. And Lord Grekory is half family, the Belmars and the Sarns were once of the same kin, there is no need for this bickering. What's done is done. Dealing with a Chosen Grandmaster is a matter that is simply beyond any of our capabilities, aside from perhaps the Council's."

"I know my history, Vinos! I do not need a lecture in the purification of Sarn blood away from the Belmars!" Umbrin collected himself abruptly from the outburst and looked harshly towards Grekory before smirking and shifting his eyes to Mikel. The king's look made Grekory's stomach churn. "But I suppose with how close we are, I can pardon Grekory. Mikel, however, is not of kin. And he has failed in every sense of the word. Bring forth the chains, the now former Captain of Eislark will be accompanying us back to Trillgrand's dungeons for his complete botchery of the single most important day in recent history."

"You must be joking! What would you have him do against a Chosen Grandmaster?" Grekory was beside himself. "Petravinos said it himself, it is beyond any of us. Had we been in any other city, the results would have been the same. The Chosen are powerful, you saw it yourself in this very room!"

"But we weren't in any other city. We were here, and the fault is Mikel's, he said so himself. He will be released when what is rightfully mine is returned. Bring me the children, and Walding's head. Any who do this will be rewarded immensely, as they will be honorary overseer of Trillgrand's Chosen!" The Blue Hearts shackled Mikel's wrists without issue, the captain's listless eyes averted to the floor as his hair concealed the rest of his face. A drop of blood fell every few seconds from his nose onto the brown stone floor as he stood motionless before the crowd.

"Come now, my King," Lady Sydnus started. "The destruction Walding caused was immense. What can a mortal man do against such power?"

"Indeed! And if you had just made your decision from the beginning this never would have happened!" Grekory spat in frustration. "Perhaps now would be a good time to lay out your decision, oh King, including your banishment of the Drifter and of one Lady Janeph!"

Umbrin lost his smirk in an instant and scanned the room for Janeph as the rest of the people searched themselves. Umbrin grew red as she and Bartellom did not immediately come forward, and he began agitatedly tapping his fingers atop the throne arm.

"Come now, Janeph, Drifter, step forward, do not be cowards! The Bonethorne is already in essence banished, he can show you the path, it won't be so terrible!"

Mikel cleared his throat uncomfortably from his chains, pulling the ire of the king upon him. "My King, I cannot say for certain, but Janeph and Bartellom were present in the dungeons before Walding let loose upon us. It may be possible that they elected to travel with the children."

Umbrin's face ranged from agitation to disgust, his upper lip quivering in repressed rage. Mikel lowered his eyes back to the floor as Umbrin stood slowly and looked over the crowd in a final scan for his sister.

"By order of the king, any who are found to be aiding Walding and this New Order he intends to bring about are hereby and henceforth traitors to the crown and to Endland. They are to be returned to Trillgrand, dead or alive, for a bounty that is to be determined. The only members of this group that shall not be harmed are the children themselves. They are to be returned to Trillgrand alive."

"Be reasonable, my King!" Petravinos stood and pleaded from his chair to the king's left. "This is a death sentence to your own blood! With such violence, we are alienating our potential liberators! The children will not come willingly by with such forceful measures!"

"The king has spoken!" Umbrin yelled as he turned his back to Vinos. "Any who oppose my decree are to be considered they themselves traitors and will be executed just the same! Now go and bring me the Chosen! Sound Eislark's horn, notify the people, search the countryside, they could not have gotten far! And until they are returned, Mikel will be Trillgrand's honored guest. We've a lovely little room in our cells that I am sure you'll find most pleasing, Mikel."

Grekory stood now too, hands clenched, white knuckles, and an open grimace upon his face. There was commotion among the people as well, questions among them, that grew louder by the second. The king did not sit, instead he walked down the aisle towards the exit of the hall, Blue Hearts flanking him through the growingly raucous crowd. Grekory desperately stepped forward to stop Mikel from being taken, but the captain raised his open hands to ward him off and offered a bloody smile.

"Not to worry, Grek, I've been in my fair share of prisons. It's been a while, but it's like a second home. You must not do anything rash, now. Stay steady amidst the swirling seas."

Grek sat back in his own throne defeated and watched as his best friend was taken out of his sight. Without room for objections or discussion, the rest of the lords and ladies began to quiet, many in open contempt given their body language. Lady

Sydnus and Frilminn even came forward as the rest of the people slowly filed out of the Great Hall.

"Lord Grekory, what was done here today is beyond injustice," Frilminn said gruffly. "We will correct this, I know not how. But we will."

"Aye, know that you are not alone in seeing how wildly our king behaves," Sydnus added. Grekory offered a weak nod.

"He will pay," Grek muttered quietly and both took the limited response to exit the brief conversation after casting foreboding looks to each other. Grek folded his hands before his mouth as they and their travelers exited the hall, leaving Councilor Lopi and several Gull at their usual posts.

"Umbrin's rule will be the end of us. It cannot be allowed to continue."

"My Lord, we must be strong and not act rashly; Umbrin will see the error in his ways in due time, I am sure," Lopi said in his squeaky voice.

"Strong I shall be, Councilor. Endland's future depends on it." He stood and retreated to the back hallway but turned in the archway and spoke with eerie calm. "Find the Chosen. Bring them to me. Send the best men we have, leak it to the vagabonds and the thieves, I care not how it gets done. And gold is no object to me; whosoever brings them to Eislark will be paid handsomely for their service. And then perhaps with these New Chosen, we will end Trillgrand's tyranny."

He turned and retreated into the back chamber as Lopi bowed low at his Lord's command.

"What a mess this will be," he muttered under his breath, and shaking his head, exited the hall to make the Lord's wishes known.

34

THE NEW ORDER

———◇———

Bryce, Zack, and Johnny sat atop the cart with hoods laxed around their necks, a burlap pouch of newly bestowed belongings from Eislark slung across their laps as the breeze from the distant bay brought the sour smell of salt and fish. The cart was open-faced and without any protection from the elements and had simple rails of wood lining three sides, each a foot or two high to corral what was being carried, while the back of the cart was open for loading and unloading cargo. Mikel had been right about the laundry area. Each of them had rather easily been able to walk through and nonchalantly grab a few items on their way out of the castle, at least a few sets of basic clothing for the trip. One of the maids had questioned them before Janeph stepped in and set her straight. Aside from that, it had been relatively easy to maneuver out, much more so than any had anticipated. With the Council and lords and ladies still unaware of their ploy, they were afforded a rather casual walk through the castle, striding confidently through the hallways with Janeph leading, before ducking into various areas for food and supplies. And as they exited the inner castle walls, Janeph managed to commandeer the cart they waited on from a group of ordinary guards. And through it all, Blark had done everything he could to stay out of the searching eyes of anyone and everyone, a shadow within the group.

They each sat upon a sleep sack that they had snatched on their trek out of the castle grounds. They were rolled tightly for easy carrying and rested on a thin layer of hay that coated the slightly aged brown-grey wood of the cart. The four other packs sat along the back rail closest to the pair of horses, one for Janeph, Bartellom, Blark, and Walding, respectively. Janeph sat at the front of the cart in the driver's seat, draped tightly in an inconspicuous dark red traveler's cloak from the laundry room. Bartellom sat next to her, his arm still slung tightly to his side from his scuffle with Jamesett the short 24 hours ago, hidden beneath a similarly mundane grey but much larger cloak. Their weapons were laid at their feet, just below the reins, beneath a concealing pile of hay and well within arm's reach should their attention be required. Blark sat at the back of the cart, legs hanging off the back, hands tucked tightly beneath his coat, hood raised to conceal his orcish features.

The boys talked quietly with each other as they all waited with increasing agitation for Walding to arrive. He had said they must leave quickly, but he had matters to attend to before leaving, "Just a few moments, I assure you." And given that he was a Chosen Grandmaster and the only one capable of training the children, Janeph and Bartellom begrudgingly obliged. Blark was very much on Walding's side, though whether he was being genuine or truckling to the Grandmaster was anyone's guess. The only unfortunate part was that he had forgotten to say farewell to Walding and now was insisting on waiting for his return before heading down his separate path. Janeph quickly had jumped into the conversation to prevent Bartellom and Blark from creating even the smallest of scenes, and she agreed to allow Blark his goodbye, despite the obvious risk. But now every second that passed increased their anxiety; it was only a matter of time before the Council meeting would end and everyone in the city, in all of Endland, would be searching high and low for the New Chosen, and Walding seemed to be taking his sweet time doing whatever it was he was doing.

"Do we send someone to search for him?" Bartellom questioned aloud to the group, leaning back towards the boys with a disarming smile, doing his best to hide his growing unease.

"We don't know where he went, but we must do something. If he was caught, I would not put it past Umbrin to have him executed behind closed doors," Janeph said as she scanned the city buildings that they sat near, a short trot from the Southern Gate, well beyond the inner walls of the Castle. It was a main road, a continuation of the road outside the walls that they had raced on to find Johnny and Zack earlier that morning. It kept its straight path inside the city walls to the inner keep, bending to the right ever so slightly. People moved about them, entering and exiting the shops on either side of the wide walkway, easy enough for two carriages to pass each other as well as for people to walk near the buildings. None that bustled past them seemed to take any special notice of their cart parked neatly to one side outside an herb and incense hut.

"Yea, is this guy senile or something? I mean, I'm still wrapping my head around like where we are, and old ass time wizards, and the king of not-England, and my own superpowers. Now this guy says he is just as super old as the old ass time wizard and can like float on wind and dodge lightning," Johnny said as he picked through the hay in the cart aimlessly.

"I don't know, but he's a Chosen like us, so if we want to get home, he's our best chance," Zack replied. Bartellom looked to Janeph quickly before looking back to the crowd, but not fast enough for Bryce to not notice.

"Didn't you hear that Petravinos guy?" Bryce said in sadness. "He said this is our actual home. We should get used to the idea that we might not be going back."

"Easy for you to say! Come on B, think of Marge and Walt! I know they aren't your actual parents, but we can't just forget about them! And the hospital got all wrecked when we left, so you know they're going to be looking everywhere for us!"

"I hear you; I just don't know what to think anymore. What if we're trapped here now or something?"

"There is a long road ahead of us. Plenty of time to discuss such things." Walding's voice came from behind them. All six looked back to find Walding walking towards the back edge of the cart, his wry lip-pressed grin greeting them. "Are we prepared to head out?"

"Yes, Grandmaster."

"Walding is just fine," Walding corrected Janeph. She smiled and nodded.

"How's come you always make me call you Grandmaster?" The heavy voice of Geaspar sounded from up the road behind Walding as the large man labored towards them.

"Because I say so, Geaspar." The hulking man scowled and smiled simultaneously but did not offer any further retort. Bryce watched intently as a shorter woman walked from behind Geaspar, golden curls protruding from her drawn hood. He smiled inadvertently and stared, pretending to look at the back of Johnny's head, who was turned to look at the group. Geaspar tossed a large sack into the middle of their cart and a few potatoes and some bread spilled out the poorly strung bag.

"You've quite the crew here, Grandmaster, are all of these Chosen?" Geaspar stuck out his hand towards Blark with jovial enthusiasm. Blark slid away from him across the edge of the cart without a word, being sure to keep his hood low and his hands hidden beneath the rest of the cloak. He instead took a look towards Walding, hopped off the cart, and bowed deeply.

"Grandmaster Walding, I had forgottens my farewell, and I did nots wants to disrespects the man who freed me. Know that the city of Kuldraz will welcomes you's when you needs rest and that I wills make sure we does not attack these humans."

Walding placed an old weathered hand on the taller orc's shoulder and smiled. "What kindness, thank you, Blark. Please know that the Chosen are with you if ever you need us."

Blark bowed again and without a word, grabbed his small bag that he had packed from the castle and slung it on his shoulder. He turned to the children and to Janeph and Bartellom and bowed again.

"I knows you humans do not keeps the legends as well as we orcs. And I knows the words of orcs mean little to you's. But you's musts know that Walding Zarlorn is maybe the greatest Chosen to ever lives. He wills guide you along your path if you listens to him."

He bowed, turned, and walked back into the city, heading along the castle wall towards the eastern edge and quickly disappeared among the crowd. Geaspar removed his small hat and scratched his wispy head.

"I'm guessing he ain't Chosen, eh, Grandmaster? And did I hear something about orcs and Kuldraz?"

"We've no time, Geaspar," Walding said as he waved his hands in front of his own face. "We will very soon be fugitives of Endland! Quickly, let us transfer the supplies and move on!"

"Apologies, Grandmaster, I suppose I'll meet everyone eventually. Lesara, if you would please, my dear, bring forward the box."

The three boys moved out of curiosity towards Geaspar as Lesara stepped forward and unraveled a purple satin cloth of extremely high quality and presented an old wooden box to her eye level, which was well above the cart's edge. The box was quite the opposite of the ornate cloth; it looked like it had been dropped a couple thousand times, showing large scuffs and flattened corners of the unusually dark wood. There were still streaks from where Geaspar or Lesara had tried to wipe it clean of the dust that it must have been collecting for many years to be as thick as it was. The dust still clung to the wood after the cloth was removed. Walding placed his hands upon the box with a fondness, lingering a moment as he gently brushed some of the dust with his fingertips. Geaspar dropped the second sack of food from his shoulder to the cart as Walding resumed contact with reality and pulled his hands from the box.

"My, I did not think I would ever get to use this again, nor that you actually have them saved! This is not the time or place, we must put some distance between us and Eislark, but I am glad to have it with us, it will make our first steps in training far easier." Geaspar smiled warmly as Walding took the satin cloth draped over Lesara's arm and covered the worn box again, wrapping it as he took it from her. He placed it carefully in the shoulder bag that was slung across his body. "I apologize to everyone for the wait, but Geaspar needed to know he too was in danger, and he was able to pull a good number of supplies from the Worn Thorn for our travels. And thankfully I do think that we are now ready to go!" he finished as he clambered somewhat strenuously atop the back of the cart and leaned his back against the rail next to Zack to balance the cart at two per side.

"You mean they are coming with us too?" Bryce asked, resisting with all his might not to look again at Lesara, though he could see her looking from the corner of his eyes as he spoke aloud.

"Aye, this is turning into quite the caravan, Walding. It will be near impossible to remain inconspicuous with such a large-sized group; it was going to be hard enough with the six of us," Bartellom said with an air of concern.

"They will not be with us. Some of the last known ties to the old Order of Chosen here in Eislark lie with the Eltenbranch blood. Sooner or later, they would be questioned. Best to get out now and begin their own journey to revive the Stars."

Bryce looked down in sadness; still restraining a look to the young lady. Geaspar came over and patted the boy's back with his oversized hand. "Not to worry, young Chosen, do not feel sorry for us. We have been preparing for this day all our lives, ready to pick up and leave should the Chosen need us! Quite an adventure to be aiding the Order in these modern times! And we shall not let you down, eh, Lesara? You'll have the Stars at your command in no time!"

The young lady curtsied in her homey dress. "It is an honor and a privilege to serve the Chosen. And to get to explore the rest of Endland while doing so is just another of Phont's blessings!"

"Yes, it is all quite exciting my dear," Walding replied, smiling, "but do remember this is as serious a journey as any of us have ever embarked on, myself included, and I've battled the Grim King firsthand! We must be wary in whom we associate. Use caution on the road and trust your instincts."

"Aye, Grandmaster, not to worry. As I said, we've been preparing for this moment since my great-grandfather passed down the Eltenbranch responsibilities! But enough chitchat, we must be off, and you as well! I suspect we are pushing the limits of our time for safe departure." Geaspar bowed low and Lesara curtsied. "Fortune unto thee, New Chosen!"

"Fortune unto thee!" Walding called as Geaspar and Lesara turned and headed up the main road and into the crowd. Bryce waved awkwardly to their backs as Bartellom snapped the reins; the two horses began to trot slowly along the road towards the Southern Gate. Johnny punched the still-waving Bryce hard in the shoulder as they moved towards the city exit.

"What the hell man?" Bryce cried, rubbing his arm.

"That girl's pretty cute, don't you think?" Johnny asked coyly, his impish smile shining through a poor attempt to look uninterested.

"Sure, I guess so, I didn't really notice," Bryce lied and looked away in red embarrassment. Turning away did little; replacing Johnny's face was a wide-grinning Zack. Bryce felt his cheeks grow warm as he looked down at the thin layer of hay.

"Oh, what's this? Do you fancy Lesara? Let us turn around and speak with her at once!" Walding said in genuine excitement and with surprising observation, waving to the Eltenbranch's direction, though where exactly they were at the moment was difficult to say in the crowd. "Young love is such a lovely thing!"

"No! Don't turn around!" Bryce said, rubbing his temples with sudden anxiety. "Let's just get out of here, we have to escape right? We don't have time."

"Yes, good point, Bryce. Sorry, Walding, next time, perhaps," Janeph said with a wink, saving Bryce further torment. "As you said, we must put some distance between us and Eislark, this journey will be difficult if we are found still within the city walls; too many eyes can still recognize us here."

"Oh yes!" Johnny said loudly, suddenly distracted from his emotional prodding as he stood up on the slowly moving cart. "I know what we need to do, I was thinking about it while we were waiting for gramps to get back! Secret identities! I've got to think about this, the secret identity name is crucial to all heroes. It makes or breaks them, if you really think about it."

"Shut up, you moron, no one needs a secret identity. And that wasn't even what Nurse Jan was talking about, she meant we're too conspicuous out here. Or I guess it's *Jan-eph*, right?" Zack said, embarrassed, as he pulled Johnny by his cloak back down onto the cart to sit.

"Yea, and secret identities don't mean anything," Bryce chimed, jumping at the chance to get off the subject of him and

Lesara. "It honestly doesn't even matter, it's the hero story, not the secret identity story."

"First off, I stand by secret identities being crucial. Imagine if Batman wasn't a billionaire and was just some random dude. Garbage story from the get go, am I right? How would he buy all his cool stuff? And second, you don't know what Nurse Jan meant. Jan, you were talking about secret identities, right?"

"I wasn't exactly, but we probably should be wary of using our actual names in public. Once they realize we're gone, we will be sought after by every man looking for a king's reward."

"See!" Johnny celebrated, as their cart approached the open gates. "Now let me think, I'll get names for everyone, I just need a minute to think it through."

"Don't think too hard, Johnny, you might hurt yourself," Bryce said with a smile. "Did I mention that I missed you guys?"

"I'm not sure anyone has ever hurt themselves simply thinking, dear boy. I say think away, Johnny!" Walding said, laughing. Johnny smiled ear to ear and stuck out his hand for a high five. Walding looked at his palm quizzically before Johnny slapped his own hand to fulfill the request and then put both pointer fingers to his temples as he concentrated.

"We'll work on that, gramps. Now let me think on this."

"In the meantime," Walding continued, "now that we are on our way, we should decide where we are heading."

"Aye, we should travel along by cart for a short while, but at some point, we will need to abandon it and go by foot. Too many travelers on the main road, and very soon those travelers will be on the lookout for us," Bartellom said as he waved calmly to the Gull just inside the gate. The Gull did not move or respond, but their helmed heads did follow the cart as they passed by. Walding waited until they were outside the walls and further from the Gull's listening ears before he shuffled up towards the front of the cart to respond.

"I agree. We should leave this cart by the end of the day, any longer promotes too much risk. Luckily there is a Chosen temple but a day or so from here. I expect we will not need to travel off the path very long before we reach it," Walding said with a smile.

"I doubt any of your temples remain, Walding," Janeph said as she turned to speak. "The Keepers wrote that they were all raided after the banishment, looted and burned to ash."

"I suspect this one in particular may have evaded the people. There were a great many temples hidden from the common folk, holding some of our greatest artifacts. I do hope I remember where it is, though. That's the problem with hidden temples, they can be so easily forgotten!"

"If you say so," Bartellom said as he lightly snapped the reins to the horses to prod them along. "Are we heading in the right direction? Towards Trillgrand?"

"Yes, but we must turn more eastward and into the Narrow Woods well before we reach the capital," Walding said as he looked up to the evening sun. "I'll recognize it when I see it, most likely. Just stay the course until I say when. You boys will enjoy it, there are a great many wondrous things to behold."

"Is one of them a bathroom? I could really use a bathroom soon," Johnny said, breaking his concentration on the group's secret identities. "I guess I could go at a rest stop on the way, but I really hate going in those places. There is always a puddle of mystery liquid on the floor and the crapper is clogged like 25-percent of the time."

Bartellom laughed. "Your world had quite the advancements in that aspect of life, Johnny. You'll find Endland is far behind what you are used to."

"Well, as long as you guys don't have the cheap toilet paper, I guess I'll just suck it up. But if you've got that off-brand crap, I'm going to demand that we stop and pick up some of the good stuff ASAP."

"J, I think you might be in for a rough time," Zack said, laughing. "You remember camping in Boy Scouts? I'm thinking its going to be that kind of thing."

"Mother of God," he muttered, his eyes going hazy as the party all laughed at his disappointment. He slunk low in the cart shaking his head as they moved towards the Narrow Woods.

HOPE

***

His hands rested loosely at his sternum, fingers interlaced save his thumbs and pinkies. Despite his decades of practice, it never got any easier to go as deep into the Medius as was required to converse. This time in particular, it felt especially difficult, though he couldn't be sure if it was from his currently clouded mind or the still-bleeding wound to his wrist. Perhaps both, they were certainly intertwined. Never in his years of searching had he encountered another with an ability so similar to his; it was quite possibly identical for all he knew. It was more than that, though. The raw power of the boy possessed was simply overwhelming. Without any formal training he had survived a trip, albeit brief, with him through the outskirts of the Medius and then had successfully repelled his blood through basic Gathering. With a little training, he would quickly become quite the adversary—or ally if they could get to him before he was turned from their cause completely.

"Quite distracted, are we?" a rumbling voice chided around him. Jamesett opened his eyes before a throne of swirling shadow, atop which sat his master, still clothed in the cold dark metallic boots he had been in all those years ago. Streaks of century-old blood of the poor souls he had personally felled at Jornun covered his metal shins, still wet, caught in his banishment. Save for the lower half of his burly long sword, which glimmered with a similar red sheen to that of his boots, the darkness of the Medius shrouded the rest of him in its misty veil.

"Apologies, Master, things have been chaotic this last day."

"Yes, I can see you've been met with quite a strike. Surprising considering the simplicity of the task of extracting unbeknownst Chosen."

Jamesett swallowed hard. "My King, the extraction did not go as planned. Endland had identified them prior to us and contacted them before we could make our move. I attempted to take them myself but it fell apart."

"Them?"

"Yes, Master, there were three Chosen in this world."

There was a shifting of the armor upon the throne, clanging mildly amidst the whispering quiet of the world between. "Where are they now?"

"In Endland, Trillgrand I believe, based on the Hunters I encountered. I can't be certain they all survived the Void, but one did for certain."

The silence that followed was far worse than the rage Jamesett had expected. He waited for a response that was not coming and did his best to correct the course of the conversation. "But the one who did survive has the gift!"

"Explain," the voice beckoned.

"My King, he managed to traverse the shallowest part of the Medius with me for a short time. He became infected with my blood—"

"Our blood," the king interrupted.

"Yes, our blood. But after arriving in Endland, he dissuaded my takeover of his mind by Gathering, and while doing so, I saw him, plain as I see you now!"

"Who, I wonder, taught him that?"

"My King?"

"Gathering."

"It is hard to say, I had not thought about it. Perhaps one of the wizards?"

A ragged helm leaned forward out of the shadows, made of the same dark metal as was played across his shins. It was a horrid shape, a scream hardened into armor, dented and gouged, with flecks of wet red splattered across it.

"Walding Zarlorn."

Jamesett nearly lost his connection at the mention but quickly refocused as Kuor-Varz leaned back into his throne and into the dark mist.

"That is impossible," Jamesett finally managed.

"I had thought so as well. But something has been nagging me all these years, an itch I could not scratch, a sight just beyond my view. It felt quite absurd. But it is him. I've felt his aura, I could never forget it after what he's done to me," he slammed an armor-clad hand to the throne. "We are here after all these years, are we not? Perhaps our beloved teacher is not as clean in spirit as he would like us to believe."

There was a pause before Kuor-Varz shifted his weight forward again, iron hands folded beneath his chin as he was visible out of the darkness once more. "Spread the word. Find the Chosen and find him quickly. Walding will taint him against us. We've Grim on the ground, do we not?"

"Yes, Master, they wait for your instructions."

"Good. Call upon them. Have them bring the Chosen to me and dispose of any who would deny this task. And emphasize this is to be done with discretion, we do not need a united Endland focused on us just yet."

Jamesett bowed in the strange manner, arm at a right angle, straight leg sliding to the side. "Yes, my King."

Kuor-Varz sat back again and shrouded himself. "If this new Chosen is gifted as you say, I may finally be out of this unbearable purgatory. And I will be able to finish what was started so many years ago. Go, I shall call you when I wish to speak again. Death beckons."

"And the Grim answer," Jamesett responded as he dissolved back into reality. The whispers faded, the scenery lightened, and he was back in the candlelit room he had left, where two eagerly waiting subjects leaned forward collectively, one a massive beast and the other a far thinner creature, both waiting patiently for the commune to end. Jamesett opened his eyes and smiled wickedly to his counterparts.

"We've Chosen to hunt."

ACKNOWLEDGMENTS

To J.R.R. Tolkien and his books for introducing me to a magnificent world of wonder in my childhood years. Your books were among the first I can remember reading and never wanting to put down. More importantly, they opened my mind to the notion that an entire world, people, and history can be created with enough time and imagination. You are undoubtedly the biggest influence on this book and if I can deliver even a sliver of the magic and wonder that your book brought to me, I would consider this writing an incredible success. Thank you.

To Nikki LaMountain for capturing the visual of my mind's eye in an incredibly beautiful cover. You were such a kind and thoughtful professional throughout the process, and I cannot thank you enough for bringing the scenery to life. Thank you.

To Lori Koetters for editing to the point where I could pass as a grammar expert. I know there were countless (that is only a slight exaggeration) fixes, edits, and suggestions throughout the book, and this writing would have given English teachers nightmares if you had not been there to save it. Thank you.

To Debra Kubiak for polishing my crude word document into a beautiful interior design and smooth read, and for helping incorporate the numerous edits from Lori. The page design and internal paging enhance the writing to such a degree that I can hardly remember what it looked like without it. Thank you.

To Uncle Keith for making all of this possible. I cannot properly express what an absolute blessing it is to have you in my life. All your work guiding this from a basic word document into this final product cannot be understated, and I can confidently say that this book would not be here without you. Of that I am absolutely certain. Saying thank you does not seem like enough, but it is all I can offer. Thank you!

ABOUT THE AUTHOR

Nick McPherson is a husband and father, which are and will always be his greatest accomplishments. He is also a fantasy genre nerd, a video game enthusiast, an engineer, a hater of yardwork, a lover of frozen custard, and most recently, an author. He splits his time between a lovely home in Cleveland, Ohio, and a less lovely work desk in a different part of Cleveland, Ohio. He is prone to demonstrating wry humor and finds writing the author bio for his book somewhat difficult. But it's done, so he supposes it wasn't too difficult after all.

CHOSEN
THE NEW ORDER

The saga continues—
BOOK TWO *coming soon!*